T0196015

DANGER IN DARK PLACES

In rural Indiana, the underground mines that once held coal and iron ore have become killing grounds. In two counties, five corpses have been discovered. Their deaths appear accidental, from drowning or suffocating in flooded and abandoned mines. But local authorities, including Chief Shaunda Lynch, have uncovered evidence suggesting they've all been murdered.

Assigned to the case as Federal Agents, Detectives Jack Murphy and Liddell Blanchard take charge of the investigation. Shaunda's proven herself more than capable of policing her jurisdiction and resents the intrusion of male authority figures. As Jack digs deep into the case, he discovers the victims have checkered pasts. But no matter who believes the killings are justified, someone still has to pay for the crime . . .

Highest Praise for Rick Reed's Thrillers

THE DEEPEST WOUND

"Reed gives the reader a genre story worth every minute and every penny spent."
—*Book Reporter*

"Whew! The murders are brutal and nonstop. Det. Jack Murphy tracks killers through a political maze of lies, deception and dishonor that leads to a violent, pulse-pounding climax."
—**Robert S. Levinson**

"The things Reed has seen as a police officer make for a great book."
—*Suspense Magazine*

THE COLDEST FEAR

"Everything you want in a thriller: strong characters, plenty of gory story, witty dialogue, and a narrative that demands you keep turning those pages."
—**BookReporter.com**

THE CRUELEST CUT

"Rick Reed, retired homicide detective and author of *Blood Trail*, the true-crime story of serial killer Joe Brown, brings his impressive writing skills to the world of fiction with *The Cruelest Cut*. This is as authentic and scary as crime thrillers get, written as only a cop can write who's lived this drama in real life… A very good and fast read."
—**Nelson DeMille**

"Put this one on your must-read list. *The Cruelest Cut* is a can't-put-down adventure. All the components of a crackerjack thriller are here, and author Reed knows how to use them. Readers will definitely want to see more of Reed's character Jack Murphy."
—**John Lutz**

Also by Rick Reed

The Jack Murphy Thrillers
The Cruelest Cut
The Coldest Fear
The Deepest Wound
The Highest Stakes
The Darkest Night
The Slowest Death
The Deadliest Sins
The Cleanest Kill
The Fiercest Enemy

Nonfiction

Blood Trail **(with Steven Walker)**

The Fiercest Enemy

A Jack Murphy Thriller

Rick Reed

LYRICAL UNDERGROUND
Kensington Publishing Corp.
www.kensingtonbooks.com

LYRICAL UNDERGROUND BOOKS are published by

Kensington Publishing Corp.
119 West 40th Street
New York, NY 10018

All Kensington titles, imprints, and distributed lines are available at special quantity discounts for bulk purchases for sales promotion, premiums, fund-raising, educational, or institutional use.

Special book excerpts or customized printings can also be created to fit specific needs. For details, write or phone the office of the Kensington Sales Manager: Kensington Publishing Corp., 119 West 40th Street, New York, NY 10018. Attn. Sales Department. Phone: 1-800-221-2647.

Lyrical Underground and Lyrical Underground logo Reg. US Pat. & TM Off.

First Electronic Edition: February 2020
ISBN-13: 978-1-5161-0460-4 (ebook)
ISBN-10: 1-5161-0459-5 (ebook)

First Print Edition: February 2020
ISBN-13: 978-1-5161-0461-1
ISBN-10: 1-5161-0461-7

Printed in the United States of America

This novel is dedicated to my brothers Tim and Mike, and my sister Betty. They will always be an inspiration.

Chapter 1

He jerked awake. He was on his back, on a hard surface, in a pitch-black world. His head felt like it would explode. He felt he was on a slight incline, covered with grit and small rocks. He pushed himself into a sitting position and the movement caused him to slide downward. He rammed his elbows and palms of his hands against the rough surface and felt the sharp rocks cut into his flesh. Before he got stopped his feet and lower legs plunged into icy cold water. He reflexively pulled his knees up and pushed with the soles of feet that were already pinpricked with pain. He dragged himself backward on his elbows. The grit and stones cut deeper into his skin.

Once his feet were out of the water he lay still, panting from the adrenaline rush, feet throbbing with pain. Using his heels and shrugging his shoulders he was able to gain a small distance from the water. He stopped and lay his head back. Mistake. Pain shot through his skull and pounded behind his eyes. He could hear his pulse pounding in his ears. His grip on consciousness was tenuous. All he wanted to do was go to sleep, but he didn't dare. He knew he had a concussion. He needed to stay awake.

"Where the hell am I?"

He twisted his head to the right and left hoping to catch even a glimmer of light. There was only the dark and the effort made him nauseous. The nausea eased and he tried to calm himself. To think. How had he gotten here—wherever here was? He remembered drinking Jack Daniels in the Coal Miner Bar and then someone was buying him Tequila shots. He didn't like Tequila, but it was free and he was out of work.

He shifted further from the water, cinders cutting into his feet and arms and elbows and palms. The incline eased to a more level surface. He rolled onto his front and pulled his knees under him. He stood. Dizziness washed over him and his legs buckled. He slid on the scree and plunged up to his waist into the icy water. His feet could find no purchase now. The incline was even steeper in the pool of water. He rolled onto his front and clawed at the slick surface. The cold seemed to climb up him as his body was drawn backward into the pool. He frantically clawed his way up the side and crab-walked up the slope. He lay on his back panting and fear hammered through him with every beat of his heart.

He lay still and took mental stock. He was naked except for his jockey shorts. He was cold but not freezing. It was mid-March. The temperature sometimes dipped into the single digits at night and reached sixties and seventies by noon. He had to get warm or he'd become hypothermic. His lower legs already felt weak to the point of useless.

He dragged himself further away from the water and with every few feet the air seemed to get warmer. He moved in the only direction possible—away from the water. He'd gone to the bar at night but was it still the same night? He couldn't remember anything that had happened after he'd drank the Tequila. He woke up here. Naked.

Someone's playing a joke, he thought. Surely the lights would come on and he'd be given his clothes back. They would pat his back and buy him a drink for being a sport. Screw that. Screw them. He could have drowned.

"Not funny!" he yelled and thought his eyes would explode out of their sockets. "Come on guys. You had your fun," he said a little less loudly. Nothing. "I'm serious. I'm cold and I almost drowned." Still nothing. He muttered a string of curse words not caring if they heard.

He shivered and felt his skin prickle with the cold. He wrapped his arms across his chest and rubbed and patted. It had little effect. His fingers were like ice cubes, felt thick and began to hurt. He rubbed his palms together and flexed his fingers to get some blood circulating. The pain eased. He couldn't see it but he felt his breath as a mist in front of his face.

"You're going to be sorry when I get out of here," he said. "Do you know who my dad is? Do you?"

He listened. There was no answer. He rubbed his hands over his upper arms and danced from one foot to the other, ignoring the sharp scree that cut into the soles of his feet. "I'm not screwing around here. My dad will have your asses. I'm dead serious. This isn't funny. Get me out of here."

The back of his head ached. He gently probed the back of his skull and felt a lump. His fingers came away sticky. *I hit my head when I was dumped in here* his rational mind thought, followed closely by *I was drugged. Rohypnol. That's why I can't remember where I am or how I got here.* That was the only logical explanation. He tried to think who had been in the bar. He had nothing. He didn't have many friends and the ones he did have wouldn't do something like this.

The effort of dragging himself out of the water had made him breathe deeply and something in the air tickled his nose. A familiar itch started in the back of his throat and in his lungs.

He hugged himself tighter and yelled, "Where am I?" His voice bounced back to him, not quite an echo. "Where am I?" he yelled again and it brought on a sudden coughing fit. The tickle in his nose grew worse. He had a breathing condition. Not COPD. Not yet. He'd never smoked anything but pot until a few years ago. Now he carried an inhaler, which, of course, was in the pants he wasn't wearing. To make matters worse he hated the dark. Wherever he was it was damp and cold and dark. He imagined spores from mold floating in the air. He slid his boxer shorts off and held them over his mouth and nose. If he could filter the musty stuff, calm himself, take slow shallow breaths, he would be okay.

He concentrated on each breath, felt his lungs expand and contract, expand, contract. It was working. The tickle was subsiding and with it the growing panic. He listened. Nothing but a steady dripping sound. The water might be from an underground spring. Like in a cave. The ground beneath him was more than just damp. Water was steadily coming in from somewhere.

"Hey!" he yelled. "Can you hear me?" His words flattened. "Where am I?" Only the steady drip answered.

He got to his hands and knees, afraid to try to stand again or fall into another pool. He hadn't gone far before his hand struck a vertical wall. The surface was pitted and uneven and smooth and damp. He ran his fingers around the ground and crawled a few feet. His fingers came upon a metal rail protruding from the ground. *A train track.* The gauge of the steel wasn't heavy enough for a train. *Not a cave. A shaft. A mine shaft.* The track was for a rail car in a mine.

The pain in his head was forgotten. The first glimmer of hope stole into his mind. If he followed the tracks they would lead to an exit. He couldn't be that far inside. Why in the hell would he wander into a mine? He'd been in one mine in his entire life and that was a high school party. He was drunk, on drugs, fearless. *Stupid.* He remembered some of what happened that night and quickly pushed the thoughts away. He had bigger fish to fry.

He got to his feet slowly this time, reached above his head and felt a hard ceiling. He was over six feet tall. The roof of the shaft was just in his reach. The water at the bottom of the shaft must be runoff from the rain.

He remembered that a lot of mine shafts were closed because they were unworkable from continual flooding.

His heart sank at the thought. The dripping sound was steady behind him and he couldn't hear a pump. If the shaft was flooded was he more likely than not in an abandoned mine? If he was in an abandoned mine he wouldn't know which direction would lead him out. There were miles and miles of shafts, some deeper than others.

He licked a finger and grimaced at the taste of charcoal and sulfur. *Definitely a coal mine.* He held the finger up to detect a hint of a breeze. If air was coming in that was the direction out. He could feel the slightest movement of air. It seemed to be coming from the direction he'd been crawling. That made sense because behind him was water.

He shuffled slowly along the tracks, one foot always touching the rail. He'd gone another few feet when the rail ended. He continued in the same direction and went a few more feet when his bare toes struck something hard. He stumbled forward and went down hard. His reflexes were too slow to break his fall. He heard his nose crunch and felt cinders grind into his lips and cheek.

He pushed himself up to his knees and examined himself with his hands. He could taste the blood running from his nose but he ignored the pain. His toe felt broken and throbbed even harder than his head. He got to his feet again and ran his hands along the wall in front of him. It was made of rough wood, like cedar planks. It was just as he thought. The shaft had been closed off.

He yelled, "Help! Someone help me!" and pounded on the wood with the side of his fist. He heard a sound like hinges squeak coming from higher on the obstruction. He reached up and ran his hand over the wood in time to feel an opening and air coming through. It was a pass-through. *A door.* The pass-through slammed shut pinching his fingers and he heard a bolt slide into place. He put his damaged fingers in his mouth and reached up with the other hand. He found the pass-through and pushed on it. It didn't budge. He beat on it with the side of his fist but it didn't give.

He yelled. "Hey! Don't go. I'm in here. Help me!" Nothing. "Help! Help me! Someone's locked me in here! I'm in here!" Still nothing. No sound from the other side of the door.

His heart pounded and he frantically scrabbled around the wood for a handle but found none. He ran his hands over the entire surface but the only thing was the small pass-through. He felt for a seam around the pass-through and then around the entire door. It was made tight. He beat on the door and yelled until he was hoarse and the pain in his head pounded behind his eyes until they felt as if they would explode.

He stopped pounding, put his back against the door slid to the floor. He was trapped. He scooted until he could put his cheek against the seam in the door. Cool air came through. Not much but it was something. *At least I'll have air and water if it's drinkable. I'll get out of here. Someone will come.*

He tried again to remember where he'd been. It was a bar. He remembered drinking Tequila. Why was he drinking tequila? Thinking made his head hurt but he had to remember. He had to know why he was here. Who he had been with. He recalled being in a bad mood and he wanted to fight someone. Maybe he'd beat someone's ass and this was payback. Was he in a fight? Is that how he got the bump on the back of his skull. Or was this part of a hallucination. Maybe the drink was laced with something, and none of this was real. His scratchy throat told him it was all too real.

He was angry and scared. He had night terrors of being trapped. In the nightmare he would be in an old, dark, musty house and going up a wide flight of stairs. As he neared the top the stairs would become narrower and narrower and the ceiling would come lower until he was forced to crawl on his belly where he would end up stuck. He would try to turn back but the stairs behind him disappeared and he was in a tight wooden box. He'd beat on it and scream until he awakened, his throat sore, his heart beating wildly.

He'd been having these dreams since high school. His mother told him it was nothing to worry about. His conscience told him he was being punished for the evil things he and his friends had done. Maybe this was his penance. A fist of emotion seemed to swell in his chest and tears streamed down his face.

He heard the bolt sliding, hinges squeaked and he felt something hit the ground near his feet. Before he could get up the small door latched shut again.

"Damn it, this isn't funny. Let me out of here. I know you can hear me!"

He knelt down and started feeling around for whatever had been dropped in with him and heard a hissing noise. It was close. His reflex was to bang on the door again, but caution told him he should remain still. Had they thrown a snake in with him? There were a lot of snakes around mine property.

The hissing was too continuous to be a snake and his eyes stung. The itch in his nose and throat worsened until he was struggling to breathe. His mind said the hissing was some kind of gas. He dropped down flat, pressed his cheek to the floor and took slow breaths through his makeshift underwear gas mask. Gas was lighter than air. He should be able to breathe nearer the floor, but it was worse.

He clenched his burning eyes shut, folded the underwear and held it across his nose and mouth. It did little to filter out the burning taste of the gas. He coughed and gagged and mucous ran freely from his nose and mouth.

A voice came from the other side of the door. "Did you think I forgot you?"

The last conscious thought he had was that he knew that voice. He slapped an arm against the wood but his strength ebbed. He slid onto his side, losing the underwear and hitching in panicked gulps of the gas. His body spasmed, his heels and hands drummed the floor. One leg kicked out, his throat hitched, and then he lay still.

Chapter 2

One week later

The early morning meeting was requested by FBI Assistant Deputy Director Silas Toomey. In attendance in the Chief's conference room were Jack Murphy, Liddell Blanchard, Chief Marlin Pope, Captain Franklin and Director Toomey.

Toomey was a doppelganger for a younger Donald Trump. As an Assistant Deputy Director with the FBI he dressed the part in two or three thousand dollar suits and smart footwear. Today he was wearing a light brown suit and vest with white and brown Oxford Brogues. He began with, "I would say I'm sorry to start your day off with this, but your country needs you, gentlemen. Need I remind you, you're not just Evansville police detectives, you are sworn agents of the federal government."

Detective Jack Murphy, third generation Irish American cop, sat in a chair across from Toomey, while his partner, Liddell Blanchard, aka Bigfoot, was squeezed into a chair near the desk.

Jack stood a little over six feet tall. He was sturdily built, with short dark hair that was spiked in the front and gray eyes that could turn stormy if he was provoked. He liked redheads, scotch, Guinness, the beach, and long walks—minus the beach and the long walks. In that order.

His partner, Liddell Blanchard, aka Bigfoot, stood over six and a half feet tall and weighed in at a full grown Yeti. Liddell was a Louisiana transplant from the Iberville Parish Sheriff Department, part French, part Creole, and all muscle.

Jack and Liddell worked as partners in the Violent Crimes Unit of the Evansville Police Department and had both been transferred into the Homicide Squad. It was composed of them and any other detective or specialist they needed at the moment. Also, as Toomey had reminded them, they were sworn Federal Agents assigned to a Task Force—USOC— Unsolved Serial and Organized Crime. This was Toomey's brainchild and his reach covered the Midwest and beyond.

Toomey launched into his packaged TED talk.

"You two have proven yourself capable, resourceful, dedicated, relentless in the pursuit of the truth and…"

"Justice and the American way," Liddell said. "Like Supermen."

Toomey ignored him.

Toomey had a strong connection with FBI profilers, the Behavior Analysis Unit at Quantico and had been made aware of Jack and Liddell's talent for catching serial killers. He recruited them to work in the Midwest Region of Unsolved, Serial and Organized Crime, or as Jack's coworkers liked to call it, "U-SUCK". Twelve states made up the Midwest region with offices in each of the state capitals. Each office reported to Director Toomey and Toomey reported to God.

Each regional office was comprised of FBI Agents, DHS, Homeland Security, ICE, DEA, ATF, and local detectives from across the Midwest who had proven records of solving high profile and difficult cases. Jack fit right in with a proven record of *being* difficult while solving high profile cases. He felt that distinguished him from the rest.

There were also contract workers and consultants in the mix when a particular talent was needed. There was a staff of lawyers assigned to tell the agents when they could shoot back. A group of lawyers is known as a 'crew.' Like on pirate ships. Individually they are called cutthroats, and privateers. Only a few qualified as swashbucklers, and these were mostly prosecutors or judges.

Captain Franklin stood by the door, dressed in his usual tailor-made suit, black pinstripe, white shirt, red tie, and polished lace up shoes. Franklin had worked his way up the ladder, rising to the very lofty and well deserved rank of captain. As captain he was the commander of the Investigations Unit, which made him believe he was Jack's boss.

Chief of Police Marlin Pope wore a 'dressed down' police uniform with few ribbons or distinctions other than his five-star collar dogs. He had worked every job, unit, and shift on the Evansville Police Department until he was appointed Chief of Police five mayors ago. Pope was the first black officer to make the rank of Lieutenant, Captain, Major, Deputy

Chief and Chief. He had the respect and loyalty of every man, woman and civilian within the police department with the exception of Deputy Chief Richard Dick, otherwise known as 'Double Dick'. He had been given the nickname because of his harsh punishments for perceived wrongdoings and his penchant for dicking someone he didn't like repeatedly. Hence the name, 'Double Dick'.

Dick was blond haired, blue eyed, tall and lean, and every bit the Aryan poster child. He hated the very air Jack Murphy breathed and hated even more that he was now indebted to Jack.

Recently, the new mayor, Benet Cato, was of a mind to clean house and intended to replace Chief Pope with Deputy Chief Richard Dick. Dick was always his own worst enemy and had screwed that up by becoming the prime suspect in an old murder case among other faux pas. Jack had saved him from total ruination. Benet Cato, as mayor of Evansville, had seen the value of maintaining Pope in office, and she knew if she replaced Pope with Dick there would be mass retirements, not to mention pissing off more than half of her constituents.

Toomey said, "As sworn federal agents you work *when* I need you, *where* I need you, and *as long* as I need you. And I need you."

Captain Franklin said, "Director Toomey, they can't wait to get to work."

Toomey raised an eyebrow.

Jack said, "That's what the captain told us to say. I need to mention that he asked if we were claustrophobic. I have to tell you that I don't do dark tight places unless it involves sex and Scotch."

Captain Franklin rubbed his eyes and groaned.

Toomey said, "Noted. Now let me brief you." Before he could say more there was a knock at the Chief's door and Double Dick entered.

"Sorry I'm late," Dick said. "My assistant must not have given me the memo. It's hard to get adequate help anymore." He came inside and shook hands with Director Toomey. "Pleasure to see you again, Director."

"Actually, Richard," Chief Pope said, "I was going to fill you in on this later. How about lunch?"

Dick awkwardly said, "That is fine, Chief. I'm sorry to barge in."

"Nonsense," Pope said. "I'll tell you all about it at lunch. My treat."

Dick smiled. He was being taken to lunch by the Chief of Police. "I'll come down at noon, Chief." With that he left.

Pope picked up the phone and punched a button. "Judy, no one else is to come near my office." He listened, then said, "That's okay," and hung up. "Sorry about that."

Toomey took a business card out of his shirt pocket and handed it to Jack. On the back of the card was a name, address and telephone number. "This case won't take you far from home. It involves Indiana, and Illinois."

Jack interpreted that as meaning he was going to be busy until he drew Social Security. That didn't fit in the plans he had for his immediate future. He and his ex-wife, Katie, had patched things up. He had a wedding to help plan. That's what Katie told him he was doing.

"On the card is the name and number of Linton, Indiana's Chief of Police. You'll meet with him and other members of a task force he has put together. You will take over the investigation."

Jack asked, "Does the Linton chief know we're coming?"

"He does."

"Does he know we're taking the case from him?" Jack asked.

"You're not taking it from him. You're working it with him but you're the boss."

Jack failed to see the difference.

"You're sworn federal officers. You're in charge because I say you are. If you get any shit from anyone let me know. By the way, you'll get plenty of it from Chief Jerrell because that's his nature. I met him when he attended the FBI Academy at Quantico. This guy's the real deal. Ex-Army Ranger, two tours in Afghanistan, two in Iraq. You don't want your name on his dance card."

"Bigfoot can handle him," Jack said. He handed the card to Liddell.

"Thanks, pod'na," Liddell said.

"What's the case?" Jack asked.

"Cases. Plural. There are a string of homicides and missing persons that may be connected," Toomey said.

"Serial killer?" Jack asked.

"Probably. The murders are in Greene and Sullivan Counties up north of here, and at least one in Illinois. A plethora of missing persons."

Liddell mouthed the word "plethora" at Jack and stifled a chuckle.

"Director, forgive me for saying this, but there is always a 'plethora' of missing persons. Are you sure you want us on this? Do Feds work missing persons? Don't we just handle kidnapping, that kind of stuff?"

"You have five confirmed deaths, some are out and out murder, some are suspicious, but you will be handling the investigations." Toomey was unable to maintain eye contact with Jack.

"How many missing persons will we be looking at?" Jack asked.

"Forty-three. However, only the five deaths have a similar cause of death. All were found in lakes. Some of those were reported as drownings or death by misadventure and the autopsies were inconclusive."

"So, we're not particularly looking into the missing persons. We're hunting a serial killer," Jack said.

Toomey cleared his throat. "We don't have enough evidence to support or exclude that theory. That's part of the reason you're going."

Jack was thinking of how he would explain a long absence to Katie and this was beginning to sound like a very long absence. They were getting remarried in a few months. For the second time. The first time around they'd split because of his job among other reasons. He didn't like to dwell on the past, and he'd vowed he would do better this time. Be a better husband. This time Katie was pregnant and he wanted to be a real father. He wanted to be married to her and not his job.

"You said, 'part of the reason'. What's the other part?" Jack asked.

"Chief Jerrell has a personal interest in this case. Too personal. He's a good policeman, sharp as a tack, but like a tack he doesn't care who he pricks if you get my meaning."

"I'm going to be blunt," Jack said. "If you're assigning us as a personal favor to Jerrell I want to know if we have jurisdiction or if we're just bullying them?"

"Don't talk to me about jurisdiction, son," Toomey warned.

Toomey had a point. Shortly after Jack and Liddell had been recruited for USOC Jack had pursued a killer across the country and had taken a suspended from duty St. Louis State Trooper with him where they promptly were involved in a murder in New Mexico and ended by killing the bad guy in shoot-out in Arizona. Both Jack and the trooper were severely injured and had totaled a couple of official cars. Jack did all this without one word to Toomey. *Murphy's Law says: "Better to kick ass and then ask forgiveness."*

Toomey said, "Chief Jerrell's son is one of the victims. He doesn't have jurisdiction in his son's case but he doesn't trust the police investigation that was done. His son's body was found in Sullivan County. Linton is in Greene County. His son's death was mishandled by the Sullivan interim Coroner who deemed it an accidental drowning. The local police mucked up the scene so Jerrell had his own autopsy performed. The coroner in Greene County ruled the death a homicide."

Jack got that. If Jack's kid was murdered he'd hunt the son of a bitch down and gut him like a catfish. It still didn't answer the question of why USOC was involved.

Toomey must have sensed Jack's reluctance and said, "Here's the crux. Chief Jerrell's family is influential in the Justice Department. They wouldn't like it if the Chief got himself into a predicament. You'll like the guy. Jerrell sounds just like you. I'm aware that under other circumstances he could work the case just fine, but these aren't those circumstances. Got it?"

Jerrell. Ranger. Mean mother. Out for blood. Maybe cut some corners. Maybe cut some throats. Yeah. His kind of guy.

"You boys are aggressive to the point of…well, let's just say you ignore rules. Sometimes it takes two Alpha's to cancel each other out. Plus, I promised that we would get this done quick."

"Who is his family?" Jack asked.

Toomey gave a typical FBI administrator answer. "You don't need to know that. Consider it a favor to me. If that doesn't do it for you, consider it an order from me. Besides, it will be good material for you to present when I send you and your partner to the profiling class at Quantico."

"Quantico? When did I agree to that?" Jack asked.

"I'll agree," Liddell pitched in.

"You agreed when you were sworn in. It was in the paperwork that neither of you bothered to read."

Jack saw no point in arguing and he wanted to meet this Chief Jerrell, ex-Army Ranger. As a detective he'd had experiences with the Feds interference. He didn't like the idea of taking some other dog's bone. Sometimes he wished he could go back to being a simple city detective. That job had its own drama but you weren't dealing with big government. Big government usually meant bigger crooks and bigger roadblocks, lawsuits, and possibly prison time.

Toomey smiled. "We'll make an FBI agent out of you yet, Jack."

Yeah. Right after I eat a cockroach.

Jack asked, "Is all this missing person and murder data coming from Chief Jerrell or from the BAU?" BAU is the Behavioral Analysis Unit of the FBI. Profilers. Think shrinks with guns.

"From me," Angelina Garcia said from the doorway.

Chapter 3

Chief Constable Shaunda Lynch was heading home from pulling an all-nighter when she spotted the Jeep peeling out of the gravel access road coming from the Dugger mine. It was a new silver Jeep Cherokee Laredo 4WD. She kept her distance and let the Jeep get off of mine property. They must have spotted her and headed for town well over the speed limit. She followed it into Dugger city limits before she turned on her light bar and lit them up with her takedown lights. The Jeep pulled in front of the library and stopped. The headlights weren't on and it was barely light enough out to see. That was an easy ticket.

She knew what they'd been doing. The abandoned underground mines and above ground stripper pits were a favorite spot with teens who wanted to smoke, drink, have sex, and do drugs. She understood that. She also knew the mines and lakes were dangerous and received little to no patrol from the state or county police. Patrolling the county around the mines was outside of her jurisdiction, but as a parent she felt it was her duty to rein in the rampant hormonal changes these little brats were experiencing.

She didn't have to call the Jeep's license plate in to dispatch. She knew the owner was Claire Dillingham, town board president. The Jeep was probably being driven by her son, Brandon, nineteen and still in high school. There were two people in the Jeep. That would make the passenger Timmy Long, drinking buddy, wingman, high school dropout. She could see a long stretch in Pendleton Correctional Facility in both of their futures.

Shaunda had moved back to Dugger five years ago after her mother died. While she was gone she'd exhausted a lot of dead-end jobs in dead-end places. Her heart had told her it was time to come home, and she'd heard at the funeral that the town was searching for a new Chief Constable, having fired the last one after he ran off with the judge's secretary. Shaunda needed a job and a place to stay. She had a GED, no police experience, was short, barely five feet five. What she lacked in experience and size she more than made up for with dogged determination.

She'd gone to City Hall to apply for the Chief Constable position and was surprised to find the interviewer was someone from her high school days, Claire DeShane, now Mrs. Claire Dillingham, president of the town board.

Shaunda stopped at an angle to the Jeep, keeping her takedown lights on the passenger compartment. As she approached she saw that Claire's son, Brandon, was inside like she thought, but he wasn't driving. She was surprised to see Patty Burris behind the wheel. The sixteen-year-old girl was grinning sheepishly. She knew Patty didn't have a driver's license yet which was a good thing because she hadn't yet learned to button her shirt up properly.

When Shaunda was hired by the city of Dugger she'd had to attend the Indiana Law Enforcement Academy in Plainfield, ninety miles drive from Dugger. Two hours of driving, nine hours of class, and then two hours home for twelve weeks. She had no choice but to commute because she had a sixteen-year-old daughter at home.

Fortunately, she had one good friend in Dugger, Rosie Benton. She and Rosie were friends since grade school and had kept in touch over those years away from home. Rosie had agreed to let Penelope stay with her while Shaunda attended the Police Academy. During that time Pen had made a best friend, Patty Burris, the driver here.

Yesterday evening when Shaunda got the panicked call from Joey saying his wife was having the baby she'd called Pen's bestie to come and spend the night. Patty said she was tied up. Now she knew why Patty was tied up.

Shaunda leaned in the driver's side window and shone her flashlight around the front and back. "You might want to zip up before you get out of the car," Shaunda said to Brandon.

Patty's face turned red. "I'm sorry Mrs. Lynch."

Not as sorry as you will be if you get pregnant.

"Brandon," she said to the boy. "I'd ask you what's up, but it's a little obvious."

"Hello Chief," Brandon said, and yanked at his zipper. "What are you doing out this early in the morning?"

Shaunda kept her expression neutral. "I was going to ask you the same thing."

"We were just talking Mrs. Lynch," Patty said. "Honest."

Brandon didn't try to hide his grin. "Yeah Chief. Just talking."

Shaunda didn't need to ask if his mother knew where he was or who he was with. Brandon's father died six years ago while working for Black Beauty Coal and Claire had had little control over the nineteen-year-old. Claire had given him everything and in return he gave her problems. Shaunda wondered when he'd get killed by some girl's father or go to prison.

"Patty, does your mom know where you are?"

Patty's head bobbed up and down, then side to side. "I told mom but she might have been asleep. You won't call her will you Mrs. Lynch."

"Patty, for starters, when you see me in uniform I'm Chief Lynch, not Mrs. Lynch. No, I'm not going to tell your mother. You are. What would happen if she knew about this?" Patty was an only child too and her mother worked two jobs to make ends meet even with what Shaunda paid Patty for helping with Pen.

Patty didn't answer but Brandon slumped in the seat and groaned. Shaunda said to him, "Brandon, I swear if you say anything to piss me off I'll tow the car and lock you up for contributing to the delinquency of a minor. I'll give you Patty's ticket for reckless driving and no headlights. You're the one that put an unlicensed driver behind the wheel."

The real reason Shaunda wasn't burying him in traffic citations was because Claire would be the one paying them, not Brandon as he never had a job. Plus, she wanted to keep Patty from getting caught up in the same old groups of bad boys that were in every high school. With teenagers if you told them no, they did just the opposite. Unfortunately, some girls had to learn life's lessons the hard way. She had.

"Here's what we're going to do," Shaunda said. "Patty, you get in the Tahoe. Brandon you go straight home and don't sass me. Claire won't be able to help you if you get on my bad side. Got it?"

Patty literally jumped out of the Jeep's door and climbed into the chief's Tahoe. Brandon scooted over the console and plopped into the driver's seat. "Can I go now Chief Constable Lynch?" he asked in a mocking voice that only a hoodlum teenager can perfect.

"Brandon, I don't have to tell you how dangerous those places are." Brandon's father had died in a mine cave-in.

Brandon said nothing. He stared straight ahead with one foot on the brake and one goosing the gas.

She slapped the roof of the Jeep and said, "Get out of here. No more warnings."

The Jeep disappeared down the road and turned back toward Main Street. When it was out of sight Shaunda heard the engine gunning flat out. She let that go and got back in the Tahoe. Patty was sitting stiff as a board, her eyes locked onto the dash mounted shotgun.

"I keep that for skunks," Shaunda said. "Like that one."

Patty's hand went to her mouth and she giggled.

"What were you thinking girl?"

Patty was silent and embarrassed but she was at that age of natural defiance. Sixteen was hard for a girl. Not a woman, not a child, adventurous, afraid of many things, trying not to disappoint, an overriding need to discover what life had to offer. In other words, vulnerable and capable of great hurt and great kindness and love. It was almost time for momma bird to shove Patty out of the nest. She made a mental note to have a sit down with Patty's mom.

"Patty, you know I appreciate everything you do for me. I appreciate how you treat Pen and watch out for her." Penelope was sixteen, wheelchair bound from the age of eight. Shaunda homeschooled her and Patty was reliable when she couldn't be home—except for last night. Because Joey was at the hospital with his wife, Shaunda had taken his shift and Pen had spent the better part of the evening and overnight by herself. Shaunda checked in from time to time. "I know I rely on you more than I should. Most girls your age wouldn't be gentle and patient and helpful and trustworthy. If you need more space I'll understand. If you need more money I can understand that, too. I can tell you one thing, you need to stay away from that boy. He's nothing but trouble. He'll hurt you."

Patty's eyes welled up and silent tears ran down both cheeks.

Shaunda got a few tissues from the console and gave them to her. "It's better to cry now than have regrets later. Trust me on this."

"I'm sorry Chief Lynch. I'm sorry if I let you down. I thought he really liked me. I can't believe how that jerk acted."

"Did he do something to you Patty?"

She didn't answer.

Patty was wearing a thin red sweater over a button-down shirt and blue jeans. Shaunda turned on the dome light and said, "Fix your shirt."

Patty re-buttoned her shirt and Shaunda saw a button was missing at the top. Patty's throat was an angry red color. A red Shaunda was all too familiar with. Brandon had choked her.

"Answer me Patty. Did he hurt you?"

Patty covered her face and sobbed until she was literally shivering.

"That little bastard," Shaunda said through clenched teeth and threw the Tahoe into gear but Patty grabbed her arm.

"Don't, Mrs. Lynch. He didn't…he didn't get that far. I don't want to see him again. I can't see him again…"

Shaunda put the Tahoe back into park. She took a deep breath and slowly let it out before saying, "Take your time hon. Whatever you tell me is between us unless I have to beat the little rat into cat chow."

Patty snickered through her tears but remained silent with the tissue hiding her eyes. "He wanted me to…to…and when I wouldn't he said I was the ugliest girl in school and I should be honored that he wanted me. He said the other girls would be jealous. I laughed at him and told him he was pathetic and that's when he…"

Shaunda waited for Patty to finish without interrupting. She had a knot in her stomach and the rage in her heart was like a living thing.

"He grabbed my throat and pushed me against the door and started feeling me all over. I tried to fight but he was too strong. Then he just stopped and told me to get out and shoved me out of the Jeep. I was afraid he was going to do it right there. Instead, he told me to get in and drive and I'd better not get caught or he'd have me arrested for stealing his car. When you stopped the Jeep, I wanted to tell you but he said I'd be arrested 'cause I didn't have a license. I was scared my mom would find out. I'm sorry."

Shaunda knew two things. One, Patty was young and didn't realize what Brandon was. A sick monster. Two, Brandon had put her behind the wheel. He was the one responsible. He knew his mom would protect him and he wanted to humiliate Patty because she wouldn't put out.

Shaunda suddenly felt old. She had put a heavy responsibility on a sixteen-year-old. Patty wasn't family but Shaunda had tried to put her in that role because she needed help, she needed family to help with her daughter, be a friend to Pen. It was partly her fault that Patty had made such a bad choice in the first place. Patty would want to date. Go to parties. Have other friends. How could she do that when she was always being asked to come and basically babysit? Shaunda knew she'd have to find some way to give Patty a break, take that responsibility off her shoulders and let her just be a friend. She wasn't sure how she would do it but she had to try.

She'd start by apologizing to Patty's mom for all the long hours she'd needed Patty to come and sit with Pen. The mother needed the money, and she was gone a lot, but if anything happened to Patty it would kill her and Shaunda would never forgive herself.

"I'll take you home, but I need you to be truthful with me. If he did anything I need to take you by the hospital and have you checked."

"Nothing happened, Mrs. Lynch. I'm being honest."

Shaunda put the Tahoe in drive and pulled away from the curb. She believed her.

"Are you going to tell my mom?"

Shaunda glanced over at the girl. She remembered Patty, the eleven-year-old she'd met in the grocery store. Pen was in the wheelchair by then and headstrong, wanting to do everything by herself. Pen wanted a box of Hostess cupcakes but there was very little money in the food budget back then. When she'd looked up Pen was gone. Shaunda had searched every aisle calling her daughter's name and then she heard giggling. She found Pen and another girl her age in the book aisle looking at a teen magazine. She couldn't remember when she'd seen her daughter so happy, or comfortable, with another person of her age. The two had hit it off immediately and became besties. Patty's mom was strict. She could just imagine what the girl would go through when they got there.

"Patty, I'm going to let you decide what to tell her. If you're positive he didn't do anything, and I mean any sexual contact, I'll let you off near your house. It's always better not to lie," she said, lying herself.

Patty was quiet for the remainder of the trip but when they neared her home she said, "I'm not going to tell her. You know how she is. She'd get into it with his mom and she hardly has time for anything now. I'm not hurt."

Shaunda pulled to the shoulder down the lane from Patty's home. The Burrises lived less than a mile from Shaunda separated by farm fields. Patty opened the Tahoe door and then came across the seat and hugged Shaunda. "Thanks Mrs. Lynch. Please don't tell Pen. I'll tell her if I can work up the nerve."

"Go on. Get out of here already," Shaunda said and Patty got out, shut the door, and walked toward the back of her house.

Shaunda watched until Patty was out of sight, then put the Tahoe in gear and pulled back onto the gravel lane. She was dead tired, but her morning wasn't quite over yet. She had a meeting with King Jerrell this afternoon for his nonsense task force and she had one or two things to do before she got to bed. Thirty minutes tops, then home, skip breakfast and get some sleep.

Chapter 4

Angelina Garcia was in her mid-twenties, with skin the color of yellow coal, dark thick hair pulled back in a ponytail, and dark eyes. She started her career as a part time temporary civilian IT person for the Evansville Police Department, fixing glitches in the data systems that linked EPD to other law enforcement agencies in the state and federal databases. What she had really longed for was to become a detective. But after seeing the result of some investigations, the body count, the damage done to victims, suspects, and policemen alike, she decided that her five feet three frame could be put to better use.

She came to Jack's attention early in her work for the EPD when he was searching for a serial killer who was using nursery rhymes to select his victims; all children. She had proven herself invaluable in finding the pattern that led Jack to the killer. This, in turn, brought her to the attention of the Chief of Police. Suddenly she was a full-time employee working with computers to crime map the city. Her expertise soon was in demand and she was assigned wherever needed.

She met her husband, Sheriff Mark Crowley of Dubois County, while working on the Mother Goose case, married, semiretired, and had started working on a consulting basis with the Evansville Police Department. Next, she established her own cyber security and consulting company.

She had recently helped Jack and Liddell when they became involved in a human trafficking ring in Liddell's hometown of Plaquemine, Louisiana. Her work on that case brought her to the attention of the FBI, ICE, DEA, ATF and DHS. The government loved their initials. She wondered why there were always three letters.

She became somewhat of a legendary computer mercenary and straddled a fine line between legal, ethical, moral, and Angelina's way of doing things.

"Pay up," Jack said holding his hand out and Liddell put a twenty dollar bill in it. Jack looked at her and said, "When we were told to come to the chief's office I bet him you were involved somehow."

"You're smarter than you look," Angelina said. "Is Double, erm, is Deputy Chief Dick going to be involved in this? I ran into him in the hall."

"He's not," Toomey said and the mood in the room brightened considerably. "Thanks for coming in, Angelina."

"Anything's better than sitting at home watching Mark try to put together a crib and changing table using directions that are barely in Chinese," she said and patted her stomach.

Liddell sidled up to her and put an arm around her shoulders. "You're just starting to show. Four more months to go. Do you think Mark will have the baby's room together by then?"

Angelina laughed and looked down at herself. "What was I thinking? I couldn't keep anything down for two months and now I can't stop eating. Do you think I'm getting fat? How did Marcie do it?"

Liddell said, "I ate things before she could."

Angelina smirked. "Yeah. Watching you eat would do it."

Toomey said, "A few weeks ago I asked Angelina to find a way to simplify our online searches. That girl could teach NASA a couple of things. She went me one better. She created a new search engine and was test-driving it when she stumbled across the things that got you here. I don't know how this thing Angelina created works. I'll let her tell you."

They all took seats again and Angelina set a stack of manila folders on the conference room table.

"I created an algorithm that searches social media, posts, newspapers, television, radio, motor vehicle records, police reports, marriage, divorce, lawsuits, courts, traffic cameras, any surveillance cameras connected to the Internet and some other stuff you don't need to know about."

Jack interpreted that as meaning she was illegally hacking government and justice department servers, satellites, and whatnot. If he didn't know he wouldn't have to testify in a Senate hearing.

"Bottom line, I can search by key words looking for just about anything or anyone. My system knows all the jurisdictional boundaries connected to the information. I haven't included all the satellites in the package yet. I would need some kind of permission according to the FBI."

Jack could tell she was lying about the satellites.

Liddell said, "Can you repeat the part after 'I created an algorithm'?"

Jack said, "Ignore him."

"I always do," Angelina said. "Anyway, I started with something simple to test my system. I searched for unsolved murders in Indiana. Then I searched active missing persons in Indiana. There was a concentration of hits in Greene County and Sullivan County. I'm still tweaking the data. I linked in VICAP—the FBI's Violent Criminal Apprehension Program—and insurance company and medical records and found some other interesting similarities. Then I..."

"I'm going comatose here, Angelina," Jack said. "Just give me the bottom line."

"In English. I kept making connections. I expanded the search to include Kentucky and Illinois and got a hit in Illinois similar to the Indiana cases. There were two in Kentucky but the autopsies ruled them out.

"I triple checked my data by calling the investigating agencies and getting hard copies of records. That was how I got involved with Chief Jerrell at the Linton Police Department. I told him some of what I thought I knew and he got excited. He told me the one case I had was his son's murder. He said he had launched his own investigation. He'd come across some of the cases I was looking through during his own research and was setting up a small task force. He asked me if I would work with his task force. I told him I was on contract with the FBI. He offered to hire me out of his own pocket. I called Director Toomey because I thought it might be a good opportunity to give my program a test run."

Toomey picked up the story. "I called Chief Jerrell and told him Angelina wasn't a tool we loaned out. In any case, the FBI is paying her to develop the software. She can't use it until we're done testing and approving it. Jerrell was—is convinced Angelina is on to something."

Jack held his hand out for a file.

"I told you they'd be interested," Angelina said and handed case file folders to everyone.

"Five victims in a seven year period," she said. "All in March. All male. Four white. One black. All would be thirty to thirty-one years old now. Except the Illinois victim, Clint Baker, who would be forty."

She had everyone's attention.

"Seven years ago, in early March, Clint Baker was found in a muddy wash along the Illinois side of the Wabash River. Near Hutsonville, Illinois, where he lived. His body was found five miles from his home. He was naked, clothes on the shore, empty tequila bottle by the clothes. His wallet and cell phone were with the clothes. His car was found in the driveway at his house five miles away. Police thought he got drunk, walked away from his house, walked or fell into the water and drowned. Drugs and alcohol were involved so it was ruled an accidental death by drowning."

"What kind of drugs?" Jack asked.

"Cocaine and fentanyl were found in the toxicology screen. It wasn't a massive dose but enough to be a contributing factor.

"Five years ago. March. Two more bodies were found. A week apart. In a Sullivan County stripper pit lake called the Coal City Mine Lake. The first victim was a black male, Willie Lamont Washington. Age twenty-six. He was naked, clothes were on a rock near the embankment. His wallet, money, credit cards, phone, and car keys were with the clothes or in his car. The car was found nearby. An empty whiskey bottle was on the floor of the car with his prints on it. An autopsy was performed. Toxicology tested positive for cocaine and fentanyl. Not enough to kill him but coupled with the whiskey might have in time. Death was ruled an accidental drowning.

"The caller to Sullivan County dispatch was anonymous. The phone number came back to a little bar near City Coal Mine Lake called —and get this—the Chute Me Bar. That's spelled C- H- U- T- E. You can't make this stuff up. A copy of the police report is in the folder.

"But wait…there's more," Angelina said like an advertisement announcer. "The second body, Daniel Winters, also age twenty-six, was found six days later in the same lake, almost in the exact same spot as Lamont Washington. He was naked except for his underwear. According to the report, the underwear was pulled over his head. The rest of his clothes were on the embankment, nothing missing. His vehicle found nearby. Anonymous call from the Chute Me Bar."

"Let me guess," Jack said. "Alcohol, cocaine and fentanyl. Ruled as an accidental drowning."

"You should be a detective," she said. "The coroner's report noted a large contusion on the back of the head. A follow-up police report merely said the two deaths, Winters and Washington, were 'suspicious' but they didn't believe they were connected. I called the Sullivan detective handling both cases, Lieutenant Nonnie Murray. She said the autopsy wasn't conclusive. The contusions on both men could have been from diving into the lake and hitting a rock."

"Both of the victims?" Jack asked.

"When I talked to her I asked that same question. She said there was the same contusion on the back of Lamont Washington's noggin. There was no water found in the lungs of either victim, but she said water isn't always found in the lungs in a drowning death. Her report is in your packet."

"She also pointed out there are two or more drowning deaths in that stripper pit lake every year. She wasn't going to get her panties in a bunch over a couple more. The guys were drunk, high, and made a poor choice. She said the investigation went nowhere. Families for the victims were nonexistent. No one seemed broke up over the deaths. Winter's personal effects are still in evidence because there was no one to pick them up. Likewise, for Lamont. Their cars were towed and unclaimed and have since been sold or scrapped out."

Jack asked, "Were there funerals?"

"Paupers graves. Both of them. Both of them were living on the county. I can try to see if there were any inquiries."

"Don't bother for now," Jack said.

"Moving right along. Three years ago, again in March another anonymous call to police dispatch. This was Greene County. Leonard DiLegge, white male, twenty-eight years old, naked, found in Dugger Lake, nothing missing except his cell phone. The anonymous call was made from that cell phone and it was never recovered. His vehicle was found near the lake. He had an older model VW Van with a wizard painted on the sides."

Jack asked, "Dugger Lake?"

She explained. "Dugger Lake is physically in two counties. Greene County and Sullivan County. This victim was found on the Greene County side of the lake. Dugger, the city, has a stretch of the lake and Sullivan County has some."

Jack nodded.

"DiLegge's clothes and wallet were found on the bank near the body, same as the others. And get this, his underwear was pulled over his head. Just like Winters. The autopsy reported a contusion on the back of the head. Cocaine and fentanyl, but no alcohol this time. Drowning was the only possibility according to the detective's report but they listed it as a suspicious death, the suspicion due to the missing phone. The official cause of death was hypoxia. Accidental drowning couldn't be ruled out. That case remains open, but no one is working on it."

"I guess DiLegge wasn't missed much either," Jack said.

"I haven't pulled all the background information yet, but the police report said he's a known druggie," she answered.

Jack shook his head in disbelief. "That blow to the head alone should have kicked the investigation up a notch."

"I agree," Toomey said. "This kind of shit is why I want you two on this."

Angelina continued. "The most recent one was a week ago. March. Troy Jerrell Jr's body was found floating in Dugger Lake. Blow to the head, some drugs, blood alcohol was sky high, and his underwear were pulled over his head."

"Sullivan County or Greene County?" Jack asked.

"Sullivan. The case is being handled by Dugger PD. The call came in anonymously like the others. His clothes were found on the bank but the wallet, phone and vehicle were missing. His truck was found three days later behind a bar in Dugger. The call came in from his cell phone."

Jack started to say something but Angelina held a finger up. "Hang on," she said. "I saved the best detail for last. Troy Jerrell Junior's cause of death was ruled as hypoxia like the others, but the pathologist found something interesting this time. Oleoresin capsaicin was found in his lungs, throat and nasal passages. He choked to death before he went in the water. Unless he was crazy and huffing that stuff, this is a definite homicide."

"Oleoresin. That's the chemical found in…" Liddell began.

"Pepper spray," Jack finished the sentence.

"Yeah," she said. "A bag of marijuana was under the seat when they found the truck. Interestingly, the truck was found by a Linton police officer—in Dugger city limits."

Jack filed that tidbit away and said, "None of the other victims showed signs of being pepper sprayed?"

"Not that I found."

Chapter 5

The home Shaunda shared with her daughter was situated in Sullivan County, just south of Dugger city limits. Shaunda turned down a packed-dirt road that ran between freshly cultivated fields and onward toward her house. The fields would be head high with corn in a few months.

An incandescent crimson, gold and cerulean blue light was hovering on the horizon in the east heralding another glorious morning. As tired as she was, she rolled to a stop to take in the God made art playing out in front of her eyes. There was something magical about a sunrise. She could understand why the ancients worshipped it and the gods that created it. She knew all the scientific explanations of the colors that made up a sunrise but sometimes you didn't try to explain a thing, you just let its beauty wash over you.

She gave the Tahoe some gas and her home soon came into view in the little L-shaped patch of cleared land at the end of the road. The house wasn't much to look at, with its peeling paint and warped porch and tar patched roof, but it was warm in the winter and cool in the summer and the privacy it afforded was worth more than money.

She rolled quietly onto the concrete pad she and a friend had poured beside the house. Pen should still be asleep at this hour. She hoped she could catch a few hours of shut-eye herself before Pen was up. She was completely wiped out and not thrilled at the prospect of being around Chief Troy Jerrell this afternoon. Not one little bit. Jerrell blamed her for his son's killer not being caught. It wasn't her fault that the County Coroner had declared the death an accidental drowning. It wasn't her fault that she had a small department. It wasn't her fault that getting resources from State Police or County Sheriff's Department was a Herculean task. It wasn't her fault Troy Junior had traded his Toyota Camry for a nondescript truck that he hadn't registered. She and her constable had spent two full days looking for the Toyota. She had to suffer the humiliation of having Chief Jerrell's officers finding out that Troy Junior currently owned a truck and then they located it in Dugger city limits. Chief Jerrell must have had knowledge of the truck and hadn't passed the information on to her.

She felt sorry for Jerrell because it was his son but there was nothing to investigate. Junior had gotten drunk and high and gone for a swim. End of story. He had a bump on the back of his head but he could have gotten that in any bar or falling down drunk. She'd done all the right things. Followed procedure. Jerrell wasn't satisfied with the way she ran the investigation and had told her so in plain English, plus a few words she was sure he'd made up. He had the Greene County Coroner do a second autopsy and their opinion was that the wound on the back of the head was from a club of some type. While Jerrell was telling her what she'd missed she'd kept her peace but if he started in on her today she didn't think she had it in her to be quiet. Especially if the FBI really showed up. She saw no reason why they should. This wasn't the Lindberg baby kidnapping after all.

She went inside, quietly shut the door, latched it and listened. She could hear the girl snoring and it was becoming a concern. She needed to get Pen into a sleep study before long. She quietly turned the deadbolt. If she was lucky, Pen would sleep a few more hours. The girl almost never got up before eight. That would give her three hours to sleep. Patty had promised to come over while Shaunda attended the meeting with Jerrell's task force in Linton. She hoped Patty got some sleep herself this morning. She didn't think Brandon would be a problem for her anymore.

Shaunda's bedroom windows faced directly east into the rising sun. The 'blackout curtains' left behind by the previous occupant did diddly-squat. She had considered nailing plywood over the windows but right now she was too tired to care. She unholstered her .357 Colt Python revolver and put it in a shoe box in the back of the closet. She unbuckled her Sam Browne gun belt and hung it on a hook on the back of the closet door. She needed a gun safe to secure her weapon even though she didn't think Pen would ever mess with her gun. Like everything else, the 'need to' column fell well short of the 'have money for' column.

She slipped out of her uniform jacket and hung it on the doorknob. She shed the remainder of her uniform on the floor and fell onto the bed. She was just dropping off to sleep when she heard the doorbell. She jumped up grabbing the thin blanket to cover up and ran to the front door before she remembered she didn't have a doorbell. Pen had programmed it as her cell phone's ring tone. She ran back to her bedroom and dug her cell phone out of her jacket pocket.

Claire Dillingham's nearly hysterical voice said, "Chief Lynch, Brandon isn't home. His bed hasn't been slept in and my Jeep is missing."

"Have you tried calling him?" Shaunda asked. She was wide awake again.

"Don't you think I've done that?" Claire said. "I've tried and tried and he doesn't answer. Something's wrong. I just know it. A mother always knows."

And some mothers are in denial, Shaunda thought. "Claire, I saw him this morning. Not an hour ago. He was in your Jeep. I sent him home." She didn't tell Claire that Brandon had an underage, unlicensed driver sitting behind the wheel of Claire's thirty-thousand-dollar Jeep. Or that her precious boy had been about to commit a rape if Shaunda hadn't come along. She didn't tell her because Claire would blame Patty for corrupting and seducing her wonderful and saintly boy.

"Maybe he has the ringer turned off?" Shaunda suggested.

"Chief Lynch, is he in trouble? Why did you stop him? What did you say to him that would make him not want to come home?" Claire asked but didn't wait for an answer. "I know you and everyone in town thinks he's a delinquent, but the boy has had trouble adjusting.

Shaunda knew that Brandon's father had died six years ago. Maybe Brandon was a boy back then but he was nineteen years old now. He'd had six years to 'adjust'.

Claire railed on, "What he needs is understanding from all of you. I'm sick of the harassment."

Shaunda wanted to suggest that maybe it was time to get professional help for the 'boy'. It was just like Claire to excuse anything her "delinquent" son did. What Brandon needed from Claire was an ass whooping. Maybe a little discipline instead of letting him lie around all day, without a job, doing whatever he felt to whoever he felt like doing it to.

Shaunda took a breath and said, "The truth is I saw your Jeep coming from the Dugger mine property. I knew you'd be worried. I stopped him and told him to go home." Only part of that was a lie.

"Did you give him a ticket, Chief Lynch? He can't afford another ticket or he'll lose his license."

Shaunda didn't know that. If she had, she would have written him a butt load of citations. Even if Claire paid all the fines, Brandon would no longer be licensed. Of course, that wouldn't stop him. Nothing stopped a kid like that.

"No Claire. No tickets."

"Well, I should think not."

Shaunda had considered Claire a friend, but friend or not, she was starting to get pissed off. She said, "Claire, I gave him a verbal warning. While I've got you on the phone, when he gets home I want you to talk to him—again—about trespassing on private mining property. You know those mines aren't safe."

The line was silent long enough that Shaunda knew she'd hit a nerve. Shaunda had been complaining at every town board meeting about kids congregating on abandoned mine property posted "NO TRESPASSING." In particular, the abandoned Dugger and Sunflower mine properties. Stopping that behavior was one thing—maybe the *only* thing—she and half of the town council agreed on. Unfortunately, half wasn't enough.

Claire's words were measured when she finally spoke. "Brandon doesn't trespass on private property, *Chief* Lynch. He knows better and he's a smart kid. He's a good boy. He gets traffic tickets and harassed because he's a good-looking young man driving an expensive vehicle. I know law enforcement officers don't make a lot of money and it bothers them to see a young man have more than them. I understand that. But let me tell you, when people in Dugger come to me with complaints about the police, I want to assure them you and your men are doing things fairly. It's hard to defend you at budget meetings when one of 'your people' has written a town leader a traffic ticket."

Shaunda almost laughed. Her 'people', as Claire succinctly put it, were a twenty-three-year-old deputy constable and the other constable was well past his expiration date. She knew exactly what ticket, and what town leader Claire was talking about.

"Claire, I wrote that ticket last year to Councilman Jackson's son, who was doing 85 miles per hour in a 40 and ran a red light. He was damn lucky I made the ticket out for ten over the limit or the kid would have lost his license for a year with a huge fine."

She had been lenient on the ticket because she knew Councilman Jackson would have paid the fine and then retaliated by making deeper budget cuts for the police department. If things got any tighter Shaunda couldn't even afford paper for their printer.

"That's not what Councilman Jackson said his son told him." The innuendo being that Shaunda was lying. "His son said you were rude and you and your people are singling out council members children because of some of the council's decisions about salaries."

Shaunda was gripping the phone so tight her hand hurt. She made herself say calmly, "I make what the city pays me, Claire. I'm happy to serve. I'm grateful for the job. I'm always grateful for having any input in council meetings. I may not always agree with the decisions but I enforce the law and respect the city's needs. I'm grateful for the house the city provided me and for being allowed to drive the Tahoe." *Even though it's ready for the scrapyard.*

She could hear Claire take in a deep breath and hold it. She hoped she wasn't laying it on too thick, but what the hell. "I appreciate everything you've personally done to help me and Pen since we came to town. If it wasn't for you I don't know what we would have done."

Claire's tone changed. "Oh. Well. Think nothing of it, Shaunda."

Bitch! "Thank you, Claire. If Brandon doesn't come home soon, give me a call back and I'll see if I can track him down."

"No. That won't be necessary if you assure me he's okay. I guess he'll come home when he gets hungry." Claire forced a laugh. "You know how teenage boys are. Always eating."

Shaunda said nothing.

"He may be at his friend's house. You know Timmy, don't you? Timmy Long?"

"Yes. I know Timmy, Claire. Do you want me to drive by Timmy's and see if your Jeep is there?"

"I said that wouldn't be necessary," Claire said sharply. "I'll call him in a little while and see if he's coming home for breakfast. Sorry I snapped at you. I just worry like any mother. I'm sure you've had more than your share of worries, what with your daughter and all."

My daughter and all, what? "I'm sure he'll be home soon, Claire. Anything else?"

The line went dead in her hand. Claire hadn't thanked her for the offer to run down her nineteen year old future felon. "Screw you too, Claire," Shaunda said louder than she intended. She heard a giggle and saw Penelope in the bedroom doorway.

"Mom," Penelope said from her wheelchair. "You okay, Mom?"

Penelope was grinning but still, Shaunda's heart ached. Pen's speech ability was deteriorating slowly. "Okay" came out sounding like "O-Tay". Just one of the many changes both mother and daughter had had to endure.

Penelope had looked like any other healthy baby girl when she was delivered but over the ensuing years Shaunda noticed something was wrong with the girl's development. Her head was slightly large for her frame but back then she'd thought the rest of her would eventually catch up. The rest didn't.

After many trips and many hours in hospital waiting rooms she was told Pen was born with a condition called spina bifida. It literally means "split spine". The doctor explained that Pen's backbone hadn't closed completely and this allowed a sac of fluid to protrude. The surgery was simple, the ensuing years of complications were anything but simple.

Although she'd lost some use of her lower extremities, Pen had become a beautiful young lady. She could get in and out of her wheelchair, bathe herself, and perform most of the functions of an able bodied sixteen-year-old, but with spina bifida there was always a risk of seizures. Pen hadn't had an episode since they'd moved to Dugger. The chance was small, but still there.

It hadn't been easy raising Pen on her own, but men were, for the most part, useless. Her father was cold hearted and miserable and her mother turned to the Bible and Baptism by wine for comfort, leaving Shaunda to raise herself. When Shaunda became pregnant at sixteen her father called her a whore and her mother disowned her. She'd had to make the choice of aborting the baby or leaving on her own.

The choice was easy. She'd lived for a short time with an aunt. It was long enough to find that her aunt's son, her cousin, wanted it to be more. She'd had to move again. She was living in an abandoned house in St. Louis, begging at intersections, doing whatever it took to feed herself when a policeman found her—arrested her for shoplifting—and instead of taking her to jail he took her to a battered women's shelter. A volunteer doctor at the shelter delivered her baby in the small bedroom she shared with another pregnant teen. She still had vivid memories of those horrid days.

Now Pen was asking *her* if *she* was okay. Shaunda felt horrible for having left Pen by herself overnight but she didn't want Pen to think of herself as an invalid. Attitude and confidence needed constant positive feeding to slow the progress of her condition. She'd given Penelope a cell phone, but still, she hated being away from Pen for more than a few hours at a time. *Some mother I am.*

"I'm just fine baby girl," Shaunda said. She went to her daughter, knelt down and hugged her. "Anything happen while I was out catting around town last night? How did you sleep?"

Pen said, "Don't worry about me, Mom. You're the one that needs to sleep. I'll answer the phone and if Claire calls again I'll tell her to go to hell."

Shaunda laughed and wiped at her eyes. "You're getting to be just like me, Tootsie Roll."

"I'm not a baby, and I'm not a Tootsie Roll."

When Penelope was about five years old she had discovered she liked candy. Especially Tootsie Rolls. They didn't have much money for

Halloween, or Christmas or birthdays, but Tootsie Rolls were the gift of choice every time.

"I know, Pen. I know. You're growing into an old hag. Getting more wrinkled every day."

Pen slapped at Shaunda's hand playfully. "You are. Not me."

Shaunda kissed the top of Pen's head. "I need a couple of hours of sleep, Pen. You can run interference for me. Don't tell anyone to go to hell. Hear me?"

"Give me the phone mom and go to bed." Penelope held her hand out for Shaunda's cell phone and it rang as if on cue.

Shaunda answered, "Chief Lynch."

* * * *

Chief Constable Shaunda Lynch watched as her young officer, Joey Trantino, waded out of the waist-deep water of the stripper pit lake, hauling a mostly naked body toward the embankment. The body was that of a young, white male and the head was covered in white material that even from the bank looked like men's underwear. Joey's cheap waders leaked and he was soaked as he wrestled the body face down onto the embankment and dropped beside it, panting. Muddy water gushed out of the tops of the waders.

"Thanks for coming so quickly Joey. I could have done that, but I needed a witness."

"I understand ma'am."

"You know I can't swim worth a shit."

"Yes, ma'am."

"How's the baby?" Shaunda asked.

Joey struggled to his feet and rubbed his palms together to remove the grit from them. "It's a boy," he said, beaming, and then remembering what he had just been doing. "Laynie thinks he looks just like me. We haven't picked a name yet."

Shaunda reminded herself that Joey was barely twenty-three. He had one year of experience as a cop. This was the second body he'd pulled out of the water in a week. She worried that he might have had enough. If he quit she'd be out of luck getting another constable for quite some time.

"You had a boy. That's great," Shaunda said. This wasn't exactly the right place or time for good news but it was welcome distraction for them both. "Laynie wants to name him Joey after you, am I right?"

Joey was staring at the body beside him and didn't answer.

"Joey, I'm sorry to do this but I need you to focus and help me for a bit." She could see a cloud cross his features. "Whatever you need Chief."

"Go to your truck and put on some dry clothes."

"Yes ma'am."

"Do you still have that video camera in your truck?" she asked.

"Sure do, ma'am. I mean Chief. I had it with me at the hospital." He smiled and said proudly, "Got the whole thing on film, too. I got one of the new high definition digital ones just for this. I mean for the baby. Not this."

"I'm sure Laynie will appreciate the sentiment," Shaunda said. *She might not appreciate the embarrassment of having everyone hear her screaming profanities while she pushed a big square peg through a little round hole.*

A pile of wet clothing—blue jeans, tennis shoes, blue sweatshirt—lay on the ground near the edge of the lake.

"Are those his clothes?" she asked.

"Looks like a guy's stuff. I didn't go through any of it yet. I was waiting for you."

"Have you got some dry clothes with you?" she asked and got a nod.

"Go change and get your camera," Shaunda said.

Shaunda had driven down the narrow path to the lake and parked beside Joey's newer Silverado truck. Joey had parked less than ten yards from the body and almost on top of the discarded clothing.

Joey went to the far side of the Silverado and quickly stripped out of his wet pants and shirt, pulling on dry clothes. He came back wearing wet boots and carrying a compact Sony digital video camera. He flipped the side of the camera open and started taking video as he approached the body and from every angle.

"Get some good footage of his head," Shaunda instructed.

Joey zoomed in and out, moving deftly around the head. He turned the camera off and slung the strap over his neck. "This thing works great."

"Well, I'm glad this guy posed for you, Joey," Shaunda said a little crankier that she'd meant to. "Sorry, Joey. Help me turn him over."

It was mid-March and the temperature was bipolar; sunny and warm part of the day, the next you could see your breath. Joey had to run to his truck for a jacket and came back slipping his arms into it.

"Chief Lynch, ma'am, if Doc Bonner's the one coming I'll have to transport the body in the back of my truck again."

"The county still hasn't got a vehicle for him," she said. The previous coroner had used his own beat up truck. The new one refused.

"I transported Chief Jerrell's son for Doc Bonner last week. If I've got to take this one, I will, but you have to promise to never mention it to Laynie," Joey said. "She'd never get in my truck again."

"I've got room in the back of the Tahoe," Shaunda said. "One day you'll get your own police vehicle."

"Yeah. Okay."

Shaunda looked the body over for signs of injuries and saw none. "You see any wounds?" she asked.

"Maybe something on the head. Should we get that off of him?"

"Let's roll him over first."

They put on latex gloves, squatted and rolled the body over onto its back.

Joey unslung the camera and filmed the front of the victim. "Ma'am," Joey stopped filming. "That looks like tighty whiteys on his head. Just like the last one."

She knelt by the body. "You're right. That's underwear. It's been knotted under his chin. I don't see any wounds on the front of the victim."

"You think this is an accidental drowning like Doc Bonner thought last time?"

"I don't know, Joey, but he didn't go swimming with underwear over his face."

"He hasn't been in the water long. What the fudge was he doing swimming like that?"

Joey was right. He hadn't been in the water very long. Death has its own essence, or more accurately the absence of essence. She'd seen enough dead bodies to 'feel' the absence without requiring a touch. The skin loses it aura of life, as if every molecule that made up a living organism stopped, waiting for the inevitable decay, leaving behind a husk, a skin stuffed with meat and bones.

"Let's see who we've got," she said, undid the twisted knot at his throat and slipped the cloth up over the face.

"Oh my God!" Joey said. "Is that...?"

"Brandon Dillingham," Shaunda said.

"Shit fire and save the matches!" This was as close as Joey Trantino came to cursing.

"Mind your mouth Joey."

"Yes ma'am."

Shaunda pulled her phone out and called Sullivan County Dispatch. They answered and she said, "What can you tell me about the call you sent me a little bit ago?"

Chapter 6

Jack drove north on Highway 41 and took the exit for State Road 57.

Liddell sat in the passenger seat watching a travel route on his cell phone. "Siri said you should have taken Interstate 69. This route is thirty-seven minutes longer."

"Screw Siri. She's not the boss of me," Jack grumped. It was the first thing he'd said since leaving Evansville.

"If you're nice to her she'll be nice to you, pod'na."

"My mom always said "be nice *and* carry a big stick", Bigfoot."

"You have a love-hate relationship with your phone. I think you're conflicted about your emotions and don't know where to put the bad feelings," Liddell countered.

"You're right. It is a love-hate thing," Jack said. "I love to hate her. Do I need to remind you that thing tried to give me directions to Kansas when I was rushing down to Louisiana to get your butt out of jail?" Jack was referring to Liddell's trip last year to see a friend, a detective on the Iberville Sherriff's Department, but instead was arrested for murdering said friend.

"It's because Siri can tell you don't like her, pod'na. I think the new phones are becoming self-aware. Artificial intelligence."

"Sending me two states out of my way is intelligent?" Jack asked.

"Point taken." Liddell put the phone away and flipped through the pages of the file Angelina had given him. Neither man spoke. They were in their own heads as they often were when going into the uncharted waters of a killer's mind.

Jack knew Liddell was right about I-69 being faster but he needed time to think and he hated traffic. Foremost in his thoughts were the elaborate wedding plans Katie and her sister, Moira, were making and their assumption that he was onboard. They were making plans far more complicated than the murder cases he and Liddell were on their way to investigate.

This was the second time around for he and Katie. They'd done all the wedding cake cutting and smearing it on each other's faces; dancing, getting drunk and making fools of themselves—well he had anyway. This time should just be for them. They could just tell each other, "I marry thee," three times. Like a biblical divorce, just in reverse. They could have a big party and invite everyone later. He loved Katie with all that he was, and he knew she felt the same. When the fluff was blown away that's what marriage was about.

He cleared his mind of the wedding and turned his thoughts to the meeting ahead with the Linton Chief of Police plus posse. Jack had worked on a couple of local task forces before. These were generally like Jerrell's. Made up of various city and county police departments. All it seemed to do was create chaos and tension and jealousy and competitiveness. He could understand. He wasn't a team player himself, or rather he had his own team that consisted of people he would trust with his life. Liddell, his partner in crime, Tony Walker in Crime Scene, Captain Franklin his immediate boss, Dr. John the forensic pathologist, Angelina the brains, and some others outside of the department. He hadn't even been told what police departments would be on Chief Jerrell's task force.

He would go to the meeting. If they were fighting over jurisdiction it would be the shortest meeting ever. He and Liddell had been ordered to take control and their authority overrode any state and local jurisdiction but that didn't mean the local agencies would agree to be their puppets.

"Five murders in seven years," Jack mused. "One seven years ago, two more at five years, one at three years, and one that just happened. All in March."

"March is important to the killer," Liddell said.

"Something got this guy started killing. Whatever it was must have happened at least seven years ago in March. Most of the serial killers we've dealt with needed symbolism. Sometimes they were sending us a message, sometimes they were sending it to other possible victims."

"Making a list and checking it twice," Liddell said. "Gonna find out who's naughty and dead."

"The two years between killings might mean something, but what?" Jack asked. "What other event happens every two years?"

"You get laid?"

"Shut up Bigfoot. I'm being serious."

"Maybe it doesn't mean anything," Liddell suggested.

"Whoever this is, man or woman, they don't seem to be in a hurry," Jack said.

"Revenge is a dish best served cold," Liddell said thoughtfully. "And speaking of a dish being served, I'm really hungry."

"You're worse than a kid sometimes, Bigfoot."

"Hey, remember that long haul trucker?" Liddell asked.

"Bruce Mendenhall. Serial killer with at least half a dozen victims. All of them women, mostly truck stop clerks," Jack said.

"The point I'm making is he was killing people along his travel route. Our killer might regularly travel State Road 54. I checked the map Angelina gave us and all of the murders are along State Highway 54. The victims this time are all males. Maybe we have a female serial killer. Like Eileen Wournos."

They rode in silence for a few miles before Jack said, "This killer is concentrating on male victims but this last one, Troy Jerrell Junior, was a big guy. Even if he was unconscious, moving him would take a lot of strength. I just don't see a woman doing that. The killings must be taking place in or right next to the water."

Liddell said, "On a different topic, if we were at home you'd be helping with the wedding plans."

Jack said nothing.

"Yeah. You'd be picking out napkins, and signing invitations, and…"

"Try a new topic," Jack interrupted him.

"Okay. I heard there's a new Denny's along here somewhere so we won't have to detour. I know how much you hate detours. I'm starving."

"Didn't Marcie feed you this morning?" Jack asked. He guessed that Liddell had found the new Denny's before they even left headquarters.

"Marcie has me on a low carb diet, pod'na. I had two eggs and one piece of toast, half a glass of milk and two pieces of bacon."

"Are you hiding food around the house?" Jack quipped. Liddell ate that much for a light snack between snacks.

"I can't. Marcie's like a bloodhound."

"Okay, we'll stop at Denny's. It'll give us a chance to read Angelina's stuff more closely," Jack said.

Liddell said into his phone, "Siri, find Lumberjack Slam."

Siri's voice came back with "There are three restaurants near you with Lumberjack Slams. The nearest is Denny's in Oakland City. Is that the one you want?"

Liddell said, "Hell yeah, Siri!" and the disembodied voice of Siri began giving driving directions.

"For crying out loud. The Denny's is just down the road, Bigfoot. Shut her up or I'll keep driving straight on to Linton."

They found the Denny's with no problem and Liddell demolished two platters of food while Jack had coffee. They then drove north on Highway 57, Jack at the wheel again and Liddell on his cell phone. Liddell was looking up the histories of Dugger and Linton, the police departments, and the restaurants.

"Dugger's population in 2010 was nine hundred and fifty," Liddell said. "Linton's was fifty-five hundred."

"About the size of Boonville," Jack remarked.

They made a left onto State Highway 58, followed by a right turn onto State Highway 59 where they entered Greene County. At the Linton city limits they passed over a double set of railroad tracks where a wooden banner stretched over the road announcing: "You'll Like Linton."

"Let's take the Interstate home, pod'na," Liddell said. "All those turns were confusing for a country boy like me."

"You drive, you can pick the route."

"Thanks Dad," Liddell said.

Linton's Main Street looked like all small towns that are trying to revitalize their businesses and attract residents. Most of the storefronts had been recently remodeled but maintained their small-town charm. The streets and sidewalks were extraordinarily clean compared to the little towns around Evansville. Couples strolled arm in arm, kids played and teased each other behind their parents back, and every head turned and stared at the unfamiliar car. Jack waved, they waved back and traffic was light and flowed steadily. It was like Pleasantville. Hard to imagine a serial killer at work in this little town.

"Go straight about a mile," Liddell said. "Highway 54 becomes East State Street. Take a left on Second Street. The station should be on the corner on the right two blocks up."

A flagpole flying the red white and blue stood on the corner of NW Second Street and A Street. The Linton Police Department was a squat stone building that had been painted gray at some point. Handicap ramps were on both sides of a single entrance in front with huge reflective windows on either side of the door. Jack turned the corner onto 2nd Street and pulled in to the curb where there was a private entrance with a keypad lock. Jack put the FBI placard on the dashboard, and said, "Let's see what Toomey's got us into."

Before they could get out of the car the side door to the police station flew open and large man came out, full tilt, heading toward a gold colored

Ford F-250 4X4 truck with Linton Police markings and a bar light on top of the cab. Another officer came flying out behind the first one and ran to a marked police car with push bars on front and back. Jack started the Crown Vic and put it in gear.

"You know I love a parade, but where are we going?" Liddell asked.

"The big guy had five stars on his collar. I guess we're following him." Jack pulled a U-turn, left some rubber and joined the race heading west on A Street.

"I'll try to get them on the radio," Liddell said. He called Evansville dispatch on the telephone and had them try to reach the Chief of Police through Linton's dispatch. Soon a voice came over the radio.

"This is the Linton Chief of Police. I don't know who the hell you are but you'd better back off. This is a police emergency."

"Tell him to bite me," Jack said.

Liddell keyed the microphone and said, "Chief Jerrell, this is the FBI Unit that you were meeting. Where's the fire—Chief—sir?"

The radio was silent but the two cars ahead increased their speed. Jack kept closing on them and traveling in excess of 80mph past a speed limit sign that showed 45mph. He wasn't familiar with these roads, but he thought if he just stayed on the tail of the car in front he'd be okay. He hoped.

"Should I call my wife and tell her goodbye?" Liddell quipped.

"Quit being a whiner," Jack said. "Maybe we'll get to do something."

"That's what I'm afraid of, pod'na. I'd at least like to know what I'm dying for."

The radio came to life again. "This is Chief Jerrell. You have no jurisdiction here. Cease and desist or I will place you under arrest."

"Did he just say "cease and desist?" I haven't heard that anywhere since *Dragnet* was on television," Liddell said.

Jack took the microphone. "Negative, Chief Jerrell. We're in pursuit of a reckless driver with no regard for human life. Yours or ours. You pull over or *I'm* going to arrest *you*." He handed the mic back to Liddell and said, "He's not telling me. I'll tell him."

Liddell was chuckling. "Yeah. You tell him pod'na. He's not the boss of us."

"Shut up."

Liddell laughed.

Jack gripped the wheel. "Now I can see why Toomey is worried. Where the hell are we? The Indy 500?"

"He drives like you, pod'na."

"I don't drive like that."

"Yeah, right. Not you. You're doing the speed limit right now."

They drove under another sign constructed over the road that read, "You'll Like Linton" and continued going west.

"I like Linton already," Jack said.

"He needs to put his lights and siren on," Liddell said, and both Linton vehicles did just that.

Chapter 7

Shaunda and Joey leaned against the faded to flesh colored paint of the Tahoe. Sirens could be heard off in the distance coming their direction.

"Joey, did you call for backup?"

"No ma'am, I mean Chief," Joey said. "I didn't call for an ambulance either. I didn't tell no one but my wife, and I told her I had to go on account of police business. This is definitely in our jurisdiction. I checked my GPS." He pulled the Tuffy jacket collar up to warm himself and stop his teeth from chattering.

Joey was barely twenty-three and had been with the department less than a year. He was honest and polite to a fault. Shaunda had yet to break him of those traits and the habit of calling her 'ma'am'.

Shaunda reached inside the Tahoe and turned the police radio volume up. She could hear Jerrell yelling into the radio at someone, ordering them to back off. She thought he might be talking to one of the Civil Defense groupies that thought a blue bubble light allowed them to run Code 3.

She heard an unfamiliar voice on the radio saying they were going to arrest Jerrell. State Police? Maybe County? Whoever it was, she hoped they'd make good on their promise.

"We're about to get company, Joey. You got your pants on?"

"Yes ma'am. I mean Chief Lynch."

"Cover the body, Joey. I'm going to the trailhead to block the entrance. I don't want anyone back here unless I'm with them. Got it?"

"Yes ma'am."

She climbed in the Tahoe and drove down the narrow path to Highway 54. She stopped at the entrance to the trailhead, switched on her emergency lights, left the police radio cranked up and got out. She leaned against the front grill of the Tahoe, thumbs tucked in her Sam Browne gun belt and waited.

The sound of sirens grew steadily louder. The vehicles topped a hill and they shut down the sirens and lights in unison. She recognized the lead vehicle, a big king cab truck, fitting for Chief Troy Jerrell, the man who would be king. The truck crossed the double yellow lines and sped toward her in the wrong lane. Behind the truck was one of Linton PD's marked police vehicles and a black unmarked Crown Vic. The Crown Vic was obviously a detective's car but she didn't recognize the two male occupants sitting in front.

Jerrell was the first out and came her direction with his John Wayne walk like a man on a mission, only moseying. Linton PD Sergeant Ditterline stepped out the Linton PD car and trotted closely behind.

"What've we got," Jerrell demanded of her.

"*We* don't have anything." She watched the two men get out of the Crown Vic. One was as big or bigger than King Jerrell. The other was also over six feet, short dark hair, spiked in front, solidly built. The big one was tense and cast glances at Jerrell and then her. The other wore a bored expression, but his eyes were taking in everything. She spotted the FBI placard on the dash of the Crown Vic and thought, *Feds don't drive Crown Vics.*

She squared off with Jerrell, thumbs still hooked in her gun belt, her five feet five against his six feet six. "What are you doing here, Troy? I sure as hell didn't call you."

Jack watched the two police chiefs square off. Jerrell was as tall as Bigfoot and built like Bigfoot but harder looking. Like he'd been chiseled out of a piece of granite; squared jaw and mallets for hands. He wore his dark hair spiked like Jack. He was in full uniform, five gold stars forming a circle pinned on both collars. He was squared away, as they would say in the military, not a piece of lint or a hair out of place.

Chief Shaunda Lynch was the opposite. Pixieish, thin but not to the point of bony, dark hair pinned up on the back of her head, no jewelry or even a hint of makeup. She too was in uniform, but only one gold star on her shirt collars. Where Jerrell's uniform was light blue with dark blue pockets and stripes down the legs, Shaunda's was light brown with dark brown trim. Her badge was scuffed and showed signs of wear, but she wasn't old enough to be the one that had worn it down. Late twenties to early thirties. Her vibe told him she hadn't been an officer very long. Her face would be pretty when she wasn't scowling.

Jerrell towered over her diminutive figure, tight jawed, mere inches separating them. "I heard you've got another floater, Shauny. These deaths affect all of us—Dugger and Linton. They're not separate events. You should have called me."

Jack noticed a flicker of annoyance in her face when Jerrell called her Shauny. *A pet name? A nickname? An insult?*

"Don't get your knickers in a twist, Troy. This is my jurisdiction but I didn't say I wasn't going to share. Who are your friends?"

Jack held up his federal credentials with its shiny gold badge. "We're with USOC, the Federal Task Force for Unsolved Serial and Organized Crime. I'm Agent Murphy and this is my partner, Agent Blanchard."

Jerrell backed up a step away from Chief Lynch and scratched the stubble on his cheek. "I wasn't expecting you boys so soon," he said.

"Crime waits for no man. Or woman," Liddell said and gave his most charming smile. No one smiled back.

"I'm Sergeant Ditterline," the Linton PD uniformed officer came forward and shook hands with Jack and Liddell. "Glad to meet you. I heard you were coming."

Chief Lynch said, "I guess Chief Jerrell has forgotten his manners. I'm Chief Constable Shaunda Lynch—Dugger Police Department. This big lug is Troy Jerrell, Chief of Linton PD. Now that everyone knows everyone else, please explain to me why you're here or I'll have to ask you to leave."

Jack said, "Chief Lynch. Chief Jerrell. We're here under orders from FBI Assistant Deputy Director Toomey to conduct an investigation into several murders in both Greene County and Sullivan County."

Shaunda wasn't satisfied. "Go investigate cases all you want. This is my case. I appreciate the offer, but you can tell your director I don't need your help." She turned on Jerrell. "I don't need you here. I didn't call you."

Jerrell said, "I invited them, Shauny. We'll need their resources. They have access to a computer whiz and maybe a profiler and lab stuff we need."

Jack said, "Chief Jerrell, Chief Lynch, you won't want to hear this but the FBI has jurisdiction now. When Chief Jerrell made a request to use our cyber specialist your situation with these murders came to the attention of Director Toomey. We were sent to *guide* your task force. I say guide but make no mistake, *we* will be making the decisions."

"I don't care for the way…" Jerrell started to say and Jack cut him off.

"Chief Jerrell, we have reliable information that over the past seven years there have been a multitude of suspicious missing persons, accidental drownings, and murders involving Sullivan and Greene counties. There is a murder in Illinois that we've linked to these murders." Jack was stretching the facts. "That makes this interstate, and that makes it our jurisdiction.

We suspect a serial killer is at work. Additionally, I have the authority to insist that both of your departments give us full cooperation."

"How's that?" Shaunda asked.

"Federal Regulation Title 21, Section 3-3. Look it up."

Shaunda smirked. "Title 21 is the Food and Drug regulations for FDA, DEA and Office of National Drug Control Policy. This isn't a drug case, and no one died from bad food."

"Ok. You got me there. Sounded official though, didn't it," Jack said, eliciting a chuckle from everyone except Jerrell. "Seriously. We can all piss and moan later about who owns the ball. Agreed?"

Shaunda thought about it for a heartbeat. "Follow me. Don't touch anything."

Chapter 8

Jack tried to get a read on the two chiefs. They were stubborn to a fault and didn't play well with others to boot. They weren't impressed or intimidated by his federal agent shtick. He admired that. He and Liddell trailed along behind Lynch, Jerrell, and Ditterline who had told them to call him Ditty. They entered a path through dead vegetation and brambles beaten down by vehicle tires and foot traffic. If there was any evidence here it was already contaminated by the law enforcement presence. They walked a hundred feet and emerged on a wide bank of dark, hard packed earth with an expansive body of water ahead. A crew cab pickup truck was parked near the water's edge. There was no yellow caution tape or other sign of a perimeter. A pile of wet clothing was on the ground by the front wheel of the truck.

"Is this a stripper pit?" Jack asked.

Chief Jerrell answered. "Dugger Lake. Dugger Mine was one of the earliest coal mines in this area. When it was abandoned they started a dragline operation and then abandoned that. The lake is split down the middle. Greene County on the far side, Sullivan on this side. This little stretch of the lake falls in Dugger city limits."

"Lucky I got here first then," Shaunda said.

Twenty feet to their right a uniformed officer dressed like Chief Lynch protectively stood blocking their approach to what Jack presumed to be the victim. The body was covered partially with a yellow rain slicker.

"They're friendlies," Shaunda said, and Joey visibly relaxed. "That's my constable. Joey Trantino. I told him not to let anyone near the body."

"Hi Chief Jerrell, sir," Constable Trantino said coming over to the group.

Jerrell acknowledged him with a nod and turned to Jack. Out of the corner of his mouth but loud enough for Chief Lynch to hear, Jerrell said, "This is what I put up with."

Chief Lynch bristled. "You don't have to put up with anything. You can turn your happy ass around and get back to your own city. I've got this."

Jerrell responded in a nasty tone, "You've got this? Are you serious? Why on God's green earth would you stomp around in a crime scene and throw something over the body? Where is Sullivan's Crime Scene? What the hell, Shauny?"

"It's not a crime scene until I say it is Jerrell," Shaunda said. "He was in the water. What were we supposed to do? Dogpaddle until you ride in and save the day? It's a drowning until we know different."

"Chief Lynch, would you mind if I take a look?" Jack asked as he walked towards the body. She didn't stop him.

The surface of the bank where the body lay was black and hard packed. They wouldn't find foot or shoe prints. There were drag marks where Joey pulled the body from the water. Jack looked up and down the stretch of ground. There were no other disturbances in the surface except for several tire tracks leading from the main road to where the new Silverado truck was parked."

"Is that the victims truck?" Jack asked.

Joey said, "It's mine. I got here before the Chief. Guess I shouldn't have driven back here."

Jack had noticed three sets of tire tracks. Two had looked similar. Chief Lynch had driven back here and then back out to the road to block the pathway. They had followed Chief Lynch back here. Any shoe or footprints would be iffy.

Jerrell seemed pretty sharp. Dugger PD had walked all over the scene and that was what he'd meant by his remark about what he had to work with. Jack remembered that Dugger PD was in charge of Jerrell's son's murder. He understood why Jerrell was pulling strings to get a better investigation going.

"Did you already search this stretch for drag marks or shoe prints?" Jack asked.

Shaunda answered, "I haven't been here long enough to start any of that. I shouldn't even have let you down here until I can secure this area."

Jack ignored her weak protestation. "Have you got a big garbage bag in your truck?" Jack asked Joey. Joey ran off to the truck and came back with a black Hefty bag. "Let's get this slicker off the body and put it in the garbage bag," Jack said. "We need to hang on to your raincoat until it can be checked by Crime Scene. Glove up first."

Jack handed Joey a pair of latex gloves and put his own on.

Shaunda said, "Take the raincoat off of him Joey and put it in the bag."

Joey walked over, not minding where he was stepping and folded the raincoat back from the head to the victim's waist. Jack noticed a white piece of cloth on the ground near the body.

"That's underwear," Joey said. "He had that on his head. The rest of his clothes is back by my truck. I haven't had a chance to go through the pockets yet."

Jack took over, lifted the slicker by the collar and pulled it over on the ground leaving the side that had touched the body facing up. He carefully folded it to preserve what evidence there might be and Joey held the bag open. Jack put the slicker inside, tied the top of the bag and set it aside.

"We'll need another bag, Joey," Jack said. Joey went to the truck and came back with a zipper top gallon sized freezer bag. Jack put the underwear in the bag and set it aside.

"You'll need to bag his clothes, too," Jack said. "Each piece separately. Did you get a picture of the clothes yet?" Joey nodded.

Jack squatted on his haunches near the body. The victim was on his back, arms down to his sides, legs straight out toward the lake. "Who pulled him out of the water?"

"That was me, Agent," Joey said.

"Did you move the body?" Jack asked.

Shaunda answered for her constable. "He was on his front. We rolled him onto his back and took the underwear off so we could identify him. Why?"

Jack didn't answer. The black grit on top of the victim's toes verified that's how it happened.

The body was that of a teenager. White male, tall, almost six feet, one hundred thirty to one hundred forty pounds, blond hair, blue eyes, no sign of blood or wounds. There was the faintest red abrasion of the skin on one side of the boy's neck. Maybe from the underwear.

"His name is Brandon Dillingham," Shaunda said. "He's nineteen years old. His mother is on the town board."

Jack mulled that over. A police chief's son and now a town board member's son. He didn't remember any of the other victims being connected to authority figures. "Chief Lynch, may I?" Jack asked.

"Who am I to say no to the FBI?" she said.

Jack lifted Brandon's upper lip and pushed the lower one down. There were two small cuts on the inside of the upper lip that looked like tooth marks. No teeth were missing or broken. He looked at the outside of the lip. No corresponding cuts or bruising. He wasn't in a fight. He fell on his face.

Brandon's eyes were open. He spread the eyelids open wider. Petechiae was present around the corneas. He pushed on the skin on the neck with two fingers, lifted an arm and lowered it, bent the arm at the elbow. The muscles weren't fixed, stiffened.

"Was he face down in the water?" Jack asked.

Joey said, "Yes sir. He was floating about six feet out in the water there. It's about five feet deep there and then it drops off and gets plenty deep."

"Is livor mortis visible on the back of the body?" Jack asked. Livor mortis is the red coloring of the skin that occurs after death because the blood no longer circulates. Gravity causes the blood to pool into the parts of the body lowest to the ground.

Shaunda again answered for Joey. "We didn't see any signs of rigor, livor or algor mortis. It's about forty degrees out here. The water is about thirty-five degrees"

Rigor mortis means the joints had locked up and the body would be stiff. Algor mortis refers to the temperature of the body gradually lowering until it reached the ambient temperature. The cold water would slow all these processes down, just like heat would speed them up.

"He's got a bump on the back of his head like he hit it. I just saw him an hour or so ago. He couldn't be dead any longer than two hours."

Jack nodded. He examined top and bottom of each hand and the fingers. The nails were intact, no scrapes on the skin or knuckles. Small particles of the black gritty soil from the bank coated the knees, thighs and tops of the toes from where the body was dragged onto shore. Joey would have had the victim under the arms, pulling the body out of the water. The chest was protected from contact with the ground.

"He's still wet," Jack said.

"That's what happens when you get in water," Shaunda said. "We just pulled him out five minutes ago."

"Can I turn him on his side?" Jack asked.

"Why not?"

Shaunda slipped gloves on and helped Jack roll the body onto its right side. Jack felt the back of the victim's head. His glove came away with a trace amount of blood. He moved the right ear forward and found a sizable laceration.

"He was hit and shoved in," Jerrell said to Shaunda but she ignored him. "Murdered. Just like my boy."

They eased the body back down and Jack stood, thinking, while Liddell recorded everything in a notebook.

"He hasn't been in the water long, Shauny," Jerrell said, barely controlling his anger.

"He has a name. His name is Brandon. I talked to him a little over an hour ago," she said. "He was supposed to be heading home. He was in his mother's Jeep. A silver newer Jeep Cherokee Laredo four wheel drive. I didn't see it around here when I came up. Did you see a Jeep?"

They hadn't.

"Did you put an alert out on the Jeep?" Jerrell asked. Shaunda didn't answer. She stripped the gloves off.

"Sergeant, see if you can locate the Jeep?" Jerrell said. Sergeant Ditterline nodded and left to get the vehicle information and have dispatch broadcast a BOLO—be on the lookout.

Shaunda asked the newcomers, "Seen everything you want?"

Jack answered. "Do you have someone to take photos, collect evidence?"

Jerrell answered for her. "Sullivan County Sheriff has a crime scene unit but I'll have my guys come over. We want to keep control of this. The task force will want to keep control. Have you called Doc Bonner? If not, I'll have my guys transport the body to the Greene County morgue."

Shaunda said, "Whatever you think, Troy." She let out a deep breath and faced the lake, fingers shoved in behind her gun belt. "I'll have to tell Claire."

Jerrell explained, "Doc Bonner is standing in for the old coroner that quit. He's new to this. I'm going to have my guys transport the body to our coroner."

Jack said, "Our morgue at home is used by several counties for the autopsies. I don't think it will be a problem."

Jerrell said, "We have an old ambulance that we've converted into a crime scene wagon. We can use that."

Chief Lynch stared down at the body. "The last time I needed help the county and the state guys acted like I'd asked them to donate a kidney." She motioned for Joey to cover the body again. He went back to his truck but this time came back with a clean folded white sheet.

Jack saw Jerrell flinch but the scene was already contaminated. Crime Scene would have to collect everything, the sheet included, for elimination purposes. In the early 1900s Dr. Edmond Locard, a criminalist, developed a theory that for any crime the suspect would leave something behind and take something away from the scene. This came to be known as Locard's Exchange Principle and the theory still held true today. The rain slicker would leave behind trace elements on the body from whomever wore it and it would take away trace elements from the body. The collection of evidence became complicated by the human need to show compassion.

"What can we do to help, Chief Lynch?" Jack asked.

She didn't answer.

Jerrell got on his phone and made a call. He disconnected and said, "My crime scene guys will be here in ten minutes." He turned to Jack and Liddell. "We're done here if you want to follow me back to the station. I'll bring you up to speed."

Jack wanted to ask Chief Lynch more questions but she didn't seem to be in a talkative mood. He'd bluffed and bullied his way thus far but he wasn't sure he truly had jurisdiction regardless of what Director Toomey said. Toomey wasn't here to make that decision. Jack gave the area a quick visual once over and he and Liddell followed Jerrell back to the road. Jerrell was far ahead of them on the path and out of earshot.

Liddell said, "Underwear over the head, the Jeep is missing, struck in the back of the head and it happened about a week after the last one. I didn't see any clothes either. This may be one of ours."

"We'll have to wait for the autopsy to see if he was drowned and if there are drugs in his system," Jack said. "We'll have to read these files more closely. I want to attend the autopsy on this kid."

"Should we get divers out here and search the lake?" Liddell asked.

"Not just yet," Jack answered. "We're thumbing our nose at Sullivan County as it is. Let's see if the kid drowned and if we can find the Jeep."

"We spending the night?" Liddell asked.

"Yep."

They caught up with Jerrell at the street. He didn't say anything, just got in his truck, cranked the engine and made a U-turn. Jerrell pulled up even with the Crown Vic, his window powered down and he said, "I'll drive slower so you won't arrest me. You know what they do to cops in jail." With that he sped away.

By the time Jack and Liddell started the Crown Vic and turned around Jerrell's truck was out of sight.

Chapter 9

Jack parked at the police station beside Jerrell's empty Ford 250 King Cab 4X4.

Liddell unbuckled his seat belt. "What do you think?"

Jack thought Jerrell was a little intense, overbearing and controlling but that's what made good investigators. It was understandable that Jerrell would want to catch his son's killer, but he was violating police procedures, ignoring jurisdiction and chain of custody issues on top of pissing off everyone around him. From what Jack had gleaned watching the two chief's interactions at the lake they had butted heads over jurisdiction in the past. It was obvious Jerrell didn't think Chief Lynch was capable of catching the killer. Being emotionally involved worked for you sometimes. Sometimes it got you or someone else killed.

"I think this will be interesting. Let's see what he's got for us," Jack said. They went to the side entrance and pressed an intercom button. Nothing. Liddell pressed it again and a voice came over the tiny speaker, saying, "Police personnel only. Come around to the front door."

"FBI," Jack said.

The voice said, "Let me see some ID."

Jack saw a camera mounted overhead. He and Liddell held their credentials up and heard a lock click.

"Down the hall to your right. Wait in the front lobby," the voice said.

They entered a wide hallway with doors on either side and an intersecting hallway just ahead. Liddell nudged Jack and pointed to a camera mounted on the ceiling at the end of the hall. Jack turned around and saw another camera mounted above the door they had just entered.

"Testing. Testing. One, two, three. One, two, three," Liddell said.

"What are you doing?"

"Sound check."

"Stop being a wiseass," Jack cautioned. "We want them to take us seriously."

"I think they take *everything* seriously."

"Point taken."

They turned right and stepped into the front lobby. The lobby was spartan, outfitted with a set of business style chrome and Naugahyde sofas, two chairs, and chrome and wood end tables. All were bolted to the floor. Canister lighting surrounded the room. Surveillance cameras were in opposing corners, one pointed toward the entrance door, the other toward a heavy wooden desk, also bolted to the floor.

The top of the desk was unadorned except for a clay flowerpot with fake petunia's and a plaque that simply read 'RECEPTION". Framed photos hung on the wall behind the lone desk. One of Chief of Police Troy Jerrell, the other of a dour looking woman with a beehive hairdo, bright red lipstick, and glasses too big for her narrow face. The caption read "Mayor of Linton Mabeline Dibney." Mabeline was the exact reverse of Jerrell in size, but the one thing they had in common was the forced smile on their faces. She reminded Jack of 'The Church Lady' on the old Saturday Night Live comedy show.

Liddell pointed to the stern looking faces in the photos and said in a deadpan voice, "You'll like Linton—but they don't."

They heard Chief Jerrell's raised voice come from somewhere down the hallway. The words weren't clear, but the angry tone was unmistakable.

There was a buzzer on the desk. Jack pushed the button several times and a uniformed sergeant came into the lobby from the hall.

"I'm Sergeant Crocker," the man said and motioned for them to take seats. Jack and Liddell remained standing. Sergeant Crocker sat down behind the desk and busied himself arranging the flowerpot, then opening and closing desk drawers. Satisfied with the desk he asked, "Now. What can I do for you gentlemen?"

Jack said, "Chief Jerrell is expecting us."

"He'll be with you shortly. He's talking to our coroner."

"More like 'talking at' him," Liddell said.

Crocker chuckled and said, "Yeah, like that. He's a good chief. A good cop. He takes care of us, and we take care of him."

To put the sergeant at ease Jack pulled out his EPD and FBI credentials and put them open on the desk. "We're detectives with the Evansville Police Department in real life, but we also work on a federal task force.

We don't like getting into your business any more than any other 'real cop' would." He stressed 'real cop' to let Crocker know they were the same. Just a couple of cops doing a job.

Crocker got up from the desk. "Well hell. You should've told me right off. The chief didn't tell me you were cops. I mean…well, you know what I mean. Can I get you guys some coffee?"

Liddell said, "I wouldn't say no. If you have a vending machine I could use a candy bar or something."

Crocker grinned. "Hell, I can do better than that. Come on back to the break room. My missus made some scones that'll make your tongue think it's gone to heaven."

They followed Crocker down the hall to a door marked 'Employees Only'. The hallway was lined with photos of police officer's and K-9's. One section of the wall held a display case with awards and trophies and snapshots of officer's playing basketball with kids and officer's in Santa beards passing out toys to little ones and the like. Jack knew that police departments were trying to forge a newer, kinder image but it was sad that the public still distrusted and disliked police. An officer's word was only as good as the video captured on their mandated body cams.

A little further down the hall was a glass fronted 'Remembrance' display with plaques for officer's and K-9's killed in the line of duty. As Crocker passed the Remembrance display he made the sign of the cross.

Crocker opened the door and a delicious smell hit them. The room they entered was a combination break room/roll call room. On one side was a podium and two huge whiteboards facing a dozen metal folding chairs. On the other side was a cafeteria style table and behind it was a complete kitchen with a counter, cabinets, sink, refrigerator and an electric oven. A petite thirtyish blond haired woman wearing a frilly white apron over a red dress was taking a tray of scones from the oven. Her clothes were right out of the 60s. She was wearing bright red lipstick. When she smiled, she reminded Jack of someone from his past.

"My wife, Betty Crocker," the Sergeant said.

That's it.

Mrs. Crocker turned and blew a strand of hair out of her eyes. "Don't tell them that's my name." She pulled off the oven mitts, wiped her hands on her white apron and gave both detectives a delicate handshake. "Hi, I'm Tina. Not Betty. I'm this one's better half. I like to bake so they all call me Betty Crocker." She playfully punched Crocker in the arm.

Jack and Liddell introduced themselves to her.

Sergeant Crocker said, "They're with the FBI, hon. They've come up here to show us farmers how it's done."

Liddell responded, "We're really here to show you how to 'com-bine' your investigations."

"Combine. I get it." Crocker laughed.

"At least someone gets your stupid jokes, Bigfoot."

"Have a seat. I just baked some scones. Coffee?"

"We'd be crazy if we said no," Liddell answered and the three men took seats at the table.

Tina brought over a platter with several small plates, mugs, butter and a large plate filled with freshly baked scones. "Should I set more places?"

Sergeant Crocker said, "I'm not sure who's doing what, hon. I'll get the coffee."

"You stay sitting," Tina said and retrieved a platter the size of a baking sheet with creamer, sugar, honey, and a carafe of coffee. She then hovered nearby and said, "Well. Dig in. Tell me what you think."

Liddell put several scones on his plate and devoured one. The expression on his face was pure ecstasy. Jack tried one and it was as good as Sergeant Crocker claimed.

"Oh my God!" Crocker said with his eyes closed and his mouth half full. He said something else that Jack interpreted as "what did I tell you?" or maybe "wah-dee-doo-doo".

Liddell lifted his coffee cup in a salute just as Chief Jerrell came into the room looking like the bull that won the bullfight. He took the empty seat at the head of the table, picked up a scone and ate fastidiously for such a large man. Jerrell sat quietly. The only activity was chewing, sipping, and refilling coffee. Jack and Liddell ignored the chief's silent treatment knowing a pecking order was establishing itself.

Crocker seemed uneasy with the silence and said, "Ditty hasn't had any luck finding that Jeep, Chief. He put a BOLO out."

Jerrell put his cup down. "Shauny said she talked to Brandon an hour before she got the call about the body. Whoever killed him and stole his Jeep had a couple hours head start." He took his cell phone out of his shirt pocket and punched in a number. "Did Ditty put that BOLO out local or did he…?" He listened and said, "Add Ohio, Kentucky and Illinois. The Jeep has a two hour lead on us. Thanks Cassie." Jerrell put the phone back in his pocket. "Cassie's our dispatcher. I'm gonna have Ditty's balls if this guy gets away. Excuse my language Tina."

Jerrell blew across the top of the cup and took a sip of the scalding hot coffee. "That's some fine coffee, Betty."

"I told you all to stop calling me that," Tina chastened him, but she smiled at the compliment and went back to cleaning up the kitchen.

"I guess we should wait for Chief Lynch and the others," Jack said and saw an unspoken message pass between Sergeant Crocker and Chief Jerrell.

"Am I missing something, Chief?" Jack asked.

"No. It's just that you got here earlier than I expected. I was kind of hoping your computer girl was coming with you. When will she be here?"

"Angelina Garcia isn't coming at all, Chief Jerrell. She briefed us this morning and we have her files," Jack said. "Is there a problem?"

Jerrell said, "It appears this is going to a small task force. We've got what you see here, Shaunda, and of course, Crime Scene and whatever of my department we need. Greene County and Sullivan County Sheriff's Departments and Indiana State Police aren't sending anyone."

"No one else is on the task force?" Liddell asked.

Jerrell said, "I'm not sure if they are planning to get involved later on. I called to get their case files on the murders and when I told them the FBI was sending agents they said they would have to get back to me. They cited manpower issues."

Mentally, Jack cursed Toomey for buckling because of his friend with DOJ and sticking them in this circle jerk. There were two reasons he didn't head back home. They were already here and these people needed help. He was interested.

"To tell you the truth," Jerrell said, making Jack guess that he was about to lie his ass off.

"I'm kind of hanging out here on my own. I'll be honest with you. We don't have the budget or resources or manpower to run an investigation this big. Not if we want to solve it in my lifetime. I got the coroner to do the post on my son by twisting the City Council's arm. Sullivan County has their own coroner, such as he is. I just told them about Brandon Dillingham before you got here. They gave me one week to finish this or the cost comes out of my budget. They said if the Feds were taking over you guys should take over the cost too."

Jack was on to Jerrell's game now. Jerrell had played Toomey. Had used the "I'm starting a task force" to justify asking for Angelina's services. If she was working for the Feds Jerrell wouldn't have to go to the Linton city council begging for the funds to pay her. This was all about Troy Junior's murder. Solving the other cases was gravy. Jack admired the man for his cunning. Toomey was right. On the other hand, he'd have to keep a close eye on him.

Jerrell finished his fourth scone, licked his fingers, patted his belly and belched. He'd gotten exactly what he wanted and was content as a tick on a hound dog. Tina cleared the table of plates and brought fresh coffee.

Jack said, "We should get on the same page with the old murders—" he handed a manila folder to Sergeant Crocker—"before we start a new investigation. I know that sounds counterintuitive but these cases are all connected somehow. Before we get started we need several copies of the file I just gave the sergeant."

Jerrell nodded at Crocker who hurried away.

"Do you mind if I use your whiteboards?" Jack asked Chief Jerrell.

"Knock yourself out."

Jack found a marker and wrote on one whiteboard:

Greene and Sullivan Counties—2012 to Present
Missing persons 43
Murders 17
Unsolved Murders 8
Drownings 27

Jack said, "These are the numbers our computer analyst pulled from police and other sources. Eight unsolved murders. Twenty-seven drownings. I guess that's not unusual since this area's crisscrossed with ponds and stripper pit lakes. Let's go through the murders first. Of the eight that are unsolved, there are five with the same characteristics.

On the second whiteboard, Jack wrote:

Found in lake
naked, (or underwear on head)
head wound, drugs,
male, 30 to 40 years old
accidental?

"If we put Brandon in this group," Jerrell said, "that makes six. He was found in almost the same spot as my son and had the head wound and underwear over his head."

"We haven't run Brandon by Angelina yet," Jack said. "Let's not jump to conclusions."

"Trust me," Jerrell said. "That boy was born to be on some killer's radar."

Sergeant Crocker brought five folders back, each containing a copy of Angelina's file. He handed them around with a yellow legal pad and a pencil. Also, Crocker had made blowups of the victim's pictures for each file.

Jerrell briefly paged through his folder and said, "This came from your little girl, Angel?"

"Angelina, yes. She wouldn't like to hear you call her a girl, or Angel for that matter," Jack said.

Jerrell made a dismissive motion with his hand. "How did she get copies of all my reports? Some of this isn't even in the file cabinet yet. She never asked me for any of this."

Crocker said, "Sorry Chief. I'm to blame for that. When she called I faxed and emailed her what we had. I thought it was okay since you'd talked to her."

Jack was losing patience with Jerrell. "Chief Jerrell, you know the area and all the good guys and bad. You said you needed our resources, but I think you need us too. We've worked more homicides in a year than you have in your career. You need to decide right now if you're going to be completely open with us because, frankly, I'm a little tired of the jurisdiction battles."

"Well, you're here and the computer girl I asked for isn't." Jerrell smiled at Jack. It was the kind of smile that said 'bite me'. "However, you have my departments full cooperation and our records are open to you Agent Murphy, or Detective Murphy, or whatever."

"Chief Jerrell or Troy or whatever, I know I do," Jack said.

The muscles in Jerrell's jaw tensed. Jack had a feeling the man wasn't used to being talked back to. The tension in the room was palpable.

Jerrell relaxed. "You're a hard man, Jack. I respect that. But let me make one thing clear up front. I'm going to be the one to arrest my boy's killer. No one else touches him. If you agree to that I'll give you everything I've got—or get."

Toomey hadn't been kidding about Jerrell being a handful. He hoped the man was on his meds. He was too big to fight and Jack didn't want to have to shoot him.

"You have our promise," Jack lied. If he had to shoot the killer he'd do it without hesitation.

Jack stood beside the whiteboard. "Seventeen murders in six years is a low number if you consider statewide statistics. There are that many murders in Gary each day before breakfast."

Crocker chuckled but stopped when Jerrell glared at him.

Jack continued. "Five murders over a seven-year period, with the most recent being your son a week ago, wouldn't set off any alarms normally. You have our condolences, Chief."

Jerrell strummed his fingers on top of the table.

"Do you have some tape?" Jack asked and Crocker brought some.

"To narrow the investigation, we've eliminated three of the unsolved murders to concentrate our efforts on the remaining five." He completely erased the first whiteboard. He taped the photos of the five victims on it in the order they had been killed. He wrote their names and dates of death under the photos.

Tina Crocker came up behind her husband and rested her hands on his shoulders. "I went to high school with Troy at Linton-Stockton High. He grew up here but I heard he moved to Dugger. I know most of the others, too, except the one at the top, Clint Baker. The face is familiar though."

She looked at the photos and said, "Lamont Washington, Daniel Winters and Troy all went to Stockton-Linton High. DiLegge went to Union High in Dugger. I'm not real familiar with him, but I recognize him as one of the baseball players on their team. Lamont, Daniel and Troy all played for Stockton-Linton High."

As there was no photo, Jack wrote Brandon Dillingham's name at the bottom of the board with today's date. "Clint Baker lived in Hutsonville, Illinois. Does that name ring a bell, Tina?"

She cocked her head and thought. "I'm sorry. I just thought his face was familiar. The name doesn't mean anything."

Jack asked Crocker, "Sergeant, do you want your wife to hear all of this?"

Crocker said, "Maybe she'll have some insight that could help. She doesn't mind. Do you, hon?"

Jack said, "I won't be going into gory details. If you can stay maybe you'll remember something about them."

"I'll try," she said. "That one at the top, Clint Baker. He's older than the rest of them isn't he?"

"He would be about forty-one years old if he was alive," Jack said. "The others would all be around your age."

"I was a year behind them," Tina said. "Was Baker a teacher, or a coach maybe?"

"We'll find out" Jack said and Liddell jotted it down. "What can you tell us about the others?"

"I heard you say that Shaunda was coming," Tina said. "Should I wait until she gets here?"

"We'll catch her up," Jerrell said.

"Have a seat, hon," Crocker said and pulled out a chair for his wife.

She sat and scanned the pictures on the whiteboard. "Winters, Washington and Troy played for the Miners."

"That's the baseball team for Stockton-Linton," Jerrell explained to Jack and Liddell.

"If I remember correctly, DiLegge was with the baseball team at Union High. The Bulldogs. They played against each other, but they were all friends. At least they were back then. I didn't keep track of them after high school. I mean I'd see one of them here or there but we never spoke. I wasn't in their circle in high school." She took a breath and let it out. "Sorry. This makes me nervous."

Crocker said, "You're doing just fine. If you don't want to do this you don't have to."

Tina pushed the errant strand of hair out of her face. "I remember Lamont Washington was a big deal ball player. He could have had done something with his life but I guess he stayed messed up on drugs or at least that's what I heard. I don't know it for a fact and I don't remember who told me that."

"Lamont was into drugs?" Jack asked.

"He had the reputation of being the guy you went to if you wanted something," she said. "I didn't hang around with any of them. I'd see them at parties. Hanging around together after games. Troy was always with them. Sorry, Chief."

Jack asked Jerrell, "Was Troy involved with drugs?"

Jerrell didn't answer but his big hands gripped the arms of his chair until his knuckles turned white.

"Was Troy Junior involved Tina?" Jack asked.

She was uncomfortable. Her husband took her hand and said, "It's okay to say what you know, hon."

"I don't think he was doing hard drugs, Troy. Not that I ever saw, anyway. It was more because of the people he was hanging out with after games. A couple of parties were…well, they had a reputation for smoking pot and doing other things."

"Smoking pot?" Jerrell asked. "You saw my boy smoking pot in high school?"

Tina quickly said, "Lamont seemed to be the one that brought whatever they were doing."

"You're saying my boy didn't bring the drugs," Jerrell said. "But he was involved."

Jack thought back to his high school days. He'd gone to a Catholic high school and people that smoked pot were rare. Doing hard drugs was even more rare back in the day. Now, it was probably an extracurricular school program.

"Troy. I'm really sorry. I didn't hang around with that group. I'm just telling you what I remember."

"Who was in 'that group', Tina?" Troy asked.

"There were a couple of others besides the four you have there. Mostly baseball players and some groupies. I don't remember the names. I've got a yearbook at home. I could try to see if I can recall any of the others if you want me to? I don't remember much else."

"If you remember anything at all later, I want you to tell us," Jerrell said. "Don't worry about my feelings. Okay?"

"Okay. I have to go run some errands." She kissed her husband on the cheek and hurried out of the room.

"I'd better go check on her," Crocker said.

Jerrell said, "I need you back here."

"Be right back Chief," Crocker said.

"Actually, Chief," Jack said, "we need yearbooks from both high schools for those years. Do you have any here at the station?"

"Not any from that far back," Jerrell said, sounding embarrassed.

"Can you get them?"

Jerrell said, "I never made it to any of Troy's games. He was an amazing baseball player. He was getting a baseball scholarship to Notre Dame. The Fighting Irish took Atlantic Conference Championship in what would have been his freshman year at Notre Dame if he had kept with it."

"What happened?" Jack asked.

"His grades slipped his senior year in high school. Any chance at a scholarship just blew away." Jerrell seemed lost in thought until Crocker came back into the room.

"Chief, I called the vice-principal at Linton-Stockton and at Union. They're going to donate some yearbooks. I told them what years we're interested in. They offered to bring them to the station."

"Go pick them up."

"I'm on my way." Crocker left.

"Don't you think we need Crocker here while we discuss the cases?" Liddell asked.

"Crocker's been here about four years. He's still a newcomer. He won't know much that I can't tell you," Jerrell answered.

"When is the autopsy scheduled for the Dillingham kid?" Jack asked.

"Lacy Daniels is the Greene County Coroner. She'll call me when she's ready."

"Do we want to continue with this now or wait?" Jack asked.

Jerrell said, "We'd better wait for Shaunda. You think she was testy earlier in Dugger, she'll be plain nasty if we do much without her. This morning was her happy face."

Jack asked Jerrell, "Do you recognize any of these victims as friends of your son?"

Jerrell said, "I was gone. Army, active duty and deployed most of the time while Troy was in high school. We kept in touch by phone and computer, but I rarely got home."

"Would Troy's mother have known the other victims? Can we show her the pictures?"

"If you can find her?" Jerrell said.

Jack was about to ask what Jerrell meant by that when Crocker came rushing back into the room. "Come quick! It's Chief Lynch. She's hurt."

Chapter 10

Chief Lynch sat slump shouldered at the desk in the front lobby with a blanket pulled around her. Crime Scene Officer Barr was trying to put an ice pack on the side of her face but she kept batting his hand away.

"I told you I'm fine," she said. "Give me my keys." She tried to stand and the blanket fell to the floor. Jack could see she was obviously not fine. Her uniform shirt was ripped down the front. Her face was bloody, left cheek was scraped, her upper lip was split and bleeding, a bluish circle was surrounding her left eye. Her shirt collar was soaked with blood, her uniform pants were damp as if she'd been swimming and her boots were coated with black grit. There was a rip in her shirt where the badge should be.

Jerrell asked Officer Barr, "What happened to her?"

"She's right here," Shaunda said angrily and took the ice pack from Barr's hand and held it against the back of her head. "You can ask me."

Jack saw the bruising on her face was worse than he'd first thought. She would end up with black bruising around both eyes—raccoon eyes.

Barr said, "We were just finishing up with the scene, Chief. Me and Rudy were putting gear in the wagon when she came crashing out of the path. She said she was ambushed. Rudy stayed with her while I searched for the guy. Sergeant Ditterline and Rudy are still out there."

"Then why are you still here? Why isn't she in the hospital?" Jerrell asked.

Shaunda looked up. "Because I don't need to go to the hospital."

Barr wilted under Jerrell's stare. "She refused an ambulance, Chief. I tried. She was getting in her own vehicle so I told her I'd drive her. She insisted I bring her here. She wouldn't let me call you or call an ambulance. She said she had to see you."

"Damn right," she said. "I think I should be here to see what *you're* all deciding about *my* investigations."

Jerrell's hands clenched and unclenched. Still ignoring her he said, "The bastard was out there waiting for her. I thought we searched that area. How the hell could he surprise her?"

"We covered the scene, Chief. Me and Rudy…"

"Sergeant Ditterline was supposed to be sweeping the area for the Jeep or any cars that were out of place or even a damn bicycle. What kind of crap operation are we running, Barr? If I'd have known…" Jerrell clamped his mouth shut, his jaw muscles working. "Well, screw me nine ways from Sunday!"

He paced around the room until he got his anger under control.

"It wasn't your people's fault," she said. "I should've been more alert. I was still down there poking around the scene. The body was gone, your techs were done and I told Joey he could go home and check on his wife. A couple of minutes after Joey left I got waylaid. I thought I saw something on the ground and bam."

Jack said, "Your knuckles are scraped. You fought him?"

Shaunda spat on the back of her hand and rubbed some of the grit off. "I guess I must have. One minute I'm bent over to see something and then its lights out. My head hurts like a category five hangover."

"I'm calling an ambulance," Jerrell said and took his cell phone from its belt holder. "You need to get checked out at the hospital. I'll ride in the back with her. You can come along if you want," he said to Jack and Liddell.

"I told you no ambulance," Shaunda said in a tone that brooked no argument. "Just let me catch my breath and we'll get to work." She attempted to rise and collapsed back in the chair.

Jerrell motioned for Crocker to call an ambulance. "You just take it easy, Shauny," Jerrell said and patted her shoulder. She winced and he took his hand away.

Shaunda asked, "Have you at least found Brandon's Jeep? This asshole couldn't have gone too far. Have you done anything, fellas?"

"We're doing everything we can. I've got guys patrolling around Dugger for you. I've notified Sullivan County and the State Police. I've called damn near everyone but Joey. Hell, Shauny, this is a homicide. You don't take vacation days off from something like this even if you just had a baby. You need to get that boy back to work."

"First of all, Troy, you know I hate that name. Secondly, Joey works for me. If anyone's going to call him back to work it will be me. For God's sake, Troy. I got beat up. It comes with the job."

"Just sit there until you get checked out by a medic. You're here. You're safe. We got this covered." To Crocker he said, "Where's that ambulance, Sergeant?"

"We're all over this Shaunda. Just you let us handle it," Crocker said and got on his cell phone again.

Jerrell pounded his fist into his palm. "Nobody hurts one of ours."

"Yeah, right," she said. In the background the familiar warble of an ambulance siren was heard growing steadily closer.

Chief Jerrell gently put his hand on her arm. He motioned for Jack and Liddell to step off to the side. "You think he's screwing with us?" Jerrell asked them. "No matter what I said earlier, I know my guys. They checked that area like they were combing lice out of a kid's hair. That Jeep wasn't around there. No one was hiding there."

"Maybe he ditched Brandon's Jeep somewhere. He had an hour or two head start before Shaunda got the call and responded," Jack said.

"That's pretty heavily forested, lots of camping, hiking trails. If a fella knew what he was doing he could have avoided our guys," Crocker said.

"Where would he ditch a Jeep?" Jack asked.

"You're not from around here," Jerrell said. "It's a Jeep. He could have gone off-road and then come back on foot. She wouldn't have seen shit if he came out of the woods."

Shaunda was watching them.

"What did you find?" Jack asked her.

"I didn't get a good look. Something was stuck in the ground. It just caught my eye is all."

Jerrell said, "Maybe the killer lost something, or left something behind. He came back for it and saw you alone out there with your back turned. You're lucky he didn't kill you girl."

"Chief, the ambulance is here," Crocker informed them.

Jack could see a small crowd of looky-loos gathered outside across the street.

"Well. Get them in here, Crocker. And go tell those people to go about their business."

Crocker held the door open and two female paramedics came in carrying medical kits. One was young enough to have pimples on her round baby face. She had blond hair that was pulled back in two braided ponytails. The other was gray headed, stocky and gave Shaunda a nod of her head.

Crocker hurried across the street and Jack heard him say, "Nothing to see here, folks," as the door shut.

"It's Chief Lynch," gray headed said to the ponytailed paramedic. "Better get the cattle prod."

"These guys wouldn't be fussing over me like this if I was a man," Shaunda said.

"You got that right," gray hair said. "Hey, Shaunda, you know what you tell a woman with two black eyes?" gray headed asked.

Shaunda finished the old joke. "You don't tell her nothing. You done told her twice."

Both paramedics laughed at the ages old, not politically correct in anyone's book, joke.

"Now hush up and let me examine you," the older paramedic said and did a visual inspection while the younger one took vitals. A penlight was shone into her eyes and flicked away. They palpated Shaunda's throat, felt her ribs, and manipulated her jaw before handing her a fresh ice pack and declaring that she would live.

"Tell these guys I'm fit for duty."

"I'm afraid I can't do that," gray hair said. "You need to come with us and have that head examined at the hospital."

Jerrell piped in, "I've been telling her for years that she needed her head examined."

Shaunda gave him the one finger salute and said to the paramedics, "You two 'ladies' can get back to your coffee and donuts. I'm refusing treatment."

"You'll have to sign a 'refusal' form."

"Stuff your form."

"Hey, don't take it out on me, Shaunda. I didn't kick your ass, but you're pushing your luck," the older medic said.

"Give me the damn form." She took the clipboard, scribbled her name and shoved it back into the medic's hands.

"You call me when you're not in such a bad mood," the older one said. "Poker's still on for next Saturday at my partner's place?"

Shaunda smiled and regretted it. She said, "I hate to keep taking your money. Why don't you just give it to me now, have a couple of beers and imagine you're hauling your sorry broke, drunken ass out to your car."

The medics laughed as they left. The ambulance left. The crowd of looky-loos lost interest and Crocker came back.

Jerrell said, "Shaunda, I want Officer Barr to get pictures and make out an incident report. You landed in my station house. Anything that happens to you from this point on is my responsibility and I don't want to get sued. You need to make out a Dugger police report or get Joey to do it."

Shaunda held the ice pack behind her ear and squeezed her eyes shut. "It happened in Dugger which you always seem to conveniently forget. Joey's with his wife and newborn. Leave him be. I don't want to press charges. I ran into a door."

"Assault on a law enforcement officer is a felony, Shauny. He might've killed you."

"Or he might've drug me off to his cave and made love to me. Just shut up. Can someone get me some water?"

Crocker got the water and Shaunda drank greedily then put the heel of her hand against her forehead.

"Drink slower," Jack said. "You feeling tired? Emotional? Like you want to cry?"

"Every damn day," Shaunda said.

"Those are signs of a concussion," Jack said. "Been there, done that."

"That describes a hangover too," she said. "I need to get back out there to see what I got clobbered over."

"Tell them to tape that whole embankment off," Jerrell barked the order at Crocker.

Crocker said, "Should I call Ditty to meet me?"

"I want Ditty searching for the Jeep. I want every inch of that bank turned over. You and Officer Barr stay here."

"Yes sir, Chief," they both said.

Shaunda stood and seemed a little steadier on her feet. "Who do I have to kill for a cup of coffee?" she asked and turned toward the break room.

"Hey, hold up there," Jerrell said and took her by the shoulders. On the back of her uniform shirt something was printed in heavy black lettering.

P IS NEXT
"Who's P?" Jack asked.

Chapter 11

Written in heavy strokes with black magic marker were the words "P IS NEXT." Shaunda went to the front door and twisted to see her reflection in the glass. "What the hell?" She headed for the outside door patting at her pockets and stopped. "Where's my keys?"

Jerrell was already on his cell phone and said, "Good. Stay there. Hold on." He said to Shaunda, "I've got your keys. You're in no shape to drive. Sergeant Ditterline is close to your house. You won't do anyone any good if you get in a wreck. When's the last time you talked to Pen?"

"I should go home. Hand me my keys, Troy."

Jerrell put his cell phone on speaker and said, "Ditty, I've got you on speakerphone. I'm in the office with the two FBI agents and Chief Lynch. How close are you to her house?"

"Chief Lynch, this is Sergeant Ditterline," the voice came over the speaker. "I'm at your front door. I can see the girls inside." There came the sound of knocking and a door opening. "Pen is just fine. The girls are fine."

"The girls? Is Patty there with her?" Shaunda asked.

"I'm here Mrs. Lynch," a young voice said in the background. Another voice came on the line. "Mom, I called Patty to come over when you left this morning. I didn't know when you'd be home. Is everything okay?"

Shaunda said, "Everything's fine honey."

"Why is Sergeant Ditterline here, mom?"

"I asked him to come by and check on you because I'm going to be tied up helping Troy for a bit," Shaunda said. "Pen, I've got to ask you some questions and I need you to be truthful with me even if you think I'll be mad. Understand?"

The silence stretched out but then the girl said, "Okay, mom. Have I done something wrong? I told Patty's mom she could spend the night if she wanted."

"No baby. That's great that Patty is staying overnight. I need to know if any strange cars or people have been around the house this morning?"

"No mom. Not for the last few days anyway."

"What do you mean? Who was there?"

"Just some guy. He was lost. I gave him directions and he left."

Jerrell said in the background, "Pen, have you or Patty seen Brandon Dillingham's Jeep this morning?"

The girls could be heard talking amongst themselves.

Shaunda said, "Put Patty on the phone hon."

Patty Burris came on the line, "Hello, Mrs. Lynch."

"Patty have you seen Brandon since I talked to you this morning? Did he come by the house?"

"Do you mean your house or my house, Mrs. Lynch."

Jack knew how infuriating it could be talking to teenage girls and having to qualify every word to get a simple answer. Shaunda said, "I mean both. Have you talked to Brandon or seen him since I took you home this morning?"

"No, Chief Lynch."

"I believe you Patty, put Pen back on."

"What's going on, mom?" Penelope asked.

"Oh Christ," Jerrell said to Shaunda and took his phone from her.

"Pen, this is Troy," he said.

"Hello."

Jerrell's face softened immediately. The only sign of the old 'take charge and kick-ass' Jerrell was his white knuckled grip on the phone. "Hey Pen. 'Ow you doin'?" he said, imitating a wise guy with a Bronx accent. Penelope chuckled.

"I'm just fine ya' big palooka. 'Ow you doin'?" she said back, then asked, "Is this about Patty and Brandon? Patty told me she was with him this morning and mom caught her driving Claire's Jeep and pulled them over and threatened Brandon with jail 'cause Patty's underage and doesn't have a driver's license. Is she in trouble? She's got her learner's permit."

Jerrell stared at Shaunda when he asked, "Where did your mom catch them, Pen?"

Pen said, "I'm sorry Patty but I've got to tell him the truth." To Jerrell she said, "They were off-roading at Dugger Mine. Patty's mom doesn't know."

Jerrell held the phone down by his side and muttered, "Just awesome." He put the phone back near his face and said, "Listen Pen. Patty's not in trouble. Your mom's helping us out on a case. She's going to be busy for a little while. I asked Sergeant Ditterline to come by and check on you. He might stay for a while so don't let him eat all the food in your fridge."

Both girls giggled, and Jerrell continued. "Tell me about this guy that was lost."

A longer pause and Jack could hear the girls whispering and Patty saying "tell him, Pen."

Pen said, "Mom already worries too much, and I don't need a babysitter."

"Sergeant Ditterline is staying there, end of discussion. Tell me what happened." Jerrell's voice was hard again. Shaunda reached for the phone and Jerrell pushed her hand away.

"Nothing happened, Chief Jerrell. Honest. Just some guy came to the house about a week ago. He knocked on the door and asked for directions to Terre Haute. I didn't see a car. I told him it was a long walk to Terre Haute. He said he needed a place to stay and some food and asked if I knew of somewhere he could crash."

"I didn't open the door. Honest. I put the chain on the door and gave him a sandwich and a Coke and a bottle of water. He sat outside on our front step and then he left. I didn't talk to him or anything, I swear."

As she was telling this story Jerrell's head drooped. "I believe you, Pen. Describe him? How old was he?"

"He was white. Older than me but not as old as mom. He was way taller than me but not as tall as you. He was real thin and had on a white long sleeve shirt over a black T-shirt. The T-shirt had 'The Walking Dead' on the front. I remember the shirt because I like that show."

"What else?"

"He seemed really tired and hungry. His hair was wavy and long and almost black. It was down on his shoulders and I remember pieces of leaf were sticking in it."

"Anything else? Beard? Mustache? Glasses?"

Pen thought and said, "He didn't have any hair on his face. He was really dark tan and he had really white teeth. I remember thinking that his teeth were awful white for someone so dirty. He was really dirty."

"Tell me about his clothes."

"I told you," Pen said.

Jack could imagine she was rolling her eyes at the other end of the call. Jerrell said, "How were they dirty? Stained? What?"

"Kind of black grime on the white shirt and in the creases in his neck and there was black stuff under his fingernails and on the knees of those old gray jeans. He had sneakers on I think."

"What did you talk about?" Jerrell asked.

"I already told you I didn't talk to him."

"What did you talk about Pen?" Jerrell asked again.

"I only talked to him a minute. I kept the chain on. He said he was on his way to Terre Haute and his car broke down. He saw me looking around to see a car and he said he'd been walking a long time. I said he should maybe call a friend to come get him. He said he didn't have a cell phone and he asked if he could use ours. Don't worry, I'm not that dumb. I said no."

"I would never say you were dumb kiddo," Jerrell said, "but it's not your brightest move, kiddo. You've got a big heart but you had better not do anything like that again. You call Shauny if someone comes to the house that you don't know. She'll come home and take care of it. Right? Safer for everyone that way. Can you do that, Pen?"

"I don't think it would have been safer for Tony. Mom would have kicked him all the way across Dugger."

Shaunda said, "That's absolutely right Pen. I would have. You never open the door when I'm not there. I can't believe I'm saying this, but you listen to Chief Jerrell." It was obvious she was trying to control her temper and was scared.

"His name was Tony?" Jerrell asked. "Did he tell you that?"

"I didn't ask him and he never told me his name. I figured that was his name because it was tattooed on his knuckles."

"You forgot to mention the tattoo, Pen," Jerrell said.

"You didn't ask about tattoos. He had a couple of them. His sleeves were rolled up. There was a fire breathing dragon on one arm and a cross on the other. He said everyone in the band had those tattoos."

"He was in a band?" Jerrell asked.

"That's what he said. He said that's why he needed to get to Terre Haute. I didn't believe him. I think he was homeless and just made that up."

"What did the cross look like, Pen?" Jerrell asked.

"It was just a cross. Like those Irish ones." She described it.

"Is there anything else you haven't told me, Pen?" Jerrell asked.

"No Chief Jerrell. I swear."

"Don't let your mother hear you swear, kiddo," Jerrell said, and Pen chuckled.

In the background Patty could be heard saying, "I'll take care of Pen, Chief Jerrell. We'll be fine if you want your policeman to do something else."

"Put Sergeant Ditterline back on."

"Chief," Ditty said, taking the phone.

"Ditty, can the girls hear you?"

"Just a minute." A door could be heard opening and closing. "No, sir. Go ahead."

"Stay put until I call you off. Don't open the door to anyone. I don't give a rat's ass if it's the pope or a politician. Stay put and call for backup if you need it. This guy might be back and he might be dangerous. Got me?"

"Yes sir."

"Don't tell the girls anything. I don't want them to worry. Play cards or something."

"Are you going to tell me what's going on, Chief? I busted ass to get over here. Is that skinny kid, Tony, involved in what happened to Brandon?"

"Possibly. Someone ambushed Shaunda down at Dugger Lake after we left. She's okay. Just a little banged up. We think there may be a threat against Pen. Stay sharp. You hear me? Radio me immediately if you even get a bad feeling. Do not go after anyone alone. You stay with the girls and call for help. Don't leave that house."

"Yes sir. I need to go lock my car up then I'll stay put. Chief, I didn't have any luck finding that Jeep. We didn't cover all of the trails. I thought whoever it was would head to the city or get on the highway. They had a good head start on us."

"Unless he's got a death wish he's long gone." Jerrell said.

"Maybe she remembers it wrong, but that didn't sound like a Celtic Cross. It sounded more like Odin's Cross," Liddell said. "A square cross with a circle interlocked over the crossbars."

"Odin's Cross?" Shaunda said.

Jerrell answered. "White supremacist. It's a hate symbol. Neo-Nazis. Militia. Drug gangs. Biker gangs."

"Great," Shaunda said. "I wish she had called me."

"How old are these two girls?" Jack asked.

"They're both sixteen," Shaunda said.

"Do they go to school together?" Liddell asked.

"I'm homeschooling Pen," Shaunda said. She's been in a wheelchair since she was ten years old. That girl's got enough on her plate without putting up with a bunch of high school pukes. Patty goes to Union High School, but she spends a lot of time with Pen helping me with her schooling. She's a good kid."

"I hate to ask but is there much activity around here that would involve any of the hate groups?" Jack asked.

"We have a lot of wannabe gang kids, a minor drug problem, but I don't know of any organized group that would have a cross tattooed on themselves," Jerrell said and Shaunda agreed.

Liddell said, "This Tony guy might be just what he seems. A guy trying to get to Terre Haute."

Or he might be dangerous as hell, Jack thought. What were the chances Tony would show up at the chief's house around the same time as Troy Junior's murder? Shaunda voiced Jack's thoughts.

"What are the odds? I live in the asshole of nowhere. It's a quarter mile walk off a main road to get back to my place. What's up with this crap written on my shirt? How would anyone even guess to write that? I'll talk to Pen some more. I think she talked to this Tony longer than she's admitting. I just hope to hell she didn't let him in the house, but I can't imagine she did."

Liddell said, "How about this? Brandon might have run into an angry father. This is a small community, right? I'm sure everyone knows about Chief Jerrell's son. Voila, Troy's killer strikes again. Whoever it was knows you and your daughter and Patty."

"Could be," Jerrell admitted. "Troy's vehicle was missing from the scene and that was in the newspapers. This would have to be one crazy son of a bitch though to come back and attack you Shaunda."

No one said anything until Jerrell added, "At least he didn't kill you."

Jack wondered why Shaunda wasn't killed? Why the warning? Why advertise what was next? Why not just kill Shaunda or Penelope or Patty? Why risk confronting an armed policewoman?

Shaunda put a hand on Jerrell's arm. "Thanks for sending someone to my house. Even if it was Ditty."

"You should have told us that you caught this kid coming from mine property. I mean that's almost where you found his body. Never mind. Why don't you go home and rest up? Be with your daughter. Ditty can stay as long as you need him. We got this."

"That's the second time you told me you've got this. While I appreciate Ditty staying with the girls, I'm good to go. Just tell him to stay out of my panty drawer."

"You don't need a hospital," Jerrell said. "What you need is a good man to straighten you out. Don't look at me like that. I'm not available."

"In your wet dreams bozo."

Jerrell's cell phone rang. He spoke for a moment, hung up and said, "That was Crime Scene. They searched the lake area again and came up with nothing. I still think you should get a CT scan, Shauny. A concussion can be a serious thing."

"When I get my hands on this guy, I'll give him a CT scan. If I wanted a man to beat me unconscious I'd get married." She looked at Jack and said, "I can see you're shocked by our lack of political correctness, Agent Murphy. Maybe you Feds don't approve."

Jack said, "I can neither confirm nor deny that. What I *can* tell you Chief is—bite me."

Shaunda tried not to smile. "You'll never do, you know that? You don't even look like a Fed, and your partner looks like an NFL linebacker."

"I played some in college," Liddell said. "Too violent for me."

Jack said, "We need your uniform for evidence. We need a full workup on you by Crime Scene for comparison. If you don't have a change of clothes with you maybe Chief Jerrell can round up something."

Jerrell said, "I think we still have a kids Halloween uniform. Unless you have a spare uniform with you?"

"No, Shauny doesn't have a spare uniform with her," she said testily. "There's some civvies in my Tahoe."

"Sergeant, would you mind getting her clothes?" Jerrell asked. Crocker turned to go.

"It's in the back. In a canvas bag."

"Yes ma'am," Crocker said.

"There's a box of Powerbars on the seat. Can you bring those and quit calling me ma'am?"

"Yes ma'am…yes, Chief," Crocker said and hurried away.

Jerrell said, "You're the most hardheaded woman I've ever had the pleasure of working with."

"You've been saying that for years."

"You look like twice baked shit."

"You've also been saying *that* for years," she gave him a tight smile. "Such a romantic."

Jerrell shrugged and said, "It's your body."

"Damn right. Got a bumper sticker."

"True love," Liddell whispered to Jack.

"I'd hate to see what they'd be like if they *were* married," Jack said.

Chapter 12

Sergeant Crocker brought in Shaunda's bag and the Powerbars from her Tahoe. She changed in the ladies room in the station house while Crocker made another pot of coffee. Shaunda had taken paper grocery bags into the restroom with her for the uniform she had been wearing. When she came out she handed the bags to Officer Barr. He had already taken photos of her in her uniform and of her injuries.

Shaunda had washed up, brushed her hair, and put on blue jeans and a Black Watch patterned flannel shirt with the sleeves rolled up. Her Sam Browne gun belt was worn loosely around her hips like a gunfighter. Holstered was a Colt Python stainless steel revolver, a big .357 magnum with a six inch vented rib barrel and rosewood grips. Two speed loaders on her gun belt held another twelve rounds of ammunition. Six in the gun, twelve on the belt. It wasn't a lot of ammo for a cop to rely on, but it just takes one well placed shot to put a bad guy down.

With civvies on she was a different woman. When she went into the ladies' room her brown hair had been pulled up into messy bun, but now it was a shiny auburn, worn down around her shoulders, framing a very pretty face. Jerrell watched her every move intently and Jack wondered if Bigfoot was right. Maybe there was something between them in spite of the catty remarks.

"Where's the rest of the Scooby-Doo Team?" she asked. "I thought you had a task force?"

Jerrell sidestepped the question and asked one of his own. "Why don't you carry a spare uniform?"

"Haven't gotten my ass kicked before. That sucker even stole my badge. The city will never spring for another. I'll have to get it back or start a "GoFundMe" page on Facebook."

Jack admired her spunk despite almost being killed. He again wondered why the killer hadn't left her floating face down in Dugger Lake. That would have sent a stronger message to law enforcement. If this wasn't a copycat he had a sick feeling in his stomach that the killer was just getting started.

"Maybe he took the badge as a memento," Liddell suggested. "The reports don't say anything about the other victims missing anything, but the killer might have taken something personal to the victims. We'll need to interview the victim's families. If he's saved something from all of his victims that will be damning evidence."

That is if Jerrell or Shaunda didn't blow him away first, Jack thought.

"Let's move this to the roll call room," Jerrell said. They went down the hall to the break/roll call room and took seats around the table. They took turns giving Shaunda the story they had pieced together before she arrived. When they finished Jerrell pushed a copy of the file across the table to Shaunda.

She began leafing through it and said, "After Troy Junior's death I did some digging around. I wasn't aware of the guy in Illinois. Do you really think they're all connected?".

Jerrell said, "They were all killed in the same manner and the bodies were found in stripper pit lakes."

"Two in Sullivan, two in Dugger if you count Brandon, one in Greene County, one in Hutsonville, Illinois," Shaunda said. "Do you think that's all of them?"

"That's all we know for now," Jack said. "Winters and Washington happened a week apart five years ago. They appeared to be accidental drownings initially. They both had narcotics in their system. Their vehicles were found at the scene. There was nothing to indicate murder. I can see why the responding detectives assumed these victims got drunk or high or both, had gone swimming, hit their head and drowned."

Shaunda said, "Maybe that's all it is. Why are we wasting time on those cases? They were drug addicts. Alcoholics. The only cases I'm interested in are Troy Junior and Brandon."

"I never said they were addicts. Just that drugs were found in their systems."

"I went to high school with Winters and Washington." Shaunda said to Jack. "Don't look so surprised. I went to high school." She looked at the victim's pictures closely. "These guys were jocks. Spell that P-R-I-C-K.

Brandon was at Union High. He wasn't involved in sports. Unless you consider groping young girls and smoking pot a sport."

Crocker said, "Tina told us she knew them from high school, but she didn't tell us she knew you."

"She didn't mention me?" Shaunda said. "How about that? I guess I'm not surprised. These guys were jocks. Tina was Miss Popular. No one ever gave me the time of day. I barely knew who these guys were. I heard about the parties they had. Come to think of it, you should ask Tina about the parties. I'm not saying she was involved with these guys. Just that I knew she was popular and why wouldn't she be. Smart. Beautiful. She was a couple of years ahead of me."

"Do you still have your yearbooks?" Jack asked.

"Now why would I keep anything like that. I didn't even get one but I guess you're going to need them. I can get the ones from Union."

"Crocker's already got that in hand," Jerrell said. "You knew these guys by reputation, right?"

"I knew they were disgusting, self-centered, arrogant, jocks," she said. "They were God's gift to women. Washington was selling pot to half of the students and most of the teachers. Winters was his wingman."

Jack said, "I thought you barely knew who they were?"

Shaunda touched her split lip and flinched. "You don't have to be a rocket scientist to know when someone's selling drugs. Washington would hang around smoker's corner and students would come to him like he was Jesus giving a blessing. I guess to them, he was. Winters," she said, "could have been king and queen of the prom."

"What do you mean?" Jerrell asked.

"You know," Shaunda said. "He batted for both teams. He liked them young. A freshman girl in my class was spending a lot of time with him until he met her younger brother, if you know what I mean."

"Did they have any enemies?" Jack asked.

"They were disgusting. I can't think of anyone that wouldn't want to kill them," she said.

"But are you sure they didn't just overdose and drown? Maybe when Washington died Winters couldn't live without him. Who knows what was going on with those two. They were carved out of the same turd."

"Are you suggesting Washington was an accidental drowning and Winters was a suicide?" Jack asked.

"It's possible," she said.

Jerrell stood over Shaunda like a drill sergeant over a recruit. "Shauny, I know you got hit in the head, but sweet Jesus girl. You can't believe that crap."

It was hard to tell what she was thinking.

Jack said, "Chief Lynch, these cases have a strong resemblance to Troy Junior's murder."

Shaunda answered defensively. "I didn't say they weren't connected. I'm just saying I can't work more cases than I have right now. Two murders in as many weeks and it's just me and Joey. I got a third constable but he doesn't count. I don't think he even feeds himself or takes a bath on his own. He belongs in an assisted living home, with heavy emphasis on the 'assisted.' I have a town board that wants to cut my budget, never listens to me, and believes their kids are immune to traffic laws."

Jack said, "I realize you have a lot on your plate but you are the investigator on two of the cases. Troy Junior and Brandon. None of us have worked any of these cases. We don't have the insight you do."

Shaunda squinted one eye at Jack. "Are you blowing federal smoke up my ass?"

"Did it work?" Jack asked.

"Oh crap," Shaunda said. "I haven't told Claire yet. If she finds out from someone else I'll be lined up at the soup kitchen. I can just imagine what I'll say. "Claire there's been another murder, and "Oh, by the way, it was your son. But I can't worry about Brandon right now. I have to investigate some old, old murders and one in Illinois."

Shaunda got up. She was steadier on her feet this time. "I gotta go."

"Do you want one of us to go with you?" Liddell asked.

"I think I'd better do this alone," Shaunda said. She picked up her bag and left.

"Should she be driving in her condition?" Jack asked Jerrell.

"You going to try and stop her?"

He had a point. "Will she come back?" Jack asked.

"Yeah. She'll be an hour if all goes well. Two if it doesn't."

"I'll go get the yearbooks, Chief," Crocker said. "Be right back."

Jack said, "We need a list of contacts for each victim. Family, friends, detectives working the cases, neighbors, employers, that kind of stuff."

"Can your girl get all that for us?" Jerrell asked.

"Probably, but we're going to have to eventually call the other agencies ourselves. We need to interview the responding officers, dispatchers, detectives, and anyone that had a hand in the investigation," Jack said.

"We need the dispatch tapes of the calls and radio traffic with the cars," Jerrell added. "We need to know who called dispatch, where they called from, if they were interviewed, what connection do they have to the victim or to any of the victims."

"All the calls were made anonymously," Liddell said. "Angelina got the locations where the calls were made from if they had any. Of course, maybe someone came forward since this happened and said they were a witness."

They all sat around the table poring over the cases, making notes, bouncing ideas off each other for the next hour until Jack said, "We're going to need the autopsy reports. We'll interview the pathologists. I wish Chief Lynch could have hung around. We're going to need her help with some of this."

"Did you miss me?" Shaunda said, coming back into the roll call room.

"I thought you be gone longer," Jerrell said.

"I saw Joey's truck when I got to Claire's house," she said. "I didn't go in. I called him and he said Sergeant Ditterline told him that I got banged up. He thought he should talk to Claire before she found out through the grapevine. He's a smart kid. He said he had just told her when she got a call from the Greene County Coroner's Office to inform her. He's still at Claire's giving her time to settle down and he'll take her to identify the body. It's probably a good thing I didn't go in. Claire and I had a little row on the phone about Brandon earlier this morning. Joey's better at compassion than I am."

"Does Joey know to ask her some questions about Brandon while he's got her?" Jack asked.

"I told him to ask about enemies, friends, that kind of stuff. He gets it. He knows his job pretty well. He had a list of questions that he read off to me. What are we doing now?"

"Crocker has gone to get the yearbooks from Linton-Stockton," Jerrell said. "Can you call someone with Union and get their yearbooks?"

"Sure," Shaunda said, and took her cell phone out, scanning down a list of names. "I assume you want all four years these guys were in school."

Jack said, "Ask them if Clint Baker ever worked for the school."

"I forgot to tell Crocker to do that." Jerrell called Crocker and passed that along.

"Come to think of it, we forgot to ask you if you recognized Clint Baker," Jack said.

Shaunda looked at his picture. "He's older than the others, isn't he?"

"He would be forty now. Everyone else would be thirty-one. Tina thought he might have worked at the high school," Jack suggested.

"Nope. Not familiar at all," Shaunda said.

Jerrell finished his call and said to Shaunda, "We were just coming up with a 'to do' list." He checked his notes and read off the list.

To Shaunda he said, "Why don't you use my office and call the Chief in Hutsonville. While you're at it, can you call the other department heads? Get them started collecting dispatch tapes and logs."

While he read the list to her, she interrupted him. "Seriously? You want me to get all that? I mean, why would they give it to me?"

Jack handed her a business card. He'd written Toomey's telephone number on the back. "Ask nicely. If they give you any shit tell them to call FBI Director Toomey and explain why they're interfering in a federal investigation. You're working under the directions of the Federal Bureau of Investigation now."

"Oh, whoopee. I always wanted to lie to people," she said, took the card and put it in her pocket.

Jack said, "We need to know these victims inside and out before we can hope to find their killer. Angelina came up with the file you have and I can…"

Shaunda interrupted again. "Who's this Angelina anyway?"

"She works for the FBI and she's really good at this stuff," Jerrell said.

"Can she tell us who murdered Brandon?"

"Can you?" Jack responded.

Chapter 13

"Take me back over all this," Shaunda said. "If Winters and Washington were accidental drownings why are we looking into them? In the meantime, Brandon's *recent* murder is going to the bottom of the pile with the clock ticking on that one. Not to mention I got my skull busted and my family threatened today. So, explain again why we're not focusing on Brandon's murder?"

"Shauny, you've got to see the bigger picture," Jerrell said.

"If you have a better idea of how to go about this let's hear it," Jack said.

"I just told you," Shaunda said and huffed out a breath. "Let's go after the guy from today. It's obvious he's the one that did them all. We don't need to be strung out over seven years of cases, talking to a hundred people, doing God knows what, when we have something right here, right now."

"I agree," Jack said.

"You do? Well, there you have it then," Shaunda said. "Let's get back out there and find Claire's Jeep."

Jack said, "I agree the one from today is probably is the one we're looking for. We don't know that for sure. If we focus on him, we may miss some important leads from the older cases. Clues that may help us find the one from Troy Junior's murder. Clues that may help with Brandon's murder. There's no solid lead from today. We can drive around hoping to get lucky, or we can work this like I intend to. The longer we sit here, pissing and moaning, the more lead time the killer has," Jack said.

All were silent.

"Okay then," Jack said, once again going to the whiteboards. "We need to know who called these deaths in." The victim's names were down the left side of the board next to their photos. Jack drew a column and titled it "Caller". They went through each victim and in each case the caller was anonymous.

Jack said, "Let's go with the two that Chief Lynch and Chief Jerrell were working before we arrived. Shaunda, how did you get the call about Troy Junior?"

Shaunda said, "We don't have our own dispatch. We pretty much rely on Sullivan County Dispatch to call us, but me and Joey have department cell phones. One cell phone actually. We take turns carrying it when we're on duty. Everyone in town has the number so they just call direct. Saves time."

"I got the call on the work phone. It displayed the number but not a name. The caller said someone had drowned in Dugger Lake and hung up. The number wasn't in my phone directory. Turned out to be Troy Junior's phone. The time and date I got the call are on my police report. I was on duty so I went to check it out. Truthfully, I thought it was a prank call because the voice sounded so young."

Jack said, "To be clear, this call didn't come in from dispatch?"

"It came in from Troy's phone," she answered.

"Male or female caller?" Jack asked.

"I couldn't tell. It was a young voice. Could've been either."

"How did you know exactly where to find Troy's body?" Jack asked.

"There's a short stretch of lake inside Dugger city limits. The lake is split down the middle. One half belongs to Sullivan County, one half to Greene County. I got my little piece of the lake. I went to the lake and saw a body floating about ten feet out in the water. It was face down and naked except for something white around the head. It turned out to be underwear."

"Like with Brandon?" Jack asked.

"Yeah. Brandon was face down, too, but not as far out in the water as Troy."

Jack said, "We'll get to Brandon. Let's stick with Troy Junior."

She said, "It took me twenty minutes to get to the lake. Troy Junior was out in the deep water. I swim like a rock. I figured whoever it was must be dead. I called Joey at home and then I called for our coroner. We don't have Crime Scene people. We do everything ourselves if we can. Joey showed up and got the body out of the water. We waited for Doc Bonner."

Jack said, "You didn't have Crime Scene come out?"

"In hindsight, maybe I should have called Sullivan County Sheriff or State Police, but they take an hour to respond if they respond at all. Besides, we got the body out of the water by ourselves and we didn't know it was anything but an accidental drowning until Troy got a different coroner involved."

"How long before Chief Jerrell got involved?" Jack asked.

Jack couldn't decide if Shaunda was irritated or embarrassed. She said, "I called Troy after Doc Bonner got the body."

"Twelve hours later," Jerrell said through clenched teeth. "I didn't have a chance to examine the scene before it was trampled. You should have called me, Shauny. You knew it was Troy when you pulled him out."

"I did," she said. "I wanted to be sure what I had before I called you."

Jerrell came out of his chair. "Wanted to be sure! What's that even mean? You knew who it was. You knew he was dead. You knew I was his father. You knew I'd help you any way I could. You should have called me and let me help with the crime scene."

Shaunda raised her voice. "Yeah. I knew you would help. Like you helped today. You'd come in like an invading army and take over, contaminating my crime scene. Get it through that thick head that you didn't belong there…"

"Didn't belong there? That was my son! You and that pimple faced deputy of yours screwed it all up. You two wrapped my boy up in a blue tarp and stuck him in the back of a truck and took him to Bonner's office. Bonner's not even a forensic pathologist. You might as well have had a veterinarian come out. What the hell were you thinking Chief?"

Jack raised his voice over both of theirs. "Stop. Stop. This isn't getting us anywhere. What's done is done. We need to concentrate on what to do now. We need each other. That means no more arguments between you two."

"Well she…" Jerrell began but stopped when Jack stood and pointed toward the door.

"If you want to duke it out take it outside. But to be honest, I don't know how much more of a beating Chief Lynch can take."

Liddell took his wallet out and slapped a twenty dollar bill on the table. "Twenty says she can take him." That eased the tension and everyone calmed a little.

"Sorry Shauny," Jerrell said.

"Yes, you are," she responded. "I'm sorry too. I could've done things differently I guess."

Before they could start in on each other about who the sorriest was, Jack said, "Okay, your report said the victim's car was missing, but Chief Jerrell said his son owned a truck and it was found by Linton officers in a field behind a tavern in Dugger. I'm confused. Was it a truck or a car?"

Jerrell said, "Troy had traded his car to a guy in Bloomfield for an old Chevy pickup truck. They didn't bother to register the vehicles and left the old license plates on them. My guys saw the truck sitting out behind the Coal Miner Bar in Dugger a few days later and thought it was suspicious.

They ran the plates and tracked down the owner of record. That's how we found out about the trade."

"In my defense, there's no way I would have known that truck was Troy's. I got a vehicle description from dispatch for a Toyota Camry."

Jack interrupted, "Okay. Okay. I can see how that would have been confusing. Who found the truck?"

"Sergeant Ditterline found it," Crocker said. "Ditty's psychic sometimes."

"Do *any* of you know if anything was missing from the body or the truck?" Jack asked.

"I can tell you we didn't find anything at the scene. No clothes or personal items." She gave Jerrell a scathing look. "How could I know about the truck?"

Jerrell said, "I searched his truck and found nothing. His apartment in Dugger was a mess but the boy was always a slob. When he was ten years old his mom gave him a gold necklace with a gold eagle charm. She told him he would soar like an eagle one day. I never found it. Not in his truck or in his apartment. He wouldn't have given it away. Shaunda said she didn't find anything at the scene. I went out there and used a metal detector and came up empty."

Crocker lay the Stockton-Linton High yearbook on the table and held it open on a page. "Here's Troy's senior picture. He's wearing that chain."

They passed the yearbook around the table. "Is that it Chief?" Jack asked.

"That's it."

"Can you get a copy of that and enlarge it?" Jack asked.

"Sure can," Crocker said. "I'll check all the pawn shops."

"He wouldn't have pawned it," Jerrell said, "but I guess you should check them too."

Jack was glad to see Liddell was keeping notes. Things were moving fast. He turned to Shaunda. "Were you able to find where the call was made from?"

She said, "I don't know where the call was made from, but it was Troy's cell phone number. I didn't have the number in my directory. I called the number back but the voicemail didn't identify who the phone belonged to."

"How did you find out it was his cell phone?" Jack asked.

"I found the phone at Troy's apartment."

Jerrell came unglued. "You had his phone all this time and didn't tell me!"

"It's evidence," Shaunda said. "I couldn't let you tamper with it. If it turned into something how could I explain handing it over to you? It was my investigation not yours. You would have done the same thing."

"Did you find his chain and the eagle?" Jerrell asked. "He would have been wearing it."

"No. I didn't," Shaunda said with finality.

Jack cut in. "Water under the bridge now. The important thing is that she has the phone." He could see Jerrell wasn't going to let it go. He didn't blame him but he'd seen other investigators hide their evidence jealously. He asked Shaunda, "Did you check the call record?"

Shaunda bristled. "I don't have the resources you big city boys have, but I'm not completely clueless. I checked and I wrote it all down. And you know what?"

She was angry. She made them wait.

"There weren't any calls except the call made to me. Someone deleted the calls made and received and the contacts."

Jerrell said in a measured tone, "Can I have the phone and a copy of your notes now?"

"Depends," Shaunda said.

"Chief Lynch, we can—" Jack said, but she interrupted him.

"I checked out the phone. There was nothing there. The last call on the phone was to me."

"You still should have had the common decency to have told me you found the phone," Jerrell shouted.

"I had my reasons, Troy," Shaunda said.

"What reason could you possibly have?"

"I was protecting you."

"If there was nothing on the phone, what the hell could you be protecting me from?"

"From yourself you moron. If we found the guy responsible you would have already ruined the chain of custody. A defense attorney would have torn you to pieces like a Cinnamon Pull-Apart bun. You can't smash everything and everyone and hope you get the right person."

Jack interrupted their brewing argument. "I agree with Chief Lynch. She should maintain control of the cell phone for chain of custody issues. I agree with Chief Jerrell that he should have been told that the phone was recovered and what information was obtained from the phone. I would like to send the phone to my computer analyst. She might be able to retrieve missing data."

Shaunda let out a breath. "The phone is in my office." Her eyes cut toward Jerrell. "This doesn't get us anywhere. Can we move on?"

Jerrell said, "Did you at least protect the phone? Tell me you did."

"Drop it, Troy. I was only trying to…"

"My protection is not your concern." Jerrell rose and marched out of the room.

Shaunda started after him but Jack held her back. "Give him some space."

Chapter 14

Jerrell came back in the room and sat down saying nothing.

"Troy…" Shaunda said.

Jerrell held a hand up. "Let's just get on with this."

Jack said, "I think we've covered Troy Junior for now. We need to talk about Brandon Dillingham. Same questions."

Shaunda had pushed her chair away from the table and rubbed at the scrapes on her knuckles. She said, "As you know, I stopped Brandon this morning. He was in his mom's Jeep. Patty Burris, my daughter's friend, was driving. Patty is barely sixteen and doesn't have a driver's license. She said Brandon was mauling her until I guess he saw headlights coming. That would be me. I let Brandon go with a warning and took Patty home and went home. It couldn't have been more than an hour later I got the call from Sullivan County Dispatch. Suspicious circumstance at Dugger Lake. Possible drowning."

"I called Joey, told him what we had and he said he'd meet me there. When I arrived, Joey was already pulling the body out onto the bank."

"We turned the body over, removed a pair of underwear from his head and we both identified Brandon Dillingham. I called dispatch back and asked who had called in the run. They said it was anonymous and gave me the number it had come from. There were no other vehicles in the area and I didn't see any traffic on my way there. We didn't see anyone out on the lake. The phone that called dispatch was Brandon's."

Jack asked, "Does anyone know if County Dispatch keeps recordings of the radio traffic?"

Shaunda said, "Dugger PD isn't a big enough department to work without a personal work phone. The people in Dugger don't tend to call the cell number unless it's a real emergency. They call 911 if they need an ambulance, or there's a fire, that kind of stuff and then dispatch calls us. If it's just some drunk refusing to leave, they call us. We try not to put people in jail if it's something we can take care of ourselves."

"Dugger is a village and we keep ourselves to ourselves. If a wife is beaten by her husband she might call me or might not. We handle things discreetly but you know how small towns are. Gossip spreads like cancer."

Jack started to suspect that secrecy was the reason Jerrell had been notified so late in the game. Shaunda said she was trying to spare his feelings, but that may have only been part of her reasoning. He'd been in other small towns that buried their secrets. Just like Las Vegas, what happens in Dugger stays in Dugger.

Domestic violence was one thing, but two murders—particularly when one was the son of the neighboring town's police chief, and the other was the son of a prominent politician in Dugger—would be hard to keep quiet. The fact that they weren't already buried in reporters backed up what Shaunda said. They'd tell each other but no one would call the media.

Jack had another mean thought. If they hadn't arrived at the scene this morning, he wondered if Brandon's death wouldn't have become an accidental drowning. Easy call. Somewhat respectful death in that there wouldn't be an investigation revealing all the boy's faults.

Jack asked, "Do you think we're dealing with a local? Two deaths within a week of each other and in the same location. Another in the same lake three years ago. I'm not big on coincidence." He didn't get the reaction he'd expected.

Shaunda said, "I don't believe it. We're on State Highway 54 which is one of the major roads that lead to the interstate. Easy access to the stripper pit lakes. I vote for it being an outsider."

Liddell and Jack had been discussing that same thing on their way to Linton. Over the road truck driver? Traveling salesman? Patterns were seldom recognized if the killer spread his hobby over numerous states, but these were all within fifteen miles of each other. The only outlier was the one in Hutsonville, Illinois and that was less than forty miles away.

"The victims were all local and our analyst didn't find any matching cases anywhere else. Someone local makes more sense. A local killer follows the pattern," Jack said. "In the Hutsonville murder the victim's car was parked in his own driveway several miles from where the body was found. The next three, Washington, Winters and DiLegge, the vehicles were found near the body. The only two where the vehicle was hidden took place near Dugger."

"You're suggesting what?" Shaunda asked.

"Two possibilities. The killer moved Baker, Troy and Brandon's vehicles because he had to. The other vehicles were found at the scene because he wasn't worried about them being discovered quickly. Dugger is central to all of the killings."

"Possibilities," Shaunda said, waving her hand dismissively at the theory.

"Okay. Let's discuss something else," Jack said. "How did the killer get to and from the lakes?"

Jerrell answered, "He could have hitched a ride. Rode a bicycle. Maybe it's a transient? Needed a vehicle sometimes to get somewhere else and carjacked the victims. If he was on a bicycle he could have stowed it in the stolen vehicle until he made his getaway. As far as Troy's murder is concerned it's possible Troy left the truck back behind the Coal Miner Bar himself. If he was drunk, and he usually was, anything's possible."

Shaunda said, "I like the transient idea. Maybe they picked this guy up, he made them take him to the lake and killed them?"

Jack said, "Or there's another possibility we haven't discussed yet." He waited until he had everyone's attention. "There are two killers."

"Now you're saying I have two homicidal maniacs living in Dugger. Nothing ever happens in Dugger. It's a quiet little place. The evidence points toward the killer being a homeless person. Like the one that came to my house. Maybe he was the same guy that clobbered me. He killed Brandon and just decided to drive a new Jeep for kicks. He realized he left something behind and came back on foot. If someone like that wanted to avoid being seen they could easily do it. Whoever it was knocked the crap out of me and got away on foot. I say it's a homeless person."

"If the killer is a homeless person don't you think they would have taken the victims money or valuables?" Jerrell asked.

"He took my valuable badge," she said defiantly.

Jack asked, "Troy's truck was found how far from the lake?"

"It's four or five miles to the bar from the lake," Shaunda said.

"Four or five miles," Jack said. "Clint Baker's body was found about the same distance from his car and home. It would take about an hour to walk that far."

"Less than that if they were hitching a ride, or going cross country on foot," Shaunda said, still pushing her homeless theory.

"I don't like a hitchhiker for the killer," Jack said. "Maybe for Brandon because he's not the right age, and he doesn't fit as part of the group of high school friends. Neither does Clint Baker at this point."

Jerrell said, "We're back to square one."

"No. We just have to keep an open mind. We can create a list of police contacts with homeless people or hitchhikers." Jack said for Shaunda's benefit. "Do the officers on either of your departments make out field contact cards?" A field contact card is created when an officer stops someone or has a situation where they need to identify the person for later use. It's not a search and seizure issue and not an arrest.

Shaunda said nothing so that was a no.

Jerrell said, "We don't have anything on paper, but we don't have that big a problem with panhandlers. My guys usually talk to them and they move on or we find them a bed in a shelter somewhere to get them off the street. Sometimes local churches take them in for short-term lodging and food. I'll put word out to my people and find out if any of them know of anyone."

Jack said, "Particularly pay attention to people who moved from the Hutsonville area to Linton or Dugger. Nothing has happened in Hutsonville for seven years. Maybe the killer moved here. I'll have Angelina get into the Bureau of Motor Vehicles database and see what she can find." He was glad neither Jerrell or Shaunda asked how Angelina was getting access to all these records.

Shaunda said, "I've had a few transients over the years but I don't keep information on them. I doubt they'd even have identification if I'd have asked." Her cell phone rang. She dug it out and had a short conversation. When she hung up she said, "That was Joey. He's on his way to the morgue with Claire. He asked her if Brandon had any enemies and she insisted that he was loved by everyone. He tried to ask her about possible drugs, girlfriends, angry fathers, and stuff but she wasn't listening to him. She was upset that Brandon's body was brought to the Greene County Coroner. He told her the FBI were assisting in the investigation and he said she seemed impressed and quit complaining. He gave me the credit for bringing the FBI in on this. I love that kid."

Jack said, "Were any of the anonymous callers identified as male or female voices?"

No one knew.

Chapter 15

Shaunda had taken Liddell with her to Dugger City Hall to collect Troy's cell phone.

Jack was going to call the Sullivan Police Department to ascertain if they still had Daniel Winters and/or Lamont Washington's property. Chief Jerrell was doing the same with Greene County Sheriff's Department asking for Leonard DiLegge's property. They were both primarily interested in the victim's cell phones. DiLegge's cell phone had not been recovered according to the reports but it was possible it had been found or turned in and that information hadn't made it into the case file.

Before they split up to do the work Jack asked, "Chief, when you had the autopsy on your son did you collect fingerprints, hair, DNA?"

Jerrell answered, "Crime Scene did that. I wish Shauny had told me about that damn phone."

"Water under the bridge, Chief," Jack said, not wanting to go down that rabbit hole again.

"I can put a rush job on it with the State Lab," Jerrell offered.

"Let's see what we get. We should send them all at the same time," Jack said. The horse was already out of the barn regarding chain of custody of the evidence but if they could get a lead it was worth a shot.

"I don't know what she was thinking," Jerrell said, his mind still circling the rabbit hole to the past.

Jack said, "What matters is that we find Brandon's phone and the Jeep. All we need is a solid lead from all this. If we get something it'll save us a lot of legwork."

"I've got two officers searching around Dugger for the Jeep. I called in a couple of reserve officers to make runs. We're stretched a little thin and I don't know what Shauny's been able to do on her end."

"The State Police and both sheriff's offices will loan us some boots on the ground," Jack suggested. "You make the call and I'll talk to them, too."

"I want to keep control of this thing."

"Call them," Jack said. "More eyes and ears. Just give them what they need to know. Murder suspect with no description yet. Possibly in Brandon's Jeep. Treat as armed and dangerous and hold for the FBI. My authority. I think you'll find them very helpful. You'll be the primary case officer working *with* me. We have to include them."

"You can use my office and I'll use Crocker's desk. Someone has to be here." He gave Jack the phone numbers for Sullivan city police and the Sheriff's Department and then headed for his office to make his calls to Indiana State Police and Greene County Sheriff's Office.

Jack called the Sullivan County Sheriff's Office first, rightly thinking that the two cases would have been in their bailiwick. He started to ask for the Adult Investigations Unit or Homicide but remembered in time that he was working for the Feds on this one. He would eventually be switched back to the investigators but protocol said he had to talk to Boss Hogg first.

He spoke to the sheriff, identified himself and went through the routine advising her of the task force and how he had become involved. Five long minutes later he was told he needed to talk to the Commander of the Investigations Unit. While he waited for his call to be transferred he hoped he wouldn't be transferred again before he found someone that could answer his questions. He was in luck.

"Adult Investigations, Captain Harvey," came a woman's gravelly voice. *Smoker's voice.*

"Captain Harvey, this is Jack Murphy. I'm a Special Agent with the FBI USOC Task Force." He had to explain what USOC was, but that was expected. "I've been assigned to investigate several murders, including two that your office worked five years ago."

Captain Harvey listened as Jack briefly recounted the cases. When Jack finished she said, "I vaguely remember the two cases out near the City Coal Mine. I was a detective sergeant back then and may have had a hand in those." Jack read the detective's names on the police reports. Harvey wasn't one of them. "That's great, Captain," Jack said. "I've got the right detective."

"Give me a moment to pull the cases up."

Jack waited less than a minute before she came back on the line.

"Got them. What do you need, Agent Murphy?"

Jack told her what he needed.

"Agent Murphy, I'm showing those files are closed as death by misadventure." That was legal jargon for accidental drowning. "You're saying they were murdered by a serial killer?"

Jack could hear the barely disguised excitement in her voice. "We're still in the early stages, Captain," Jack said. "If you have what I want we may be able to confirm our theory about a possible serial killer. We just got into Linton this morning."

"Yeah," she said. "I heard about the drowning in Dugger Lake. You looking into that one too?"

"We are looking at everything for now. You know how that is. Everyone's a suspect and every case is connected until you can prove differently."

"You got that right. I'm more on the administrative side now but I remember my days working cases. I suppose you want me to see if we still have any of the property and pull the files for you?"

"You read my mind, Captain."

"I'll check for you myself. Do you need a place to set up shop? We can give you our big conference room, phone lines, computers, personnel? Be happy to help."

"We are still in early stages so I'll get back to you on that," Jack lied. "Any assistance you can give us is greatly appreciated."

Shaunda had told them she never had cooperation from Sullivan Sheriff's Office but they were rolling out the red carpet. He'd keep it in mind, but he had no intention of moving the investigation. He was having too much fun watching Jerrell and Lynch take each other apart.

Captain Harvey didn't sound happy that she wouldn't be running lead on this, seeing her face on television, but she was smart enough not to push it.

"I'll get the tapes of the calls, property, copies of the case files and any notes we may have. I'll have an officer drop them off for you in Linton. I'm not positive we still have the dispatch tapes. We live in the technical age so you'd think we'd keep everything digitally forever."

"My thoughts exactly, Captain," Jack said. "Don't forget the cell phones of the victims. I'll sign the chain of custody."

"You want us to run phone records?"

"Not necessary, Captain. We have an intelligence analyst that works miracles with this stuff."

"Anything else, Agent?"

"We might want to talk to the detectives that worked the cases. Will you send copies of your crime scene photos?"

"Okay. When do you need my detectives? I'll can make them available today."

Jack said, "Like I said, we're just getting started. We have some things to sort out but we can come tomorrow, if that works for you?"

She said, "Just call. I'll get the detectives that worked the case to show you anything you need. Well, one detective anyway. One of them retired last year and is down in Florida. Lucky stiff."

"I hear you," Jack said.

"Detective Minnie Park will be your contact. The retired detective's name is Bob Parsons. Minnie will take care of you. If you need anything else just call."

Captain Harvey gave Jack her work and personal cell phone number, and Detective Park's numbers. She took Jack's contact information and promised he'd hear from Minnie Park by the end of the day with an answer about the items he'd requested. She said she'd make sure Minnie had a phone number for Parsons in case Jack needed to talk to him.

Jack met Jerrell at the front desk and they headed back to the roll call room. Jack put on a pot of coffee while Jerrell got them mugs and condiments.

"I put out another statewide BOLO for the Jeep," Jerrell said. "I called Greene County. They never found DiLegge's cell phone, but the call to dispatch was definitely made from his number. It hasn't been used since. They don't have the tape of the call to dispatch anymore, but I found the dispatcher that took it. She remembered taking the call but she didn't remember anything. I called the State Police to see if they could send a couple of troops to help search around Dugger since Shauny's low on troops."

Jack told Jerrell about his conversation with Captain Harvey.

"If we get the dispatch tapes and cell phones from Sullivan County I want to get it all to the FBI lab ASAP. I'll call Toomey and have a rush put on it. If they have dispatch tapes I think the lab can do a voice analysis to tell us if it's the same voice and maybe if it's a man or woman. Who knows? If we can find some phones maybe we'll get DNA."

"At least we'll have Troy's phone. Shauny's DNA is probably all over it," Jerrell said.

Jack said, "We have air service at our disposal. Let me make a quick call."

Jack went outside and called Director Toomey and explained what he needed. He came back in and said, "Toomey is going to call Sullivan PD himself and get this expedited. That'll save about a week of our time."

Jack's phone rang and he answered. "Detective Parks, that was quick." He listened and said, "You'll be getting a call from the Deputy Director of the FBI if you haven't already. He's going to send someone to pick up the phones and tapes if you found them."

He listened again, then said, "You do? That's great. Can you have someone email the crime scene and autopsy photos to Chief Jerrell, Linton Police?" He gave her Jerrell's official email address and disconnected. Jack called Liddell, updated him and asked if they could take Troy's cell phone by the Sullivan County Sheriff's Office.

Jerrell said, "You should come to work for me."

"We'd kill each other inside a week," Jack kidded.

"Probably."

Chapter 16

Liddell and Shaunda came into the roll call room. Jack and Chief Jerrell had the case files arranged on the tables along with steaming mugs of coffee.

Shaunda said "You boys haven't made an arrest yet, I see," Shaunda said.

"That was fast," Jack said.

Liddell explained, "She was flying low. I may need to change my pants."

"Had him crying like a baby," Shaunda said.

"I was. I admit it."

"Meanwhile," Jack said, "we were slaving away trying to solve multiple murders."

"I told you he doesn't have a sense of humor," Liddell said.

"Neither does the big ugly one," she said, meaning Chief Jerrell. "We gave the phone to Sullivan County. They said your private FBI plane was on its way. What did we miss?"

Jack answered. "I called Angelina and told her to expect downloads from the sim cards in the phones. She found Brandon's cell phone number and said she could track it if the "Find My Phone" thing was turned on."

"Can she find DiLegge's like that?" Liddell asked.

"It's been too long," Jack said.

"Too bad," Shaunda said. "Joey called and said he'd taken Claire to the morgue and she almost had a meltdown. He's taken her home and I told him to stay with her as long as she needed. Poor woman."

Sergeant Crocker came in with an armload of hard bound books. "I got all the yearbooks, Chief."

Jerrell flipped through the Stockton-Linton books. He held it open and said, "Here's the eagle pendant I was telling you about."

Everyone gathered around him. The portrait photo was of a teenage boy with a shock of blond hair, a big smile on his face showing a full set of braces. He was the spitting image of his father. Around Junior's neck was a heavy gold chain with a gold eagle pendant the size of Jack's thumb.

"You sure you didn't see that, Shauny?" Jerrell asked her.

She didn't answer.

Jerrell went through the other three yearbooks, finding the pictures of his son and in each he pointed out the eagle around his son's neck, reinforcing his statement that Troy Junior would never have parted with the gift from his mother. Jack was glad Shaunda didn't suggest that Troy Junior may have sold it or traded it for drugs which was very probable.

"Someone needs to go through the yearbooks completely, every picture, see what clubs the victims belonged to, who their friends were. It's too bad we can't get their personal yearbooks to see what everyone wrote about them," Jack suggested.

"I'll do the yearbooks," Crocker said.

It was going on lunchtime. Liddell reminded them.

"We need something to eat. I don't do my best thinking when I'm hungry." Jack asked, "Is there anything we need to do first? Did we miss something?"

Jerrell said, "Go ahead without me. I've got some calls to make."

"We have to find a place to stay," Jack said. His phone rang. It was Angelina.

Liddell and Jack sat in their Crown Vic on the west side of Linton City Park, backed into a space in the parking lot of a motel aptly named The Park Inn. South from them, across the two lane highway, was an O'Reilly Auto Parts store. Further East was a Chuckles gas station and a Taco Bell. They had a good view of the west and south side of the park where a Vietnam Era Army tank, an M60 Patton, was on display. A concrete drive, the Phil Harris Parkway, named after the 1950s comedian/actor Phil Harris, encircled the park.

Angelina's call had given Jack the general location of Brandon Dillingham's cell phone. That fact that his phone had made the call directly to Sullivan County dispatch that morning and hadn't come in through 911 was unusual. Not many people would know the direct number. Angelina told Jack the phone was currently near the Linton City Park and was stationary and pinging. She was trying to narrow down the location.

Chief Lynch had ridden with Chief Jerrell. The two Chiefs were parked on the southeast side of the park where Highway 54 intersected with County Road 1100 West. Crocker was watching the east side. Two more Linton PD cruisers were told to stay in the area but to stay out of the park. Angelina was passing the phone location info to Liddell who was in turn relaying it to Jerrell via a borrowed portable radio.

They had been sitting for the better part of an hour when the radio squelched in Jack's lap causing him to jump.

"Is it moving yet?" Jerrell asked.

Jack keyed the mic. "It hasn't moved for a while, Chief." He let up on the talk button and muttered, "Not since the last five times you've asked."

Jerrell said, "I say we go ahead and do a walk through. For all we know the phone is in a trash bin. Or it might be in Chuckles. Who knows. I thought that little gal of yours knew where it was."

Jack keyed his mic. "It's stationary, Chief. Angelina's trying to narrow its location down."

"How narrowed down can she get it?"

"To a gnat's wingspan," Jack said.

Liddell was on an open phone line with Angelina. He held a finger up. "Angelina just pinpointed the phone. It's not in the park. It's in a residence just north of the park." Liddell gave Jerrell the address.

Jack keyed the radio. "Chief Jerrell, keep someone out here in front of the park to watch for the homeless guy Chief Lynch's daughter described. He's the best lead we've got."

Jerrell's truck started moving and Jack hurried to follow. Jerrell was on the radio giving instructions. Jerrell would take the front door with Chief Lynch. Jack and Liddell would cover the back door. Crocker was to set up at the intersection to block traffic from entering or exiting. Jerrell ordered his roving cars to close in on the park and keep a loose perimeter.

They followed Jerrell's truck down the county road. On their left was the city park; to their right was a mobile home park. As they passed through the intersection Crocker angled his car blocking the intersection behind them.

"I hope Angelina's right about this," Jack said. "We don't need to break into some granny's house and cause a heart attack."

Angelina's voice came over the phone. "I can hear you Jack."

Liddell smirked and silently mimicked her words.

"I can see you Liddell," Angelina said.

"Cannot."

"Hey, guys, the phone signal just disappeared," Angelina said.

"What?" Jack asked.

"It's just gone. Someone could be taking the sim card out or destroying the phone."

Jack passed the info on to Jerrell.

Jerrell said, "I'm on the phone with our prosecutor for the search warrant. I just told him the signal went blank. He says we have exigent circumstances."

An 'exigent circumstance' is an exception to the Fourth Amendment search and seizure requirement. The exception says when officers have probable cause to search, and reasonably believe contraband or evidence is being destroyed, it is allowable to enter and search without a warrant.

"I agree, Chief," Jack said, knowing that Jerrell didn't give two hoots whether Jack agreed or not.

Jerrell bumped his truck over the curb and drove into the front yard of a white vinyl sided cottage. The truck slid to a stop and Jerrell and Shaunda exited and rushed up a wooden handicap ramp to the front door of the house. The ramp and yard were decorated with brightly painted yard gnomes that stood like sentries on the sides of the front stoop.

Liddell hurried to the right side of the house and Jack went to left where he could watch the side and the back. Jerrell was preparing to kick the door open when Liddell yelled, "Wait! Hold up. The signal's on the move again."

Jerrell hurriedly spoke into the radio mic on his shoulder. "All units stand down. Stand down." He turned to Liddell who had come to the front. "What do you mean it's moving. Moving where?"

Liddell held the cell phone to his ear. "She says it's going west. No. Yeah. West."

"Are you sure?" Jerrell asked.

"It's headed west. She says it's moving fast toward the park."

Jerrell passed this on to his troops.

Crocker came on the radio. "Chief, you want me to go into the park?"

"Damn," Jerrell said and asked Liddell, "How sure is your gal that the phone isn't in there?"

Liddell put the phone on speaker and Angelina said, "The signal is still moving away from you heading west at a good pace. You're going to have to hurry to catch it."

Jack had come around to the front. "What do you want to do Chief?"

Jerrell said, "You and your partner follow the signal. We'll knock and see if we're let in." Jerrell keyed his radio and gave instructions to his troops.

Jack and Liddell went back behind the house through a copse of trees and entered the park. The land was flat once they broke out of the trees and gave them a good view into the park.

They couldn't risk putting Angelina on speaker. Liddell quietly passed the directions on. "She's got our phones pulled up on GPS. We're a hundred yards north of the signal. It's heading south still. We're coming to a swimming pool."

"I see it," Jack said. They crossed the narrow paved road they had seen from the parking lot of The Park Inn. "Left, or right?" he asked.

Liddell said, "Neither. Go straight through and past the parking lot for the pool. It's moving faster."

"Put her on speaker," Jack said, and Liddell did. Jack said, "Angelina, can you task a satellite and see who we're chasing?" Jack asked, knowing the answer would be…

"So solly, Cha-lee. Me go prison long time," she answered. "Maybe if Toomey didn't know what we were doing I could, but federal laws and regulations kind of frown on my hacking satellites without permission. Go around the pool, straight ahead. You'll see another bunch of trees and on the other side of that is tennis courts. The signal has slowed down but if it keeps moving it'll be out of the park before you catch up."

Liddell keyed the radio and passed this on to Jerrell. Jerrell told his perimeter cars to converge on the front of the park and to stop anyone trying to cross Highway 54. He said they were still trying to make contact with the occupants of the house. You could hear one of them knocking loudly before the radio went quiet.

Liddell and Jack picked up the pace and jogged past the pool just in time for Jack to see a small figure in dark clothes and a dark hoodie enter the trees behind the tennis courts moving away from them.

"There they are, Bigfoot," Jack said.

"I don't see anyone."

Angelina's voice came from the tiny speaker. "The signal has stopped about five hundred feet ahead of you. On the map I can see a skate park right where the signal is located."

Jack saw an old man sitting on a bench beside the tennis courts reading a book. He didn't pay any attention as they ran past him. As they entered the trees Jack saw the skate park where four teenagers were skateboarding. One was the figure wearing the dark hoodie. Jack saw it was a young girl and none of the four resembled the man the Chief's daughter had described.

Jack and Liddell stood at the edge of one of the concrete slopes watching the teens effortlessly jump ramps, land gracefully and go up another ramp seeming to float in the air. The teens ignored them which struck Jack as odd. Bigfoot always attracted attention.

"I've got an idea," Jack said, and stepped into the middle of the ramp with his arms out at his sides. The skateboarders stomped down on the back of the boards flipping them up into their hands and started walking away. At the same time Jerrell's voice came over the radio. "We've made entry. Just an old couple here having a late lunch. They said they didn't hear us knocking. Chief Lynch and I have permission to go through the house. Standby."

Jack keyed the radio. "Chief, we're going to talk to some skateboarders in the park."

"10-4," Jerrell said.

Jack called to the teens, "Hey guys. Twenty bucks for some information." Instead of taking out his badge he pulled a twenty out of his pocket and held it up. The teens immediately stopped and came back like a choreographed group.

There were four of them. The one wearing a hoodie was definitely a girl. The hoodie came down revealing a girl of about thirteen with light purple Kool-Aid colored hair. Her head was shaved to the scalp on one side and the remaining hair combed over like a horse's mane. She rode her skateboard up to within five feet of Jack, expertly flipped it up and caught it. The others had made room for her. She was the leader.

A boy, approximately the same age as the girl, taller, but with the same hair and metal studs in his eyebrows put his board down and balanced on it. The other two boys were younger, maybe ten to twelve years old and clung to their boards like they were childhood binkies.

"Twenty-five dollars," the Kool-Aid girl said.

Jack said, "Okay, ten dollars. Going once, going twice…"

"For what?" Kool Aid girl again.

"To answer some questions." Jack and Liddell showed their FBI badges, but to this age group, all badges meant the same thing. Cops.

Liddell asked, "Where's the phone?"

The boys all shook their heads.

Kool Aid hair crossed her arms defiantly. "I didn't steal it, I swear. I got witnesses." All of the boy's heads bobbed up and down in agreement.

Chapter 17

Kool-Aid was fourteen years old and identified herself as Cretin. The older boy was also fourteen and went by the name Crabs. The younger boys were ten and eleven years old and were too scared to give a made-up name. Liddell took notes while Jack questioned them. Jack had a way with kids. He scared them.

Kool-Aid girl's real name was Lucia Bowles. She lived with her grandparents in the house Jerrell had just searched. Crabs was Wesley Niles III. Jack could understand why he went by the name Crabs. They hadn't gotten far into the questioning when Jerrell came trotting up with Chief Lynch following.

"Hey Chief," the girl said.

"Hello Cretin. What are you doing on this side of town?" Jerrell asked.

She lost the aggressive stance. "Juvie Court gave me to granny. Pop's in rehab. Mom's—somewhere."

"Where's your little brother?"

She let out a breath and shrugged. "He's with some old bag on a farm over by Lyons. He's there with a bunch of *orphans*. She's probably making Jinky milk cows or shovel horseshit."

"Jinky is your brother's nickname?" Jack asked.

Jerrell turned to Jack. "Kids' real name is Jinky. He's eight."

Jack said, "Lucia—I mean Cretin—gave me this." He unfolded a latex glove and revealed an iPhone. "She said she found it in a trash can up near the front entrance of the park." Jack's expression said he didn't believe her.

Jerrell pulled on some gloves, took the phone and punched a button. The screen lit up with a screensaver picture of a cannabis leaf. Jerrell brought up the contacts and scrolled down.

Shaunda said, "That's Claire's number in there as 'Mom'. This is Brandon's phone."

"When did you get the phone?" Jerrell asked.

"I didn't steal it. I found it in a trash bin over by Chuckles. I was going to bring it to the police station and turn it in. Is there a reward or something?"

"He asked you when you 'found' it?" Shaunda said.

"A couple hours ago."

"What's a couple?" Shaunda asked.

"I don't have a clock," Cretin said. "It was a while ago." The other kids were nodding.

Jack checked the time. It was coming up on 1:30. If she was telling the truth she found the phone around ten-ish. The call to Sullivan dispatch had come in at 6:48 a.m. That would mean the killer had to do the deed, drive to Linton City Park, call 911, then ditch the phone. That would make sense except Jack didn't believe Cretin. The word 'cretin' means a stupid person. This kid was far from stupid.

"Did you use the phone?" Jerrell asked.

"You think I'm ignorant? Everyone knows if you use 'em that's theft," she said and Crabs sniggered.

"Were you going to sell it?" Jerrell asked. Cell phones went for fifty to a hundred bucks on the street.

"I told you. I was going to turn it in to the police and get a reward. I'm not a thief."

Jerrell said, "We just talked to your grandparents."

"If you charge me with something they'll send me to that stupid farm with Jinky."

Jerrell called Sergeant Crocker on the portable. "Crocker, I need you to ask the grandparents if they are the legal guardians of Lucia. If so, I need them to meet us at headquarters. Tell them Lucia is helping us with an investigation."

A pause, then Crocker said, "They said they aren't the legal guardians. The mother took off somewhere and father is in rehab. She's a ward of the court."

Jerrell said, "Lucia Bowles, you're being detained for questioning and will need to come with me. What I need to know right now—and don't try lying to me or you will be in big trouble and you spell that F-A-R-M." He let that sink in before asking, "Where did you get this phone?"

"If I don't get arrested I'll tell you."

"You're not in a bargaining position. If you're helping us with our investigation I won't have to charge you. Let's start over. Do you know Brandon Dillingham?" Jerrell asked.

She hesitated only a breath. "Who?"

Jack said, "Brandon is dead."

"He's dead." She turned pale. "I told him he'd better stop messing with those people."

"What people?" Jack asked.

Instead of answering Jack's question she said, "Am I under arrest?"

"We should take all of them to the station," Jack said.

"Yeah. We'll take Cretin and Crabs. You want to take the little ones?" Jerrell asked. Jerrell radioed Crocker and advised him to have the grandparents come to the station.

Jack gave the younger boys his best doom face. "It's a school day. You want to head back to school, or do you want your parents to come and get you at the police station?"

Both boys jumped on their skateboards and vacated the area.

Crocker called over the radio and said the guardians were on their way to the station.

Chief Lynch took the girl by the arm, "You can ride with me and the Chief."

Cretin made a bored face. "Oh goody."

Jack said to the boy named Crabs, "I guess you're going with us."

"Hey. You can't take me nowhere. I'm a juvenile. I got rights."

Liddell towered over the boy. "You got the right to march, son. Just so you know, if you run you don't want me to catch you. Got it?"

Crabs nodded his head at the behemoth that was Liddell.

They marched back through the park to their vehicles. Liddell opened the back door of the Crown Vic and put a hand on top of Crabs head to help him in the backseat.

"Seatbelt," Liddell said, and Crabs hurriedly buckled up.

"Watch your head," Shaunda said, stuffing Cretin in the crew cab door of Jerrell's truck. "You know the drill kid. Get your belt on." Shaunda slammed the door shut harder than necessary.

"I take it you know this young lady?" Jerrell asked.

"I caught her with Brandon trespassing on Sunflower Mine property a few months back. I took her home and left her with what passed for parents. She didn't have any identification on her and her parents were so stoned I'm surprised they recognized their own daughter."

Jerrell and Shaunda got in the truck. Jerrell checked the rearview mirror. "Buckle up buttercup," he said. Cretin let out an exaggerated sigh and fixed the seatbelt.

"We'll drive around the area a few minutes. Keep your eyes peeled back there. You see the guy you got the phone from shout it out."

"I told you I found the phone," Cretin said.

"This is a murder investigation kiddo," Shaunda said. "You don't want to get caught lying like you just did back there to the FBI. Did you know that lying to Feds is a crime all by itself? Lying about a murder case makes you an accessory. You hear me? Fifteen years minimum."

"Don't put me in a room with Crabs and I'll tell you the truth. If those guys find out I'm talking I might need witness protection."

Jerrell grinned. "She's a pistol. I like her."

Shaunda said, "She's definitely marriage material, but don't you think you're a little old?"

Jerrell answered by firing up the big 8 cylinder engine and peeling out. He drove around the side streets, around the park and behind the businesses along State Road 54 but they didn't see anyone that matched the description given by Lynch's daughter and Cretin didn't give a sign she recognized anyone.

Chapter 18

They met up at the Linton Police Station. Cretin was put in a small office they used for interrogations. Her grandparents had arrived and were seated with her while she was read the juvenile Miranda and the three of them were left alone for the mandatory fifteen minutes to discuss her options.

Crabs was sitting in the lobby in a chair next to the front desk with Sergeant Crocker keeping an eye on him. Crabs lived alone with his mom and a cadre of his mom's boyfriends. There had been no luck finding Crabs's mother or anyone willing to act as guardian. Mom was a waitress and was supposedly at work, but she wasn't and no one seemed to know where to find her. Crabs didn't expect her to be home for a few days or weeks. He didn't seem bothered by her absence. Since Crabs wasn't a suspect and as his mother was unavailable Crocker called the State Welfare Department.

Cretin's grandparents said they were not her legal guardians and refused to get involved with whatever the girl had gotten herself into. They refused to sign the Miranda form, told Cretin they would wait for her at home and left. Fourteen-year-old Cretin was on her own.

Jerrell said to the girl, "You said you didn't steal the phone. I'm prepared to believe you but you're fourteen. By law I'm supposed to have a relative or guardian sit in on the interview."

"Screw them," Cretin said. "I want to hear the FBI say I'm not going to jail and I'll tell you anything you want to know? I didn't do anything."

Jack said, "We're wasting time."

Cretin turned her face toward the wall. "I didn't find the phone. I lied about that. I got the phone from some creep hanging out at the park this morning."

Jack didn't interrupt.

"When they took my brother to that farm I ran off. I wasn't going there. I hate the smell even. I was on the street for about a week and I decided to go to my grandparents. I just got there yesterday. I knew some guys that hung out at the skate park so I went out the back window this morning after breakfast."

She said this as if it was normal to leave by climbing out a window.

"I was telling the truth about not knowing what time it was. Anyway, I went to the skate park but no one was there yet. I went across the street to Chuckles and got a couple of candy bars and some smokes. I hung around long enough to burn a couple. When I got back to the park a creepy guy was there. He asked if I wanted to buy a phone. I didn't have any money. I blew him off but he said he'd trade me the phone for some cigarettes. We traded." She stopped talking.

"Go on," Jerrell said.

Cretin gave an exaggerated shrug. "That's it."

"Did the other boys see the guy you traded with?" Jack asked.

"He was gone by the time they got there. I hung around with them a few minutes and went back to my grandparents. I thought about calling the police but I knew you'd say I stole it."

"Did the others know about the phone?" Jerrell asked.

"I showed it to them. They were all like, "It's stolen. You're going to jail." They wanted me to sell it. I was going to bring it to the police station and see if the owner was giving a reward. I'm not a thief."

"Did you tell them about the guy?" Jack asked.

"Yeah. Kind of. I told them some creep traded me for some smokes."

Jerrell said, "Blind Pete is working Chuckles today. The kids all know to steal when he's at work. He can't see more than the end of his arm. She's probably telling the truth."

"Describe the guy in the park," Jack said.

She said, "He was old. Twenty at least."

"Okay. Good. Go on," Jerrell said.

"He was skinnier than Crabs, but a lot taller. Blue eyes, real tan like he lived outside. A homeless guy."

"Why do you say he was homeless, Cretin?" Jerrell asked.

"His clothes were really dirty. His pants were crusty gray and real worn out. Everything about him was dirty. His hair came down to his shoulders."

"What color hair?"

"Dark. Black," she said.

"Anything else you can remember," Jerrell prodded.

"He had tattoos on both arms. Here and here." She indicated her own forearms.

"Describe the tattoos," Jerrell said.

"One was a dragon that went from his wrist all the way up past his elbow. Some kind of cross was on his other arm."

"Any other tattoos?" Jack asked.

"He had something tattooed on his fingers, but I didn't see what."

"Anything else you remember?"

Jerrell continued to ask open ended questions until Jack was sure they'd squeezed her dry. She'd remembered some other things about the homeless guy that supported Pen's description. She also said the tattoo of the cross had blood dripping from the circle shape. She was adamant that she hadn't seen where he went after her encounter with him."

Jack asked her, "How long have you lived with your grandparents this time?"

"Not long," was the answer.

"Have you seen this guy anywhere before today?"

"No."

Jack waited for her to elaborate. She didn't.

"If you saw him again would you recognize him?" Jack asked.

"Hell yeah. He was creepy."

Jack said, "We're going to talk to Crabs now and if he tells us a different story our deal is off."

"I don't want to get anyone else in trouble. Crabs can't know I talked to you."

"Why is that?" Jerrell asked.

"Because he used to hang out with the same people Brandon hung out with. If they find out I talked to you they'll kill me. Or worse."

Jerrell knew the names she gave of the people Brandon was hanging around with. Two adult men and a woman. All regulars with Linton PD.

"You said you warned Brandon not to hang around with them," Jerrell said. "Why was that?"

"They carry guns. Brandon said people that messed with them disappeared."

"Were you with Brandon when you saw the guns?" Jerrell asked.

"I never saw guns. Brandon told me about them. That's where he got his…" she stopped and turned her head away.

"Where he got what?"

"I never did any of that stuff. He tried to give me some LSD one time but I wasn't having nothing to do with it. I'm not a drug addict like my mom and dad."

For some reason Jack believed her. Contrary to common belief, children of drug addicts don't always follow in the parent's footsteps. Children of criminals likewise. If anything, they are embarrassed into doing just the opposite.

"Empty your pockets on the desk," Jerrell said.

She did.

Jerrell pulled a latex glove on one hand and pushed the items around. A pack of chewing gum, two quarters, a toothpick, pack of Virginia Slims and a Bic lighter.

"That's my stuff."

"It's mine now," Jerrell said and picked up the cigarettes and lighter. "You're underage. I could write you a ticket for the smokes but I'm just holding onto this stuff until you're eighteen."

"I won't be here by the time I'm eighteen. I'm getting the hell out of this town."

Jack asked, "Did the homeless guy touch any of this?"

"How do you know?" she said.

"The lighter. You gave him a light, didn't you?"

"It's my lighter," she answered.

"We need to get your fingerprints," Jack said.

"Not necessary," Jerrell said. "We have her on file. Don't we Cretin?"

"Boy, this is all kinds of wrong," she said.

"I'm going to let you walk out of here," Jerrell said, "on one condition. You keep an eye out for this guy. If you see him you call me right away." He wrote his number on a scrap of paper and gave it to her. "No one will know we talked. You let me know where he is and if we catch him I'll think about giving this stuff back to you."

"He lit the cigarette himself," she said. "I had to ask him for it back three times and threaten to call some friends over. What a jerk wad."

Jerrell opened a desk drawer and took a Bic lighter out. He handed her the cigarettes and a lighter. "Don't set anything on fire. Don't let me catch you smoking or I'll confiscate the cigarettes and arrest you and Blind Bob too."

"Don't worry, Chief. You won't catch me," she said and grinned.

"Did Brandon come on to you?" Jerrell asked.

She said too quickly, "Ewww!"

"The guys Brandon hung around with have girlfriends, don't they?"

"So?"

"How old?" Jack asked. "No one will know you talked to us. You'd be doing us a big favor and the FBI never forgets a favor."

She said, "I'm fourteen. These guys are messing around with girls in training bras."

"What are they doing with the girls?" Jack asked.

Cretin smirked at him.

"What's that mean?" Jack asked.

She said, "What do you think? They get them to try some weed and then something stronger and then when the girl really needs the stuff they make her do things…you know…to get it. They get what they want, she gets what she wants."

Jerrell's cheeks turned red and then his face turned pale. "This is going on in the park?" he asked.

Cretin didn't answer, which was the answer.

Jerrell said, "I have patrols go through the park every night. We've never ever seen anything like that. What kind of car are they in?"

"Different ones. One time it's a truck. Next, it's a van. Something big enough for them to all get inside it."

Jack asked, "Do you know what Brandon drives?"

"Yeah. A Jeep."

"Are you sure these guys were giving the girls drugs?" Jack asked.

"I seen 'em."

"Do you know any of the girls' names?"

"I'm done. Can I go or not?"

"No, you can't go. Are these guys working for someone else? Someone older?" Jack asked.

"I don't know. I heard they have a boss. He's supposed to be really old. Forty at least. His guys hang around schools and recruit kids to work for him. I mean, I'm screwed up but that's really screwed up."

Jack took Jerrell off to the side out of earshot of Cretin.

"Chief, sounds like you have a real drug problem. Maybe sex trafficking. Were you aware of any of this?" Jack asked.

"Not a bit but we had a murder last year that resembled this setup. Two high school buddies started dealing and they decided they wanted to know what it felt like to kill a woman. They picked up one of their customers, a fifteen-year-old girl, took her out and drugged her up, beat, raped and strangled her. They weighed the body down and dumped her in Sullivan Lake. They were all from here so we worked part of it with the State Police."

Jack said, "Unless she's going to tell us something relating to the previous murders I'm going to leave the questioning to you. Maybe we can tie this drugs for sex ring into what happened to Brandon but I don't see that happening with her."

"You're right," Jerrell said. "I guess she won't be leaving here anytime soon. I'll have to get Child Welfare here to take custody just to cover my ass."

They walked back over to Cretin. Sergeant Crocker came in long enough to give her a Coke and she guzzled half of it down, belched, and looked pleased with herself.

Jack said, "Nice one."

"I can belch on command," she said and belched louder.

"You have quite a talent, Cretin. I have a couple more questions and then Chief Jerrell is going to finish this. Okay?"

"Do I have a choice?" she asked.

"No." Jack went back through her story with her filling in any blanks. She stuck with her original statement. She had never seen the homeless guy interact with Brandon or any of the drug for sex people. She hadn't see Brandon's Jeep in or near the park that morning and had no idea how the homeless guy got Brandon's phone.

Jerrell took Cretin to the front lobby, left Cretin in Crocker's care and told him to fingerprint her again, collect hair and get a DNA swab. He also told Crocker to hold her and crooked a finger at Crabs. "Your turn."

They were finished interviewing Crabs in a short time. He had little to add to what Cretin had told them. He was fourteen. Kicked out of school or suspended, he couldn't remember which, but he didn't intend to go back.

"What's your first name?" Jack asked.

"Crabs," the boy responded and slouched in his seat, one arm over the back, one leg stretched out front, and he'd tied a red bandana half covering his eyes.

Jerrell took the bandana off the kid's head and said, "Stick that in your pocket or lose it."

Crabs sat up straight in the chair and stuffed the bandana in his back pocket.

"How do you know Brandon?" Jerrell asked.

"Everyone knows Brandon," he said. He went on to say the last time he'd seen Brandon was on the street near the park talking to some guys in a dark colored SUV with tinted windows. He didn't know who the guys in the SUV were but they always seemed to have some 'hotties' hanging around.

"Did you try to meet any of these 'hotties'?" Jerrell asked.

"Nah, man. That's not my thing. I don't know what they were doing but I don't like little girls." He seemed to realize what he'd said and quickly said, "I don't like boys. I'm straight."

"I never thought anything about it," Jerrell said. "Can you tell me any of the names?"

Crabs affected an indifferent attitude. "I told you. Not my thing. How would I know any of them? What'd Cretin tell you?"

"We'll talk again about how you don't know any of these guys or the 'hotties'. Right now, I'm more interested in the homeless guy that's been hanging around the park," Jerrell said.

He'd seen the homeless guy the first time about a week ago. The guy was hanging out by the skate park, leering at them, acting like a lecher. He gave the same description as Cretin, including the tats. He claimed he didn't see Cretin get the phone and didn't see the homeless guy that morning. Jack knew that if they pushed him much harder on this that the kid was liable to start making stuff up just to shut them up. Now they had to decide what to do with him.

Crabs was on his own. There was really no place to drop him off or an adult to take him in. He was truly one of the forgotten children. Jerrell explained to Jack and Liddell that if he took the boy to child welfare he'd be back on the street in less than an hour.

They were getting ready to kick Crabs loose when he said, "His name is Tony. The guy from the park. I just remembered he had his name tattooed on his knuckles. T-O-N-Y. You know, like you see some guys with L-O-V-E and H-A-T-E on their knuckles."

Chapter 19

Child Welfare had contacted Cretin's grandparents. They agreed to take responsibility so she was taken back there. Crabs was a different story. He had no one to contact except his mother who had disappeared. It wasn't the first time he'd been a ward of the court. He was taken to a juvenile detention facility until he could be placed with a responsible guardian which didn't seem to be likely.

Jack sat on the edge of Crocker's desk and watched the boy leave. Crabs didn't look nervous or upset. He was resigned to this place in life. It made Jack sick to see kids being thrown away. His wife, Katie, dealt with kids like this almost every day where she taught school. The castaways, the abused, the unloved and uncared for, were more numerous than anyone would like to imagine. Thinking about it hurt your soul, but there was little that could be done. There was a rush to adopt children from other countries but the children in need here seemed to be forgotten. It was a fault with the bureaucracy that created such a paperwork nightmare that it was simpler and faster to get a child from somewhere else. That, and everyone wanted babies or very young children. Kids like Cretin and Crabs didn't stand a chance.

Jerrell was in his office. He'd excused himself to call his troops and hand out assignments. Shaunda and Liddell were sitting quietly in visitor's lobby chairs. Liddell had dozed off and Jack felt guilty for not ordering food. He teased Liddell frequently about his eating habits, but there was no one else he would ever want to work with.

Shaunda was slouched in a chair, staring out the front doors and seemed lost in thought. Either that, or the beating she'd taken was catching up to her. She sat up slowly when Jerrell came back in the lobby.

Jerrell said, "We've got the whole state alerted to look for this guy and for the Jeep. I guess it won't hurt to call the news media and get them involved."

"Your call," Jack said. "Personally, I'd wait and see what turns up today before I chum the waters. The guy's been in the area for at least a week if you believe Crabs. He doesn't seem to be in a hurry to move on. We've called all the homeless shelters, and churches where he could go. If we don't find him tomorrow let's revisit the media angle. We don't have anything definite to tell them except that we're looking for a possible suspect and even that is a long shot."

Jack wasn't as hopeful as Jerrell about the homeless guy being their killer. For all they knew he'd found the phone. They had to find him. They needed to eliminate him from the investigation if they could. He was their best, if not only, lead. If they found him they could detain him for a while without charging him with the murder. If the guy was really homeless he wouldn't mind having food and shelter for a few days, even if it was in the pokey.

"Actually, it's your call Shaunda," Jerrell said, surprising both Jack and Shaunda.

She sat up straighter. "We gave his description to the state and county police. We still haven't found Brandon's Jeep. I want to put his description out to the public. But I can see where that would backfire on us if this turns out to be the wrong guy. Which I don't think is the case. He's the guy. He's got to be." She leaned back in the chair and let a breath out. "There's just so much to do—I don't even know where to begin."

Jack could hear defeat in her voice and he could understand how she was feeling. If they'd gotten to the park a few hours earlier they would have the guy. If they called the media she would have to go home without a suspect in custody or even identified. Two murders on her turf in a week with no resolution. Not an easy thing for a small town chief whose job was always on the line. Realistically she was doing a good job considering she had a two person department, and both with limited on the job experience. Plus, she had no forensic resources.

Jack said to her, "If he's out there we'll turn him up. If he's the guy we'll know. Right now, we're wasting daylight. Patrols are out. We've got Brandon's phone. Maybe he's hunkered down somewhere and goes to the park to bum smokes."

"Or he's a pedophile with a skateboard fetish," Shaunda suggested.

"I hope to God not," Jerrell said, suddenly remembering what Cretin had told them about the guys that were trading dope for sex with minors.

No one spoke for several minutes.

Jerrell asked, "Can you get an FBI profiler?"

"It's a bit early for that," Jack answered. "Let's exhaust our efforts first. We still have a lot of ground to cover and they'll want to know what we know. That's not much at this point."

This wasn't the first time Jack wished he could call Special Agent Frank Tunney. Tunney was known as the serial killer hunter for the FBI. When Tunney died last year, someone had replaced him but Jack hadn't heard who it was. Didn't really care. Tunney's death had come as a blow. Jack didn't think he could work with another profiler.

It was almost three o'clock and Liddell's stomach was growling. Liddell opened his eyes and said, "I don't know about you people, but I'm hungry. Where's a good place to eat?"

Shaunda asked, "Where are you planning on staying tonight? You *are* staying, right?"

It didn't make sense to commute to and from Evansville. Besides, something might break in the case and they didn't want to miss it.

"Any suggestions on a hotel?" Jack asked.

Shaunda said, "This is happening in my town. I'll take care of you. I know the perfect place."

Jack drove and followed Chief Lynch's Tahoe down state highway 54 West at a more reasonable speed than earlier. They were nearing the place they'd first met Chief Lynch this morning.

"This part of the state must be fishing heaven," Liddell remarked. "The whole area is riddled with lake sized ponds."

Jack said, "When I was in high school my dad used to take me and my brother on fishing trips up around this area. The stripper pits were stocked by the Department of Natural Resources, sometimes by the coal company to show what good public partners they were. We'd buy bait, and beer. We'd sit in a boat and fish most of the day. When we got hungry Dad would find a little roadhouse. Sometimes he'd let us have part of his beer. They never complained about underage boys eating in the roadhouses, or if they did, I guess Dad took care of it. It was the best food I've ever had."

"Is that when you started drinking Scotch? In high school?" Liddell asked.

"That's kind of insulting, Bigfoot. I'm Irish. When I was born I slapped the doctor and told the nurse to bring me a Guinness."

Liddell chuckled. "I thought you pulled a gun on him and told him to put you down?"

"Yeah. That too," Jack said.

They passed the access road to Dugger Lake and Shaunda slowed, turning onto a wide gravel road that paralleled the railroad tracks. They followed this a quarter mile until the tracks split, one set running southwest and the other staying with the road to the south. Both sides of the tracks were densely wooded. The trees were bare until mid April but grew so close together you couldn't see far into the woods. They had passed no houses or structures of any kind.

Shaunda slowed again as they came to a clearing on their left where a two-story building sat smack-dab in the middle of it. She turned into the parking lot and stopped in front of the building.

Except for having a second floor, the building resembled a repurposed train station with brick and wood exterior, iron window frames and iron bars bolted across them. A wooden portico covered a wood plank step up porch complete with unpainted wooden benches and rockers evenly spaced across the front. An antique sign hung from the portico that read:

DUGGER STATION
Est. 1889

The front of the property was defined with heavy black railroad ties laid end to end forming a square. Inside this were pieces of mining machinery. In an enclosure near the front door sat a six-feet-by-three-feet wooden mining cart on a light gauge steel track. The cart was overfilled with chunks of coal. The mine cart was wood sided held together with iron bands. On the side of the cart facing visitors, burnt into the wood were the words:

Coal Miner Bar & Grill

Shaunda stepped up on the porch. "Come on in. She doesn't bite."

"Chief Lynch…" Jack began.

"Shaunda."

"Okay, Shaunda. We don't really have time to take a break. I thought we were going to find a place to stay and get back to work," Jack said.

Shaunda held the door open. "Trust me. If you're nice she might even feed you."

Liddell patted his stomach. "I guess we could use a bite to eat."

Jack and Liddell followed Shaunda through the front door. The inside continued the theme of an old railroad station. The tabletops were worn smooth as were the bench seats that may have been the original seating when it was a train station. The floor was solid hardwood, worn down by foot traffic. Antique gray steel dome lighting hung from the ceiling bathing the room in a warm glow. The walls were covered with wooden and steel framed train schedules and railway maps yellowed with age and tools of all varieties associated with rail crews and mining. In contrast with the mining and railway décor in half of the room were comfortable sofas and chairs lined against the walls in a U-shape facing a bank of wall mounted sixty inch television screens. Narrow counter tops ran along the walls on the other half of the room with padded barstools stowed underneath. Colorful blinds painted with depictions of steam engines and rail cars covered the windows from where the railroad tracks could be seen.

On the back side of the spacious room a polished mahogany bar sat in front of batwing doors that led to a good sized kitchen. A variety of beers were on tap and every kind of liquor filled the shelves mounted behind the bar.

"I could use a drink about now but we need a place to stay, Chief," Jack said.

A voice coming from behind the bar said, "Passed all the health code inspections. You can eat off the floor but I highly recommend a plate. We have rooms upstairs."

A woman straightened up behind the bar holding a dust rag and a can of Pledge. She was in her 30s, close to Jack's height with thick copper colored hair worn in a weave tossed over one shoulder. She reminded Jack of a young Reba McEntire, but taller. There was merriment in her pale green eyes and a hint of a smile on her lips that faded when she saw Shaunda's face. "What happened to you?"

"Had a little accident," Shaunda said.

"That must've been one hell of a little one." She obviously didn't believe Shaunda's explanation. She eyed Jack and Liddell. "You said these guys are FBI."

Jack didn't know whether to show his badge or order a Guinness. He preferred the latter but opted for the badge. She put the cleaning rag down and examined his credentials closely before handing it back and shaking their hands.

"I'm Rosie. Rosie Benton. The owner, operator and sole employee. Shaunda called and said you're helping her with an investigation. How long are you planning on staying in town?"

"We'll be here as long as it takes," Jack said. "If you have two rooms that would be great."

Rosie smiled. "Well, you're in luck. Bill Gates and his wife just cancelled their reservation and I don't expect Oprah until next week. Let's go see the rooms. They're nothing fancy but it beats sleeping at The Park Inn in

Linton. I imagine you're used to fancy hotels, what with being Federal Agents, but the closest four star hotel is in Terre Haute."

Shaunda said, "You all go ahead. I'm going to wait for them."

"Wait for who?" Jack asked.

"My daughter and her friend Patty are going to stay with Rosie until this is over," Shaunda said. "Sergeant Ditterline is bringing them."

Rosie said, "Follow me G-men."

Jack smiled at her use of the old moniker for an FBI Agent. 'G-man' was underworld slang for anyone working for the government. It meant government man.

Rosie opened a door to the left of the bar marked 'PRIVATE' and started up a hardwood stairway. Something crunched under sole of Jack's shoe. He picked it up. It was a tiny stone that resembled pumice.

"That's a cinder," Rosie said. "Damn things get in like sand from a beach. I'd have the parking lot paved but I don't think it would help. The road here is full of cinders."

The walls of the stairway were shiplap adorned with framed black-and-white photographs of mines and miners. The miners were young and old, mostly male with a smattering of females. In one picture the miners were bent over at the waist to fit in the claustrophobic shaft, shoveling coal into a rail cart like the one out front. In other pictures child miners in hard hats that were too big for their small heads held pickaxes over their shoulders. The pickaxes were as big as some of the kids. The hard hats were made of steel with carbide lanterns fixed on the brims. Some smiled for the camera, others seemed to stare hopelessly into the distance. He'd seen the same lost expression on prisoners.

The caption under each photograph gave the name of the mine and the year. One photograph was of the Dugger Mine (1873), another was the Sunflower Mine (1900) and the City Mine in Sullivan (1921). Some mining operations were without names or dates, just pictures of adults and children in heavy coveralls and web belts holding unnamable pieces of mining gear. In all of these they were underground with soot smeared faces and hands.

They reached the top of the stairs and turned down a hallway. On their right was a steel mesh door behind which led to an industrial lift. "Do you store supplies up here?" Jack asked.

"For years I had to lug it all up here with a dolly but I had the elevator put in when Shaunda moved back to Dugger. Pen stayed with me for a while. The entrance to the lift is in the kitchen. It was originally a dumbwaiter.

It's big enough for one person but it does the job. Can't hardly expect the girl to take the stairs. You know the kid's in a wheelchair?"

Jack said he had heard. "How old is her daughter?"

"Penelope? She's sixteen going on thirteen. Don't get me wrong, the girl is smart as all get out, but she's been sheltered. Shaunda homeschools her and I think the longest trip she's been on was when they moved here from St. Louis. Shaunda dotes on that girl. I guess I do too."

"Why doesn't she go to Union High?"

"You'll have to talk to Shaunda about that."

Rosie paused in front of a sepia tone portrait of a middle aged gentleman wearing a suit, vest, and buttoned down white shirt with a stiff collar. "That's Francis Dugger. He was fifty-two when that was taken. Francis and William Dugger and Neal Henry discovered coal here in 1879 and sunk the Dugger Coal Mine. Dugger was still a viable coal producing town until the 30s when the Depression hit. That's when he when he started mining. William was seventeen. They both fought in the Civil War under Jefferson Davis."

Jack was impressed. When he was thirteen he was still doing pushups after class as punishment for something he'd done. The nuns at St. Anthony Grade School were like ninja's on a mission for God.

Rosie continued giving the tour as she led them down the hall. "This building was originally a stagecoach stop. Then it was part of Railway Station #3 for the Indiana railroad that ran between Bedford and Terre Haute and west into Illinois. When the demand for coal dropped off the railroad closed the station. The building and acreage were bought by a family who turned it into a bar and restaurant and rooms for rent. The rumor is that John Dillinger spent a night or two here."

"Now the FBI are here," Liddell quipped.

"You laugh, but during the prohibition era, a basement was dug out and a bootlegging operation was run out of here. That's why the dumbwaiter was here. There were tunnels leading to the railroad tracks and a place in the woods where they'd keep a car. When I had the elevator installed the contractor found the basement. He said most of it had caved in and it wasn't worth the cost of fixing."

Liddell said, "You should try to see what's down there. It could put you on the map. Lots of people would like to tour a real bootlegging operation."

"Are you sure you're FBI?" Rosie asked.

"I ask myself that question all the time," Liddell answered.

The uneven boards squeaked underfoot as they walked down to the rooms. There were brass plaques on the doors to identify three of the rooms as Truman, Roosevelt and Hoover. The other rooms farther down weren't marked.

Rosie said, "They're named after the presidents that stayed in them. Each has its own bathroom. Plus, there's another bathroom down the hall on the right. Central a/c and heat, mini-fridge, microwave, telephone and internet." She opened the door to the Hoover room. The room was spacious with an antique four piece burl walnut bedroom suite. The flooring was highly polished hardwood plank. The bed was massive with a thick mattress. A framed photo of President Herbert Hoover shaking hands with a young couple sat on top of the dresser. A watercolor painting of Herbert Hoover hung on the wall above the headboard. An old Royal typewriter set atop a desk in front of one of the two windows that faced the parking lot. Another small frame depicted Hoover sitting in profile at the same desk contemplating something outside the window."

"The original owners posed for that picture with Hoover," Rosie said, proudly. "There was a box of old photos, papers, newspapers and books in the storage room when I was clearing it out for my bedroom. Hoover stayed in this very room. That's the real typewriter he used. I found drafts of notes and some letters. Did you know Hoover was the president that made the Star-Spangled Banner the national anthem?"

"I did not know that," Liddell said.

Jack remembered from history class at St. Anthony's school that Hoover was also the president blamed for the Great Depression.

Rosie continued the historical tour. "Hoover was a mining engineer. He traveled the country searching for mineral deposits. My place here was one of his regular haunts according to rumor. This whole part of the state is rich in coal, iron ore, sulfur, fluorine, zinc and limestone. All the ingredients needed for steel production."

"That's very interesting, Mrs. Benton. We'll take the rooms," Jack said.

"I'll let you fight it out over who gets what room but if you damage anything I'll report you to the Secret Service," Rosie said with a straight face. "Just kidding. I'll put you in the president's rooms. Would you like to see the Roosevelt Room?"

"Not necessary," Jack said. He was anxious to get back to work.

"What's down the hall?" Liddell asked.

"The one on the right is mine. The other was Shaunda and Pen's room. I don't rent those out unless I get a handicapped guest—which is about never."

"Did someone famous stay in your room?" Liddell asked.

She laughed. "Rats and mice maybe. It was a storage room until I remodeled. The historic tour ends here."

"Mrs. Benton, we really don't want to be an inconvenience," Jack said.

"Really. Mrs. Benton again? I'm younger than you are. Call me Rosie."

"Okay, Rosie it is," Jack said.

"You can call me Liddell," Liddell said.

Jack said, "You can call me Supreme Commander. My cell phone does."

Rosie clapped her hands gleefully together. "Wow! A FBI agent and a stand-up comedian. I'll call you Jack unless we're in public and then Supreme Commander it is. You'll bring some life back into the place. I have to warn you the bar gets a little noisy sometimes, mostly just during football season. Lately we've been kind of empty."

She squeezed Liddell's bicep. "You played football."

"Louisiana State University Tigers. Half back. I knew I wasn't going to go pro. I graduated and went to the Sheriff Department. Plus, I wanted to keep my brains intact."

"Do you ever regret giving it up?" Rosie asked.

"Nah. I've got Marcie and baby Jane. Plus, I get to work with this guy."

Rosie asked Jack, "How about you? Quarterback?"

Jack said, "I never had time. I was always in detention."

Rosie laughed and they walked back to the stairway.

It wasn't exactly the Ritz Carlton, but the room was what Jack's wife, Katie, would call cozy or quaint or historical and would comment on the ambiance. Jack was more practical. It was a room, it was convenient, and it had the advantage of keeping them near the scene of two of the cases they were investigating. "How much?" he asked.

"I'll make you a deal," Rosie said. Sunlight coming through a window glimmered in her copper colored hair. "You catch the guy that killed Troy and we'll call it even. Plus, I'll throw in meals. Breakfast is whenever, lunch is on your own, and dinner is at five. I normally serve pizza, pizza, and pizza, but I've got a full kitchen down there. It'll be nice to cook for someone again. As you can see I'm kind of out in the sticks. I don't get steady business."

"The Federal Government is footing the bill, Rosie," Jack said. "I don't think we can put zero dollars down on our lodging expense sheet. Your normal rates are okay, and we'll probably eat out."

"In that case I'll charge you double what I charge my other guests." She told Jack what the room rate was and even doubled it was a fair price. He agreed and she said, "It's about time I got something from the government besides an IRS audit. At least have breakfast with me."

Liddell agreed wholeheartedly. With lodging sorted, the three of them went downstairs where Shaunda sat at a table with two young ladies, one of them in a wheelchair.

"Aunt Rosie," the girl in the wheelchair said, excitedly rolling over to Rosie. She gave Rosie a tight hug around the waist. The other girl merely nodded.

"Hello Tootsie Roll," Rosie said.

Penelope's smile widened into a huge grin. "My name's not Tootsie Roll."

"You'll always be my Tootsie Roll," Rosie said.

Penelope Lynch gave an exasperated grunt and said to Jack and Liddell, "Hi, I'm Pen. That's short for Penelope." She shook hands with Jack and then Liddell and then with appropriate awe, said, "You guys are the FBI."

"That's right," Jack said. "We're helping your mom."

"I've never met a G-man before."

Liddell asked, "Do you even know what a G-man is?"

"Sure. I watch all the old detective shows on television. *FBI Files* is one of my favorite shows. John Dillinger, Bonnie and Clyde, Machine Gun Kelly, Pretty Boy Floyd, Ma Barker's Boys. You must live a real exciting life."

Jack said, "We're old, but not that old. I'm Jack and this is Liddell."

"If I call you Jack and Liddell you call me Pen. Not Tootsie or Tootsie Roll."

"Okay, Pen. Who's your friend?" Jack asked.

"That's Patty."

Patty cut her eyes toward them and then toward the floor.

"She's kind of shy," Pen whispered.

"Are you two old enough to be in a bar?" Jack asked with a serious face.

"I'm going on seventeen. I've been in here a bunch of times." Pen put a hand to her mouth. "Rosie won't be in trouble, will she?"

"I guess not. Just this once."

Rosie pushed Pen back to the table and sat.

Shaunda came over and asked the men, "Have you got kids?"

"Bigfoot just had a daughter. I've got one on the way," Jack said.

"Pen's my life," Shaunda said. "You know what she said when she saw my bruises?"

"Tell me."

"She said, 'That's a good look on you, Mom. The eye shadow is perfect.'"

Jack said, "She takes after you. She looks like you and talks like you."

Sergeant Ditterline came out of the kitchen carrying a soft drink in one hand and a half eaten cold cut sandwich in the other.

"I helped myself," Ditty said and Jack was struck with how much Sergeant Ditterline resembled a middle aged Clint Eastwood. Almost as tall as Bigfoot's six feet seven inches, slim but solid, square jawed, exuding confidence.

"I see you're making yourself at home," Rosie said "Can I ask why you're raiding my kitchen?"

"I told him it would be okay," Shaunda said. "I need to ask a big favor, Rosie."

"I told you the girls could stay with me as long as you need."

Shaunda said, "Let's go outside." To the girls she said, "Be back in a minute."

They followed Shaunda and Rosie out onto the porch.

Shaunda took a deep breath and let it out before saying, "Rosie, there's been another murder."

"Who?" Rosie asked.

"Brandon Dillingham. We found his body in Dugger Lake this morning."

"Claire's Brandon?"

Shaunda nodded.

"Why is the FBI involved? I mean, don't you guys go after bank robbers and terrorists and the like?" Rosie asked Jack.

Shaunda answered for them. "There are more murders going back to before I came back to Dugger, Rosie. Several more, in fact, and we think Brandon is the most recent."

"Oh my God!" Rosie said. "I can't believe it."

"My little accident happened this morning down at the lake after Brandon's body was taken away. We think the killer came back for something he forgot and knocked me out. He spray painted a warning on the back of my shirt saying that P was next."

"P? You mean Pen? Does she know?" Rosie asked.

"She probably knows something's going on because Ditty stayed with them until I could make arrangements for them. I don't want to tell her. We don't know if the P was for Pen or Patty."

"Patty?" Rosie said. "What does she have to do with this?"

"I stopped Brandon real early this morning coming from the old Dugger Mine. He had Patty with him. Then Brandon turns up dead. I'm just playing it safe here. Plus, there was a guy came by my house last week while I was gone and Pen talked to him. The way she described him, he might be homeless, he might be harmless or he might be involved in these murders. I can't leave Pen at home. Even with a guard. That's why I need you to keep the girls."

"Of course, I'll keep the girls."

Jack noticed that Rosie didn't ask if she, herself was in danger. Her only concern was for Pen and Patty.

"I knew I could count on you," Shaunda said and hugged Rosie. "I know it's asking a lot. I already called Patty's mom and asked if she could spend a few nights with Pen. I don't have the manpower to watch them *and* run an investigation."

Sergeant Ditterline said, "Chief Jerrell said I should stay with the girls. I'll be here to protect all of you."

"Who's going to protect my kitchen. God help us," Rosie said.

"I was hungry," Ditterline complained and reluctantly dug out his wallet but Rosie waved it away.

"I guess one more mouth can't hurt, but you'll have to sleep in here on one of the sofas or I have a roll out bed." She said to Jack, "I can close for a couple of days if you think that's best."

Jack said, "That might be best. Liddell and I will be here but not all day. Is that okay with you, Sergeant?"

Ditty said, "I don't have plans."

Shaunda said, "I doubt this freak knows much about me except where I live."

"He knew about the girls," Rosie reminded her.

Shaunda said, "I'll be checking in regularly until we can find the guy that came by the house. If it's him, he had Brandon's cell phone. Traded it to a kid in Linton City Park. We got the phone back and a description of the creep." She told Rosie and Ditterline the description they'd gotten from Cretin. "Chief Jerrell has the troops out searching for Brandon's Jeep."

Rosie said, "I haven't seen the guy you described around, but thought I saw Brandon's Jeep this morning."

Chapter 20

Sergeant Ditterline stayed with the girls while Rosie led the way out the front and behind the building. Twenty feet from the back door were train tracks. Rosie pointed to the northwest where Jack saw sunlight glinting off something.

"I was out here putting some things in the trash this morning and I saw a Jeep going down the tracks. It was pretty far down there and I couldn't see who was driving but it was a Jeep. I'm sorry I didn't pay more attention. Do you think that's the Jeep?"

Jack squinted into the glare and could make out the shape of an SUV. "What time was it?"

"Maybe nine or ten o'clock. I was cleaning the kitchen after breakfast. That sounds about right."

"We'll check it out," Jack said. "Why don't you tell Sergeant Ditterline what we're doing? Tell him to call Chief Jerrell."

"You know they found Troy Junior's truck right over there," Rosie said pointing to the northeast. "Just on the other side of the track almost in the trees."

Jack thanked her and Rosie left. Jack, Liddell and Shaunda hiked along the tracks. As they got closer Jack could make out the back hatch of a Jeep Cherokee Laredo 4X4. The Jeep had been ditched nose down in a steep drainage ditch running parallel to the tracks. The front bumper was smashed into the grill and the driver's door hung open. The tires on that side were flat.

"That's Claire's Jeep," Shaunda said. She took out her cell phone and called Joey, her deputy. The call went to voicemail. She left a message to call her. She then called Claire Dillingham's telephone and it also went to voicemail.

"Joey should have called me by now," Shaunda said.

Jack said, "Chief Jerrell will get his crime scene people and a wrecker out here."

"I really should call Sullivan Sheriff's Department for their crime scene people. They'll get their nose bent out of shape if I don't," she said.

"I talked to them earlier and agreed with Chief Jerrell that we would keep this in-house as much as possible," Jack said. "If anyone gives you grief you can blame me. Linton PD has a K-9 don't they? We need to get it out here."

She nodded. "They do, but it's mean as hell."

Liddell said, "The Jeep hasn't been here long. If we're lucky we can get the killer's direction of travel. Maybe there was a vehicle stashed back here somewhere."

Jack thought the same thing. He would have needed some way to get to Linton. The guy Cretin described as homeless could have stolen another car and used it to get to Linton. The timing was right. Shaunda gets knocked cold, the Jeep gets ditched, then Cretin trades cigarettes for the phone. It was perfect.

"Shaunda, have you had any reports of stolen vehicles recently?" Jack asked.

"None that I know of. We haven't had a stolen vehicle report since one of the local miners 'misplaced' his truck after a night of drinking. This is a pretty safe place. I've got to touch base with Claire now that we found the Jeep. She's probably not answering her phone so I'm going over there. There's nothing I can do here right this minute anyway."

"I'll go with you," Liddell volunteered.

"I wouldn't say no," Shaunda answered. "Would you mind driving? You probably won't have to climb to get into the cab of the Tahoe."

Chapter 21

Jerrell arrived behind Rosie's place with the Crime Scene wagon. Jack could see why the killer had chosen this spot to abandon the Jeep. No witnesses. If Rosie hadn't seen the Jeep they wouldn't have found it for a while.

A Toyota Highlander with police K-9 markings pulled into the parking lot.

"You might want to sit in my truck until Rusty gets Rinnie some little ways down there. That dog's bite is worse than his bark. In fact, he doesn't bark first," Jerrell said.

Jack didn't have to be told twice. He got in Jerrell's truck. He'd learned early in his career not to stand in the path of a police K-9.

Jerrell said with half a grin, "Should've named that dog Killer instead of Rinnie. He even bit Rusty once."

The back door of the K-9 vehicle opened and Rusty led Rinnie up to the Chief's open window. Rinnie sat obediently, but Jack swore every muscle in the shepherd's massive chest was vibrating. The dog was as excited as a two-dollar hooker watching a Corvette payday pull to the curb.

Rusty asked, "Are there any friendlies down there?"

"I hope not," Jerrell said and rolled the window up.

"Hear that Rinnie?" Rusty said and the dog gave a thundering bark.

Rusty was early 20s, nearly bald, short and slight of build for a police officer. He reminded Jack of EPD's K-9 officer, Johnny Hailman, minus Johnny's thick rug of hair. Johnny was short, but no one messed with him, with or without his dog. Rusty was wearing a tailored khaki uniform and green Latex gloves. Rinnie was wearing Rusty's arms out. It was hard to tell who was leading who.

"Yo Rinnie," Rusty said and man and dog took off at a trot.

"Must be K-9 humor," Jack said.

"What is?" Jerrell asked.

"The names and commands they give these dogs. Our K-9 officer named his dog "Glinda", as in the good witch from the *Wizard of Oz*. Glinda's cross-trained in explosives and she is very protective of her handler. The command for her to search is *Toto*. Your dog is named Rinnie. I assume by the command 'Yo Rinnie' he named the dog after that old series, *The Adventures of Rin Tin Tin*? Come to think of it wasn't the dog's handler named Rusty in that show?"

Jerrell shrugged. "K-9 guys are all frustrated comics. Rusty still reads Green Lantern comic books in the station."

Jerrell started the truck and slowly rolled toward the railroad tracks for a better view. He pointed to a spot almost straight ahead of the truck. "My boy's pickup was found parked back over there in the tree line. No telling how long it had been there."

"Rosie was just telling us," Jack said.

"No one remembered seeing it there, but everyone said that if they had it wouldn't have meant anything. Troy was known to frequent a couple of the bars, but this was one of his favorite bars. I told Shauny that we found Troy's truck and all she said was he might have parked it there himself. I think he might have had his eye on Rosie. She is one fine looking woman, but she's got no heart," Jerrell said.

"That brings me to the question of why Rosie didn't notice your son's truck before you found it."

Troy said, "She was gone for a couple of days and that's when my guys came across the truck. Shauny should have seen it but I guess she doesn't do patrol like I do. I checked with Rosie about video. No cameras. I told her she needs to get them to protect herself and her property. The closest building with a surveillance camera is nowhere near here."

"I talked to the manager at First Financial Bank in Dugger and she let me view the surveillance footage. There wasn't anything worth seeing but I got a copy. There's two ways to get a vehicle back here. Come through Rosie's parking lot or come down the tracks."

"There's a lawnmower repair shop by the bank but he didn't have any cameras. I talked to the owner and he said he'd been drinking with Troy the night before he was found. The Sportsman's Bar is just down the street from his shop. I went over his story with him. He'd seen Troy in that bar before and here at Rosie's. He said Troy was doing tequila shots. He asked if there was a reward for information. I told him he was full of shit. Troy hated tequila."

Jerrell sat quietly thinking. "I talked to as many of the regulars as I could find at the Sportsman's Bar. Everyone said the same thing. Troy was in there sometimes. Stayed until closing. No one remembered when they saw him last. They remembered the lawn mower guy in there—alone—drunk on his ass and talking to himself. Troy was a generous sort and when he was working he'd buy everyone drinks. When he wasn't buying drinks, he was leeching them off everyone. Shauny said she had to come to both bars a few times and escort him off the premises."

"I take it you don't think much about Chief Lynch's investigation," Jack said. "What can we do that you think she didn't do?"

"Alright, let's talk about that. Shaunda means well and she's an adequate law officer for a little town like Dugger..." he trailed off.

"But?" Jack asked.

"But she's no detective. You saw for yourself the way she and her constable treated that crime scene today. Not her fault for the most part because she doesn't have any experience except for what she might have been told at the police academy. This town doesn't have the money to send her to specialized training, or to get up to date on the newest crime scene methods. We have in service training at our station at least once a month and she's brought her constable, Joey, to a couple of them, but that's about it. Dugger doesn't have serious crime. A rare burglary and those are committed by drunks who've gone to the wrong house."

No one really paid attention to drunks, Jack thought.

"Troy wouldn't have left that truck unlocked, I can tell you that. He would not have gotten a ride with someone he didn't know. No one admitted to giving him a ride or remembered him leaving the bar with anyone."

"How far to his place from the bar?" Jack asked.

"It's possible he walked home, but not likely. Why would he hide it way back behind Rosie's and leave it unlocked?"

Because he was shitfaced drunk, Jack thought. Jack mulled this over and watched the K-9 working. Rinnie crossed the tracks several times, snout to the ground, then making a sudden turn back toward the Jeep, then back over the same ground.

"What did Troy do for a living?"

Jerrell said, "He was a union electrician and he was hardworking when he had a job, but he never stuck with anything. Let his union card expire. Did odd jobs when he needed money. He had issues. His mother disappeared about ten years ago. We never heard from her again. He started going downhill after that and just never got over it. Blamed himself. Blamed me.

Started drinking, couldn't hold a job more than a few weeks. Gave up his friends. Went through girlfriends like a kid through candy."

"What was his demeanor like recently?" Jack asked.

"He was drinking more than usual and even stopped dating, if you could call what he did dating. All the regulars I talked to said he had a thing for Rosie but I don't buy that. He'd never said anything to me about it and to tell the truth, I think he was intimidated by her. I asked Rosie point blank if she had had something going on with Troy and she laughed. I've never known her to date anyone. She flirts with guys, but you always see her with gal pals. Her and Shauny are damn near inseparable. More than sisters if you ask me. None of my business. I'm telling you this in case she comes on to you."

"It was nice of Rosie to take in Patty and Penelope for a while," Jack said. "She offered us rooms here at no charge."

"Well, now, that surprises me because Rosie would pinch a penny until it threw up."

"You've known Rosie a while then?" Jack asked.

"Not that long. Shaunda introduced us and I've been over here to eat a few times." He sat quietly staring out the windshield.

Jack could tell Jerrell wasn't going to say more on the subject. He asked, "How did Shaunda feel about you running your own investigation on her turf?"

Jerrell scratched his neck. "How do you think she felt? I had Ditty and Crocker come over and go through Troy's place. It was unlocked and we never found his keys. Now I know that Shaunda had already been there. She probably didn't lock up. Anyway, Ditty called all excited and thought there had been a burglary. He said someone had tossed Troy's place. They described what they saw to me and there was no break in. Troy was a slob."

"Shaunda showed up just as my guys were. Said she got a call from a neighbor about Linton Police cars being out there, and someone was in the house. She threatened to arrest my men for breaking and entering and interfering in a police investigation. There was no crime scene tape, no coroner's seal on the door. Nothing."

"I got on the phone with her and kept my guys from being humiliated. I guess she's got a right to be mad at me, but he was my only kid." Jerrell hung his head. "I can't believe she almost got killed today and I been busting her balls."

Jack said, "Don't beat yourself up. We've got the Jeep. Things are moving along."

"You think?"

"I know," Jack said and the Chief's radio crackled.

"Chief, I got something here," the K-9 Officer said.

They exited Jerrell's truck and walked beside the train tracks.

"What did you find in your son's truck?" Jack asked.

"The usual. Beer cans, trash, clothes on the passenger side—pants, shirt, boots—might have been what he was wearing when he was killed but we didn't find blood on any of it. Maybe it was just a change of clothes. Like I said, he was a slob. Got that from his mother. Fingerprints, a folding knife, chewing gum stuck under the dash, pair of panties hung from the rearview mirror."

Jack said, "The anonymous call came from Troy's cell phone and the phone was found in his apartment. Did Troy live with someone? You said he'd quit dating."

"He was living by himself," Jerrell said. "When we went through his apartment there was evidence he'd had women over but it didn't appear that anyone else was staying there with him."

"The 911 call would have been made at the lake," Jack said. "We can assume the killer made that call because the phone was found in his house. They would have wanted to give them some time to get rid of the truck and go to the house."

They were talking about a drunken, possibly drugged young man that made horrible life decisions. No matter what his dad thought, Troy Junior could have gotten a ride from Rosie's that night, gone to the stripper pit and been killed. Maybe Troy Junior was more into drugs than his dad thought. He might have been cheating his supplier and they tore his place up searching for their product or money. But why not call from the stripper pit and leave the phone and clothes there? If they wanted it to look like another accidental drowning they'd screwed the pooch. But they'd been so adept at the other scenes, maybe this one wasn't a screw up. Maybe there was a good reason for cocking the scene up. He'd have to find them to ask them.

"Can you think of any reason someone would want to search Troy's place?" Jack asked.

"Search for what?" Jerrell asked. "I know what the autopsy results were, but that boy was not on drugs or selling drugs. He drank more than he should and I take the blame for a lot of that. What about his truck? It's four miles or more between Rosie's and his place. How did the truck get out to Rosie's?

"Troy was such a slob. My crime scene guys didn't find anything to indicate he was killed there. Maybe he left with whoever it was, or never even got home from the bar. Maybe the killer came here to see if he had any valuables laying around," Jerrell suggested.

"Just getting things clear in my head," Jack said. "A lot of what you just told me isn't in the file."

"It's in *my* file," Jerrell said.

"Which file is that?" Jack asked.

"What? You never keep anything to yourself?"

"The detective part of me says, hell yeah. The fed side denies everything and wants a lawyer."

Jerrell chuckled. "You got issues. You know that?"

"So, I'm told. Let's see what Rinnie has found."

Jack was grateful to see Rinnie was wearing a muzzle. Rusty pointed to a copse of evergreen trees south of the Jeep and said, "There's a camp fifty feet in." The ground there was thick with scrub.

Rusty stayed behind while Jerrell and Jack made their way down the gravel incline to a spot where the wild blackberry bushes and scrub brush were trampled down to a narrow path, maybe a deer trail. They took the trail and came to a tall pine tree where pine needles were gathered into a thick mat. Someone had slept there. Jack wasn't much of a tracker but even he knew that deer didn't gather material for a bed.

There was a scorched area where more of the pine needles and small twigs had been swept or scraped into a small pile and burned. Jack held his hand above it. It was still warm. Someone had been there recently. It looked like someone had attempted to smother the fire with a couple of handfuls of earth. There were scrape marks in the soil nearby where they had dug, possibly with their hands. He pointed it out to Jerrell. "DNA?"

"My Crime Scene unit is coming. I'll tell them to collect some of the soil. The Jeep was abandoned right over there," Jerrell said. "Maybe this is our guy. Maybe we're close to the bastard."

"Maybe," Jack said. In his gut he didn't believe it. This was too obvious. Almost as if they were meant to find the fire. He had thought that they may never have found the Jeep if not for Rosie but now he thought Rosie had been meant to see the Jeep. But why? The Dugger Lake scene had been swept by several policemen this morning and the killer still got the drop on Shaunda and got away. He was changing his modus operandi. That was never a good thing.

Jerrell squatted and stared into the blackened mess. He took out an ink pen and dragged it through the ashes until it struck something. "What have we got here?"

Chapter 22

Jerrell had found a long cylindrical metal object buried in the ashes of the fire. His Crime Scene techs identified it as a carbide tipped drill bit used in coal mining. It weighed two pounds, was tapered to a point at one end and was thick at the other. It was at least twelve inches long and the surface was rough and worn.

Jerrell had Crime Scene bag the drill bit but he signed a chain of custody form and took possession. They walked back to the Coal Miner Bar. Jack's Crown Vic was parked in front and Liddell and Shaunda were back.

"You thinking what I'm thinking?" Jerrell asked.

"It definitely could be the weapon," Jack said. "Are you taking it to the coroner?" It was the right size and shape to have inflicted the wounds on both Brandon and Shaunda. The coroner would be able to say whether the drill bit could have made the abrasions, but it would take laboratory tests to determine if it had been used in any of the other murders.

"I saw the marks on my boy's head. It matches. I'll call you in a bit. Tell Shauny what we found."

"Do you want us to meet you at the morgue? I'd like to be there for Brandon's autopsy."

Jerrell said, "I'll find out what's going on. Come on when you're ready. Bring Shauny if she feels like coming. Personally, I think she should take some sack time. She's had one hell of a week and she might have a concussion to boot."

Jerrell got into his truck, peeled out in the gravel and disappeared inside a plume of dust. Jack went inside. Liddell and Shaunda were talking to Rosie. The door that led up to the rooms was open and Jack could hear the girls and Sergeant Ditterline chatting. Pen was saying, "You have to do whatever we say." Sergeant Ditterline said, "I don't think so. I'm the adult here."

When Jack heard both girls giggling he knew who the real bosses were.

"We talked to Claire," Liddell said. "Shaunda's constable was still there. She's pretty messed up. She didn't even ask about the Jeep. Where'd Chief Jerrell go tearing off to?"

"He's going to check on things in Linton and make arrangements for the Jeep to be processed."

"Shaunda said it was definitely Brandon's Jeep," Rosie said.

"It was," Jack said. "You've got good eyes."

"Why, Agent Murphy, more than my eyes are good."

Jack felt his face reddening. She held his eyes until he blinked.

"How about it?" she asked.

Jack cleared his throat. "How about what?"

She smiled. "We were talking about having dinner."

Liddell said, "I wouldn't turn down something to eat."

"No fooling," Jack said. "Jerrell's going let us know when the autopsy is scheduled. We need to be there. The K-9 found a campsite close to the Jeep. Someone had made a fire and it was still warm. Jerrell found an old mining tool in the ashes that might've been used as the weapon."

"What kind of tool?" she asked.

He described it holding his hands a foot apart. "It was heavy."

Shaunda gently touched the back of her head and winced.

Rosie put an arm around Shaunda's shoulders and hugged her. "Poor baby."

"It only hurts when I breathe," Shaunda said.

"I'm not talking about you. I'm talking about the asshat that hit you. If you don't kick his butt I'm going to."

Shaunda hugged Rosie back. "My protector. What would I ever do without you?"

"We're not ever going to find out. Come on. Let's eat before you all rush off. The food is already made and you'll hurt my feelings if you don't say yes. Besides, I want to hear everything."

"She's a CSI Miami fan," Shaunda said.

Rosie yelled up the stairs, "Dinner. Get down here or I feed it to the pigs." She looked sheepishly at them and said, "You know what I mean, right?"

Liddell grinned. "You can call me anything you want as long as food is involved."

"Okay. A quick bite and then we head to Linton. Jerrell's expecting us," Jack said.

"You want to give me a hand?" Rosie asked, and Shaunda followed her into the kitchen.

Liddell walked around the bar room admiring the antique pieces of mining equipment mounted on the walls and hanging from the ceiling. Hard hats, kerosene lamps, sledgehammers and pickaxes, interspersed with framed photos of mines and miners and coal trains and the monstrous hulks of bucket trucks. A deep wooden frame on one wall held several mining drill bits of the kind Jack had described. "Was it like these?"

Jack came over and stood by him. "It narrowed down like that one," he said and pointed to one of the bits. "It wouldn't take much strength to lay someone low with one of those."

"Marcie would just love this place," Liddell said. "There's a lot of history right here."

"Yeah. It's right out of the 30s," Jack agreed. "Makes me feel like yelling "FIRE IN THE HOLE!"

"You think Katie would like to stay here?"

"Katie likes 'romantic getaways' which translates to far away from home and far too expensive." Jack didn't care for driving twelve hours to sit on a beach with a horde of strangers. He had a twenty-five-foot cabin cruiser and a fishing cabin equipped with all the comforts of home. He liked places that were familiar. Places where he always knew where a gun was within reach.

"With a baby on the way, and the wedding bells due to be ringing, you'd better get some traveling in," Liddell said. "Marcie didn't want to leave the house for a month after Janie was born. She was on alert all the time and neither of us got much sleep. Then we got used to the routine and broke chores up."

"Did that help?" Jack asked.

"We still don't get much sleep."

"I'll tell you something, Bigfoot, but you have to keep it to yourself."

"I'm the soul of discretion pod'na."

"I'm taking Katie to Maui for our wedding and honeymoon," Jack said. "The resort where I booked calls it a 'wedding-moon'. It's all inclusive, flights, transportation to and from the resort, food, drinks entertainment, more drinks and they threw in a rental car."

Liddell was uncharacteristically quiet.

"I thought you'd be excited for us," Jack said.

"Oh, I'm excited for you. Not so much for me. Now Marcie will expect me to take her somewhere tropical? When are you going?"

"Next month," Jack said. "Whether we're finished here or not."

"Does Katie know?"

"It's going to be a surprise."

"You're going to elope. Just going to tell her to pack, take her to the airport, fly over an ocean, and say 'Surprise!'"

"I'll think of something," Jack said.

Liddell shook his head. "She's got the wedding plans in full swing. Marcie's the maid of honor. I thought I was your best man."

"You're a nice enough guy, Bigfoot, but I wouldn't go so far as to say the best. Besides, I have to pay for the catering. I'd have to rent the whole luau to feed you."

"Won't she suspect something when you don't start doing 'groomly' things?"

"That's part of the surprise. We won't need to plan the wedding anymore. Part of the wedding-moon package is getting married on the beach. There's a short pier with a gazebo on the ocean. Very private. Just us, a minister, a string quartet, the moon and stars."

"You said there's a short pier at least so you can take a long walk off of it. I can't believe you're not going to have your big day here where your family can congratulate you and your buddies can castigate you and tie you naked and drunk to a light pole."

"I want to keep this low key. We've already been married once. This time it will be just us. We'll send you a postcard. 'Having a great time. Wish you were here.' That kind of crap."

"You really think Katie will go along with this?"

"I've already made most of the arrangements. I've got a travel guide setting up some romantic dinners, cruises, a glass bottom boat, snorkeling, even a little sub that takes us along a reef. We'll tour some of the smaller islands by Jeep. Shops, clothes, trinkets. I've got all the bases covered. It's romantic. It's far away and it's expensive."

"Well, you get to tell Marcie. She'll be thrilled to *not* be at your wedding. In fact, Janie will probably be upset too. This is all on you pod'na. I'm not touching it with a ten foot pole."

Jack said, "I saw this package and called them. I already worked out tickets, resort fees, cars, meals, wedding venue, the whole nine yards. I can't get my deposit back."

Liddell's eyes grew wide. "You said cars. Plural. Does that mean…?"

"Yeah. You should have seen your face. I'm pulling your big foot. If Katie doesn't kick the plan to the curb I was hoping you and Marcie—Janie, too, of course—would be the maid of honor and best man. You can dress Janie up like a maid of honor. My treat."

Liddell didn't speak and turned his head away.

"What?" Jack asked. "I thought you'd be happy."

Liddell wiped at his eyes with the back of one big arm.

"Are you crying? You big sissy."

"I'm just...I just don't know what to say."

"Say you'll be on my side when the poop hits the fan," Jack said. "I might need to sleep in your basement."

"You just surprised me pod'na. You're a true romantic. We'll need a suite and a crib..."

"And you'll need vacation days from work," Jack finished the thought. "I've already cleared the time with Captain Franklin for both of us. I was going to tell you this morning but we got stuck on this case. Keep it under your hat until this thing over."

"Yeah. You might not need to sign invitations."

"She'll be excited." He hoped she'd be excited in a good way.

"She'll have to see her doctor to see if she can fly at this stage of the pregnancy," Liddell said.

"I forgot. I guess I will have to tell her sooner than later."

"Let's eat and I'll forget all about what you said that I didn't hear," Liddell said.

"I think we can have one drink with our meal. To celebrate. Who's going to arrest us?" Jack said.

Liddell pointed up with one finger and mouthed the words, "There are spies everywhere."

"Don't be paranoid, Bigfoot. Angelina can't really do all that stuff."

"Don't bet on it, pod'na. She's like George Orwell's big brother character in that book."

Rosie and Shaunda came out of the kitchen carrying oversized serving trays. On one was a carafe of coffee and coffee mugs, soft drinks, tumblers of ice, plates and utensils. On the other tray was a gigantic bowl of spaghetti with fist sized meatballs, a platter of toasted garlic bread and a shaker of Parmesan cheese. The trays were set on one round table and the plates around another table.

Rosie said, "Dig in."

Rosie went behind the bar and brought a bottle of Glenmorangie whisky to the table.

"No liquor for us sadly. We're on duty," Jack said.

"You think those drinks are for you? Cripes! The scotch is for me and our wounded warrior. Who's going to arrest her?"

"Not us," Jack said. "Someone tried to kill her today. Maybe I should taste her drink before she does?"

"Nice try." Rosie popped the tops on two soft drinks and sat them in front of the men.

"Are the others eating with us?" Jack asked.

"I took a platter up to them. Ditty will eat with the girls," Rosie said.

"What're we having for dessert?" Liddell asked.

"Carrot cake with sour cream topping, or a hot fudge walnut brownie with ice cream," Rosie said.

"I'll have both. I'm counting my caloric intake."

"How's that going," Shaunda said and patted Liddell's gut. She was smiling.

They loaded their plates and Rosie said, "The girls are upstairs. Tell me what you're going to do."

Jack took a sip of his Coca Cola and eyed the Glenmorangie. "This is good."

"Talk about the murders. The suspense is killing me," Rosie said.

"First, we pray," Shaunda said. Both women lowered their heads and said the Lord's Prayer. Coffee was poured and they all dug in. Rosie picked at her food while Shaunda attacked her meal as if it was the enemy. When they were finished eating Rosie brought out dessert, thick slices of warmed carrot cake dripping frosting. Shaunda and Liddell devoured what was on their plate and got seconds. Jack was used to the carnivorous atmosphere from Bigfoot, but he was surprised that Shaunda packed away as much. Rosie had tried to make conversation several times but Shaunda shut her up with a look.

Liddell pushed his dessert plate away and gave a satisfied sigh.

Jack said, "Everything was excellent Rosie," and reached for his wallet.

She put her hand over his. "Food is included with the room. Don't act so surprised. I'm a very good cook."

Shaunda belched her agreement, patted her stomach and smiled at Liddell.

Jack said, "That was probably the quietest meal I've had in a long time."

Shaunda said, "If you're going to talk—talk. If you want to eat—eat."

Rosie said, "Shaunda was raised with wolves."

"Bite me Rosie," Shaunda said, causing Liddell to give Jack a grin.

"They sound like us, pod'na. You just sit there picking at your food being all grumpy and thoughtful while I eat."

"I don't do that," Jack said.

Rosie smiled at him. "That's what Shaunda says I do, too."

Liddell nudged Jack's arm. "See. Twins."

"Bite me Bigfoot."

"He calls you Bigfoot?" Shaunda asked.

"I came up here from Iberville Parish Louisiana," Liddell said. "I worked a Sheriff Patrol Boat in the swamps and bayous."

Rosie asked, "Tell me what you are going to do next? I watch CSI and Cold Case Files on television. Does it all get solved in forty-five minutes with commercial breaks?"

Jack laughed. "Hardly."

"Do you get in car chases and shootouts? Do you always get the girl in the end?" Rosie asked Jack in a seductive voice.

"Put a sock in it, Rosie," Shaunda said. "Pardon my friend."

"I'm just curious," Rosie said. "Nothing ever happened here in Pleasant Valley until this killer."

Jack and Shaunda exchanged a look.

Shaunda said, "You can trust her."

Jack gave Rosie the Reader's Digest version, leaving out things only the killer might know, hoping Shaunda hadn't already said too much. Rosie listened without interrupting. When Jack was finished Rosie took a pen and wrote on a drink napkin. She put the napkin in Jack's hand. "That's my personal cell phone."

Jack put the napkin in his shirt pocket and stood.

Liddell got up brushing crumbs from his front. He said with a big smile, "Rosie, it's been a pleasure. Thank you for the food and the rooms and finding the Jeep. You've been a big help."

Rosie's face lit up.

Shaunda said, "Now you've done it. She'll be insufferable for a week."

"She did find the Jeep," Liddell said.

"Yes. I did," Rosie said proudly. "You never told me what was in it."

"We don't know yet," Liddell said.

"Do you think that campsite belonged to the killer?" Rosie asked.

"No telling," Jack answered with a half-truth.

"You can tell me all about your adventure with Jerrell when we get to Linton," Shaunda said. "I'm going to cruise by my place and then go check the stripper pit one more time."

Rosie said with a pout, "I'll just stay here with Ditty and the girls twiddling my thumbs and being kept in the dark. Don't feel bad for me."

"We won't," Shaunda said.

Jack and Liddell followed Shaunda out to the parking lot. "I'll ride with you if you like," Jack offered Shaunda. He didn't like the idea of her going to the stripper pit alone. She hadn't fared well last time.

Her mouth tightened into a straight line and her eyes into slits. "You don't have to do that."

"I'll tell you about my playdate with the chief."

Her face relaxed a bit. "Okay. Don't back seat drive. I hate it when a guy does that."

"I'll call Chief Jerrell and see where he is," Liddell said. "See you at the PD or wherever." Liddell slid into the Crown Vic and pulled out.

"Should I ride in the back seat?" Jack asked. He watched her open the door of the Tahoe and climb up on the running board to get in. It reminded him of the Deputy Coroner at home, Lilly Caskins, who had been aptly named Little Casket by the troops because of her diminutive size and evil demeanor. She drove a Suburban and needed a ladder.

"I didn't know the FBI approved of a sense of humor," Shaunda said.

"I told you. I'm a hybrid. Half Fed, half cop."

"Get in and don't mess with me. Remember I have a headache and a gun."

Chapter 23

Jack got in the passenger side. A shotgun was mounted on the dash. An ancient Motorola radio was mounted on the floor with a yellow happy face sticker on top of it. Someone had written in magic marker on the smiley face, "Make My Day."

The Tahoe was at least ten years old. The brown and tan paint gave it the profile of a sheriff's vehicle but the faded colors said it had spent its life in the sun and harsh weather. The front passenger seat didn't show much sign of use, but with as small of a department as Shaunda had there wouldn't be a partner riding shotgun. The driver's side seat springs were sunken deep from the weight of someone three times the size of the petite Shaunda Lynch. Her predecessor must have been a very large man. Or woman.

Shaunda backed out and instead of heading toward Linton she turned left on the gravel road that ran along the railroad tracks. Her expression was unreadable. She wore no jewelry, earrings, gold chain, rings. A simple leather thong was tied around her left wrist. She tugged on this as she drove in silence. Jack knew she must have a dozen questions about what they found in the Jeep. She was bright enough to know he hadn't told everything in front of Rosie. He had the impression that she was trying very hard to show him she was tough. Trying too hard. She had a biting way of talking to everyone, even her friend Rosie. He noticed Chief Jerrell had the same habit. He'd seen the way Shaunda and Chief Jerrell snuck peeks at each other when they thought the other wasn't looking.

They were headed northwest, with nothing around them but trees, farm fields and railroad tracks. Jack saw combines out working in a few of the fields and asked, "Why aren't all the fields being tilled?"

Shaunda pointed to a large tract of land to their left between the road and the railroad tracks. "That's the Oberman place. They can't get in their fields for maybe another week if the rain holds off. It's been cold, but the problem is the moisture. The ditches running along the tracks are steep but not deep enough to keep the ground from being flooded. If the ground is too wet when they plow or till it will just turn to hard mud when it dries. The ideal time to till is when the soil is dry on top and moist an inch or so below."

She changed subjects. "I told you something you didn't know. Now you tell me something I didn't know. You can start with what it was you weren't telling me in front of Rosie?"

"What?"

"I told you Rosie can be trusted but I can understand you holding back," Shaunda said.

"I told you we found a campsite about fifty yards from the Jeep. I didn't want to get into much with Rosie there. Best not to share too much with civilians." He couldn't tell if she was nodding understanding or if her head bobbed from the uneven surface of the road.

"I trust Rosie," Shaunda said.

"I know you do. That's why I wanted to ride with you and talk in private. We don't want things to go public that will hurt a confession when we find the killer. The less in the papers or on TV, the better for us. Right?"

"Everyone is a suspect until they aren't," she said glancing at him. "I see what you're saying. I'll follow your lead G-man. Now tell me everything."

"I've told you everything," he said. "I just want you to understand why I don't want to discuss this outside of our small group. That means Rosie's out."

"We've known each other since grade school," Shaunda said, taking her eyes off the road to see if he understood. "She keeps my secrets and I keep hers. She's watching my daughter so I get to decide what she hears and what she doesn't. She's not a blabbermouth."

Jack gave in. "Okay. Part of the reason I didn't want to talk in front of her was so she wouldn't worry. The Jeep got hung up in the ditch and the driver's door was still open. The K-9 searched on both sides of the track and followed a scent back almost to Rosie's but lost it. We think they had a car parked back in the trees behind Rosie's. About the same area where Troy's truck was found."

"You think the killer was going to Rosie's?" Shaunda asked.

"There's no reason to think that. But whoever this is they're starting to get sloppy. They leave both cars within five hundred yards of Rosie's place and they must have left something incriminating enough behind this morning that they went back for it."

"That was a big risk."

"Unless he wasn't afraid to be seen," Jack said.

"What do you mean?"

Jack said, "I'm just thinking out loud."

They came to a road heading north. She bounced over the tracks and up onto the road. She turned west on Main Street at Newkirk's Funeral Home and they were suddenly back in civilization. She zigged and zagged through the south end of Dugger, then due north past Casey's General Store, turned west again onto State Road 54. Jack saw a Country Porch gas station across the road and was tempted to have her pull over so he could put his kidneys back where they belonged from the teeth jarring ride along the tracks.

"Who's the killer, Mister FBI man?" Shaunda asked.

"I have no idea," Jack said. "If we can match the DNA we found at the campsite to some of the other murders that'll be our big break. He'll screw up if he hasn't already. They always do."

"You found DNA at the campsite?" Shaunda said, turning her head and almost going off the road.

"We think so. Whoever was sleeping there made a pine needle bed under a tree with a campfire. The K-9 officer tracked from the Jeep to the campsite and back, then back towards Rosie's before the scent disappeared. The person at the camp definitely went to the Jeep. It might not have been the killer, but whoever it was might have seen the killer stash the Jeep."

"Holy cow!"

"Yeah. Crime Scene thinks they'll find blood in the Jeep. They're taking it to their garage to process with luminol. There were still some embers in the campfire. I think the guy must have made the fire late last night or early this morning to keep warm."

"You don't seem too happy. Come on. Give."

Jack was quiet

"You've got doubts," she said.

"Yep."

"Listen, if Jerrell thinks that's the weapon—and I was hit with it remember—and then you find it in a campfire near the victim's stolen Jeep, that's case closed."

"Yeah."

"But?"

"But there are a lot of unanswered questions," Jack said.

Shaunda exhaled loudly. "You know, my mama always said, "If it looks like a dog and bites like a dog, it's a dog.""

Instead of answering, Jack took out his cell phone, pulled up a picture of the drill bit and handed his phone to her.

She glanced at the picture and handed the phone back. "The tip will be carbide. I've never handled one but I've seen something just like it in the Mining Museum in town. Rosie's the expert on this stuff. Did you see all the mining paraphernalia on the walls at Rosie's?"

"Yeah."

Shaunda thought for a bit and said, "If that was in the fire any DNA would be destroyed."

"We're sending it to the FBI lab anyway," Jack said. "They work miracles sometimes."

Shaunda gave him a questioning look and then focused on the road again. "You think?"

"Who knows," Jack said and shrugged.

"If I was hit with that, maybe I should get an X-ray," she reached back and gingerly touched the spot behind her ear. "I'd hate Jerrell to think he'd won. He's an ass sometimes."

Jack said, "My partner thinks you two have history."

"Mind you own business."

"Sorry," Jack said and changed the subject. "We need to narrow down when your daughter had the visitor. She said she gave him a drink and a sandwich. Is there any chance the can or bottle he drank from is still around?"

"Why would I keep something I didn't even know about? By the way, do I look like a complete slob? I'll have you know I keep a very clean house. Take the trash out and everything."

"I meant we need to ask Penelope if the guy took the drink and food with him. When is trash pickup?"

"Boy, you don't quit, do you? If he left it behind it would have been picked up by now and thrown away. I keep a neat yard too. The trash was picked up two days ago. Once a week. Just like in the big cities."

"Okay. That's off the table."

"Do they teach you that in the FBI Academy?" Shaunda asked.

"What? To be thorough?"

"To be annoying," she said, and grinned. "Loosen up. I'm enjoying our chat."

"Me too," Jack said, and thought, *she's bipolar.*

He'd made a mistake telling Jerrell they should wait to have the composite drawing made. He would have to interview Pen and Cretin again and have composite drawings made. He hadn't asked if Cretin or Penelope—or Patty—knew each other. He'd been so caught up in the chaos this morning that he hadn't had time to think this through. That was true of a lot of his cases. Sometimes stumbling through worked best.

"I wish to God she'd told me about this guy back then," Shaunda said. "I could have tracked him down and at least have a name. I don't know what that girl was thinking. I told her about Troy Junior when it happened. She didn't say a word about any hitchhiker. It pisses me off."

"She's a teenager," Jack said. "She came clean with us today."

"I'm not pissed at her. I'm angry with myself for being the kind of mother that she didn't feel like she could talk to. She was right about how I would have handled it though. I would have picked him up and dropped him off in Sullivan."

She laughed. "Don't give me attitude. I know you guys do it too. You stick them in the car and take them out of town to be someone else's problem. Hitchhikers are nothing but trouble."

"I'll bet Sullivan loves you," Jack said.

Shaunda turned south and drove down a graveled one lane road that turned into a hard packed dirt lane and led between freshly tilled fields. Jack could smell the fresh soil. Down the road he could make out a small wood sided farmhouse painted white with the red asphalt tile favored by farmhomes in the early 30s and 40s.

"Is that your place?" he asked and she nodded. It was at least a quarter of a mile from the main road. The hitchhiker couldn't have been after directions.

"You have a lot of privacy out here," Jack said.

"It's a dead-end road. You don't get surprise visitors. Or at least that's what I thought."

"Does your daughter complain about being out in the sticks?"

"Pen likes it out here," Shaunda said defensively. "She's got friends. Patty comes over and spends the night all the time."

"Rosie said you were homeschooling her."

"Yeah. Hey, if you're saying I don't take care of my kid just spit it out."

"Whoa. I merely brought it up because my wife is a teacher."

"Rosie told me you weren't married."

"Shaunda, there's no reason for us to fight. I shouldn't have said anything. I'm sorry."

"Forget it," Shaunda said. "I'm just sore. Not at you." She drove over the dead grass beside the house, shut the engine off and got out. Jack got out too.

"I'll check the house for you," Jack said. "Anyone else live here?"

"I'm quite capable of checking my own house, thank you."

"You're right. You stay here and keep an eye out. If I need help, I'll yell. Now give me your key." Jack held his hand out.

Shaunda shoved her keys in his hand. "I'm in no mood to argue with you. If the kitchen's messy someone planted that stuff to set me up."

Jack smiled. He had no doubt she could hold her own if she was attacked, but she hadn't done too well at the lake. He put the key in the front door lock but it was already unlocked. He unholstered his .45 and tensed with his hand on the doorknob.

"That idiot forgot to lock the door," Shaunda said.

Jack hadn't noticed her come up behind him. She took the keys, pushed the door open, stepped around him and went inside. "Come on in."

Jack stepped inside and scanned the room. Shaunda seemed amused as Jack moved from room to room clearing them. He came back into what served as a front room/office. The room was divided in half by a leather sofa. To the right of this was a loveseat with a fold-up table tray in front, a rocker, and a small ancient television.

To the left of the sofa the walls were covered with bookshelves full of books and file boxes. An olive green metal desk—the kind favored by the Army in the 70s—was pushed against the back of the sofa facing toward the front door. The top of the desk was piled high with file folders and office supplies.

Shaunda squeezed past Jack to shut the door.

"You can put that away," Shaunda said. "Sergeant Ditterline just forgot to lock the door. If someone wanted to break in they wouldn't pick the lock. This isn't the big city. Our burglars and miscreants just kick doors open. Unless you think our killer is a considerate person. Besides, if someone broke in here they'd probably leave money so I could buy a decent television."

Jack holstered the .45 and examined the locks and frame on the door. They didn't show signs of being tampered with. The lock was cheap. "You really should have better locks installed."

"I'm a girl. Don't you know girls are helpless? Besides, I've never needed more than a deadbolt."

"You don't seem helpless to me."

"Well, don't tell Jerrell that," she said. "He still calls me Little Shauny behind my back. You heard the cracks he made about my size."

"He's protective of you," Jack suggested. "Is that a bad thing?"

"Yes. If I made those kinds of jokes about him he'd get his nuts in a toaster and file a lawsuit."

Jack had to laugh. He'd never heard that expression before.

"Have a seat. I'm going to put on a uniform. It might be the last time I wear one after the town board meets this week." She went to her bedroom and shut the door.

Jack had noticed the bathroom was outfitted with handicap necessities. He'd also noticed that everything in the larger bedroom that must be Penelope's were handicap equipped with even a hospital type bed and better furniture. Shaunda had spared no expense when it came to her daughter, while her own bedroom seemed a little shabby.

She came out of the bedroom wearing a freshly starched uniform, sans badge. She'd put a light coat of makeup over the bruises. It didn't help. Her brunette hair was brushed to a high shine and worn in a ponytail.

"Is this your office away from home?" Jack asked, indicating the old desk and book covered shelves. The shelves were filled with text books, resource books, dictionaries, classical literature, and history and so on. The worn covers indicated they were well read or had come from library sales. "Have you read all of these?"

"Pen has. They're mostly books recommended by a teacher friend of mine. I'm supposed to be homeschooling Pen, but the truth of the matter is, she's teaching me some of this."

"Well, you taught her how to have compassion for someone down on their luck and needing help," Jack said. "She may not have made the wisest decision, but she's okay and she learned a good lesson."

"Believe me, she doesn't get that from me."

"I think you might need to put a bandage on that." He could see the wound on her head clearer with her hair pulled back.

"I've had worse," she said.

They went back to the Tahoe, got in and she backed out to the gravel road.

Jack said, "Last year a bank robber threw a live grenade at me. I was deaf for most of the day. Still have some ringing in my ears."

"You catch 'em?"

"I shot her."

"Her?"

"Yeah. It was a family of bank robbers. They'd been pulling jobs all over the country wearing flak jackets and carrying military ordinance. She was the baby in the family. Fourteen. I still feel guilty for shooting a kid."

Shaunda let out a low whistle. "Is that supposed to make me feel better?"

Jack laughed. "No. I just wanted to tell you that it bothered me to shoot a kid. For all we know this guy could be a teenager."

"I'll tell you to turn your head when I shoot him."

Shaunda drove back to State Road 54 to the cut through that accessed Dugger Lake, pulled the Tahoe down to the water's edge and cut the engine. She pointed to the rocky area fifty to seventy feet from where Brandon Dillingham's body had lain. "Before I got hammered I was over there poking around. I thought I saw something on the ground near that scrub brush growing under the ledge. I had to get in the water to check it out."

Where she was pointing the bank was restricted by solid rock, six feet high, scrub and blackberry bushes grew out of the rocky ledges around the base but there was a small area of embankment visible underneath the brush.

"A rabbit wearing body armor would have a hard time getting through the sticker bushes," Jack said. He wondered how thoroughly that area was searched by Crime Scene techs, but on the other hand, how the hell could a person get through that without Shaunda noticing.

"These stripper pits are as dangerous as the mining that caused them. When they dug the coal out of the ground they hit pockets of gas or underground springs or older mining shafts. When they abandoned those, they came up top and scraped some more up. Some places in the lake are fifty feet deep. It's public land. Idiots come out here and snorkel or dive in those underground caverns. The water's not clear enough to see anything. I was worried I'd step into a drop-off or a hole when I walked into the water to check under that cliff ledge. I didn't get too far because it started getting deep."

"You can't swim."

"I swim like a rock," she said. "Been afraid of the water since I was little. When I was three years old my dad threw me in a pond to teach me to swim. I nearly drowned."

Jack's dad had done the same thing to him, but it was into deep water at the end of a pier they were fishing from. He'd learned to swim fast. He'd learned everything the hard way since then. Sink or swim.

He changed the subject. "Did you find anything at all?"

"Yeah," she said. "If you walk into a lake you're going to get wet."

"Were you still in the water when you were hit? You were soaked when I saw you at the PD."

"My legs were in the water when I was bent over, but I wasn't anywhere near the bank when my fuse got blown. Whoever it was must have dragged me out of the water unless I crawled."

"Can you show me the spot where you were standing when you were hit."

"I'm not going back in that water."

"You don't have to. Just show me where you saw whatever it was you saw," Jack said.

They exited the Tahoe. Shaunda walked to the water's edge and pointed out a rock shaped like a saddle that jutted from the ground near the bank. "I thought I saw something at the base of that rock. I can't describe it, but it could have been that drill bit. It was dark colored."

"No one else was down here? Crime Scene? Your deputy?"

"All I know is I woke up. I had already sent Joey home. Jerrell's Crime Scene people were still up by the road. I still had my gun but my badge was gone."

Jack said nothing.

"Maybe they realized they'd lost something and came back for it. Maybe they were surprised to see me, knocked me out and wrote that stuff on the back of my shirt to warn us—me off."

"There were armed policemen on the road and you were armed. This guy took one hell of a chance."

Jack had learned from experience that nothing was impossible. No matter how improbable it sounded. Even knowing that he was still bothered by the fact that someone had been able to sneak up on Shaunda. A kid had just been found killed. Her senses should have been working overtime.

She walked to the water's edge and stood with her hands resting on her gun belt and stared across the lake.

Jack got as close to the rock ledge as possible without getting into the water and ran his eyes over the brush and stickers and rock. He didn't see anything that didn't belong, but he smelled something like rotten eggs. He sniffed and wrinkled his nose. "What is that smell?"

Shaunda came up beside him and sniffed. "Sulfur."

"Sulfur?"

"This is mining country. There's sulfur damn near everywhere."

"I didn't smell it when we were here this morning," Jack said.

Shaunda raised an arm and swept it through the air. "All around here," she said. "Mines and stone quarries. I grew up with the smell of burnt charcoal and coal dust from the trucks and train cars that ran through here day after day. One of the chemicals in coal is sulfur. Smells like rotten eggs."

Jack made a mental note to ask Penelope and Cretin if they smelled anything when they had met the hitchhiker/homeless guy.

"Can you think of any reason Brandon might have been down here?" Jack asked.

"Yeah," she said. "I mean, this whole state is honeycombed with mine shafts. Some of them were closed because they were flooded. A good hard rain, or the shaft is drilled into an underground spring and the shaft will collapse and fill with water. If Brandon was a spelunker I'd say he might be exploring the flooded shafts like some idiot. He was an idiot but I don't think he was brave enough to do that. Like I said, I've run him off the Dugger Mine property a couple of times. This time he'd taken his clothes off. He might've had some girl down here to go swimming—or something else. The angry father angle makes more sense to me than anything."

"This is a make out spot?" Jack said.

"This and any other place," Shaunda answered. "The abandoned mine property doesn't have security. Maybe a fence, but that doesn't stop anyone. You could put a fence all around this lake and it wouldn't matter one bit."

Jack thought about it. Brandon gets caught down here doing the nasty with some underage girl, dad shows up, bim-bam-boom, Brandon dies. Maybe murder wasn't the plan, just an ass kicking. But Brandon dies from the blow to the back of the head. What do they do now?

"I'm sure we have some news clippings in the file, but do you recall how much of the details of the case got into the news, Chief?" Jack asked.

"This is a small community. The death of the son of Linton's Police Chief would get around, even without the news media."

"That's what I thought." They must have heard about where Troy Junior's body was found. A lot of the details had leaked to the public by word of mouth. Jerrell and his troops had been charging around like a bull, asking questions, searching. Brandon's murder is made to look like Troy Junior's. He, or she, dumps Brandon in the water, uses Brandon's phone to report the body. As there are two of them, father and daughter, or brother and sister, they drive both vehicles away from the scene.

That just left the attack on Shaunda to be explained and the use of a similar weapon to the other killings. A drill bit is an unusual thing to carry around with you but maybe the killer had something like that in his, or her, vehicle for work or as a tire knocker or whatever. If the killer knew Shaunda it would answer the question of the warning written on her uniform shirt.

That's a lot of coincidence and too complicated.

"What're you thinking," Shaunda asked him.

"Nothing."

They got back in the Tahoe and didn't speak again until Shaunda was entering Linton city limits and Jack's phone rang. It was Liddell.

"Jack, I'm with Jerrell at the Greene County morgue. We're just finishing. Are you close?" Liddell asked.

"How close are we to the morgue?" Jack asked Shaunda

"Fifteen minutes."

Jack passed that on to Liddell and disconnected.

Chapter 24

Shaunda stayed on SR 54 going east, which turned into US Highway 231 and then into Main Street as she entered downtown Bloomfield. The coroner's office was a gray squat brick building that resembled a funeral home. Like in Evansville they had to ring a buzzer to gain entrance.

Inside Jack and Shaunda were met by the forensic pathologist, Lacy Daniels.

"You must be Agent Murphy," she said, taking his hand in both of hers and giving it a friendly squeeze. "I'm Doctor Daniels. Coroner, forensic pathologist, secretary, and staff."

She turned her attention to Shaunda. "What happened to you? Accident?"

"You should see the other driver," Shaunda said.

Dr. Daniels was wearing a stark white lab coat over a set of gray scrubs. She still wore paper booties over her shoes but had stripped off the latex gloves. Her hair was jet-black contrasted with a creamy white complexion. She was short like Shaunda, a little older, maybe in her forties, with a little more meat on her bones, but she wasn't pudgy, just well filled out. No jewelry or makeup, of course, given what she had just done. She was pretty with a charming smile and pleasant manner. Jack had been expecting someone rough around the edges, like the Chief Deputy Coroner back home, Lilly Caskins, aka/Little Casket. In fact, Lacy was the opposite of Little Casket.

"We've just completed the post on Brandon. I'd offer you coffee but no food or drink is allowed. Follow me," she said, and led the way down a hallway. "Your constable was here with the mother to identify the body." They came to an unmarked steel door with a keypad lock on the wall where she punched in the code and they entered.

The autopsy room was laid out in the same fashion as the one in Evansville. Two steel tables were bolted to the floor canted slightly into an industrial sized steel sink. Microphones were mounted from the ceiling above each table. On the left side of the room light boards for viewing X-rays were mounted to the wall. Chief Jerrell stood staring at X-rays clipped to the light boards. Liddell still wore white Tyvek zip-up coveralls, a paper hat, mask and paper booties.

Jack said, "You look like someone threw a sheet over a mountain."

Jerrell said, "I asked your partner if he'd do this one. Three Big Macs, three fries, a chocolate shake and two bags of cookies and here we are—finally," Jerrell said. "Don't you ever feed this guy?"

"I was hungry," Liddell said pulling off the protective gear and disposing of it in the hazardous waste receptacle. "The cookies are for Janie when I get home. Janie's my little girl. She's teething."

Jack ignored them and focused on the body. White male, pale chalky skin, medium length brown hair, no tattoos or scars, fingernails on the first two fingers of the right hand were ripped from the quick and hanging. He'd missed this at the scene. The body would have been washed down after the examination and before the autopsy. The Y incision ran from the top of the breastbone to below the navel and was expertly stitched together.

Jack examined the face closely. The eyes were half open in that accusatory stare only the dead could acquire. Brandon appeared to be younger and more pitiable than he had been at the scene. Even if he was the bad boy everyone said he was, he didn't deserve to die like this. If he'd lived maybe he'd have gone on to do great things. Or maybe someone would have shot him. Jack stared into the dead boy's eyes and said in a whisper, "Who did this to you?"

Shaunda spoke up close to his ear and made him jump. "There's a waiting list. I always knew he'd end up badly. I wanted to kill him myself a few times. Don't feel too sorry for him. Feel sorry for his mother. She had to live with him."

Jack glared at her.

"Don't look at me like that. You didn't know him. Tell him, Troy."

Jerrell continued examining the X-rays. "Shauny's right. He was a dip-shit. Had to happen sometime. Barr just called me. He found two bags of marijuana under the seat of the Jeep and around a thousand dollars. He also found a kit with an 8-ball but no syringe or spoon."

Dr. Daniels stood by the corpse's feet. She slipped Latex gloves on and spread the toes of the right foot. Jack could plainly see new and old needle marks in the web between his toes.

"Speaking of which," she said. "He's not a newcomer to cocaine. You don't usually see this until they're in for the long haul. I'm surprised no one noticed he was a junkie before now. Surely his mom must have suspected but she seemed angry that we pointed it out."

Liddell said, "The doc's getting a full toxicology workup."

"What's the cause of death?" Jack asked.

"Hypoxia," she said. "I think he quit breathing before he went in the water. I'll know for sure when we get toxicology back. The contusion on the back of the skull would have rendered him unconscious. He might have shot up before he was hit, or someone might have shot him up afterwards. It happened before he went in the water. The mark left on his scalp is almost identical to the one on Troy Jerrell Junior."

Jack asked, "Were there any differences in Jerrell's and Brandon's cases that you can think of, Dr. Daniels?"

"Not really, except for the O.C. in Jerrell's lungs. Did they tell you about that?"

Jack nodded.

"Brandon didn't show signs of exposure to an irritant."

"Is there anything else?" Jack asked.

"I did notice something, but it's not odd considering where we live."

"What do you mean?" Jack asked.

"When I did the post on Troy Junior I noticed something under his toenails. The same thing was on Brandon's clothes, on the bottoms of the blue jeans and shoes."

Jack waited.

"I didn't have the equipment to test it here but I put it under the microscope and it is sulfur."

"Do you still have the sample?" Jack asked.

"I've got it, but it doesn't mean anything. Sulfur is common around here. You can get it on your clothes walking across the yard."

"Does sulfur smell like rotten eggs?" Jack asked.

"If you have enough of it, or if it's in a gaseous form. You're not going to smell anything like that on the bodies unless they were coated with it."

Jack said, "We stopped by Dugger Lake just now and I smelled something like rotten eggs. Chief Lynch said she smelled it earlier when they were at the scene."

"I didn't smell anything like that when I was down there," Chief Jerrell said.

"I asked her to show me where she was standing when she was hit," Jack said.

"Someone hit you?" Dr. Daniels asked.

"I've had worse," Shaunda said.

Jack said, "Anyway, we were over by that rocky ledge near the water. She said she thought she saw something under the brush. When she went to bend over to see what it was she was hit. She said she smelled sulfur just before that."

Jerrell, Liddell and Dr. Daniels all turned toward Shaunda.

"So what?" Shaunda said.

Jack said, "Why didn't we all smell it the first time we were down there? Is it possible the person that attacked you had somehow gotten into a bunch of the stuff and was hiding in that thick brush?"

Shaunda shrugged the question off.

Jerrell said, "I didn't smell anything like that coming from the Jeep. Or around that campsite. Why? Did you, Jack?"

"I smelled all kinds of stuff. I thought it was because we were near the railroad tracks. The campfire was fairly recent. It could have covered the sulfur smell."

Shaunda rubbed the back of her neck. "Seriously? You think what's important is the smell of rotten eggs? We searched the whole damn area and didn't find anything or anyone. No one else mentioned that smell. I shouldn't have said anything."

Jack wasn't done. "Didn't you say you stopped Brandon this morning after you saw him coming off mining property?"

"Yeah. So?"

"Bear with me here," Jack said. "Dr. Daniels tells us she found sulfur on the bottom of Brandon's blue jean legs, bottoms of his shoes, and under Troy Junior's toenails."

Jerrell grinned. "I think you city boys have a lot to learn about this part of the country. You just made Shauny's point for her. You're going to find that shit just everywhere. If that was a clue to who the killer is, we'd have to arrest damn near everyone in four counties."

Jack wasn't one hundred percent convinced the sulfur wasn't important. Jerrell and Shaunda were locals and had more experience with it than he did but their insistence that the presence of sulfur wasn't a clue didn't mean it wasn't.

"Did you get a time of death?" he asked Jerrell and the doctor.

Jerrell said, "What you'd expect. Sometime after Shaunda stopped him and before she got the call about the body."

Dr. Daniels said, "His death was very recent. If I guessed I'd say he wasn't in the water more than an hour. Probably less. The water temperature this time of year is about forty-five degrees. That would be enough to slow down deterioration, but not very much."

She took them back to the table and pointed at the backs of Brandon's heels. There was specks of black rock embedded in the flesh.

"He was dragged into the water," Liddell remarked.

"Constable Trantino told me he'd pulled the body out on the bank and he was face down. There wasn't any sign of abrasions or embedding on the knees or tops of his toes. He must have been dragged a long way across that bank to the water," Dr. Daniels said.

"What does he weigh?" Jack asked.

"One fifty-two," Dr. Daniels answered.

Chapter 25

Chief Jerrell had gone to his office when they arrived at Linton PD, leaving Jack, Liddell and Shaunda in the roll call/break room poring over the case files, making notes on the whiteboards with the new information. They had divided the six case files into separate piles of information that now took up the tabletop and most of the floor. Merely reading the files became more confusing, frustrating and overwhelming. Jack ripped the six photos from a whiteboard and flung them into the air.

"We're not getting anywhere. We need to know these guys inside and out. We need to find that guy from the park. At least we'd be doing something," Jack said.

Shaunda got up from the floor where she'd been arranging sheets of paper. "You're the one that said we should go through all this crap. Now you say we should go get the hitchhiker. Make up your mind."

"Hey, it's not his fault this is such a mess," Liddell said. "You guys let it get like this."

Jerrell came back through the door and cleared his throat loudly.

"If you're through ripping each other's throats out, I might have a solution to the paperwork." Jerrell held the door open for a small woman in her mid-twenties to enter.

Liddell rushed forward to hug her.

Jack introduced Angelina Garcia to everyone. She shook hands and her eyes roamed the room. Introductions finished, she said, "What a mess. Toomey said you needed me, but wow! What did you guys do without me?"

Jack was relieved and happy to see Angelina. Toomey had not said a word about sending her.

Liddell said meekly, "Help."

Shaunda started to stack piles on the floor.

"Leave all that. Fill me in on what you've done. I'll put all this in some kind of order later," Angelina said, stopping Shaunda.

"Some of us have been too busy to type up reports," Shaunda said.

Angelina put her fingers gently beside Shaunda's cheek and checked out her black eye. "I can see that. I don't suppose one of these guys did that?"

Shaunda smiled and said, "They're alive, aren't they?"

Angelina chuckled. "The director didn't tell me any of you got hurt. He just said you needed computer support. Should I carry a gun?"

"You don't need a gun. You've got me. Did I tell you how glad I am to see you," Liddell said and gave her another hug.

"'Bout damn time," Jerrell said. "No offense angel…" He hurriedly added, "…ina." Jack smiled. Jerrell hadn't called her gal, or hon, or little lady or angel or any other politically incorrect stuff that was meant as friendly, not insulting. Jerrell wouldn't have to worry about being sued by Angelina. Being punched was a possibility.

"What do you need?" Jerrell asked. "Name it and I'll make it happen."

Angelina looked around the room and up at the wall clock. "Looks like I'll be here overnight at least. I'm going to need a place to stay, something to eat, a Coke or twelve, and would one of you erase those whiteboards. They're scaring me."

"That's all Jack's doing," Liddell said.

"I believe you. I've got my equipment in the car. Do you have Wi-Fi?"

"We do and I can get more computers and a projector if you want. Just name it Angelina," Jerrell said.

"This is your roll call room. Do you want me to set my stuff up here, or do you have another office? I'll need a desk and both of these whiteboards."

"I'll put you in my office. Lots of room. We'll move this for you."

"I'll get my stuff," she said.

"I'll help you," Shaunda said. "Jerrell has a bottle of emergency whiskey in his desk drawer. You might need it later."

After the women left Jerrell said, "She can't stay at Rosie's. I don't want that little gal staying in a bar. I got the perfect place about fifteen minutes outside of town. I'll call. My office is down the hall in the front. First door on the right if you don't mind moving those boards."

Jack and Liddell began rolling the large whiteboards toward the door. Jerrell called after them, "Stay out of my desk."

"Your emergency whiskey is safe," Liddell said. "Jack only drinks high end Scotch."

"Stay out of my desk," Jerrell repeated.

Shaunda was helping Angelina get set up in Jerrell's office when Sergeant Crocker stuck his head in the room. "Where's the chief? I mean my chief?" he asked.

Shaunda pointed down the hall and Crocker took off at a quick pace. Shaunda said, "I'd better go see what's got his hormones firing." She walked into the roll call room just in time to hear Crocker's news. An employee at the Humane Society had spotted a hitchhiker matching the description Cretin had given them. He was cutting through the field and heading west into the trees.

Jerrell and Jack rode together. Shaunda rode with Liddell in the Crown Vic. Sergeant Crocker grabbed extra shells for his riot shotgun and then followed on his own.

Jack asked Chief Jerrell, "What's behind the Humane Society?"

"Farm fields, trees, railroad tracks and Black Creek. Maybe he's got a camp set up near the tracks like he did behind Rosie's."

"How far is it from here?" Jack asked. They were headed the opposite direction from the City Park.

"Just a couple of miles."

"Don't call the K-9 or other cars out just yet, Chief. Let's talk to the person that sighted this guy. I hate to waste time and manpower if it's not the right guy."

"You're right," Jerrell said and got on his radio. He advised the officers that were watching the City Park to continue the roaming stakeout there. He advised Rusty to bring the K-9 to the Humane Society but wait there.

Jerrell veered off State Road 54 at Linton Sporting Goods and drove west on Price Road. Price turned into County Road 75. They passed a Baptist Church and there was nothing but farms ahead of them. Straight ahead was a forest.

"We'll take Atlas Road. We're a half mile from the animal shelter?"

"The guy's on foot. He won't get that far ahead of us."

Jerrell sped up turning north on Atlas Road and down a long gravel drive to the Humane Society. A middle aged woman with bleached blonde hair with purple highlights, wearing a camouflage jacket over a bright flower print dress stood outside watching for them.

"What the hell did you do to your hair, woman?" Jerrell said as they got out of the truck.

"Well ain't you something," she said. "Here I go and find your bad guy for you and that's all you can say."

"I'm sorry, Sissy. It's just that your natural color was pretty. Now all you need is a skateboard and some tattoos and you can hang out at the Dollar General."

The woman named Sissy laughed. "You got me there Troy. My niece did this to me. She said it would make me younger. Younger than what is what I want to know." She laughed again. She had a very pleasant laugh.

"Tell your niece she's under arrest," Jerrell said back. "What've you got?"

"The guy I saw came walking down the driveway pretty as you please. I thought he was coming here and was about to lock the door, but he just kept going across the field, that way." She pointed west. "If he's planning to hop a train he's going to be surprised. Nothing stops around there."

"Describe him," Jerrell said.

"He was a hobo," she said.

Jack hadn't heard someone described as a hobo for quite a while. The politically correct term was "homeless." Hobo was right up there with vagabond.

The description Sissy gave was very close to what Cretin and Pen told them, minus the tattoos. Sissy didn't get close enough to see that. "I saw him coming and I saw him going. I didn't check him out all that close, Troy. He was creepy."

"How long ago, Sissy?" Jerrell asked.

"Ten, fifteen minutes. What's he wanted for? Is he an escapee from the prison?"

"Nothing like that, Sissy. Are you expecting anyone?"

She said she wasn't.

"Go inside, lock your door. I'll see you when we find this guy. Okay?"

"You don't have to tell me twice, Troy," she said and headed indoors.

Liddell and Shaunda arrived and they all talked. It was decided Liddell and Shaunda would drive east a quarter mile down the road to the big curve. They would then hike south toward the tracks. Jack and Jerrell would follow the direction the hitchhiker was seen going. Sergeant Crocker arrived and was told to go farther west and come up the tracks where they would all hook up somewhere in the middle.

"Hopefully one of us will run across this guy's trail," Jack said. They split up and headed out.

* * * *

Liddell and Shaunda drove east and before they reached the curve Shaunda said, "Let me out here. You go to the crossroad. I'll go in here and you can start from there. Divide and conquer."

"I don't think that's a good idea Shaunda," Liddell said. "We should stay together."

"If you're worrying about me, don't. I welcome another round with this asshole. You're not afraid, are you?"

"You're trying to make me defend my manhood and it won't work. We can spread out a little, but I want to be close enough to hear you in case it gets scary and you cry."

"Bite me," she said.

"Likewise," he answered. They checked their weapons. Satisfied they were loaded and ready she got out and he drove on for a hundred yards. She was entering the tree line by the time he got out of the car.

* * * *

A runoff ditch ran alongside a huge farm field that was dotted here and there with stunted maple and red bud trees. Jack and Jerrell followed the ditch south into the trees, many of which were evergreens, eastern cedars and white pines. There were splotches of green among the leafless oak and maple trees. They walked quickly but quietly and stopped frequently to listen for sounds. Cretin said the guy had traded her the phone for cigarettes.

The railroad tracks were dead ahead and they'd seen no sign of the hitchhiker. When they reached the tracks Jerrell said, "You angle off to the east and hook up with Shaunda and Liddell. I'll go a little west and meet Crocker. We can cover more ground that way."

Jack didn't think splitting up was a good tactical move, but this was Jerrell's home turf. "If you see something don't try to grab him alone, Chief."

Jerrell stood tall. "I think I can handle the little fella." Jerrell was six feet and five inches of solidly built muscle.

"If he's got a gun size doesn't matter," Jack reminded him.

Jerrell grinned. "Don't worry about me."

"I'm not worried about you. We need this guy in one piece to talk," Jack said.

"I hear ya," Jerrell said.

They split up and Jerrell disappeared in the thickening woods. Jack angled slightly to the east, the idea being to cross paths with Liddell and Shaunda who were supposed to be going due south. After what seemed like an hour, watching for obstacles and holes in the ground and scanning around him, Jack heard two gunshots. The shots were close together and came from a large caliber weapon. A handgun, not a rifle or shotgun.

He drew his .45 and headed toward the sound as quickly as possible. He keyed the mic on the borrowed walkie-talkie. "This is Murphy. Respond." No response. He tried again, calling for each unit individually. His radio squelched and a voice said, "This is Crocker. I heard shots."

The soft ground beneath his feet slowed him down as he called out to Jerrell. There was no response. He called out again, louder and again there was no response. He called Jerrell's cell number and it was answered almost immediately. "That wasn't me," Jerrell said. "It came from where Shaunda and your partner should be."

Jack said, "You try Shaunda and I'll try Liddell's cell phone."

Jerrell agreed and Jack called Liddell's cell phone. Liddell answered. "What's going on?" Liddell sounded out of breath.

"Those shots didn't come from you or Shaunda?"

"Not me. I'm not with Shaunda," Liddell said. "We split up and I haven't seen her for about ten minutes. She took the radio."

"It wasn't Jerrell or Crocker. Hang on," Jack said, and called Jerrell on the radio. This time he answered. Jack said, "I've got Liddell on the phone. Shaunda took their radio and went off on her own. She's headed in your general direction. What do you want to do?"

Jerrell advised, "I'm going on. Black Creek is just ahead. She couldn't cross that on foot. You keep heading south until you hit the creek. I'll find you. Keep trying her radio. I'll call her cell phone. This guy might have a gun, or her gun. Be careful."

"Did you hear that?" Jack asked Liddell.

"I'll head a little west. She was moving a lot quicker than me. I'll meet up with you along the creek."

Jack got on the walkie-talkie and called for Shaunda until he could see Black Creek ahead. Not getting a response he called for Crocker and told him to head back to the railroad tracks and come east in case the suspect doubled back.

The radio squelched. Shaunda said, "I got him."

Chapter 26

Shaunda had walked toward Black Creek and was able to give them a landmark, an ancient poplar tree that had been uprooted in a storm. Jack followed the creek until he spotted the tree. It was hard to miss with the thick roots taller than Jerrell who was waving his arms.

Jack came into a small clearing the fallen tree had made when it took down several smaller trees. The tree roots held the trunk several feet into the air. Shaunda sat on the ground, knees drawn up, arms wrapped around her chest. Her left hand was pressed tightly against her right rib cage and the front of her shirt was covered in blood.

Jerrell knelt in front of her trying to assess the damage but she kept twisting away. "Shauny, let me see how bad you're hurt."

"I'm okay dammit," she said and tried to get to her feet. "You'd better check on him." Shaunda motioned with her head over her shoulder where a body was partially hidden by the large roots.

The man's body was lying face down. His arms were up as if he'd tried to stop his fall. The back of his head was a bloody crater filled with red and gray goo. The missing parts of his head peppered the tree trunk above where he lay in blood and bits of skull and brain matter. "Told you I got him," she said in a weak voice.

A Colt Python revolver lay on the ground beside Shaunda's right foot. A stag handled hunting knife lay in the grass in front of the dead man, the blade covered in blood.

"He doesn't need my help," Jerrell said. "Let me see." Jerrell gently removed her hand from her side and a trickle of blood ran down the blood soaked fabric of her shirt. He placed her hand back on the wound and said, "Keep that right there."

"What do you think I was doing?" She grimaced and tried to get up but couldn't.

Jack had already called 911, requested an ambulance and handed the phone to Jerrell who gave them an approximate location and told them one of his men would meet them on Highway 54 and lead them in.

Liddell searched his pockets and came up with a wad of brown napkins. Jerrell took them and put them under Shaunda's hand and pressed her hand over the wound. He put his hand over hers and kept pressure. "You're going to be okay. They're sending help right now."

Sergeant Crocker ran up and Jack said, "Sergeant, can you go back to the nearest road? You'll have to direct the ambulance back here."

"There's a wide shoulder along the tracks that cross Highway 54," Crocker said. "They can get back here to the tracks but it's a long haul with a stretcher to get back here."

Jerrell said, "I'll get her to the tracks."

Crocker took off at a sprint. He was just out of sight when they heard more than one siren wailing far off in the distance.

"What the hell did you think you were doing, Shauny," Jerrell said.

"We're going to need your Crime Scene people, Chief."

"There's one coming," Jerrell answered. "One of those sirens is the Crime Scene wagon. Let's carry her out of here."

Jerrell pulled the retaining snaps loose and handed Jack his gun belt. He pulled his belt from his pants and wrapped it around Shaunda's right arm and chest and buckled it tight to hold her arm against the wound. "Keep your arm down tight," he said and put an arm around Shaunda's back, the other under her legs. She was able to wrap her free arm around his neck and he lifted her as if she weighed nothing.

Jack saw a lot of blood on the ground. He hoped the knife hadn't hit anything vital. The wound was trickling blood and she didn't have blood coming from her mouth. The blade hadn't penetrated a lung but she could still go into shock.

Liddell said, "I'll stay here and wait for Crime Scene."

Jerrell carried Shaunda effortlessly but quickly over the rough terrain. He slowed often to check that the compress hadn't slipped. He never seemed to tire and he barely spoke except to assure Shaunda that she was going to be okay.

Shaunda said in a weak voice, "I guess I'll take that ambulance now," and Jerrell grunted.

Jack asked her, "What happened?"

She took a breath, let it out and said, "I saw his trail." She grimaced with pain.

"Shut up, Shauny," Jerrell said. "There will be an investigation. Don't say anything."

"Screw that," Shaunda said. "I didn't do anything wrong. He attacked me with a knife and I shot him."

Jack ignored the stern looks Jerrell threw his way and asked, "You saw his trail. Then what?"

"He came out of nowhere. I pulled my gun but he ran. I grabbed his jacket but he pulled away. I thought he was trying to get away." She took a deep breath through her nose and let it out slowly through her mouth. "He could have got away. But he turned and came at me."

She stopped talking again and Jack let her rest. All the huff and puff had gone out of her voice. Jack understood the emotion. It had felt the same way the first time he'd killed a man. His strut and cocksureness evaporated like a bad dream leaving a fog of nightmares to be endured for years to come. It was one thing to carry a gun, another to use it.

"It happened so fast. I thought he punched me. Then I saw the knife. We were right there...at that tree. He had this look in his eyes. He's dead...isn't he?"

Shaunda's eyes opened wide and she stiffened. "Where's my gun?"

"Don't worry about your gun," Jack said. "We've got it."

She relaxed and nodded. She tensed and said, "I feel sick, Troy. You'd better put me down."

Jack saw drops of perspiration were dotting her brow. Her skin was pasty pale. She was going into shock.

Jerrell was on the same wavelength. "Are you thirsty, Shaunda?"

She answered with a nod.

"You're probably going into shock. You need to relax. Think of something else. Think about Pen and how much she likes Tootsie Rolls."

Shaunda gave a weak smile and settled in his arms.

"We're almost there."

If she was going into shock they had very little time before medics would need to get her warm and start IV fluids. Jerrell picked up the pace, carrying Shaunda as carefully as if she were a china doll.

Jack had slung the gun belt over his shoulder. He keyed the mic on Jerrell's mobile radio. "Where's that ambulance, Sergeant?"

Crocker's voice came back. "Just turning onto the tracks. We'll be there in two shakes. How's she doing?"

Jerrell muttered, "How do you think she's doing, idjit."

Jack keyed the mic and translated, "Make it one shake."

"Roger. 10-4," Crocker said, and Jack could hear the siren growing closer and just as they made it to the railroad tracks he could see emergency lights flashing.

Jerrell said with a shaking voice, "Don't give up, Shauny. You're going to be okay. I got you."

Shaunda let out a long breath, closed her eyes and lay her head on his shoulder.

Jerrell picked up his pace again, heading down the tracks in the direction of the ambulance. He yelled, "Come on Crocker. Get the lead out."

When they met the ambulance the paramedics popped the back doors. Jerrell helped paramedics put Shaunda on the wheeled gurney and load her into the back. Jerrell climbed in over the medics' protests. Jack shoved Jerrell's gun belt in the back.

Shaunda's eyes opened as a medic hooked up an IV. "Asshole stabbed me," she said. The medic was able to hook her to the monitors without removing the makeshift compress Jerrell had rigged.

Jerrell tossed his keys to Jack. A medic squeezed in past Jerrell. As the other medic prepared to shut the back doors Jack could hear Shaunda ask Jerrell in a weak voice, "Where's my gun?" and Jerrell's answer, "Shut up and hold still girl."

Chapter 27

Jack got on the walkie-talkie. "Murphy to Sergeant Crocker."

"Crocker," the sergeant said.

"Give any State Police or County Sheriff cars headed to our location a disregard." He listened as Crocker passed the 10-22—disregard the run—on to dispatch and other units. He then said, "Sergeant Crocker, please give Crime Scene and K-9 my location." Crocker passed the location on to Crime Scene and K-9.

Seeing the knife sparked a memory of a past injury. He fingered the thick white scar that started next to his ear and ran down his jaw and chest in a jagged almost life ending wound. He'd gotten the scar compliments of a career criminal named Bobby Solazzo. A stakeout had gone wrong. Two robbers were exchanging gunfire with SWAT while he'd chased Solazzo down an alleyway in a blinding rain. He remembered a lightning flash and the glint off the blade of Solazzo's knife as it came down across Jack's face. The memory still made his blood run cold, but he'd gotten off easier than Solazzo whose head he'd blown away much like the dead guy that Liddell was body sitting. Jack remembered lying in the alley, watching his blood mix with the heavy rain. It was a nightmare he often had. Knife wounds could be as fatal as bullet wounds. Sometimes worse. Internal bleeding, punctured intestine, infections. It could all be bad. He would rather face a gun any day.

He had to believe they had gotten Shaunda medical attention in time. The paramedic seemed to know what he was doing. Jerrell would keep her alive by sheer strength of will.

Something nagged the back of Jack's mind. When a case came to a positive result he always felt a rush. The bad guy was dead and maybe the cases were wrapped up but he didn't feel the rush. Maybe it was because he knew Shaunda would be facing a shooting board and a lot of criticism. It was a sad comment on the public's lack of belief in law enforcement.

Unfortunately for Shaunda this had to be handled as if it were a murder investigation with her as the suspect. He and Liddell would be involved. Toomey would hold their feet to the fire. This is exactly what Toomey had hoped to prevent. Toomey had sent them to solve a case, not kill a suspect. Especially not their lone suspect.

He called Liddell's cell phone. When Liddell answered Jack said, "Pizza Hut delivery. I can't seem to find your house."

"Oh, ha ha," Liddell said.

"I'm on the tracks," Jack said. "Jerrell left with the ambulance and the prognosis is good. Crocker is escorting them. Crime Scene is on the way and K-9 will be coming. Watch your six."

"What about you, pod'na. You don't have any safe place to hide when Rin Tin Tin gets there."

"I've got a gun and no conscience, Bigfoot. Just protect that scene as much as you can. Something's bothering me about this."

"I was going to talk to you about that."

"Let's compare notes later. I'm going to call Angelina and see if she has satellite imaging of this area. Maybe we'll get lucky and she's got the whole thing."

"Good idea. Warn her that I had to stop and take a number one in the woods," Liddell said.

"Great. We can get the photo blown up and hang it in the squad room."

"I'm sorry I mentioned it. I should have stopped Shaunda from going out on her own. I feel pretty bad she got hurt."

"She's hard headed, Bigfoot. You couldn't have stopped her without cuffing yourself to her. This is on her. The fact that we won't get to interrogate this guy is on her as well. If she would have stayed back and called for backup we wouldn't be doing this. I just hope to hell this guy is guilty of something besides being homeless."

"It was a righteous shooting."

"Probably. I've got to go," Jack said and disconnected as the K-9 and Crime Scene vehicles bumped toward him down the gravel.

Rusty got out of the K-9 vehicle first and approached, followed quickly by both CSU officers, Rudy and Barr. Rusty didn't waste any time. "Do you know where I'm going?"

"We came out of the woods right here," Jack said, pointing to a trail of blood droplets on the gravel leading back south. "Before you get going I need you to do me a favor."

Jack asked Officer Barr for a couple dozen marker flags in green, yellow and red. Barr got them out of the wagon and Jack handed them to Rusty. "Rinnie can discern between different scents, can't he?"

"Sure," Rusty said.

Jack told him about Jerrell carrying Shaunda out of the woods to the ambulance. He advised that it was just him, Jerrell and Shaunda and they'd stayed together.

Rusty said nothing. Rusty was a man of few words.

"Liddell is with a dead suspect. Liddell and Shaunda came across the tracks somewhere down there," Jack said and pointed east. "I was with Chief Jerrell. After we found her we came out right here to the ambulance. She's been stabbed."

Jack was kicking himself for not coming up with a better plan. They should have been able to see each other even if it was in the distance. The hitchhiker could have been just out of sight and they all would have walked right past him.

"Shaunda split off from Liddell when they crossed the tracks. According to Liddell she was heading southwest. By the time your chief and I made it to the tracks we heard two gunshots. We rushed in and found her about a hundred or two hundred yards in there. There's a huge poplar tree that uprooted. You can't miss it. The body is by the tree."

"Okay," Rusty said. "Flags?"

"There are going to be several scents to track. I want you to mark a trail from here to the scene. Crocker was at the scene but he left to direct the ambulance in. I'm not sure what direction he took."

Rusty said, "I'll use your scent to track back to the scene. It'll be mixed up with Chief Lynch's but that's okay. What else do you need?"

"Use green flags for the trail back to the scene. When you get there, you'll be able to pick up Shaunda's scent from her blood. Liddell can show you where she was. The body is near there. I want you to mark anywhere his scent takes you. His scent and Shaunda's should be together from the scene back to where she said she ran across him. Then I want you to mark Shaunda's trail from the scene back through the woods to the railroad tracks. Use green flags to mark our trail back to the scene, yellow flags for Shaunda and red flags for the suspect. Can you do that?"

"I can try. It might take a while if a bunch of you were back there."

"Do what you can. She's been hurt and a suspect's been killed." Jack didn't have to say there would be a shooting board.

"Want me to mark your partner's path too?"

"Not necessary," Jack replied.

Rusty raised a questioning eyebrow but didn't ask. He put Rinnie to work.

After the K-9 disappeared through the woods, Officer Barr asked, "What are you hoping to find?"

Jack didn't answer that question. He said, "Let's give the K-9 time to work and then all we have to do is follow the green flags back to the scene. Which is good because I probably couldn't find it again."

Ten minutes later Liddell called. "The K-9's been here and headed out on another track."

"How is the K-9 doing?" Jack asked.

"He had to take the dog about twenty yards away from here to get him on the scent again. Rinnie kept wanting to go behind the tree. The green flags end where we found Shaunda. He got on to the suspect's scent but the dog kept going around the tree. Rusty had to bring him back towards you to get on the track again. He put red flags for the suspect and then the red and yellow seemed to come in together back to the scene. I can't see or hear him anymore."

"Call when it's okay to come to you," Jack said.

"Oh, and something else, Rusty said the K 9 wanted to keep following a scent south. I think the creek is back there. He hasn't followed that up yet."

Jack thanked him and saw the Crime Scene officers had heard most of the conversation. They stopped and put their hard side cases down.

Jack said, "I'm just trying to cover all the bases guys."

"Sounds to me like you don't believe Shaunda's story," Barr said.

"It's Officer Barr and Rudy...uh?"

"Rudy Pitzer, Agent Murphy."

"I won't lie to you guys," Jack lied. "In a case like this we are ordered to follow procedures. I have final responsibility for the case. I have to justify the shooting. Understand?"

"Yeah sure," Rudy said.

Barr said, "It'll speed things up for us if we know where everyone walked. We won't have to search as wide an area as last time."

Officer Rudy Pitzer reluctantly agreed, but it was obvious he wasn't happy with the idea of treating another officer like a suspect. "It's a clear case of self-defense if you ask me."

Jack wasn't asking him. These guys hadn't been to the scene to decide what the case was. He hated lying to them. They were excellent Crime Scene officers.

Jack called Angelina.

She answered. "You didn't leave a working radio for me and I didn't think you'd want your cell phones ringing wherever the hell you are."

"We were tracking the guy that was seen out by the Humane Society," Jack said. "I was hoping you might be able to do me a favor."

"Hold on," she said and he heard keys clacking. She came back on the line. "I don't have anything in the sky over the area where your phone is. What happened? Did you lose him?"

"You haven't heard?" Jack asked.

"I told you. No radio. I figured you'd call if you needed my help."

Jack gave her a rundown. She said she would check to see if there were other eyes in the sky that had covered the area for the last couple of hours. She asked about Shaunda and Jack promised to keep her updated. He disconnected and called Jerrell who must have lit a fire under the ambulance driver because they were already at the hospital.

"What?" Jerrell said. He sounded angry and exhausted.

"How is she?" Jack asked.

"Meaner than a rattle snake," Jerrell said. "Tough as one too. The doctor said she just needs stitched up, plenty of liquids and they're putting her on antibiotics overnight. The knife hit her rib. She was lucky. They want her to spend the night. I'm staying until she gets settled and then I'm coming back to the scene. Where are you?"

"Still at the scene," Jack said. "I've got Rusty marking the trail with different colored flags in case we need that for a shooting board. You know what kind of questions they ask, Chief. Do you need K-9 somewhere else?"

"No. I don't. Feel free to order my troops around however you want," he said sarcastically. "You've got this under control. Find anything?" Jerrell asked.

Jerrell's voice wasn't trembling like when Shaunda was being put in the ambulance. If Jack had any doubt about those two having a romantic history, there was no doubt now. Tears had welled in Jerrell's eyes when he was carrying Shaunda out of the woods and he barely spoke. Not that it was a bad thing if the two were romantically inclined but their connection might have an impact on the current investigation.

Chapter 28

Jack and the two Crime Scene officers waited until they got the call from Liddell.

"K-9 was here and left again. He wasn't too happy."

"Not his problem," Jack said. "Are we safe to come in?"

Liddell answered, "Yeah, you're safe, but I didn't like the way that dog was looking at me."

Jack said, "Now you know how a double quarter pounder with cheese feels." Jack disconnected and said, "Safe to go."

Officers Barr and Rudy picked up their cases and headed out. They followed the trail of flags with Jack trailing behind.

"I read up on you this morning," Barr said to Jack.

"It's all lies," Jack said. "I was never there and I never had sex with that woman."

Barr snorted out a chuckle. Rudy grinned and said, "Spoken like a true cop. I wasn't sure if you really were a cop until now. Any chance we could get FBI badges?"

"Why would you want one?"

"Chick magnet," Rudy said.

"You're much better off just being a cop. Trust me. FBI stands for 'Functional But Incompetent.'"

"Federal Bureau of Idiots," Barr pitched in.

"Fancy Boys Incorporated," said Rudy. "No offense."

"None taken." Jack said, "My dad was a street cop for over thirty years and his dad before him. I'm mostly Irish with some Scottish mixed in. We came over from the old country. My great-great-grandpa was a horse thief. We had to move."

Rudy and Barr were laughing now. They told each other stories to kill the time and each story was a more blatant lie than the last. They saw Liddell waving them down.

"Your chief should be back shortly and..."

Jerrell came over Jack's radio. "I'm back. I see Rusty heading this way. I'll wait and see what he's got and he can direct me back there. I want to be there when Barr does his thing."

"We'll wait for Chief Jerrell," Jack said.

Crime Scene put on protective wear. Barr asked, "Did any of you touch the body?"

Jack said, "No one got that close. The chief lifted Shaunda. I guess he was the closest. Maybe two feet away."

"The knife and the gun are the only weapons?" Rudy asked.

Jack said, "As far as we know. We didn't touch the body. He was obviously dead unless he was a congressman. They don't need half their brains."

Barr seemed satisfied with that answer.

While Crime Scene worked, Jack and Liddell walked several paces away and spoke in lowered voices. Liddell asked, "What's bugging you, pod'na?"

Jack had his back to the Crime Scene officers and spoke in almost a whisper. "Let me walk through this and you jump in where you see fit.

"We heard two gunshots. Jerrell was with me. A few feet apart. We ran down the tracks in the direction of the shots and met you coming alone from about fifty to a hundred yards east of us."

"That's sounds right," Liddell said.

"Jerrell calls her on the radio. No answer. He calls her cell and she answers. She says 'I got him' and we find her over there about two feet in front of the body. Looks to me like he tried to crawl under the tree."

"Agreed," Liddell said.

Jack paused to organize his thoughts then went on. "Shaunda's bleeding from the right side of her chest. The right side of her jacket and sleeve are soaked with blood. She's acting like she's going into shock. Jerrell is more concerned about her injury than where the suspect is. He has to ask where the guy was. She said, 'I told you I got him.'

"We see the back of the head is blown out. He's more than dead. Where did the second shot go?"

"Maybe she fired a warning shot?" Liddell suggested.

Jack could see Barr and Rudy occasionally casting looks their way. He said, "Shaunda said she saw this guy. Told him to stop. He ran. She chased. He stopped and she thought he punched her in the side. She said she saw him draw his arm back, like he was going to hit her again. That's when she saw the knife and shot him in the face."

"Maybe she shot him twice and missed one of the shots?"

"She shot him point blank in the face, Bigfoot. The gunshots were close together. If she shot him in the face twice I don't think we would have found his head."

"Hard one to call, pod'na. Strange shit happens when you're fighting for your life. You should know that better than anyone. We've become hard after all the crap we've been through, but if this was the first time she shot someone, much less killed anyone, she may not be thinking straight."

Liddell was right. Jack hated to be suspicious. But there were other questions that added to the ones he was already asking. Each question brought up another one.

"The red marker flags are the suspect's. The yellow are Shaunda's. Hers seem to go behind the tree and then she's confronting him in front of the tree. Did she crawl underneath? Did he? Their flags don't converge until they are both in front of the tree. It doesn't show she was chasing him. Surely she'd remember if she ran around that big tree."

"What are you getting at?" Liddell asked.

Jack made sure the Crime Scene techs weren't watching them. He said, "What if she saw this guy first. What if she worked her way around the tree and waited for him. She comes around behind him. He turns. Bam! Bam! Bye bye."

"How do you explain her injury and the knife?"

Jack didn't know. Yet. He'd talk to Angelina about satellite imaging. Then he'd ask her to run a history on Shaunda, Jerrell, the Crockers, Ditty, Rosie and Pen and Patty just to cover the bases.

"There's little we can do here," Jack said. "We should find out when the autopsy is and be there for that. Then I guess we stop by the hospital and check on Chief Lynch."

"You mean interview her?"

"Can't slip anything by you, Bigfoot."

Jerrell came crashing up giving sidelong looks at the colored flags. "I was hoping you'd still be here. I'll take over and let you two go back and get your paperwork done. You're welcome to use the offices at the police station. I guess this wraps it up."

"Wraps what up?" Jack asked.

"This is the guy. Shaunda got him. End of story. Cases solved. Your boss will be happy that his little gal could test her whatchamacallit and you'll look good. I'll be happy because the town council can kiss my ass about the money spent."

"Chief, I think we might be premature calling the investigation off. This might or might not be the guy that visited Penelope or gave Cretin Brandon's cell phone. Even if it is it doesn't place him at any of the murder scenes. It would barely connect him to a stolen cell phone."

"Now why do you want to go and ruin my happy day?"

Jack could see the muscles in Jerrell's jaw working. The chief wanted nothing more than this to be the killer and, even more, the guy that had ambushed Shaunda.

"Chief, I just want to be positive we have the killer. If we don't there may be other victims. *That* would ruin everyone's day."

Jerrell said, "Yeah. Okay." He didn't sound convinced.

Jack said, "We have the drill bit from the campfire. We have the cell phones and the dispatch tapes. We need to get results back on those. After the autopsy we should send the drill bit to the FBI lab."

Jack asked Officer Barr, "Have you found any identification?"

Barr had stopped working and was watching the exchange between Jack and his boss. "Just a sec," Barr said, and felt inside the dead man's jean pocket. He removed a leather wallet. "Got a wallet," he said.

"Well, open it, numbnuts," Jerrell said.

Barr opened the wallet. "Here's a Tennessee driver's license in the name of Thomas Anthony Anderson. Address in Nashville."

Liddell took out his notebook and Barr gave him all the pertinent information. Liddell called Angelina. She retrieved the info in less than a minute. Liddell repeated what she told him.

"Thomas Anthony Anderson. The description matches the body. He has a record for vehicle theft. Possession of narcotics. Assault and battery on a police officer." Angelina said all that was from the same arrest. "Last arrest was a month ago in Louisville. Another vehicle theft."

Liddell held a finger up. "There's more." He listened. She gave him a list of addresses for Anderson, none of them in Indiana. Then she gave him a list of tattoos and he repeated them to Officer Barr. Barr nodded. "This is our hitchhiker."

Jack took the phone. "Angelina, where was he living during the other murders?"

"He's not your guy, Jack," she said. "I just checked prison records. He was in Angola Prison in Louisiana for the last six years. Was released three months ago. No record in Indiana. He doesn't have anything prior to that stretch. He might be responsible for Clint Baker in Illinois."

"Plus, the chief's son and the one today," Jack said.

"I'll see if I can find anything else to track him but the new system should have brought all that up."

Jack thanked Angelina and disconnected. "He was in Angola in Louisiana during most of the murders. He was released three months ago."

Liddell added, "Angola Prison is called the 'Alcatraz of the South'. Super maximum security prison."

Jerrell was quick to say, "He could still have killed my boy. She could be wrong. Never trust them damn computers. He could still be responsible for Brandon and the attack on Shauny. He's a drug dealer and car thief, and don't forget that battery charge."

Liddell's phone dinged. Angelina had sent him pictures of Anderson. He showed these to Jerrell and Jack.

Jack said, "Except for the hole beside his nose I'd say that's who we have here."

Jerrell agreed but said, "You haven't convinced me this isn't the guy that killed Brandon or assaulted Chief Lynch. Not by a long shot." He got on his cell. "Hey Ditty. I'm going to need you to stay there a bit longer." He put the call on speaker.

"Chief, I heard most of the radio traffic and kept it from the girls but Rosie's a different matter. Did you identify the knucklehead?" Sergeant Ditterline asked.

Jerrell told him and Ditty asked him to repeat it so he could write it down. "I'll stay with the girls, but Rosie got a phone call and shot out of here like her ass was on fire, if you'll excuse my language."

"You don't know where she went?" Jerrell asked.

"She just blew through the door without saying boo or howdy, Chief."

Jerrell said, "She's probably on her way to the hospital. You stay with the girls."

"Does Patty still need to stay here?" Ditty asked. "Her mom's wanting her to come home. Apparently, word is out about Brandon's death."

Jerrell said, "Her mom can come and get her. I don't think this had anything to do with the girls in the first place but you stay put. If you get hungry you can charge whatever you eat to me. Is that going to be a problem?"

"I'll stay with the girls until you say different, Chief. I'm not spending the night again, am I? If I am I'm smelling kind of ripe."

"I'll be there as soon as I can or I'll send a relief," Jerrell said and disconnected.

Jack's phone rang. It was Angelina. "I'm putting you on speaker Angelina," Jack said.

"I checked and there is not going to be any help from the eyes in the sky," she said.

"I need you to do something else."

"Shoot," she said.

"Do a thorough check of the following." He gave her the names of everyone involved in the case from the chiefs, officers, detectives, to the coroners. "I don't have identifiers on them."

"That won't be a problem. I have the case files. I can get the rest. When do you need this?"

"Yesterday."

"That's what I thought. I'll call. Oh, and by the way."

"What now?" Jack asked her.

"Your teenage victim, Brandon Dillingham."

"I'm getting older here," Jack complained.

"He's a father. I'll text you the information," she said.

"Well that little asshole," Jerrell said. "I wonder if Claire or Shauny knew about that? Now what?"

Jack said, "We'll go to Rosie's and show her Tony Anderson's picture. I'll text the photos to you and you can have one of your guys run Cretin down and show her. Let's hope there are prints from this guy on that phone at least."

Officer Barr said, "Chief, I got another tattoo here."

They all went to see. Barr was holding the suspect's right hand up. The letters T-O-N-Y were tattooed, one letter on each knuckle.

"Well, we don't need to show anyone pictures anyway," Jerrell said.

"Let's show the girls the photos anyway," said Jack. He believed in tying everything up in a neat bundle. He sent the photos to Jerrell's phone.

Chapter 29

The sun was setting and with it the temperature dropped almost ten degrees when Jack and Liddell hiked back to the Crown Vic. They got in the trunk for heavier jackets and put them on. Chief Jerrell had stayed with his Crime Scene unit. Rusty still had his K-9 partner out doing ever widening circular sweeps of the area hoping to come across another campsite like the one behind Rosie's.

"I forgot how far we'd walked," Liddell complained by the time they reached the parking lot of the Humane Society. Sissy of the blond and purple hair and large glasses was waiting for them.

"I heard gunshots," she said, her eyes made even larger by the glasses.

"It's all taken care of," Jack said. "You can unlock your doors and go about business. Thank you for calling us."

"Someone get killed?" Sissy asked.

Jack was tired. He didn't need the news media to start hounding him. He said, "Your name is Sissy, right?"

"Yep."

"Sissy, we're federal agents. The man you told us about was involved in a federal investigation that involves this county and Sullivan County. We have him in custody." *Dead.* "You can't tell anyone. Not a soul."

"Not a soul," Sissy repeated.

"Swear it," Jack said, with his most serious expression.

"I swear," Sissy said and held one hand in the air and the other on an imaginary bible.

"I'll make sure your assistance goes in our report to the FBI Director," Jack said.

Sissy's face split open in a grin. "You think I'll get on television?"

"Very possibly," Jack lied, "but not today. Remember, talk to no one about any of this. We weren't even here."

"Yes sir."

Jack and Liddell got in the Crown Vic, Jack driving. Jack said, "I swear she'll be plastered all over the local television tonight."

Liddell chuckled. "You were pretty impressive, pod'na. Maybe she'll wait a minute before she calls the news media."

"Let's go to Rosie's. We have to tell Penelope about her mom," Jack said.

"Did Jerrell say what hospital they'd taken Shaunda to?"

"Sergeant Ditterline should know," Jack said.

They bumped over the railroad tracks and took the narrow road to the Coal Miner Bar. They pulled in front and parked next to the Linton PD cruiser. Penelope opened the door. She had wheeled her chair to the doorway, her face pale with concern, lips thin and trembling. "Is my mom going to die?"

Sergeant Ditterline said, "Rosie heard most of it on my radio. Sorry. She flew out of here and I had to tell the girls."

"Understood," Jack said. "Penelope, your mom's going to be okay." He could see the relief on the girl's face.

"I thought…because you came, I mean. Mom says I watch too much TV."

"Your mom's at the hospital right now and being taken very good care of. Chief Jerrell went to the hospital with her."

"I want Chief Jerrell to take me to see her."

Jack said, "Chief Jerrell will be busy for a little while."

"But I want him to take me," she said, sounding like she was twelve and not seventeen years old.

"Rosie is going to be with her, hon. Sergeant Ditterline is going to stay with you," Jack said.

Ditty picked up the clue. "I'll be right here. We can play cards or do something fun."

"I want to see my mom," Pen said on the verge of tears.

From what Jack knew Pen was raised by her mother alone. It was always the two of them dealing with the crap life threw at them. They'd moved here and connected with Rosie. Now the girl was all alone in a place that might be familiar but still wasn't home. He imagined the panic that was running through the girl's mind at the possibility of her mother not coming back.

Jack came to a decision. He would take the girl to see her mother. It was the right thing to do.

"Get a jacket and something to read," Jack said to her.

Penelope raced through the batwing doors of the kitchen and soon Jack heard the whir of the elevator.

"Where's the other girl?" Jack asked.

Sergeant Ditterline said, "Her mother picked her up. I'll take Pen. She's my responsibility until Chief Jerrell says otherwise."

"You'd better check with the chief," Liddell said. "He's at the scene and might need another warm body." He realized what he'd just said. "Another officer to search the area. They still haven't found a campsite."

Ditty got on the radio to Jerrell and didn't get a response. The elevator started again while Ditty tried the radio. Penelope came back in the room and watched the men intently.

Ditty said, "I'll try his cell."

"There's no great immediacy to get to the hospital, Sergeant. Chief Jerrell wouldn't have left the hospital if she wasn't in good hands. Besides, he said she's a tough old bird."

Ditty agreed.

"Who's a tough old bird," Shaunda said from the doorway.

"Mom!" Penelope said, her strong arms working the wheels as hard as possible.

Shaunda and Rosie came inside. Shaunda was wearing a faded green hospital scrub top with Rosie's heavy button up sweater around her shoulders. She barely winced as she bent to hug her daughter.

Penelope drew back and tears ran down a smiling ecstatic face and the words exploded. "Patty already went home with her mom. Did you catch him? I'm sorry I talked to the guy. I didn't mean for him to hurt you. It's my fault."

Shaunda drew her daughter's head into her uninjured side and hugged her. "Never say that. It's not your fault that you're a good person. Sometimes bad people take advantage of goodness. You did nothing wrong, my precious girl," she said. Shaunda straightened up and gently lifted Pen's face. "You'll always be my little Tootsie Roll."

Penelope said, "I'm not a Tootsie Roll," and sniffled. "Where did he hurt you, Mom?"

Shaunda released her daughter and lifted the scrub top enough to show a thickness of white gauze.

"Did he shoot you?"

"No, I didn't get shot, nosy."

"Why is Aunt Rosie carrying your gun belt?"

Rosie pushed the gun belt in Jack's hands and said, "So I am. I hate guns. I don't allow them in here. Except for Johnny Law that is. I don't even like that."

Jack held the gun belt and saw the big revolver was missing from the holster. It would have been taken by Chief Jerrell to be tested against the bullet that killed Anderson. In its place a small five shot .38 caliber Smith & Wesson Chief Special revolver was strapped in loosely. No policeman that's been involved in a police shooting wants to go around disarmed after. No matter how many officers are around you it's comforting to have your own weapon handy. The public would never understand that need or agree, for that matter.

Jack had been involved in several gunfights. Each time the weapon was taken by a sergeant and given to Crime Scene for ballistics testing. Each time he'd slept with a backup gun under his pillow at night. It never changed.

Chapter 30

"I'll make my famous chicken and noodle soup," Rosie said. "It's always good for what ails you." She headed for the kitchen and Sergeant Ditterline loped off after her, insisting that he help.

Shaunda eased into a chair with Pen's wheelchair pulled close beside her.

Liddell excused himself to make some phone calls. Jack dragged a chair up next to Penelope. He found the photo of Anderson on his cell phone. "Penelope, is this the guy that came by your house a week ago?"

She took the phone. "That's the guy. Is he the one that hurt Mom?"

"Take another look at the picture. Are you sure this is the guy that came to your house?" Jack asked.

Shaunda said, "She already said it was. Leave her alone. He's the one. It's over. What else do you need?"

Jack calmly said, "I'll need to write a report and I want to cover all the bases. Have you ever been involved in something like this before?"

"No. I never want to again," Shaunda said. "End of subject."

"Well, I have been." He cleared his throat. "Can we talk alone for a few minutes."

Shaunda put a hand on Penelope's. "Why don't you help your aunt Rosie in the kitchen?"

Pen started toward the kitchen. "Yeah. I know. The grownups need to talk."

"That's right. Now git," Shaunda said.

When she was out of earshot Jack said, "Chief Lynch, I'm sure there will be some kind of investigation into the shooting."

Shaunda protectively put her hand over the bandage on her right side. "What do you think this is? He stabbed me. I protected myself. It was self-defense and no one can prove any different."

What she said bothered Jack. No one can prove any different was a statement that was made by many a guilty person. It was like starting a sentence with "I swear to God" or "I'm not lying" or "To tell the truth." It was a dare to Jack to prove she had done something. In Shaunda's case, she might have felt his incredulity at the scene. He had a niggling doubt that her story was the way things really happened but now she'd turned it up a notch.

He'd spent most of the day with her, but he really didn't know what made her tick. Outside of her daughter and her friend, what meant the most to her? Did getting beaten up put her on the dark path of revenge? Or someone threatening her daughter? He supposed, if he was in her place he might be out for blood. She had stated she was going to make the guy sorry. She'd just had a life or death situation and here he was asking questions. It's normal to be defensive. She was in law enforcement. She should know there would be questions.

Shaunda winced as she got up and said to Jack, "You won't be the one investigating the shooting. Why do you care? I read up on you. Jack Murphy. The hero who saved hundreds of lives on the Blue Star floating casino. How many people did you kill that day, Jack? Did you wait until they killed someone else before you put them down like the nasty turds they were? After all that you shot a fourteen-year-old girl. Three years younger than my Pen. And I'm just getting started."

Jack couldn't defend any of those incidents, except to say they were necessary, and who was to say Shaunda's shooting wasn't. Why hadn't she stayed with Bigfoot? And when she saw the suspect why didn't she just keep him in sight and call for backup. She knew the area. She knew the woods ended at Black Creek. They would have caught him there. Or they could have set a perimeter and found him. If she wasn't so convinced the hitchhiker was the serial killer would she still feel justified?

"You're ready for this to be over, aren't you?" Jack said, not rising to her bait.

"Damn right I am," she said. "I want a win. I want the murders to stop. I'm sick of all of this."

Jack saw desperation in her eyes and something else too. Rage. A fire was burning inside her and she was trying to put it out. He imagined he'd had the same look when the heat of battle made common sense, uncommon. When reason was on vacation. When stopping the fear and pain was all that was left inside. At the end of a warrior's mental rope is pure seething rage because that's all that will serve you.

He changed the subject. "I'm going to call Chief Jerrell and see how they're doing out there. You shouldn't be at the autopsy. You shouldn't go back to the scene. You do understand?"

"Don't worry," she said and started for the kitchen. "I'm done. I'm all in. I'm going to eat some miracle chicken soup and crash for twenty-four hours. I worked last night and all day."

Chapter 31

Jack and Liddell opted to skip the food. They said their goodbyes and assured Rosie they would be spending the night.

"Think she'll double the rate now, pod'na?" Liddell asked as they drove away.

Jack checked the rearview mirror and saw Ditty's car was still in the parking lot. Ditty was no longer on guard duty. He wondered why Jerrell wasn't calling all his troops back to the scene. He had the uneasy thought that Jerrell believed the investigation was at an end.

"Call Jerrell," Jack said. Liddell did and put it on speakerphone.

When Jerrell came on Jack said, "Hi Chief. We're just leaving Rosie's. Where we at on the scene?"

The line was silent too long and Jack looked at the screen to see if he'd lost the connection. Jerrell said, "We found a campsite."

Jack noticed Jerrell said "a" campsite and not "the" campsite. "It that good or bad news, Chief?"

"I'll tell you when you get here." Jerrell gave them directions from the railway tracks to where they were setting up a second crime scene perimeter and ended the call.

"Maybe he's found some evidence," Liddell suggested.

"Yeah," Jack said. In his gut he believed it was more than that. Jerrell sounded disappointed and hurt.

* * * *

Jack drove down the side of the railroad tracks heading to the place they'd entered the woods earlier. If the flags were still in place they could easily find their way back to the shooting scene. From there he watched for a glow in the woods from the floodlights Crime Scene would need.

Jack felt a cold spot in his chest, anxiety maybe. Neither Jerrell nor Shaunda seemed to be on board with Jack and Liddell running the investigation. It had been like pulling teeth to get information from them. They appeared to cooperate but he felt their resentment.

When Jack was still just a detective he always hated it when the feds horned in on one of his cases. He had resisted and gone around them most times. This felt different. It was almost like they didn't want these murders solved. Like they were just putting on a show and the FBI's computer analyst was all they wanted. Jerrell wanted to use Angelina to catch whoever had murdered his boy.

"Did you get the feeling from Jerrell and Shaunda that we were a surprise when we showed up?" Jack asked.

"They knew we were coming, so no."

"But when we first got there we had to engage in a high-speed chase with Jerrell."

"That was odd, I'll admit that. We have to remember his kid was killed the week before and he thought Shaunda had screwed up the investigation. I'm telling you pod'na, even if Anderson is the right guy, if he'd lived and gotten himself a half decent lawyer, they'd never make any of these cases stick."

Jack was silent.

"What are you thinking Oh Wise One?" Liddell asked.

"Nothing," Jack lied.

"C'mon. I know you. What?"

"I just think it's a little too convenient. Too much coincidence. We're pursuing a serial killer that's evaded police for seven years. They didn't even know they had a serial killer until Angelina got involved."

"They don't have our resources, pod'na. Give them a break."

"It's not just that. We barely get here and there's another murder. This time they find the victim's vehicle almost immediately."

"Luck."

"I don't believe in luck. I believe in what I can prove. We can't prove this guy did anything except have a cell phone that belonged to a dead guy and likes to live in the woods.

"You found the big coal mine drill bit. It matches the marks on the victims' heads. It even matches Shaunda's. That's evidence."

Jack stopped when they spotted the red marker flags. They got out and followed the flags until they met Officer Barr back at the shooting scene. Officer Barr pointed over the top of the fallen tree. "If you want the chief, he's up that way. Just before you get to Black Creek. Rusty put out flags for you city boys."

Jack and Liddell made their way around the massive root cluster of the downed tree and saw two sets of flags, one red, Shaunda's, the other yellow, Anderson's. The yellow flags led south deeper into the woods. The red flags stopped behind the tree. Liddell was the better tracker of the two but even he would not have found the campsite were it not for the flags.

Jerrell was alone, sitting on the ground, knees bent, army boots planted firmly, lit up by the crime scene floodlights. His attention was on something in his hand. "It belonged to my boy. His mother gave it to him when he turned thirteen years old. She sent me one while I was overseas."

Jack stood closer and saw that Jerrell held a gold chain with a gold pendant swinging from the end. The pendant was a soaring eagle. Jerrell reached in his shirt front and lifted out a gold chain with the same pendant.

"Where did you find it, Chief?"

Jerrell ignored the question. "I joined the Army when I was seventeen. My mom and dad had to sign me in because you had to be eighteen. Before I left for boot camp I gave my high school sweetheart a present. Troy Junior. When I found out Peggy, that was her name, was pregnant I married her. Troy was born on the base at Fort Campbell. Hell, we were still kids ourselves when we had him. Neither of us thought a thing about packing up and traipsing all over the country from one year to the next, one posting to the next."

"She finally had enough and moved herself and Troy back here to Linton. Said Army posts weren't a place where a kid should grow up. I stayed in the Army. He almost got a full ride to Notre Dame. My wife said he was one hell of a baseball player. I missed most of his games growing up because I was deployed. Always in some godforsaken country dealing with other people's problems, and not a clue what was going on at home. Troy started getting in trouble at school. Fighting. Drinking. Girls. He lost the scholarship, moved into his own place. I didn't know that for a couple of years. I was a horrible father. She got us matching necklaces one Christmas, I guess it was right before he moved out, maybe hoping it would make him stay home. I don't know. She said the necklaces were so we'd never forget we were connected. Troy never took his off. He still wore it up to when he…"

He looked at Jack and Liddell. "You don't want to hear all of this."

"We're really sorry for your loss, Chief," Liddell said.

"Now that you know my life story you can call me Troy. Not in front of my men," Jerrell said, the military man had reasserted himself.

Jack scanned the immediate area. He saw a place where the pine needles were matted down under a huge pine tree. It could have been a campsite, or the beginnings of one, or where deer had bedded down overnight. There was nothing to show a person had been here at all were it not for the yellow flags stuck in the ground. The campsite they'd found near Rosie's had a burnt-out campfire. There were no remains of a fire here. No backpack. No clothes, or food wrappers, or cigarette butts. If Anderson had come back here he maybe intended to bed down for the night but didn't get the chance before he was shot and killed.

"Did you find that here?" Jack asked Jerrell again.

"No. Barr found it in his pocket."

Jack wanted to remind him that was a piece of evidence and should have been collected and processed but the man was in no shape to even care.

Jerrell pocketed the necklace and got to his feet. "I was hoping we'd find something back here, but there's nothing. He was just setting up camp. He had some junk food in his jacket pocket and a pack of cigarettes and matches in his jeans. He must have been on his way back here when Shauny came up on him."

"She's at Rosie's with her daughter," Jack told him.

"Hardheaded. That woman is a danger to herself," Jerrell said.

"I don't think we need to stay here," Jack said. "Your guys already took pictures and collected whatever they could, didn't they?"

"Yeah," Jerrell said. "Guess I should have let Barr take that, but it won't matter. We got this guy nine ways from Sunday."

"You have another problem," Jack said.

"What do you mean?"

"Now you've got another death to investigate. We have to find definitive evidence Anderson killed the others."

"I don't believe you just said that. I've got the proof in my pocket. He attacked Shaunda at Dugger Lake and he tried to kill her here. He's got my boy's neck chain in his pocket. What more do you want?"

"I want what you want Troy. I want to catch the killer. Or killers. I don't want this psycho to stay free to kill again. I want to clear Shaunda of any wrongdoing on the shooting. I want all that done with no doubt in anyone's mind."

Jerrell remained quiet.

"We're going to continue with our investigation," Jack said. "You're free to believe whatever you want, Chief, but I don't believe this is our guy. At least not the guy for all the murders. He was in town according to Penelope around the same time your son was killed. He was here when Brandon Dillingham was killed. He had Brandon's cell phone. Your son's necklace was found in his pocket. We know he was in a deadly confrontation with Shaunda Lynch. That's all we know right now. We haven't talked to anyone that might be able to alibi him for the times of these murders and we know he was in Angola for at least three of them. Shaunda didn't see who hit her from behind or wrote on her shirt."

Jerrell's fists were clenching and Jack could tell he was about to go nuclear.

"To be frank, Chief, this crime scene doesn't explain some things. We need to take a statement from Shaunda. What she said back at the ambulance doesn't jibe with what's here."

"What do you mean?"

"Your K-9 officer marked our movements with flags," Jack said and paused. "If the dog is right, Shaunda was behind the tree at some point. That's not what she said. She said she caught up with him from behind and it all happened in front of the tree."

Jerrell hurriedly said, "Maybe she didn't tell us everything."

"You may be right. Until I know for sure we can't rule out that she shot him out of anger. Revenge. She truly believes he's the guy that hurt her and threatened her family. You heard what she said she was going to do when she caught up with him."

"She was stabbed," Jerrell protested. "Do you think…are you telling me she stabbed herself?"

"I'm not saying that." Jack had seen crazier things. "This doesn't end till the fat lady sings. Let it end with Shaunda being the hero, instead of a cop under suspicion."

Jerrell let out a breath and stood. "I can handle it from here. Thanks for your help. You're done here. I'll call your boss and take full responsibility."

"Not going to happen, Chief," Jack said.

Chapter 32

They left Officer Barr to work the crime scenes—the shooting location and the campsite—and hiked back to their vehicles. With Jerrell leading the way it took no time at all before they were pulling in front of the gray brick building that served as the Greene County morgue. Officer Rudy Pitzer, one of the Crime Scene officers, was waiting for them, holding the door open. He had followed the coroner's wagon that brought the body in.

"I didn't think you could get Dr. Daniels back in here tonight," Rudy said. "You feds must have some tall to get an autopsy that quick." 'Tall' is a term police use to mean influence.

Jack didn't tell Rudy that he'd called Director Toomey after they'd left Rosie's to update him. Toomey wanted the autopsy done pronto, and Toomey got what Toomey wanted.

Rudy led them into the autopsy room with a seemingly endless stream of chatter. "We already got him X-rayed and I collected the clothes and went through them. Did Chief Jerrell tell you about the necklace? Of course, he did. There wasn't any chance of getting fingerprints off something like that and it had special meaning to the chief." Rudy pulled a receipt pad from his shirt pocket and flashed it at Jack and Liddell. It was no doubt a receipt for the necklace containing the signature of Chief Jerrell. "I'll put that in my report. Just like it says."

They said nothing and Jerrell pushed past Rudy without commenting on the receipt.

Dr. Daniels was slipping X-ray films onto the lightbox. She motioned the men over. The deceased was laid out on one of the steel autopsy tables, the back of his neck propped up on a block of wood, arms at his sides. The back of his skull was ragged pieces of scalp and hair. Whatever evidence there was on his body or clothes had already been collected and bagged by Rudy. Several paper grocery sacks were folded closed and sat out of the way against a wall.

"Your boss can be a very convincing guy," Lacy Daniels said to Jack. She wasn't smiling.

"Welcome to the club," Jack said. "Is this guy going to live?"

"Very funny, Agent Murphy. She pointed to a side view of the skull in the X-ray. "About four inches diameter of skull was blown out, and maybe a third of his brain went bye-bye with it."

"Where we work, losing thirty-three percent of your brain would make him a captain," Liddell said. No one smiled but Rudy.

Lacy pointed at several places on the X-rays, speaking in medical lingo that Jack couldn't spell or much less care to.

"In a nutshell, doc. Please," Jack said.

Lacy said slowly. "Gunshot. Forehead. Explode brain. Dead."

"Were there any signs of a struggle?" Jack asked unperturbed by her sarcastic streak.

"I didn't find anything on the cursory examination to make me believe he had been in any altercations recently. However, he has several old bruises, cuts and scrapes that have scabbed over, and there is petechial hemorrhaging in the eyes. Of course, the petechiae could be explained by the pressure caused when the bullet tore through the skull. I'll have to crack him open to give an informed opinion." Petechiae are ruptured blood vessels in the white of the eye.

She was once again wearing the white lab coat, but the gray scrubs had been replaced by a sheer black dress that stopped just above the knees showing off perfect legs. Her jet-black hair was down around her shoulders and fell across one eye.

"Did we interrupt your evening, Dr. Daniels?" Jack asked, nodding to her dress.

"I do have a life outside of death," she said.

"I'm not arguing, doc," Jack said.

"There's gloves and gowns over there if you need them."

"I'm good, doc," Jack said. "I won't touch anything."

Liddell put on gloves. Jerrell stepped back to the wall, arms crossed.

"Let's do this," she said and they stood on the opposite side of the autopsy table while she briefed them.

The body was that of a malnourished twenty-three-year-old male with bruises on his stomach, chest, arms, right shoulder, back, backs of his thighs and calves. There were numerous shallow cuts that were scabbed

over. Scrapes on his left knee and shin, bottoms of both elbows, and a
nasty road rash on the side of his right hand. The bruises were long and
wide. He'd been beaten with something shaped like a club or stick. The
top of his right shoulder was bruised and swollen.

"How old are these injuries?" Jack asked.

"The cuts and bruises are about five to seven days old except for the
one on top of the shoulder. It's more recent. Hard to say. Cause of death,
like I said, is the gunshot to the face."

"You said gunshot. Just one," Jack said.

"One was enough."

"It couldn't have been more than one?" Jack persisted.

"Not unless more than one bullet went through his face."

Jack didn't see stippling on the flesh around the wound. If the shot was
fired up close, say within three feet, there would be some signs of the burnt
gunpowder stuck to the skin.

"Can you guess the range?" Jack asked.

"I've seen a few of these. I'd say the distance from the gun to the victim's
face was two to three feet," Dr. Daniels said.

Jack thought it was more distant than that. Jerrell did too by the look he
gave Dr. Daniels. "Can you show us the trajectory of the bullet?" Jack asked.

Lacy took them to the X-rays and pointed to a side view of the skull. The
bullet entered just to the right of the nose and angled slightly upward. Lacy
lay a pencil across the X-ray to show where the trajectory was indicated.

"Rudy, where do you think this guy was when he was shot?" Jack asked.

"What do you mean, Agent Murphy?" Dr. Daniels asked.

"Sorry. Was he standing, sitting, lying on the ground? Did you find the
bullet or pieces of the skull?"

"We didn't find a bullet or any tissue or skull pieces on the tree that
would have been behind her. He must've been standing like Shaunda said."

Jack wondered how Rudy knew what Shaunda had said. Rudy wasn't
there when the ambulance arrived. Jack knew he and Liddell hadn't said
anything in front of Rudy.

"Chief, you have Chief Lynch's revolver," Jack said. Not a question.

"It's locked up until my guys are ready to do ballistics. Why?"

"I was just wondering how many shots were fired. I heard two," Jack said.

"I didn't tamper with the gun to check. There was a spent round in
the cylinder. I'm assuming there's another under the hammer. I heard two
shots as well."

Jack asked, "Drugs?"

Dr. Daniels said, "Toxicology won't be back for a few days."

"Brandon Dillingham had needle marks. Does this guy?" Jerrell asked.

"As I said, I haven't done the post yet."

"Did you examine him for needle marks?" Jack asked.

"Not yet. I will call you when I'm ready to do the post and you'll be able to see for yourselves."

"We'll wait," Jerrell said.

"You can sleep in your cars if you want. I'm going out for the evening. Can't this wait until in the morning?"

"Of course," Jerrell said contritely.

"I'll call the director of the FBI and tell him we're spending the night in your office," Jack said.

Dr. Daniels stormed out of the room. The sounds of locker doors banging could be heard. She came back in wearing scrubs and protective gear.

They all stepped back to let Dr. Daniels have room to work. She was fast and precise. The autopsy was completed quickly.

"In layman's terms," she said, "he died of a single gunshot wound to the face, entering to the left of the nose, traveling through the brain and taking a large part of the brain out the back of the skull. It was a large caliber. That's all I can say about that. There are no fragments of the bullet left behind and no stippling around the entrance of the wound or on the face."

"Can I see the bottoms of his hands?" Jack asked.

Rudy positioned the right hand, palm up and then the left hand.

"Okay?" Lacy asked.

"That's all I needed," Jack said. "Now can I look at his shirt and pants?"

Rudy looked at Chief Jerrell who nodded. Rudy brought one of the paper grocery sacks over to Jack and Liddell and opened it. He pulled out a black T-shirt that was worn thin. It was imprinted with zombies and a title. "The Walking Dead."

Rudy said, "He was wearing a white, or at least it was at one time, button up shirt over this." He opened a second paper sack and lifted out a long sleeve shirt. There was blood on the collar and a small amount in a downward pattern on the middle of the front.

Rudy opened a third sack and held up a pair of worn-out, filthy, gray colored blue jeans. The pockets had been turned inside out.

Rudy then opened a fourth sack and took out a dirty blue jean jacket. The elbows were shredded.

Jack examined all of these closely without touching them and without speaking.

"Satisfied?" Jerrell asked him.

"That does it for me, Chief," Jack said.

"Well?" Jerrell asked.

"I need to think about all of this. We'll talk in the morning."

"Well, if you gentlemen are done, I need to close this guy up," Lacy said.

Liddell gave her a business card. "Can you send us a copy of your report to my email?"

Lacy said, "On one condition. Don't call me again tonight. I've got a date and now I'm going to have to go home and shower and change."

Jerrell followed Jack and Liddell outside.

"Agent Murphy, there's nothing to think about. Shaunda shot him in self-defense. That's what it will say in my report. Anything else is pure speculation on your part and I don't even want to hear it." Jerrell went back inside.

Jack was sure that no one in a four county area wanted to hear anything to the contrary. Except maybe the news media. They fed on this stuff.

"He didn't ask for our portable radios," Liddell commented as they got back in the Crown Vic.

"That may be all we get from him for a while," Jack said.

"Do you really think Shaunda executed that guy?" Liddell asked.

Jack drove away from the curb. "Let's go eat. Then we need to discuss this."

"Now you're talking, pod'na. I thank you and my stomach thanks you."

They were halfway through Linton before they spoke again, each lost in their thoughts.

Jack had spoken to Director Toomey and Toomey agreed they needed to continue the investigation to Jack's surprise. Apparently, word hadn't yet reached Chief Jerrell's father that Jerrell was satisfied he had the guy that had killed Troy Junior. Jerrell's father had enough clout to get an expensive FBI operation launched, he could change his mind. When that happened Jack didn't know if Toomey would change his tune and demand their immediate return to Evansville and an end to the investigation. *Screw that.*

"Let's check on Angelina," Jack said. They were a block from the police station.

They found Angelina at the Linton Police Department, packing up her computers and gear.

"Where are you going?" Jack asked her.

"Jerrell called and told me you got the guy. He's considerate, unlike some detectives," she said.

"Did you check with Director Toomey?"

"What do you think?" she answered.

"He didn't tell us you were being pulled," Jack said. "We might still need you here. We're going on with the investigation."

"I know." Angelina wrapped up some power cords.

"If you don't mind staying I'll call Toomey and get the okay."

She put the power and various cords in a large hard side case with computer accessories Jack couldn't identify. "I'm going to set up again, but not here. Jerrell had suggested I stay in a cottage at Pleasant Grove Farms in Lyons. It's about a twenty-minute drive from here. Toomey paid for a week and I plan to take advantage of every minute. It's beautiful out here and I haven't had a vacation in forever. Besides, Mark is at some police thing for a few days and I hate cooking for myself. I'm going to get some takeout, check in, and watch *The Voice* on television. If you need me you know how to reach me."

Chapter 33

Jack and Liddell helped Angelina carry the equipment out to her car. After she drove away Jack called Rosie.

"Agent Murphy," she answered. "I guess you'll be checking out."

"Actually, I thought we'd stay the night."

"Yes. Of course. Good. You can help me talk some sense into Shaunda. She wants to take Pen and go home. She can't even drive."

"Put her on the phone," Jack said. He heard Rosie call Shaunda. Rosie said, "It's a man. He wants to talk to you." Shaunda came on the line.

"What do you want now?" Shaunda asked.

"I want what everyone wants. World peace," Jack said.

"Ha ha. Now leave me alone. I'm taking my daughter home."

"Not a good idea," Jack said. "Pen doesn't have a driver's license and you aren't in any shape to drive. You need to rest. The pain will get worse before it gets better and you'll need someone to bring you alcohol. She's not old enough."

This got a chuckle out of Shaunda.

"We're going to stay the night at Rosie's," Jack said. "We've got a ton of paperwork to do and we'll have to give a report to Chief Jerrell on the incident."

"You want to ask more questions," Shaunda said. "I'm not stupid. I know this part is going to be nasty. I have nothing to hide."

"Maybe you should get an attorney, Shaunda. It doesn't mean you did anything wrong. It's just the smart thing to do before you talk to anyone."

"Then you won't mind if I do this," she said and the line went dead.

"She hung up on you?" Liddell asked.

Jack put the phone in his pocket.

"You didn't ask Rosie if we could eat there."

"I didn't want to push things," Jack said.

"Well, I'm hungry," Liddell grouched.

"If Rosie doesn't offer anything we'll get takeout."

"Or," Liddell said, "we could stop on the way there and sit down and eat like real people. You know. Use real silverware and eat off of real dinner plates. Maybe get some dessert that doesn't have Ronald McDonald on the cardboard wrapper."

"She's wanting to go home. If she leaves before we get there and we go to her house she'll think we're investigating her."

Liddell said, "Aren't we?"

"Well, yeah."

"You're going to question a woman that's been beaten unconscious, then later stabbed, killed someone and to top it off she's the Chief Constable. You're going to do this with her handicap daughter present?"

"Yeah."

Liddell turned the car around and headed back toward Linton. "I'm going to keep you from doing something you'll regret. We're going to Pizza Hut, have a couple of brews and talk this out. Then let's go back, get some sleep and leave that poor woman alone for tonight at least."

Jack gave in. They went to Pizza Hut and ate, but they didn't have any beer and they talked very little. Angelina called and was excited about her cottage. She said there was another cottage for rent on the property. Jack declined. Murphy's Law says, *"Keep your friends and your enemies equally close in case you have to shoot one of them."* Right now, he wasn't sure who was who. He'd stay near Shaunda.

When Jack and Liddell returned to the Coal Miner Bar the sun was already down and there were no floodlights outside. Lights were on in the downstairs but it was dark upstairs. Shaunda's Tahoe was parked next to Jerrell's Ford F250 4X4. On the other side of the Ford a white Geo Metro mini-car was almost hidden by Jerrell's massive truck.

Jack called Angelina and had her check out the owner of the Geo and run some background histories. He was still talking to Angelina when the door to the bar opened and Jerrell stood in the light.

"Thanks Angelina. Get back to me when you get the rest."

"Who owns the Geo?" Liddell asked.

"Somebody named Lizzy Parson. Let's go see what they have to say," Jack said and they went inside.

Jerrell greeted them with, "I thought you guys had given up and gone back to the big city of Evansville."

"The rooms are paid for tonight so we thought we'd take advantage of the government's generosity. Rosie said we could stay as long as we wanted. Is there a problem?"

"Not with me there's not. Have you boys eaten? Rosie made pizza and I can tell you it's to die for," Jerrell said.

Rosie was behind the bar. She said, "Kitchen's closed, but I can heat you some of the leftovers if you want?"

Jack ignored her and asked, "Who's driving the Geo out there?"

A slight man in his mid sixties to early seventies came forward. He had a thick head of wavy white hair and wore bell-bottom blue jeans and a Linton-Stockton High sweatshirt. "That'd be me," he said and introduced himself.

"Detective Bob Parson. Retired from Greene County Sheriff's Department. Sorry I couldn't be here before now. I was in a trial on an old case and will be back there in the morning. Chief Jerrell called and told me you caught the guy."

Jack remembered Parson was the Greene County Detective that had worked the Leonard DiLegge case. "Leonard DiLegge, aka Wizard?" Jack said.

"That's right. I retired after that one. I knew Wizard from my days working in Narcotics," Parson said. "I was the reason he was in prison. Then they moved me to Violent Crime unit right when he got out on parole. I always knew he'd turn up dead somewhere. I shouldn't say it but I'm not sorry the bugger drowned."

Jack said, "Detective Parson, I'm glad you came, but I think it's a little premature to say we caught the guy that killed DiLegge."

Parson said, "Troy, you told me this was definitely the guy. Son, I had that one cleared as an accidental drowning. What's going on?"

"Don't ask me, Bob. Ask them," Jerrell said. "You said you've seen this Anderson guy out in the county before. You said he's been bumming around out there for a couple of years."

Parson said, "Oh, yeah. The guy you described is a vagrant. I had a couple dozen calls on him stealing out of people's gardens and taking clothes and such. Even broke into a shed about five or six years ago and made himself at home."

Jack pulled up the BMV picture of Anderson on his cell phone. "What about this guy?" he asked Parson.

Parson took a long time before saying, "Can't honestly say I recognize this guy, but it could be him. I never really saw the guy up close and personal. I just had his description from other deputies and the people that called in on him. He's been out there at least five or six years."

Jack took the phone back. "Do you know if he was ever arrested?"

"I'm retired," Parson said. "I wouldn't be here now if you hadn't told me you got him, Troy. I'm getting back home. Good luck with this mess."

Parson walked out and Jack heard the lawnmower engine of the Geo start up and fade away.

Jack heard the elevator humming the doors open and Shaunda came from the kitchen. "Let's get this done. I've got Pen to bed and I want to get some sleep. It's been a very long day."

Jack said, "I don't have any questions tonight. I think we're done for today."

"Amen to that brother," Jerrell said and walked behind the bar. He put a bottle of Scotch and several glasses out before Rosie pushed out from behind the bar.

"I'll do that. This is still my place, and I think we all need one."

Chapter 34

Jack woke well before sunup after a restless night. He'd had too much Scotch. He missed Katie. He hated what he was thinking and what he might have to do. It wasn't the first time he was sick of being a cop.

He'd asked Angelina to do an extensive background on Shaunda Lynch and Rosie Benton. He'd learned that Shaunda's parents were not legally married, and ironically, they were religious chauvinists up to the day they died five years past. An aunt was the only living family left besides Shaunda and Penelope. What was most interesting was the aunt, Eunice Lynch, who, according to Angelina had never married, lived in Hutsonville, Illinois.

Jack had taken the address and telephone number down and intended to visit Eunice Lynch this morning. Angelina couldn't find much else on Shaunda besides the school records at Union High School that showed Shaunda had left school at the end of her junior year and didn't return. Angelina was unable to find out if Shaunda had enrolled in another school, and due to her age, there was no financial paper trail. Angelina was still digging.

However, there was a font of information on Rosie Benton. She had completed high school at Union and went to Indiana University where she obtained a bachelor's degree in psychology with a minor in history. She had also earned a bachelor's degree in business administration and was well on her way to an MBA when she suddenly dropped out five years ago. That was coincidentally the same time that Shaunda had moved back to Dugger, and Rosie had become the owner of the Coal Miner Bar three years before that. Rosie's parents were also deceased and she was an only child.

There were a few newspaper articles concerning Shaunda's occasional mention in reference to Dugger town business. There was an article in the

Sullivan Times touting Rosie's academic accomplishments after graduating from Union High, but nothing after she dropped out of her MBA program.

Angelina was trying to come up with the name of someone Jack could talk to about Rosie, but she had come up empty. Both women had spotless records.

Jack's phone showed it was 5:30 in the morning. He could hear Liddell snoring like a buzz saw across the hall. He got up, showered and dressed in clean clothes. He rolled up the dirty ones and stuffed them in one side of his bag. He hadn't thought to bring a second sport coat, or jacket for that matter. He had thought he could run back to Evansville if he needed more clothes. Bad idea.

He went downstairs to make some coffee. He was in luck and Rosie had an old Mr. Coffee. He scrounged around in the cabinets and found coffee but no filters. He used a paper towel for one and was soon smelling the wonderful aroma of coffee. Now all he needed was some Alka Seltzer.

He poured a mug of coffee, took it out to the barroom and sat by a window. The horizon was all trees, with a luminescent glow rising in the east. This time of morning was always his favorite time of day. Coffee, sunrise, quiet.

His thoughts turned to Rosie, to Shaunda and Jerrell. There was an unspoken bond between them all. It was as if they had been friends forever. Friends that were occasionally mad at each other. Friends that verbally abused one another and seemed to enjoy the playfulness.

Angelina had performed a search and could not find any marriages for Rosie or Shaunda or Troy Junior. Jerrell had been married for quite a while, but as he had said, he was absent most of the time. The only victim that was married was Baker in Hutsonville. Baker's wife wasn't a widow for long. He knew Chief Jerrell's ex-wife's name was Peggy. Peggy had no record, was remarried, lived in Atlanta, had a fourteen year old daughter and taught grade school. Sixth grade just like Katie. He couldn't imagine Peggy as a serial killer.

The door to the stairs opened and Bigfoot plodded toward the kitchen. He came back with a steaming mug. He'd found donuts somewhere and brought a couple out on a plate and sat down across the table from Jack. He offered one of the donuts to Jack who declined, then took one to Liddell's disappointment.

"Couldn't sleep?" Liddell asked.

"You didn't seem to be having any trouble by the sound of it."

"I don't snore."

Jack said, "You're right. That's not what I'd call that noise."

"What was with all the questions at the morgue, and then you didn't ask Shaunda anything?" Liddell asked.

"Did you notice which side Shaunda wears her gun on?" Jack asked.

"Right."

"She's right handed," Jack said.

Liddell found the donut more interesting than Jack.

"Where was her stab wound? Which side?" Jack asked.

"Her right side," Liddell answered.

"Did you notice at the autopsy if this Anderson guy was right or left handed?"

Liddell put the donut down. "I didn't notice."

"His right hand was calloused more than his left. I'm going to bet he's right-handed."

Liddell pushed the donut away. "Where we going this morning?"

"Hutsonville."

"Hutsonville?" Rosie said from the stairway. "In Illinois? What's in Hutsonville?"

Rosie's makeup was perfect as was her hair. She was dressed in tan slacks and a blue wool turtleneck sweater. She stood in the doorway waiting for an answer.

"I hear they're famous for kettle corn," Jack said.

"I haven't had my caffeine yet. Save your jokes for later." She went to the kitchen and came out with coffee and sat at the table with them. She held up a finger for them to wait. She took a sip of coffee, made a face, and said, "Who made this crap? It tastes like paper towel. Weak paper towel."

"I couldn't find your coffee filters," Jack said.

"I'm kidding," Rosie said. She put a hand on Jack's arm and left it there. "I use paper towels, too, and make it twice this strong. I'll put on another pot before Shaunda and Pen come down."

Jack said. "We're going to be leaving in a few minutes."

"For Hutsonville?" Rosie said. "You're not joking?"

"We have to find the scene where one of the victims was found," Jack said.

"Was that a recent one?"

"It's a seven year old case."

"What do you expect to find seven years later?" she asked. "Oh wait. Was this guy married? I'll bet the killer is his wife. I know I've felt like killing some of the guys I've dated."

"He was married," Jack said. "I don't think the wife killed him but if you're confessing..."

Rosie laughed and snorted into her coffee. "Now look what you made me do. This crap tastes so bad I don't even consider pouring it out wasted. I'll go make some real stuff now. Hang around a bit. I want to get caught up." She headed to the kitchen.

"I like her," Liddell said.

"You like anyone that feeds you, Bigfoot. You're like a dog."

"Am not."

"We can get coffee on the road. If you've got your stuff, let's go."

Liddell finished the coffee in one gulp and stood. "I was born ready."

Jack collected their mugs and the empty plate and sat them on the bar. They made it to the door when Shaunda came down the stairs.

"Where are we going?" she asked. She had on a clean uniform, sans badge. Her gun belt was draped over one shoulder. She moved stiffly but there was no other sign that she'd been beaten and stabbed yesterday.

"We're going to follow up on something," Jack said. "You should get some more rest. You can't even patrol Dugger in your condition."

"Joey's going to patrol," she said. "I can't stand to sit around. What are you following up on? Or is it a secret?"

"It's not a secret," Rosie said from the kitchen batwing doors. "They're going to Hutsonville, Illinois to badger a dead guy's wife."

"I've got a Girl Scout badge in badgering," Shaunda said.

"She really does," Rosie agreed.

"We're not going to badger anyone," Jack said. "We're just following up on the earlier information. It's been seven years. Probably nothing to find."

"If you're going to waste your time, I've got plenty to waste. Besides, there are two of you big bruisers to protect me. All I have here is this pitiful excuse for a bartender."

Jack gave in. "No guns allowed. I don't want you getting any more hurt."

Shaunda handed her gun belt to Rosie, saying, "Will you feed Pen when she gets up? Don't throw those hospital scrubs away. I might need them again."

"Very funny," Rosie answered. "Get out of here."

Chapter 35

Shaunda climbed into the back behind the driver's side. Jack was driving and Liddell had the passenger seat pushed all the way back. She said, "Thanks for letting me tag along."

They were soon on State Road 54 headed west toward the Illinois state line. Angelina had supplied Jack with GPS coordinates of where the body was found, and an address for Shaunda's aunt. Speaking to the aunt wasn't possible this trip but they could view the scene, plus he thought it would give him a chance to get Shaunda to talk. He was wrong about the latter. She spoke very little until they reached the narrow two lane concrete bridge that crossed the Wabash River into Illinois.

"I don't feel as bad as I thought I would," she said. "The stitches are holding. They haven't started to itch like the doctor said. I took a handful of ibuprofen but I haven't needed any of the OxyContin they gave me at the hospital ER. We should have waited for Rosie to make coffee. She has to-go cups."

Jack was half listening and trying to pay attention to the GPS directions on his phone.

"What's really hard is the waiting," she said.

"Waiting?" Jack asked.

"You know. Waiting for all this to be over. I mean the whole enchilada. Not just Brandon. The guy I shot. I had to shoot him. You believe me, don't you?"

"What I believe doesn't really matter," Jack answered.

"What an asshole," Shaunda muttered just loud enough for Jack to hear.

"Why don't you tell us what happened. We haven't heard it all," Jack said.

"Where do you want me to start? Don't start with the attorney shit. Okay?"

"Okay," Jack said. "Why don't you start with the dumb idea of splitting up with Liddell?"

"You got me there. That was a dumb move. I really wanted to find this guy. I mean, if he's the one that hit me and threatened my baby girl, I had to know."

Jack translated that as meaning that she was afraid if she found him while she was with Liddell that Liddell would have kept her from bashing this guy into a confession.

"I got in the trees and imagined which way the guy would go. I was right. I saw some weeds tramped down, and scuff marks where the dead grass was kicked out of the dirt. I followed that but I lost it. I just got lucky and spotted him off to my right. I tried to flank him. He must have heard me because he started walking faster. I had to run flat out to keep up and I know he had to hear that. I cut across and just about caught him but he was faster than I thought. I grabbed for his jacket and he twisted away. I grabbed for him again and he stopped like he was going to give up. He was fast. He turned and punched me in the side. He was getting ready to do it again and I saw the knife. I had my gun out and shoved it in his face and pulled the trigger. I don't really remember all of it. It happened so fast. I don't even remember drawing my gun. I thought he'd punched me. Then I saw the knife."

Jack hoped Liddell had listened close because she was rambling and he didn't want to ask questions until she was talked out.

"I had to shoot him," she said and went quiet.

"You didn't hear us calling you on the radio?" Jack asked.

"I don't know. Maybe. I just remember hitting the ground. Then I pulled myself up. I saw him lying there and the knife was still in his hand. I might have moved it. I was scared. He tried to kill me. He would have killed me. I could see it in his face."

"You saw his face before you shot him?" Jack asked.

"Yes. No. I mean, I think I did. It's all messed up. I killed him."

In the rearview mirror Jack saw tears running down her cheeks. If she was acting, she was damn good.

"Do you remember how many times you fired the gun?" Jack asked.

"I'm not sure. I just remember his face when I shot him. I'll never forget his expression."

"Listen, Shaunda. I'm sorry for being a dick. I guess I've gotten paranoid. We really needed to talk to this guy."

"I know," she said. "I'm sorry. I should have stayed with my partner. It was a dumb, stupid, asinine thing to do. I don't blame you for thinking that I was..." Her voice trailed off.

"That you deliberately killed him?" Jack finished for her. He could hear a dry sob.

She said, "Yeah. That. I don't know. Maybe I wanted to kill him."

Jack turned his head toward her. "Don't say that unless you mean it. Don't say that to anyone else. You hear me."

"Yes."

"Now let me concentrate on the road. I hate these electronic thingies and this one is getting on my last nerve," Jack said.

Liddell reached over and took the phone from him. "I'll navigate."

"'Bout time," Jack said.

They followed the directions through the east end of Hutsonville and turned right onto North Pleasant Street and right again at Mill Street which according to the map was a dead-end. It was. At the end of the road they all got out. Liddell led the way using the GPS coordinates Angelina had given them. They walked through a dense area of trees and Jack could feel the ground getting softer until they were into mud. Through the branches Jack could see a little wash just ahead. It was like a pond, an overflow from the Wabash River.

"According to Angelina the body was found right over there about twenty feet," Liddell said.

Shaunda said, "If you want to wade through the mud be my guest. I'm not changing clothes again."

"Not me," Liddell said.

They headed back to the car. Jack thought he would have to call the detective or Crime Scene officers to get a better feel for the scene and for the victim. The ground was soft. Surely Crime Scene had gotten shoe impressions. He was leaving perfect ones. It was March when the murders happened and it was March now. The weather may have been similar. The ground was wet but not sloppy until you got close to the water where the body was found.

"Had enough?" Shaunda asked Jack when they got back in the car.

"I've got the victim's old address," Jack said. "Angelina said it's almost three miles as the crow flies. Five by road. His car was still at his house when his body was found."

They drove the route the victim might have taken if he was on foot. If he was in the trunk of a car the route was anybody's guess. Jack stopped the car and let Liddell drive. Shaunda had to move over in the back seat.

Backtracking to SR 54 Jack told Liddell to turn right towards the heart of downtown Hutsonville. He gave Liddell the address and Liddell pulled it up on Jack's cell phone.

"What are you hoping for?" Shaunda asked.

"Surveillance cameras, and homes where rich or elderly people might live," Jack said.

"I think I get the cameras but why rich and elderly?"

"The rich are more likely to have alarm systems and cameras. The elderly may not have cameras but they have great memories and they see more than other people do. A strange car down a back road like the one we just took to the river for example. They also pay attention to the news, read the newspaper."

"See anything?" she asked.

Jack turned to face her. "I didn't see anything promising. Most likely the detectives canvassed all this and didn't find anything either. There's nothing in the reports that said they did or didn't do a sweep."

Shaunda leaned back against the seat and closed her eyes.

"Do we need to go back?" Jack asked her. "You're hurting."

Shaunda took a deep breath and let it out. "I'm okay. Let's see this house."

Liddell followed the GPS directions and after zigging and zagging down some side and back streets they pulled up in front of an old Victorian style home in a neighborhood of homes built only feet apart.

Jack said, "I talked to Angelina and she had done a little more digging on Baker. He didn't have much in the bank but he was within walking distance of the high school where he worked as a janitor. He was a substitute teacher at Union High School when you were there. Do you remember him?"

"Do you remember all your teachers?" she asked.

"He was part time until about six months before his body was found. There's nothing on record of why he left the Hutsonville school. He was let go by Union High School for keeping a common nuisance at his home. Underage parties, drugs, drinking, exploring," Jack said.

"Exploring," Shaunda repeated. "That's a nice way of putting orgies and rape. He was probably up to the same garbage here. Guys like that don't stop."

"Like Brandon?"

"Brandon was a predator. He wouldn't have stopped."

"Unless someone stops them," Jack added.

Shaunda faced the car window and remained silent.

The house where Baker lived had kids in it now. There were toys all over the front yard. Two bicycles. One adult sized, one tiny with a pink basket and pink streamers coming from the handlebars.

"Want to talk to the owners?" Liddell asked.

"According to Angelina the family has only been here two years. It's a rental."

"Next stop?" Liddell asked.

"We have the address of the widow," Jack said. "Let's see what she has to say."

Liddell drove back to West Clover Drive which was on SR 54 and headed west into more farm country. Most of the fields were still being cultivated in readiness of the Spring planting, April and May for sweet corn and beans. Several structures that looked like Quonset huts covered in opaque plastic sheets were on tracts of land behind the farmhouses.

Shaunda said, "We do hoop houses in Sullivan County."

"Hoop houses?" Jack asked.

Liddell said, "You've never heard of a hoop house? And you live in Indiana, the corn belt of the nation. Shame on you."

"My life doesn't revolve around food like some people," Jack answered.

Shaunda leaned forward and pointed out the front windshield. "See those over there." She pointed to several of the 'hoop houses'. "They grow lettuce, asparagus, lima beans, snap beans, carrots and other things all winter in those places. If it snows a couple of feet the sun can get through and the snow acts like insulation. I made a small one, about the size of a school desktop, for science class in my sophomore year."

Liddell said, "We're getting close. The place should be right up...I guess we're here." He stopped, backed up and turned down a gravel drive. A split rail fence ran down both sides. The front acreage was used for pasture. A sign at the entrance to the road said, "Rockin' Round the Clock Horse Boarding".

"Angelina said it's a horse farm. Boarding, riding lessons, and they have a veterinarian living on the grounds. It's huge," Jack said.

Instead of the massive house Jack expected, the main house was a one story sprawling ranch with wood siding and a cinder block foundation. Behind the house were two barns, both twice or three times as large as the main house. Both had a hayloft above them. Unpainted wood rail fencing surrounded at least a hundred acres where a dozen or more horses paid no attention to the newcomers.

Liddell stopped in front of the house and they got out. Liddell walked toward the barns while Jack knocked at the door. Shaunda stayed near the car looking disinterested. There was no answer at the door, Jack stepped off the porch to see if Liddell was having any better luck. He was.

Liddell was with an attractive woman walking back towards them. She pulled off a pair of leather work gloves and dusted hay from the front of her plaid shirt and blue jeans. Her bright red hair was pulled back in a tight ponytail that ran halfway down her back.

"C'mon," Jack said to Shaunda.

"This is your gig, but okay," Shaunda said and walked with him.

Liddell made introductions. "This is Stacy Bronson. Stacy this is Jack Murphy and Shaunda Lynch. Jack is FBI like me and Shaunda is with Dugger, Indiana police."

Jack could see a smattering of freckles on Stacy's cheeks and nose. Her skin was smooth, her eyes ocean green and cautious but not afraid. Friendly, but businesslike.

Stacy wiped her hand on her shirt and shook hands with Jack and Shaunda. "I'm flattered to have a visit from the law, but Tommy, that's our vet, is checking the stock and I'm needed inside. What is this about?"

Chapter 36

Shaunda walked toward one of the rail fences facing out over the near pasture. "I count twenty-five."

Stacy Bronson turned her attention to Shaunda and walked to the fence. She leaned on the rail and gazed proudly at the horses in the pasture. "Twenty-six. One is out for a ride with its owner. I don't breed here unless it's a special request. We mostly board for people and provide care, of course. Do you ride?"

"When I was eight my aunt took me to a stable for my birthday. I got to ride, groom, clean the stables. I wore myself out. It's not all fun but I loved being around them. They were like people, you know? Only better."

Stacy looked at Shaunda and her features softened.

Shaunda said, "You need at least an acre a horse. I'm betting that pasture is thirty acres or more. How many acres is your ranch?"

Warming to the subject Stacy said, "Good eye. That pasture is the thirty acres we started with. Eli, that's my husband, inherited most of this land and the house from his family. Other family members owned farms around us and little by little we bought more. We have close to a thousand acres now. Some we lease to farmers. Some we lease cheap in exchange for feed for the horses."

"Wow," Shaunda said and whistled. "You farm any of it yourself?"

Stacy laughed. "I have my hands full with what I'm doing. I'm a working owner. I hire temporary workers, of course, but I learned to shoe the horses and help the vet. That's what I'm doing this morning."

"This must be a whole different world from when you were married to Clint?" Shaunda asked.

Stacy's face froze. "Is that what you're here about?" She backed away from the rail and seemed to notice Jack and Liddell again. "Of course it is," she said. "At first, I thought it might have something to do with the fight in town. Some of my clients want to play at being rodeo cowboys and like to go to the western bars and mix it up." She looked at Jack and said, "You look like you're in charge. Ask your questions and let me get back to work."

Jack asked the easy questions as tactfully as he was capable of doing and with each one Stacy became more reticent to answer. They learned that she had been married to Clint at a young age—she was seventeen and he was twenty-nine. They were married for two years before his death. She refused to talk about the drugs. One of Jack's last questions was, "We know he was let go by Union High School where he was a substitute teacher. Do you know about that?"

An irate Stacy answered, "The principal had it in for him. That's what that was all about. That and those stupid, immature little bitches who needed to get attention. Clint never touched any of them. He was a kind man."

Jack's last question was, "What happened to the job at Hutsonville High School?"

It went unanswered and they were ordered off of her property. Stacy, red-faced with anger, turned and stomped off toward the barn.

"That went well," Shaunda said when they got back in the car. "She's a lying bitch. She knew what he was doing. They always know. I don't understand why she's protecting him. It's been seven years. He's dead."

"Feel better?" Liddell asked her.

"No." She was about to say something else but sat back and shut up.

Liddell still had Jack's phone. "Want it back or are we going somewhere else, pod'na?"

"Moonshine Pub," Jack answered.

"Is that where the call came from?" Shaunda asked.

"That's where the anonymous call came from," Jack said.

Driving east toward downtown Hutsonville, Jack watched the farm fields recede as they neared city limits. The houses encroached on the fields, first becoming streets, then small blocks of homes built in the 30s, 40s and 50s. Most of the homes were in mint condition despite the warping eighty-year-old wood siding and trim. One home sat behind a chain link fence with just a mustache of grass in front. Most of the homes had brick fireplace chimneys. Homes that old generally had poor to no insulation and used the fireplace to keep the home warm in the cold, cold winters here.

Following the GPS, he watched as the homes turned into small businesses that turned into block long lengths of storefront of brick and glass and

Bedford stone. All the businesses were of the flat roof design. He slowed and watched the windows for signs of the Moonshine Pub. Just like in Dugger many of the businesses had been multipurposed or were closed and for lease. A Yoga studio was in what was once a bank. Some sported apartments on the second floor of the building. Even these had 'for rent' signs on the doors. Just like every other small town there was a problem keeping or attracting residents and workers. Kids graduate and can't wait to go away to college. Most never come back. Businesses are vacant because there is little need for a small clothing store, grocery store, or even a gas station/garage on a corner when you can drive five miles outside the city and go to a super Walmart, or a JCPenney, or cineplex, or get gas ten cents cheaper than what the little guy can afford to charge for it.

Liddell must have been reading Jack's thoughts. He said, "In fifty years these businesses will all become yuppie apartment/condos with roof gardens and pubs and art galleries."

Shaunda said, "If it doesn't turn into tattoo parlors, vape shops, massage parlors, Quick Cash, liquor stores and a church on every corner to save their misguided souls."

"You sound like you're speaking from experience," Jack said.

"I'm not very old," Shaunda said, "but I've heard all the old stories about Dugger. It was a booming town once, and blind tigers were all the rage. Then the state legislature made blind tigers illegal and then came Prohibition and the Depression and everything went down the toilet."

"Blind whats?" Liddell asked.

"Blind tiger. It's an illegal liquor establishment. They predated the speakeasies of the Prohibition Era. In 1907 the Indiana legislature outlawed unlicensed liquor sales. A blind tiger was operated out of a closed up bar or store. They would take some bricks out of the wall and you could walk down an alley, reach inside the hole, give them ten cents, and get a beer."

"Why did they call them 'Blind Tiger'?"

"There was a sign on the wall outside of the one in Dugger that read: 10 cents for a peek at the blind tiger. Everyone knew what was going on, but no one was going to stop it. Even the cops were in on it back then," Shaunda said.

"Where did you get all that?" Jack asked her.

"Rosie. She's a history buff. I guess you noticed all the coal mining stuff she's collected. She's given a bunch of it to the Coal Miner Museum or the upstairs of her place would be full of it."

"Coal Miner Museum," Jack said. "Is that in Dugger?"

"You need to see it sometime. I've taken Pen there a bunch of times. I saw how little I knew about Dugger's history. Rosie's helping me teach Pen at home. One reason I don't want her in high school is I don't want her to graduate with her only knowledge being what drug to take or how to party down. She's going to have a better life than me."

Jack thought that was every parent's wish for their kids. Somewhere along the way money and work interfered and the kids were taught values by each other and hormones lit the way. No more did you hear of families sitting together at the dinner table or going to church as a family or believing in a power higher than the dollar.

Jack's mom had stayed home, his dad worked long hours, but they spent every dinner together, talking, discussing school, plans, good or bad things that happened. He didn't understand how he'd let his career as a cop take over his life, but it had happened. That obsession had kept him away from home when Katie was pregnant last time. When she had really needed him, he was gone. When Katie had lost the baby, he'd drawn away from her rather than closer. They should have comforted each other. He would always feel guilt for her losing their daughter and he would feel guilty for abandoning Katie emotionally.

Katie was pregnant again, they were back together, planning to get married. He'd do it right this time. He'd loosen up and not treat every case as if it was the world. Instead he'd try living in the world and enjoying it with his wife and child. Maybe a son this time. Jake, after his father. Or Jackie if it was a girl. He thought he was getting obsessed with these cases. Not a good sign.

He was pulled out of his reverie by Liddell saying, "Whoa, pod'na! Pull over."

His thoughts had put him on autopilot and he had driven right past the Moonshine Pub. He turned around, went back and almost drove past it again. It was easy to miss. Whoever made the 911 call from here must have known of its existence. Any stranger would have driven right by like Jack had done.

The pub was squeezed between a vacant store and an antique store. A green shingle awning protected the entrance. Wrought iron rails were in place on each side of the two concrete steps to give the pub the appearance of complying with handicap regulations. There was a sign on the door glass, white print on a black background:

IF YOU NEED HELP

GETTIN' IN
OR GETTIN' OUT
GIVE A SHOUT

So much for ADA compliance.

"I'll wait in the car," Shaunda said.

"We need you," Jack said. To her questioning look he said, "Show of force. Never go in a bar except in numbers."

She grunted, got out and went with them.

Jack pulled the thick oak door open and they all entered the shotgun style pub. It was a 1930s building that still had all the furniture from the period. Heavy wooden tables with wooden chairs ran down the left wall. A well-worn pathway ran down the middle of the scuffed plank floor. A wooden bar ran at least twenty feet down the right side of the room. Behind the bar were the customary displays of hard liquors, no wines, and big jars of pickled eggs and pig feet. Beer taps were at the front by the register.

A scrawny man with a wrinkled face, prominent brown teeth and dressed in gray Dickie pants and long sleeve Dickies shirt was wiping down the already spotless bar top with a dishtowel. He looked over the newcomers through the thick lenses of gray plastic-framed glasses. Seeing Shaunda in uniform gave him a start.

Jack guessed the bartender was in his 50s but he gave off the vibes of someone that had lived a long, hard life. Jack asked, "Have you got a phone I can use?"

The bartender hitched a thumb towards the gloomy back of the business where sunlight seemed afraid to penetrate. The law had changed disallowing smoking in most places, but this place smelled like it was made from second hand smoke. Jack started to walk to the back.

Without taking his eyes off Shaunda, the bartender said, "Paying customers only." He wiped his hands on the now dirty rag. "You buying something?"

"We'll all have canned Cokes to go," Jack said.

"That'll do," the man said, and motioned with his head at the back of the room.

"You're buying," Jack said to Liddell and walked to the back. A hallway led down the right wall to an exit sign that glowed red over a door. The door was propped open with a brick. There were two doors on the left of that hall. One door was marked "PRIVATE" the other "NECESSARY ROOM". On the wall next to the exit was an old-fashioned pay phone. Jack dug around for a quarter, lifted the handset, slid the quarter into the slot and heard a dial tone. He dialed Angelina's number and she answered with "Jack?"

"How did you know it was me?" he asked.

"You're at the Moonshine Pub and no one else would be calling me from that number."

"This is a pay phone hanging on the wall," he told her.

"It's the same number as the bar's business line. Did you put money in?"

"Yes."

"Hang up and try calling me again without money this time," she said. He did. The call went through easily.

Angelina said, "You may be able to get your quarter back if you ask the bartender."

"It's a small amount to pay to hear your lovely sarcastic voice."

"You romantic dog," she said. "Do you need something?"

"Yeah. You told me Shaunda had an aunt. Can you find out if the aunt is still alive? If she is, see if she still lives at the address you gave me." Angelina said she would and they disconnected.

He looked inside the bathroom. It was a one-seater and empty. He tried the door marked PRIVATE. It was locked. He walked back to the front where Liddell was waiting with two canned drinks and several packages of Fritos. Shaunda had gone back outside.

Jack leaned on the bar and held his FBI credentials open. The bartender deliberately ignored him.

"I'm here on federal business," Jack said in a not too threatening voice and got the man's attention.

"I'm trying to locate some witnesses. I figure if they live within fifty miles of this fine place they would spend time in here. I know I would."

Liddell pulled up the photos of all the victims and handed his phone to the bartender. Without asking what the witnesses had witnessed, the man disinterestedly flipped through the pictures. He paused at the picture of Clint Baker, eyes sharpening, before going on. He flipped quickly backward through the pictures and handed the phone back.

"Did you recognize any of them?" Jack asked.

"A lot of people come through here," the man said.

"I'm sure they do," Jack said. "You stopped on one picture. Do you know him?"

"I don't know any of them."

Jack could see he wasn't going to get an identification from this guy. He asked, "Do you remember a guy's body being found down by the Wabash about seven years ago?"

"My memory ain't as good anymore," the man said. "But come to think of it, I do remember hearing something about a man drowning himself. Long time ago."

"Did the police come in here asking about that?" Jack asked.

"You mean today?"

"Not today. Seven years ago. Did they police come in and talk to anyone about the guy you thought drowned himself?"

"I don't recall that."

"Do policemen come in here?"

"No need. Never any trouble here. We keep ourselves to ourselves," the old man said and smiled, showing only gums and rotted brown teeth.

Jack thanked him for being open and honest and they went outside. Shaunda was already in the back seat of the Crown Vic.

"He tell you anything?" Shaunda asked.

"He was lying but he seemed to recognize Clint Baker," Liddell said, starting the engine.

"Maybe he wasn't working here back then?" Shaunda suggested.

"He's been at the Moonshine Pub since God said 'let there be light.' If you'd have stayed with us you would know all this," Jack said to her.

"I thought my uniform was intimidating him," she said.

"He couldn't take his eyes off of you, that's for sure," Liddell said, and pulled a bag of Fritos open.

"You're going to get my steering wheel all greasy," Jack complained.

"He's like a vacuum cleaner. The Fritos don't even touch his fingers," Shaunda remarked.

"Et tu Brutus," Liddell said to her.

"If you're quoting Julius Caesar," Shaunda corrected him, "what he said was, 'Et tu, Brute.' Not Brutus. Brute. Silent e."

Liddell crunched some Frito's and mumbled, "I was quoting Jack Murphy."

"Oh. That's perfectly understandable then," Shaunda said.

"Where to now Brutus," Liddell asked Jack.

"Hutsonville PD. We don't have much information in the file. It's been seven years but maybe they can shed some light on Clint Baker's life… and death. Maybe they have a report on talking to Gumby back there at the bar."

Chapter 37

They found nothing helpful in the visit with the Hutsonville Police. Detective Sergeant Steven Bohleber had worked the case, but he and his wife had died in a suspicious house fire a couple of months after Clint Baker's body was found. The captain in charge of the Investigations Unit had told Jack that Bohleber was a very meticulous investigator and had a reputation for overworking his cases if anything. Holidays, weekends, days off. He was dedicated. He had taken his notes and most of the case files home. The only thing the captain could tell them was that Bohleber was the only one that was convinced Baker's death wasn't a drug overdose, or an accidental or intentional drowning. Bohleber believed Baker had been killed and the scene staged.

The captain said it 'looked' like a suicide to his Crime Scene folks and there were heavy duty drugs found in his system at autopsy. Baker had no known enemies, but he was known to hang with youngsters and teenagers. Baker's wife insisted the suicide was because the high school administrators had accused him of messing with the kids and harassed him after firing him.

They thanked the captain and were heading back to Dugger, Liddell driving.

"I thought this was the case you didn't think was involved with the others?" Shaunda asked from the backseat. She'd begun holding her arm against her ribs and it was obvious she needed to get some pain medication and rest.

"No stone unturned. We'll rework all the cases from the beginning," Jack said. "Maybe exhume the bodies for a second autopsy." He hoped that didn't become necessary.

"You still don't believe this Anderson guy is the killer?" Shaunda asked. "Maybe Baker's wife knocked him off for insurance? Or because he was abusive to kids like that captain said. Or maybe because she had a chance at a real life, with money and doing the thing she loved like boarding horses and giving riding lessons. What will it take for you to let this go? Does your boss have to call and order you to drop it?"

Liddell chuckled. "You don't know Jack. Once he's like this he doesn't stop and I trust him. If he says there's someone else, you'd better believe there is someone else."

They were nearing Dugger and turned toward Rosie's place. "We're dropping you off, Chief. You need to take some of the pain pills they gave you at the hospital and get some rest before you go anywhere. You've got your daughter to think of. You're no good to anyone right now."

"Are you saying I'm bitching too much?"

Neither man stepped on that landmine.

"Well, welcome to the real Shaunda Lynch," she said. "I can take a hint. I want to keep in the loop. Tell me what you're doing next. After all I have an interest in this too."

"We're going to the Chute Me Bar in Sullivan to talk to them since the call to dispatch was placed from there. We need to find family, friends, coworkers, enemies, drug dealers, favorite restaurants, library, that kind of thing," Jack said.

"Library? What the hell could you possibly hope to find there?"

"These guys all went to high school. Maybe one of them could read. Librarians are a good source. They notice things. I'm not saying Sullivan dropped the ball on the investigation. I'm just collecting the scraps."

They stopped in the lot of Rosie's place and let Shaunda out. She leaned in the open door and asked, "You're not coming in?"

"Places to go. Rights to violate," Jack said.

"Knock yourself out," she said and headed inside.

Liddell asked Jack, "Back to Hutsonville?"

"Eunice Lynch," Jack confirmed. "Angelina texted me while we were on our way here. Shaunda's aunt Eunice is alive and well in Hutsonville."

"Shaunda lied?" Liddell said.

"Yep. Did you see the way that bartender stared at her?"

"I did, but Shaunda said it was the uniform."

"He couldn't take his eyes off of her," Jack said. "He recognized Clint Baker."

"Yeah."

Jack said, "Shaunda said she wanted to be in on this but she sure didn't want to spend any time in that bar."

"Maybe she was in pain, pod'na. Give her a break."

"She seemed to be okay when she got out of the car. I don't think her wound is as serious as we thought."

"She's a police officer and she's under pressure to find the killer. Her job might depend on it. Don't forget someone clobbered her and threatened her kid," Liddell said.

"She was no help this morning. All she did was drag her feet once we got there. She lied about her aunt. She's asking a lot of questions about what we plan to do."

"Yeah. I guess that isn't normal behavior for a policeman. Policewoman I mean. After the aunt are we really going to Sullivan and check out the bar?"

"How could we not go to a place called the Chute Me Bar?"

Liddell pulled out and turned toward State Road 54 again. In less than thirty minutes they had found the aunt's house. Eunice Lynch was Shaunda's father's older sister. Angelina told them that Shaunda's mother had an extended family that branched out across the country, but the father only had the one living sister.

Eunice's house was typical of the farmhouses in the area. The old wood siding was newly painted white, as was the wood railed front porch and wooden steps. The house was closely bordered by tall cedar trees for a wind break from the empty farm fields that surrounded it.

Liddell parked on the shoulder of the graveled road. The oval glass pane in the front door was covered with a blind. A wood framed double paned window overlooked the porch. The curtain was being held back. Jack and Liddell stepped up onto the porch and an unsmiling heavily made up woman opened the door. She was dressed smartly in a dark skirt and white turtleneck sweater. Her hair was dark and worn short and wavy. According to Angelina she was seventy years old, but only her eyes gave her age away. She was short and slightly built like Shaunda, with dark alert eyes. She wasn't surprised to see them.

"Come in," she said. "I'll put coffee on. Unless you'd like some tea."

"Tea would be great," Liddell said, before Jack could answer.

They entered the house into a small foyer and she led them into the front room from where she had watched them arrive.

"Have a seat," she said and walked away.

They sat on each end of a curved, brown leather sectional sofa facing a wood burning fireplace. A glass topped oval coffee table sat in front of the sofa. A matching chaise lounge sat where it faced the sofa and the fireplace. There was no sign of a television. The mantelpiece over the fireplace was filled with paperbacks. Jack got up and looked at the titles. *The Highlander Comes, Her Castle Keeper, Bound by Love*, and so forth. Most of the books showed a muscular man wearing a kilt and wielding a gleaming sword, while a long blonde haired damsel was at his feet in lustful distress.

Jack heard a tea kettle begin steaming and hurriedly stood by the sofa just as Eunice came back carrying a tray with two tea cups, sugar, honey, cream, and two tiny spoons. "For goodness sake, have a seat. I'm sorry for the mess. I haven't cleaned today yet."

Jack looked around the room. You could eat off the floor and it was still very early. He and Liddell sat on the sofa and then got back up to introduce themselves. She again didn't seem surprised the FBI had come to her house far out in the country.

"I'm assuming this is about my niece," she said.

Jack just nodded. He wondered what she thought she knew about their reason for being there.

Eunice said, "I read the papers about the murder of that man last week. The paper said he was the Linton Police Chief's son and the body was found in Dugger. That poor girl."

Jack waited for her to continue.

"Would you like some cookies to go with the tea?" she asked. "I'm afraid I have a beauty appointment this morning and I haven't had time to bake anything."

"No ma'am. We just ate and my partner's on a diet," Jack said.

"Nonsense," Eunice said. "He looks perfectly healthy to me. I'll get you something." With that she left again.

Liddell muttered to Jack, "Diet?"

"She's taking too long to spit out what she knows," Jack muttered back.

From the kitchen, Eunice said, "I'm going to tell you but you have to be patient. I don't get many visitors, and you can't be in that much of a hurry or you wouldn't have driven all the way out here from Evansville."

She came back in with a plate of sugar cookies with white icing and sprinkles.

"How did you know we're from Evansville?" Jack asked.

"Your license plate number," she said and settled into a chair. "82 is the prefix for Vanderburgh County. I have friends in Evansville. I have good hearing and eyesight too."

"You were going to tell us why we're here," Jack reminded her.

"No, I was telling you that I'd heard about that young man's body being found in Dugger. I read it in the newspaper. That article also mentioned my niece, Shaunda. She's the Chief of Police there I gather. The article wasn't very complimentary of her and I felt sorry for her. That girl's had more than her share of pain."

Liddell asked, "Have you had contact with her recently, ma'am?"

"Call me Eunice. Please. No. I didn't know she was back in Dugger until I saw the article. Why she would ever go back there I haven't a clue. That place was nothing but misery for her."

Jack had a thought. "Liddell is going to show you a picture."

Liddell pulled up the picture of Clint Baker on his cell phone. Eunice looked at it closely and shook her head. "Am I supposed to know this person?"

Jack said, "Probably not. He was a murder victim from seven years ago."

"That would be the high school janitor," Eunice said. "I recall that one because we don't have murders around here. All our residents go somewhere else to get killed."

Jack couldn't help but smile. "Do you recall his name?"

"Of course. It was Clint Baker. His wife got remarried less than a year after he died. She married some big shot and runs a horse farm out in the county."

"Just how do you know all that?" Jack asked.

"This is a small town, Agent Murphy. That's why I don't want to miss my hair appointment. That's where you hear all the juicy gossip."

"We won't keep you long. Just a few more questions please."

"I guess you don't want more tea then." She sat back.

"Was there ever a rumor of a suspect in the Baker case?" Jack asked.

"Not a word. We heard he was into drugs, and that was why they fired him from the high school, but then we heard he was doing things to the young people."

"Like what?" Jack asked.

"You know. Like being one of those pedophiles. I heard he was always hanging around the freshmen girls...and boys."

"Did Shaunda know him?" Jack asked her.

Eunice looked away. "I don't know if he was the one—" she began and stopped.

"The one?" Jack asked.

Eunice said, "Hang on a minute. I'm going to call the shop and tell them I'll be a little late."

She left the room and Jack mouthed the words at Liddell. "The one?"

Liddell took out his digital recorder and checked that it worked. When Eunice came back in the room and sat down she saw the recorder and said, "I guess if you must."

Liddell turned the recorder on and set it on the table.

* * * *

They said goodbye to Eunice and were back in the Crown Vic. Jack headed towards Sullivan. The calls reporting both Winter's and Washington's bodies were made from a bar called Chute Me. The one in Sullivan would be another little dive bar with a public phone available and little or nothing in the way of witnesses.

Liddell turned on the recorder and put it on the console. They listened to the recorded conversation. When the recording ended Liddell put it in his pocket.

"What do you think?" Liddell asked.

Jack drove in silence, thinking. "Where is the Chute Me Bar?"

Liddell asked Siri and she gave directions. He told Jack, "You have to stay on Highway 154 to Sullivan. We should drive right by it when we get through town."

Jack took a breath and let it out slowly. He said, "What do *you* think?"

Liddell crossed his arms and looked out of the car window at the fields and farmhouses passing by. "It makes a good case for a revenge shooting. Your turn."

Jack said, "I wonder if Chief Jerrell knows about Shaunda?"

Liddell turned toward Jack. "You think Jerrell would help cover something like that up? I mean a murder? I don't believe it. He said he was gone on deployment a lot during the time all that high school shit was going on. He may not have even heard about it because he didn't get along very well with his wife and kid. Eunice said what happened to Shaunda was never in the paper and no one knew about it except Shaunda and her parents."

"Eunice and Eunice's son who is now deceased," Jack said. "If it makes you feel any better I agree that Jerrell more than likely had no knowledge of this."

"Can you imagine carrying that around in your head all those years. She deserves a medal for getting through all that and raising a handicapped daughter to boot. Holy cow!"

Chapter 38

The Chute Me Bar was wedged between a gun shop and a walk-in medical clinic. The brick walls of the inside of the bar were covered with genuine coal chute trap doors made of iron, the kind that allowed coal to be loaded into basements of homes that burned coal in their stoves or fireplaces for heat. The top of the bar was made up of two conveyor belts that were each ten feet long and three feet wide. The conveyor belts still worked and delivered drinks to patrons. It wasn't pretty, but it worked.

The bartender this time was a woman of about twenty-five going on sixty. Her hair had been bleached so many times it stuck out like straw on her head and was currently tipped with purple and green Kool-Aid colors. She wasn't old enough to have been working in the bar—legally—at the time the victims were still walking, breathing and drinking and she didn't know anything helpful except how to call the boss. The boss was an attorney who worked just down the street. He was more than happy to talk to the FBI.

He was also of no help but he did call a long time employee that had bartended at a time where he might remember something. The man came in from home. He was in his sixties, wearing stone washed jeans, Hawaiian print shirt and sandals. His gray hair was pulled back tightly into a knot on his crown. His eyes were sharp and he sized up Jack and Liddell as they showed him their FBI credentials. He was reticent at first to answer any questions until Jack reminded him that his boss was an attorney and would gladly represent him for lying to the FBI.

The owner told the man to give the FBI anything they wanted, excused himself and seemed to vanish. Jack asked a simple question. "What is your name?"

"Jack Spratt," the man said. "Like the Jack Sprat in Mother Goose, but with two T's and not one."

Jack said nothing and Spratt explained further, "You know that rhyme. 'Jack Sprat could eat no fat,' and so on." While saying this Pratt patted his generous midsection and chuckled. "Obviously I can eat fat and do, all the time."

Liddell took out his cell phone and showed Spratt the same set of victim's photos as the other bartenders.

"I've seen these two," Spratt said, and pointed at the photos of Daniel Winters and Lamont Washington. Those were the boys they found in the stripper pit. Committed suicide I thought. Is that right?"

"Something like that," Jack said. "I guess there was a lot of commotion going on that night?"

"This is a bar. Lots of commotion most nights," Spratt answered cautiously. "I didn't see anything if that's what you're after."

Jack laughed. "You are one sharp customer. I guess you must come by it naturally. How long have you been tending bar, Jack?"

"Almost as long as you've been alive I'll bet," Spratt answered with a smile. He was relaxed now.

"Jack, all we want to know is who came in here and called the police the night the bodies were found."

Spratt considered the question. He said, "It was two different nights. About three or four years ago now, I imagine. I remember the police coming in here asking the same questions. Both times. They called me a liar. Said I had to see who came in. I ain't no liar."

Jack said, "We're not going to call you a liar. We just want to know if your memory is better now that you've slept on it."

Spratt's face broke out in a grin. "After three or four years you mean. Well I'll tell you what I told them then, and it's the truth, I swear to God and my momma."

Jack prepared himself for the lie to follow that remark.

"You see that phone back on the wall? That's one of them old rotary dial phones. The boss man put it in for calling a cab. Most of my guys here don't cause any trouble. They can get a cab ride home and the boss picks up the tab. Nice, huh?"

Jack nodded, although he thought that the attorney that owned the place was just covering his ass from a civil suit in case one of the 'good ol' boys' left the place too drunk and crashed.

"The phone on the wall," Jack prompted him to continue.

"Whoever came in must have used that phone because that's the number the cops said the call was from. Lots of people use the phone. I never noticed anyone in particular using it around the time they asked me about. I swear on a bible and you can give me one of those poly tests."

"That's not necessary. I believe you," Jack lied. "Just a couple more questions and we'll get out of your hair. The two guys you remember. Were they regulars?"

Spratt didn't have to think about it. "They came in together. By themselves usually."

"What kind of customers were they?"

"I might as well cut to the chase," Spratt said and dug his hands into the pockets of the jeans. "They was nothing but trouble. I had to run them off from hanging around out front."

"Drugs?" Jack asked.

Spratt gave Jack a serious look. "That too. They started bringing underage girls in here or try to sneak them in. I can't 'bide by someone that does that. I was thinking about barring them from coming around here altogether, then they turn up dead and I say good riddance to gutter trash."

"Last question," Jack said. "Did you ever see them in here with a woman?"

"Never," Spratt said. "They was into young girls, you know. Never a woman."

"I lied," Jack said, "I have another question. Was there ever a woman in here that was interested in either of them? Tried to pick them up? Bought them a drink?" He turned to Liddell and said, "See if you can find a picture of Shaunda."

"There was a woman cop in here asking about one of the guys," Spratt volunteered. "The picture of the black guy you showed me."

Lamont Washington. He saw Liddell had found a photo. Liddell had pulled up a newspaper photo of Shaunda from years back when she was sworn in as the first female Chief Constable of Dugger.

Liddell showed the photo to Spratt.

"Might be her," Spratt answered.

"Was she wearing a uniform?" Jack asked.

"No. I knew she was a cop the minute she came through the door. Not that I have anything against cops."

"Of course," Jack said. "What did she ask about the black guy?"

"I don't quite recall. Been a while you know."

"Try," Jack persisted.

Spratt looked at the ceiling as if calling for divine help to be rid of these pestering Feds. "She was asking where the black guy's buddy was. She described the other one."

Liddell pulled up the photo of Winters and held it out. "Is this the guy she was asking about?"

"That's who she described to me I guess. She didn't show me a picture or anything, but the black guy only seemed to have one buddy," Spratt said. "Can I get home now. The missus is waiting, if you know what I mean." He had a gleam in his eye. Jack knew what he meant. He'd seen that same look in the mirror when Katie was waiting for him.

"Do you know where the lady was a cop? Sullivan?" Jack asked.

"No. Not from around here," Spratt said. "I'd know her. Never seen her before that night and never seen her since. Well, maybe one other time."

"Are you positive she was a cop?" Jack asked.

"I knew it right off. And another regular pointed her out to me in case she was in here to cause trouble."

Jack translated 'in here to cause trouble' as meaning she might arrest someone for criminal activity. He asked, "Where did this regular customer say she was from?"

"Maybe over in Linton or Lyons or some little town over that way."

"Was she with a woman or a man any of the times you saw her?"

"I don't recall. I remember she was a cop," Spratt said.

Jack and Liddell watched Spratt greet the younger Kool-Aid haired bartender in an unchaste hug and they left.

"You drive," Jack said, throwing the keys to Liddell.

They got in the Crown Vic. Jack said, "Let's see if Jerrell is available. Maybe we can get him onboard. I'll call the director and update him."

Liddell headed toward Linton while Jack made the calls. Jerrell agreed to meet them in his office. Toomey was more of a concern. He was beginning to waffle. Someone was putting the pressure on.

"The director didn't say we were done, did he?" Liddell asked.

"He didn't say much of anything," Jack replied. "I think he's at the stage of 'don't know, don't care to know.'"

"He pulled Angelina off the job here. I wonder what he'll think when she doesn't go back home?"

"She's basically a civilian. He's lucky to have her at all. I don't think he wants to mess up that relationship."

"How did Jerrell sound?"

"I don't think he can be convinced. It doesn't matter if he is or not. He'll get over it."

"I was just getting to like it."

"You mean in the situation we're in?" Jack asked.

"You know what I mean. I like Rosie. I like Shaunda. These are good people. Where I came from the people might take potshots at each other but outsiders would find them standing together if push came to shove. I think it's the same way here."

"I hear you, Bigfoot," Jack said. "I was down there with you, remember. I hope we don't run into more of the same here." Jack and Liddell had run into several corrupt and deadly officials in Liddell's hometown and a lot of people had died before they'd put a stop to them.

They passed through Dugger on their way to Linton, not speaking, dealing with their own thoughts and emotions at what they might have to do here.

"Linton straight ahead," Liddell said.

Jack looked up as they passed under the big wooden banner running across the road that said, "You'll Like Linton". He remembered what Liddell had said when they first entered the town. "But will Linton like us?"

Chapter 39

They pulled into the police parking lot of the Linton PD and were met at the side door by Sergeant Ditterline. Jack saw the defensive look on the man's face. Word had already spread that they were trying to make a federal case out of a justified shooting. To his surprise, Ditty said, "You guys do what you have to." His meaning was clear. No one wanted to work with a cop whose behavior was questionable.

"Thanks, Sergeant. We will," Jack said.

"My friends call me Ditty."

"Thanks Ditty. That means a lot to us," Jack said and could feel his blood pressure lower.

Not that he was any stranger to pissing other cops off. However, this wasn't his home turf.

Jack and Liddell went in the side entrance and walked to the chief's office where Liddell knocked. The door was opened by Jerrell and Jack could see it was a full house. Sergeant Crocker, the two Crime Scene guys, even Rusty the K-9 officer minus his trusty sidekick were present and all eyes were on Jack and Liddell.

Jerrell said, "We're a close-knit department. All these officers have worked hard on this. I was the one that hired them. They deserve—no, they need—to hear what you have to say. I'm not meaning to intimidate, you understand."

Jack replied, looking around the room, "Good. You're not intimidating us."

Ditty had come in behind them and said, "He's a hoot. For a Fed that is." Not everyone smiled.

Jack made the decision. He was going to trust them. "Can we get some chairs? This might take a while."

Sergeant Crocker got up and Jack added, "Can someone watch the door and make sure we're not interrupted?"

Jerrell nodded at Rudy. Rudy could still hear but wasn't essential to the discussion because Barr knew everything Rudy did. Rudy stood in the doorway. Crocker brought extra chairs and Jack and Liddell took a seat.

Jack began with asking Jerrell, "What has everyone been told about the need for this meeting?"

Jerrell replied, "I haven't discussed it with them. I thought you'd tell us what you know."

"First of all, this isn't the way the FBI would normally conduct an inquiry into a shooting. You men need to understand that everything that's said in this room is in confidence and will go no further than Chief Jerrell. No wives, girlfriends, not anyone. Tell me you understand or it ends here."

All around the room Jack got an affirmative answer and it made the mood even more tense. Jack said, "Secondly, you're all sworn law enforcement officers. You took the same oath that we took to uphold the law of the land. When something is questionable we are sworn to look into it and not sweep it under the rug because it's a fellow officer, politician, or your bookie or someone that holds your mortgage."

The latter remark about the bookie and mortgage got a few grins.

Jack said, "You know that we were here to investigate five separate, but possibly connected murders. Before we got to town yesterday a sixth murder occurred. We developed a suspect for the last murder. Tony Anderson."

Officer Barr said, "We found Troy Junior's neck chain in Anderson's pocket. He had the cell phone from Brandon Dillingham. I'd call that a little more than being a suspect."

"Possession might be nine tenths of the law in the civilian world, but in police work possession is just probable cause to investigate further. A defense attorney would say the guy found the phone and the necklace. That they were discarded by the real killer. Or maybe given to Anderson to throw us off the track. After all, the previous murder scenes were staged to look like suicides or accidental drownings. The victims were drugged or drunk or both." He reminded himself that he needed to check all the local pawn shops and jewelers from here to Hutsonville to see if they carried that medallion. He doubted it was rare.

No one said anything, nor did they argue the point that the scenes may have been staged. Jerrell sat like a statue not looking at anyone, like the bartender in Hutsonville had said, "Jerrell was keeping himself to himself."

"Greene and Sullivan Counties both have a lot of drug activity," Jack said. "Most of you were aware of Dillingham's preference for young girls.

We discovered today that the other victims shared the same traits. Drugs. Alcohol. Young girls."

He could feel a shift in the room from cold to cool. It was a start but he didn't want to convince them. He wanted them to convince him. "When we all started this yesterday Sergeant Crocker's wife, Tina, told us there was a connection between some of the victims through Union and Stocker-Linton High School. She also told us that four of the victims played baseball as rival's but they would hang out together and party."

Crocker said, "While we were waiting for you guys to get here I went through the Union High School yearbooks. I found a picture of an older guy hanging out with a couple of guys in baseball uniforms at Union High. You'll never guess who it was."

Jerrell said, "While we're still alive, Crocker."

"Yes, sir, Chief. There were three people in the picture. Two were in Union High School baseball uniforms. One of them was Leonard DiLegge. I got the name of the other student but he wasn't someone we were interested in. If you want it I got it written down." He dug his notebook out of his pocket but Jerrell gave him an impatient look.

"Anyway, I've got it if you want it. Okay, the third guy was in slacks and a sport coat. It didn't give his name but I got out the pictures of the victims. It was Clint Baker talking to DiLegge and the other guy. They were talking like buddies."

Officer Barr said, "We already know the victims have some things in common. What we don't know is how Chief Lynch fits in the picture. Dillingham didn't go to school with these guys. We don't know that he even knew any of them."

"Let him finish," Jerrell said.

"Thank you Chief. I'll tell you what we did this morning and let you decide for yourselves."

The room was quiet. All eyes were on Jack.

Jack began. "I had my computer analyst, Angelina Crowley, run background on everyone involved in these cases. That included Chief Shaunda Lynch. Angelina told me that Shaunda had one living relative. An aunt named Eunice Lynch who lived in Hutsonville, Illinois."

Some of the officers exchanged looks, but Jack forged on.

"We were leaving Rosie's this morning and Shaunda was there. She asked where we were going and we told her Hutsonville. She insisted on going. I mentioned her aunt and she told me her aunt was dead. Angelina advised otherwise. Angelina's rarely wrong. We took Shaunda with us and reinvestigated what we could in Hutsonville and I'll tell you about that in a bit."

"When we were finished in Hutsonville we brought Shaunda back to Rosie's and she stayed there. Liddell and I went back to Hutsonville to find the aunt. She is alive and wasn't surprised we had come to see her. She apparently had seen something about Troy Junior's death in the news or there was some gossip, and she saw a photo of Shaunda in uniform. Before that she'd had no contact since Shaunda was seventeen. Didn't know where she was, but knew she was pregnant. We're going to let you hear the recorded conversation with Shaunda's aunt."

Liddell put the recorder on the table and they all gathered around as he turned it on. It started with Jack asking her name.

Eunice: "My name's Eunice Lynch."

Jack: "Are you related to Shaunda Lynch?"

Eunice: "She's my niece."

Jack: "When was the last time you saw Shaunda?"

Eunice: "She was almost seventeen years old."

Jack: "When did you become aware of her again?"

Eunice: "I was at the beauty shop a few weeks ago. We all gossip, I know it's shameful, but one of the girls asked if I'd heard from Shaunda recently. I said that I hadn't talked to the girl for a long time. My friend, Trudy, said she'd just seen Shaunda in the newspaper. She went out to her car and brought a Sullivan Times newspaper in and showed it to me. There was a story about a man drowning in a stripper pit lake in Dugger. That's in Indiana."

Jack: "We've just come from there."

Eunice: "You've talked to Shaunda? How is she?"

Jack: "Shaunda's fine. Continue with how you became aware that she was in Dugger."

Eunice: "Okay. I saw the article and they had a photo of Shaunda in a police uniform. It said she was the Chief Constable and went on about how she was the first woman ever to hold that position. I think it's shameful when they make a big fuss about a woman doing something. It's like they're saying, 'Can you believe that?'"

Jack: "Go on."

Eunice: "Well, that's about it. The article said she'd been with the Dugger Police for around five years. I never heard a word from her. I didn't know she'd come back until that day. Not that I expected her to call or come by. We didn't part on good terms."

Jack: "Tell me about that."

Eunice: "It's a long story."

Jack: "We've got time."

Eunice: "Well, I don't. Let me make a call and tell my hairdresser that I won't make it."

The recording stopped. It started again.

Eunice: "Now, where was I?"

Jack: "It's a long story…"

Eunice: "Shaunda visited me a couple of times when she was around nine or ten. Her father was my brother. He's deceased. His wife too. They died in a house fire. So tragic. He was my brother but he was a mean bastard. Excuse my language, but there's no other way to describe him. He was my younger brother. He got religion when he married that woman and they were so strict on Shaunda. Poor girl was treated like a slave and couldn't have any friends. They didn't approve of anyone, those two. I convinced them to let Shaunda come over and stay for a few days now and then. My brother found out I was taking Shaunda over to a neighbor to let her ride a horse and he had a hissy fit. Said I should have asked him and he didn't know who this neighbor was. I told him it was divorced man and all the sudden the man was a sinner that was going to molest his daughter and such. That was the end of Shaunda's childhood to my way of thinking."

Jack: "When did you see her again?"

Eunice: "Not until she was a sophomore in high school."

Jack: "Tell me about that."

Eunice: "She came to the door one night. It was dark outside. She said she'd been kicked out of the house and she didn't have anywhere else to go. She'd hitchhiked and walked all the way here from Dugger where they lived. She was tired and hungry and upset and I wanted to kill my brother and that woman for the way they treated this girl. Anyway, I put her in the extra bedroom and told her she could stay as long as she needed. She started crying and said I would make her leave like her parents did when I knew why they kicked her out. I made her tell me and she said she was pregnant."

Jack: "She was a sophomore. That would make her about sixteen, correct?"

Eunice: "Yes. My son lived with me then. He was twenty-one. It was hard for him to find a job back then you see, and he'd never finished high school. He was good about her staying and they got along fine for a while."

Jack: "Shaunda?"

Eunice: "Shaunda stayed with me a few nights before she would talk to me how she got pregnant. She told me that she had been invited to a party for some of the seniors. She had sneaked out because my brother would have skinned her alive if he knew. When she got to the party there was a lot of drinking and drugs and—well you know what raging hormones will do. She said she wanted to go home but she was coaxed into having one drink before they took her home. You know how young people are. She gave in and whatever it was they gave her made her sick. She said she couldn't move or talk and they were laughing at her and carried her down into a mine."

Jack: "Mine?"

Eunice: "I'm sorry. The party was outside an abandoned coal mine. Those animals carried her inside the coal mine and raped her repeatedly. She said there was more than one of them. They beat and hurt that poor girl and left her there. I don't know how she got home.

Jack: "Did she go to the hospital?"

Eunice: "No. She said they caught her coming in and saw the condition she was in. Of course, they were horrified that she had shamed them. When they found out she was pregnant they didn't let her go back to school. They starved that poor girl half to death until she was skin and bones by the time she came here. You could still see the scars on her back and arms and legs where those boys hurt her in that mine. My brother wanted her to have an abortion."

Jack: "What month did she come to your house, Eunice?"

Eunice: "It was in late May. She was about two or three months pregnant. Or at least she thought she was at the time. They never took her to a doctor. I tried to take her but she refused. She was that ashamed."

Jack: "Did she tell you what month the rape occurred?"

Eunice: "Sometime in March."

Jack: "Did she tell you the names of the boys that did this to her?"

Eunice: "She wouldn't say but I'm sure she knew. You could see it in her eyes. She would wake up in the night screaming bloody murder. I found her one morning sleeping in the closet. She was here a couple of months. She needed help, to see a doctor and check on the baby. She flat out refused and got mad when I would bring it up."

Jack: "Then what happened?"

Eunice: "I don't want to say."

Jack: "Eunice. We need to know."

Eunice: "The longer she stayed with me the more I got to see the girl underneath the one I thought I knew. She'd changed. I don't know if it was because of my brother or if it was because of what she'd been through. She had this anger building inside. Oh, she was courteous, but her sarcasm was cutting at times. She'd say please or sorry but you knew she didn't mean it. Then one day she came to me and said my son had tried to have his way with her. I told her she shouldn't tell lies after everything we'd done for her. She said it had happened more than once. He'd come into her room at night and was touching her while she was sleeping. Well, I finally had enough of her lying and told her to get her stuff and I'd take her to the bus station the next morning. I didn't want her telling lies about my son."

Jack: "Where did she go?"

Eunice: "I don't know. I didn't care. She just disappeared in the middle of the night. I was so mad and disgusted I didn't look for her."

Jack: "You said your son is deceased?"

Eunice: "I'm sure you'll find all this out, being FBI and all, so I'll tell you. Not long after she left my son got arrested for robbing a bank and shooting a guard. The guard died. He went to prison and died there."

Jack: "Is there anything else you want to tell us?"

Eunice: "Just that I didn't understand why Shaunda would ever come back here. Her life in Dugger was pure hell on earth. Why would she come back?"

Jack: "Before we started this recording you said something about Clint Baker being 'the one'.

Eunice: "Clint Baker was a janitor here at the high school. He was fired and a few months later he drowned himself in the river."

Jack: "Do you know why he'd drowned himself?"

Eunice: "He was fired for messing with the young ones at school. Young girls. Young boys. Disgusting. He must've been ashamed."

Jack: "Eunice, you said he was 'the one'. What did you mean by that?"

Eunice: "Shaunda said something that stuck with me. She said when these boys were raping her that a man from school was watching. He didn't do anything to her, but he didn't try to stop what they were doing. He was smiling. That made me sick. He could have stopped them."

Jack: "Did she tell you the adult was Clint Baker?"

Eunice: "Not in so many words. She just said it was a man from the school."

Jack: "What makes you think Baker was the man she was talking about?"

Eunice: "When he drowned himself there was talk. He had worked at Shaunda's high school and had a better job than janitor. He was a teacher. They fired him for the same thing as here. I maybe be wrong and I don't want to gossip."

Liddell turned the recorder off.

Chapter 40

After the recording ended Jerrell and his men sat silent, stunned, exchanging brief looks. Jack understood what they were going through. The knowledge that one of your brothers or sisters in law enforcement wasn't what you thought they were was a loss. A loss of respect for them, trust in them, and also a loss of your own self-confidence for not seeing it sooner.

Jerrell was the first to speak.

"I've known that woman since she took office. She was in one of the classes I taught for the Police Academy. I was impressed with her passion for the job. She would call me from time to time for advice, one chief to another. I went over there and helped her straighten out the paperwork. You'd think with only three people on the payroll, herself included, it would be simple, but the last chief hadn't kept anything current. He was still using a notebook to keep tabs on equipment and expenses. I got to know Pen because she would have the girl at work with her sometimes. We got to be buddies, but when my son was killed we butted heads and we've kept our distance."

"I'll admit, this doesn't look good for Shaunda. It gives her a lot of motive *if* Winters and Washington and all the rest were the ones that raped her. This is just conjecture at this point," Jerrell said.

"What do we have that connects the victims?" Jack asked the assembled group.

Jerrell said, "They were found in a stripper pit lake. Naked. Drugs and/or alcohol was in their systems."

"They were made to look like accidental drownings or suicides," Rudy offered.

Rudy again. "Three of them had underwear tied on their head. That seems personal to me."

Jerrell. "They were all hit on the back of the head. Some of the calls were made directly to police dispatch and not a 911 call. Someone knew the direct dispatch number." Only a handful of people, usually officers or their families had access to the direct dispatch phone number.

Jack. "I went through the reports again. All the anonymous calls were made by a female voice, or the dispatcher couldn't tell if it was male or female. I haven't heard from the FBI lab yet on the dispatch tapes."

Jerrell held his hands up. "Whoa. Slow down. Are we looking at Shaunda for all the killings, or are we just looking at her for the hitchhiker she shot?"

Instead of answering that question, Liddell said, "All the deaths took place near a coal mine. Shaunda told Eunice that she was raped and left in an abandoned coal mine. In March. All the killings were in March."

Jerrell put his hands down and hung his head. Jack asked him, "Do you know when Penelope's birthday is? What month?"

Jerrell said, "December first."

Jack. "That fits, too. Nine months. March to December. It fits with Shaunda not going back to high school and telling her aunt that she was kicked out of the house by her parents." He asked Crocker, "Can you look through the Union High School yearbooks and see when Shaunda ended school?"

"Ahead of you Chief," Crocker said. "I went through them all and made sure the victims were in school all four years. I ran across Shaunda's pictures. Shaunda was in the sophomore one but not after that."

"Shaunda moved back to Dugger a little over five years ago," Jerrell said. "Two years after the first victim in Sullivan County was killed."

"She knew all these guys from high school, Chief," Crocker said. "But she didn't act like she did. My wife said these guys all partied together from both high schools. Tina went to one or two parties and she said there was marijuana there but she didn't say any of what Shaunda's aunt said was going on."

Jack thought, *and she wouldn't tell you if she knew.*

"Second question," Jack said. "We've answered most of this, but what connects these guys prior to their deaths?"

"High school. Baseball. Parties. Maybe drugs but not the heavy stuff I wouldn't imagine," Sergeant Ditterline said.

"Although they did find cocaine in some of the autopsies," Barr said.

"It would be nice to know if any of these parties took place on mine property," Jack said.

"Who was at that party in March," Liddell said. "Maybe Clint Baker was there. He was a substitute teacher at Union when Shaunda was there. That was fourteen or fifteen years ago. We'll have to talk to every student that attended both high schools during those years to see if they remember a party in March. It's going to be hard to find witnesses now."

Jerrell stood. "I'm going to ask Shaunda. I can tell if she lies to me."

"I don't think that's a good idea, Chief," Jack said. "She's already suspicious that we're on to her. Otherwise she wouldn't have insisted on coming to Hutsonville with us. I think she was keeping eye on us. If you confront her she could flee. Disappear. We'd never know the truth."

"Or she could confess to me."

"Or she could kill you," Jack said.

"Not going to happen," Jerrell said. "We need to find out one way or another. If it was you or me we'd want to get cleared of this."

Jack said, "We need to build probable cause first. Get as much information or evidence as we can. Or to clear her. We need more."

"She knows me. If these assholes did that to her she had good reason to end them. I know that's not up to us, but I…" his words trailed off.

"What about Dillingham, Chief?" Jack asked. "Or Anderson? Did they deserve to be killed?"

"We don't know who killed Dillingham," Jerrell answered without conviction.

"We know she killed Anderson," Jack said and everyone agreed.

Chapter 41

The meeting broke up. Jerrell told his men to start finding any video that was available in Linton. All of it. He didn't care where it was from or how old it was. He was going talk to the students that went to high school with the victims in his county. Find out who else was friends with them. Maybe he'd get lucky and find out who was at that party in March.

Jack suggested that he have someone go through the voter registration office to current addresses of the yearbook students. Jack and Liddell were back in the Crown Vic with Jack driving. Liddell asked, "Where do you want to start?"

"We're going to have Angelina check Shaunda's background deeper. Financial records, telephone calls, social media, teachers, friends, anyone we can talk to. We need to find out where she went when she left her aunt's house. We need to determine where she was when Baker was killed."

"Do you really think Jerrell will find anything on the video?" Liddell asked.

"No, but it will keep him busy and away from Shaunda for a while."

"We hope."

"Yeah," Jack said. "You know he's going to talk to her sometime. Probably heading over there now."

"That's why we're going to set up somewhere close to Rosie's in a little while. If he tries to interfere I won't have any choice but to arrest him," Jack said.

"You're going to arrest a Chief of Police?"

"We've done worse, Bigfoot. He'll live."

"Yeah, but we might not," Liddell said. "He's big enough to break us both in two."

"You're big enough he'd have to break you into three," Jack said.

"You a funny man, pod'na. Anyone ever tell you that?"

"Just you."

Liddell said, "It's a good thing Shaunda wanted to come with us this morning. If we hadn't caught her in that lie about her aunt we wouldn't have gotten this far. With Shaunda staying at Rosie's I'm not looking forward to being there tonight. Maybe we should get rooms somewhere else?"

"She would think we were avoiding her," Jack said. "My mom always said, 'Keep your friends close, but 'keep your enemies close too because you might have to shoot one of them.'"

"Did your mom really say that?"

"It might've been one of the nuns at St. Anthony Grade School, come to think of it. Sister Alphonse Capone," Jack said.

Liddell said, "Let's go check on Angelina before we get tied down. I'll text her and get directions."

Angelina texted right back with the address.

"It's about fifteen minutes south of here," Liddell said and told Siri the address. Siri responded. "Here's the address. Would you like me to navigate?"

"Yes, please and thank you," Liddell said.

"I'm glad you can get some sense out of that thing. She hates me. If I asked for the address she would send me to Kansas."

Liddell said, "You should be nice to her. She doesn't like it when you call her names."

"It's a program, Bigfoot. Not a person. It doesn't recognize the words I say."

"Oh, I'm sure Siri does. You even sound angry when you're just asking Siri a question. I'm surprised she even lets you make a call."

"My cell phone doesn't 'let' me do anything. I'm the human. It's just a piece of talking junk. You hear that Siri?" Jack said in a loud and angry voice.

Siri's voice came from Liddell's cell phone. "I'm sorry. I don't understand that command."

"I have the voice activation turned on, pod'na. You called. She answered," Liddell said and chuckled.

"Bite me, Siri!"

The phone didn't answer. "Now you've hurt her feelings," Liddell said. "I apologize for him Siri. He doesn't mean it."

"Where the hell am I going?" Jack asked Liddell.

They were soon on State Road 59 going south. Where State Road 59 took a 45 degree turn to the west they got off on County Road 200 South. The roads were paved until they were halfway down a farm road. Plumes of limestone dust filled the air. Without the verbal instructions from the GPS Liddell would have missed the turn into the Pleasant Grove Farms Resorts.

Not far down the road the dust settled and a sign on their left pointed to Pleasant Grove Farms Main House. A little farther down a sign pointed to the south for "Quail Run Cottage." A grove of trees and evergreens hid the cottage from the road until they made the turn into the driveway. The cottage looked newly built with cedar plank siding, a wood railed porch with rockers and a two person swing. The tin roof was painted blue. A flagstone walk worked its way around the cottage. Angelina's SUV sat in one space and Jack pulled into the other.

Angelina was sitting in the wooden swing beside a distinguished looking gentleman in his seventies. Even sitting, he was clearly tall and lanky. A full head of white hair, a bushy walrus mustache that drooped over his lip, western boots, faded blue jeans and Levi jacket gave him the appearance of a cowboy. All that was missing was a Stetson a rope and a Marlboro.

They got out of the car and Liddell said, "Wow! How'd you manage this? It must cost a few coffee beans and the director is definitely a bean counter."

Without getting up Angelina made introductions. "This is John Cline. He's the owner of all you see. The director was going to put me in a little cabin on the property but when I got here John upgraded me for free."

John Cline came off the porch and shook hands with Jack and then Liddell. "She's been telling wild stories about you two," Cline said. "Makes you sound like lawmen in those old westerns that I love. Like that show, Tombstone, where Kurt Russell was a sheriff."

"Tombstone," Liddell said. "Yeah, Jack would make a mean Wyatt Earp."

"Well, I've got to get back to the ranch," Cline said with a grin. "I came over to help Angie get all that equipment inside. Hey, you're not Russian spies, are you? All that computer stuff can't be for bird watching."

"Don't mess with them, John. Jack's shot people for less," Angelina said.

Cline chuckled and said, "No offense intended Agent Murphy. Angie said you might need some education on coal mining operations, equipment, things like that."

Jack gave Angelina a curious look and wondered what kind of stories she'd been telling.

"We might at that, Mr. Cline," Jack said.

"I come from a family of miners but my grandparents gave it up when the Depression hit and started farming. My dad still did some mining but this farm became more than he could handle. He had to put all his focus here. I'm actually an accountant, but I inherited this place from my dad. I didn't want to run a farm so I built this into a bed and breakfast and it just kept growing. You like it?"

"It's beautiful out here," Jack said.

"If you need a place to stay I can let you have rooms inside the main house."

Cline said goodbye to Angelina and left, his western hand tooled leather boots crunching on the gravel.

"Let's see the place," Liddell said.

They went inside and Jack was surprised at the spaciousness of the rooms. The cottage didn't look that big from outside but inside was a large living room slash kitchen. Two bedrooms and a full modern bath were off the living room. A stairway led up to a loft where another bedroom and bathroom were located.

"You've got a three bedroom cottage in a primo location and we're stuck in small rooms over a bar," Liddell said.

"There's enough room for you two if you decide you can't go back to the Coal Miner Bar. Speaking of which, how did the interview with the aunt go? She was alive, right?"

"She is. The interview was good. Mostly about Shaunda's early life, before Penelope was born. Let's sit down and we'll tell you everything."

They sat on the comfortable furniture in the living room and Jack repeated what they'd talked about at Linton PD while Angelina put on a pot of coffee. He felt comfortable here, relaxed, and realized that he'd missed the comradery of his own crew of which Angelina had become an essential part. He could trust Liddell and Angelina. With his life, if need be. It was more than that. He liked running his thoughts by Angelina. She was his mini-Watson. She found crumbs of details they'd missed and had helped them solve a few cases with her insights. He hoped she could come up with a magic pill for this one.

Angelina came back in holding three mugs of black coffee. "Sorry. No creamer."

"It's fine. Have a seat. Liddell recorded the conversation with the aunt."

Liddell took out the recorder and turned it on. She listened without expression to the gruesome tale of the gang rape, beating, and being left naked and injured in the abandoned mine.

"Before you say anything, let me finish the story," Jack said. He told her about the interviews in Hutsonville, Clint Baker's widow, the bartenders in Hutsonville and Sullivan and then the meeting with Linton PD. When he finished he asked where the bathroom was and excused himself to let her sit and digest the information. When he came back Angelina had brought the coffee pot and topped everyone up.

"What do you think?" Jack asked.

"The skater chick got Brandon's cell phone from the homeless guy, Anderson, whom Shaunda later gunned down. Did the skater chick or Penelope identify Anderson as the homeless guy?" Angelina asked.

"Jerrell talked to Cretin, skater chick. He said she did. Penelope Lynch identified Anderson as the guy that came to her house asking for directions."

"Crime Scene found the eagle medal and chain in Anderson's pocket after Shaunda shot him," Angelina said. Not a question. "With what the aunt told you it all makes sense. Shaunda has the knowledge, ability, and the training to make these murders look like something they're not. She also has one hell of a motive. Except for Brandon."

"Also, there is a sexual overtone to the murders. They were personal. The drugging, stripping, beating, leaving the bodies in plain view to be found in a humiliating condition. Even finding two of the bodies herself. Which would give her an excuse for any trace evidence she might have left at the scene."

Angelina twisted the wedding ring around her finger. Something she was prone to do while she thought. She said, "She'd been lucky so far, but when she heard the FBI was sending investigators she got scared. Then she saw an opportunity. She could stage another murder, same pit, same method, show up at the scene and no one would suspect her. She killed Brandon, staged the scene, took his cell phone and gave it to the homeless guy. She may not have known who Anderson was but she knew he was hanging around. She may have even known he'd been at her house. I don't think you could get much past that gal."

"You're on a roll. Go on," Jack said.

"All this would require her to bust her own skull with something," Angelina said and twisted the ring. "Maybe she knew you weren't convinced Brandon's murder was related to the others. She was still going to have to kill Anderson, but she needed to give you more convincing evidence. The drill bit was a red herring. She busts herself in the head with whatever, goes to you guys all beat up and it looks like the killer is still in the area. That would kick up the search a notch and make her a victim instead of a suspect."

Jack said, "We tried to get her to go to the hospital but she refused. She left to go tell Brandon's mother he'd been killed but said her deputy had already done that. That would have given her time to set up a camp near the stolen Jeep and leave the drill bit to be found."

Liddell said, "Yeah. That would make us look for someone that was camping out. A homeless person. Pen told us about the guy coming to the house, then we found the phone, learned about the homeless guy and it all came together. Her plan would be perfect. If you hadn't suspected she shot the homeless guy out of revenge."

"It wasn't revenge," Jack said. "It was a plan and we walked right into it."

They were all silent, sipping coffee.

"She was very convincing," Liddell said.

"Both times," Jack added. "She stabbed herself, too, remember?"

"She's a psycho," Angelina said. "You need to stay here tonight. You don't want to wake up dead in the morning."

"I wish we could but we need to keep her close," Jack said. "She's killed seven people. She's not sure what we know, or what we're doing."

"What are you going to do?" Angelina asked.

"I plan to let her stay inside the investigation," Jack said. "I'll rattle her cage a little and see what happens."

"She's killed seven men that you know of, Jack. Do you think that's a good idea?" Angelina asked.

"If you have a better one, let's hear it."

No one said anything.

"I've just thought of something," Jack said. "Excuse me." He went onto the porch and called Greene County dispatch. He got the telephone number he wanted and punched it into his cell phone.

The call was answered, "Dr. Lacy Daniels."

Jack identified himself and asked his questions. When he got his answers, Lacy said, "You and Troy are not going to leave me alone, are you? He was just asking the same questions. You two need to compare notes."

He hung up and called Chief Jerrell's cell phone.

Chapter 42

The Crown Vic was enveloped in a cloud of limestone dust as Jack and Liddell made their way back to State Road 59.

"Tell me again what Dr. Daniels said," Liddell asked, not taking his eyes off the road. There were deep drainage ditches on each side of the road for the farm fields.

Jack said, "I asked her about the sulfur she found on Troy Junior and Brandon. She found sulfur under Troy Junior's toenails, and some on the bottom of Brandon's jeans. Remember how we were told that was common around here. Shaunda said she smelled it at the lake before she was attacked. I asked Daniels if it could have come from inside a coal mine."

"Shaunda was raped inside a coal mine," Liddell said.

"Exactly. Dr. Daniels said Troy had capsaicin in his lungs. Angelina had looked that up and it would have to be inhaled in quantities for that to happen."

Liddell said, "Like in an enclosed area."

"I asked Jerrell if Troy Junior had breathing problems. He said his son had to carry albuterol with him. He didn't have asthma, but he had trouble catching his breath when he got nervous."

"You think these guys were killed in a mine? Why weren't there traces of sulfur on any of the other victims?"

Jack said, "I'm not sure. Maybe no one was looking for it but Dr. Daniels. Shaunda said Brandon was trespassing on Dugger Mine property and that's why she stopped his Jeep that morning. What if there's something in that mine she doesn't want anyone to find? What if there are more victims that we haven't found?"

"Shit!"

"Yeah. Shit!"

"How are we going to find the mine?" Liddell asked. "We'll need some equipment. We need someone that knows what the hell they're doing to take us in."

"I know just the guy."

"Cline?"

"Cline."

Liddell made a wide U-turn and headed back to Pleasant Grove Farms. Jack was about to call Angelina when his phone rang in his hand.

"Agent Murphy," Sergeant Ditterline said.

"You got me Ditty," Jack answered.

"I thought you should know something. I don't want to cause problems between you and my boss, but I don't think he should be going out there by himself."

Jack listened, disconnected and said, "Turn back around. We've got to get to Rosie's. Jerrell's going to confront Shaunda and Ditty said he wasn't in a good mood. He's afraid someone is going to get hurt."

"Probably Jerrell."

"You read my mind, Bigfoot. Now put that foot to good use."

Liddell fishtailed in the gravel and punched the accelerator until he hit blacktop. The tires peeled out rocketing the car ahead down the narrow county road.

"We'll never beat him there," Jack said. "I'm going to try his cell again." He called. "He's not answering."

"Is Ditty going after him?" Liddell asked.

"No one will dare to," Jack said and he didn't blame them. Jack didn't want to piss the big man off, but he was giving him no choice.

The trip to Rosie's took longer than Jack had hoped. If Jerrell was there he had already done all the damage. Jack now had to consider the possibility that Jerrell was involved in a cover up and wasn't going to confront Shaunda at all. Director Toomey seemed to think Jerrell would be prone to impulsive behavior. Jack had only known the man for two days. He didn't know what was going through Jerrell's head.

They were on State Road 54 when they heard a siren coming up on them fast from behind.

"Linton PD," Liddell said looking in the rearview mirror.

The squad car pulled around them. The bar lights danced off the shiny hood of the Crown Vic and Jack's cell phone rang. He answered.

"Agent Murphy, I thought you might need some help," Sergeant Ditterline said.

"Just get us there, Ditty, and then you can take off," Jack said.

"10-4, Agent," Ditty said, the call disconnected and the police car shot forward, the speed increasing until they reached ninety miles per hour. The sun was drawing down and dark clouds cast shadows that outraced the cars. Liddell skillfully stayed with the squad car as it managed to move traffic out of their path until they could turn off the main road.

Ditty dropped back and waved as Liddell pulled past and headed to Rosie's. Liddell reached the parking lot and slid to a halt behind Jerrell's big truck. Shaunda's Tahoe was there but Rosie's little Ford Ranger pickup was gone.

"The front door is open," Liddell said as they automatically ran their windows down to listen.

"Back up toward the road a little," Jack said.

Liddell shifted into reverse and backed until the car faced the front doors from twenty feet distant. They opened their doors and prepared to get out, all senses alert.

"Let's go," Jack said and drew his .45. It was quiet. The lights were on in the bar and one window upstairs. Pen's room. Nothing moved and even the air seemed to still.

"I really don't like this, pod'na."

They exited the car and split up, approaching from angles. Jack reached the porch first and put his back against the wall, the .45 Glock up and ready. Liddell did the same on the other side of the door.

"I don't hear anything," Jack whispered.

"Smell," Liddell said.

Jack sniffed the air again. The smell was faint. Burnt gunpowder. He nodded.

"I'm going in," Jack said in a lowered voice. Liddell steadied himself to give cover fire if necessary. Jack bladed around the edge of the door, gun pointing the way. The bar was straight ahead. He cleared the doorway, ran and dropped to the floor with his back against the bar. He scanned the room quickly.

Jack crouched and he crab walked to the end of the bar. He lay prone and crawled until he could see behind the bar. Nothing.

He got back in a crouched position. He pointed at himself and then pointed at the batwing doors that led to the kitchen. He pointed at Liddell and then at the door leading upstairs. Liddell took a two handed stance using the door frame to support his gun hand and trained the barrel on that door.

Jack moved to the kitchen and cleared it. He came back into the bar, stopped and listened. He felt more than heard something upstairs. He moved to the other end of the bar, slowly opened the door and leveled his gun at the entrance. Liddell came in and edged around the room coming up on the other side of the stairway door. Jack went first with Liddell covering him. He took the steps slowly, pausing on each step to listen for movement or sound. He heard a soft moan and ran up the remaining steps, motioning for Liddell to follow. He stopped before entering the hallway and peeked around the sill.

"Gun!" he yelled to warn Liddell and leveled his .45 at the figure standing over Jerrell's prone body. Shaunda was in full uniform holding the big Colt Python .357 in both hands, legs straddling the body. She turned slightly toward Jack and the gun came up.

"Drop it or I'll drop you!" Jack ordered.

She kept turning and Jack's finger tightened on the trigger, taking up the three pounds of pressure needed to fire a .45 bullet right into her brain. Time seemed to slow. Jack could see everything clearly and all at one time. He could see Shaunda turning impossibly slow. Jerrell lying on his side. Blood seeping out of a wound on his chest. Blood pooling around his upper arm that was twisted at an impossible angle. Jerrell's light blue shirt blooming red like a rose opening its petals. Jerrell's eyes drifting shut. He could see the door to Pen's room and the door to Rosie's room were shut tight and no one was behind Shaunda or in the line of fire. He could clearly smell the burnt gunpowder. Shaunda was still turning toward him and he could feel his finger tightening, speeding her death. The sound of his voice ordering her to drop the gun seemed to have barely receded when time resumed.

Shaunda froze and held one hand up in the air, the gun still in the other hand.

Jack yelled, "I will kill you." He said the words slowly, succinctly. "Drop it!"

"It wasn't me," Shaunda said and Jack could see tears running down her cheeks. "It wasn't me."

"Put the gun on the floor, Shaunda," Jack said. "I won't tell you again." He stepped into the hallway and quickly advanced on her gun and pushed the gun under her chin, lifting her head. He didn't need to remind himself that this woman had dropped the homeless guy like he was a bag of shit. Had conceivably killed six other men. If she turned another inch with that gun he would end her. Guilty of one, all, or none of the murders, she was an imminent threat to his and Liddell's lives. There's an old police adage, *"Better tried by twelve, than carried by six."*

Jerrell's eyes opened suddenly and he tried to lift his head from the floor. He made it an inch with great effort and said one word. "Rosie." His head dropped to the floor and his eyes closed.

Liddell was coming down the hall. Jack held his gun under Shaunda's chin, took the gun from her hand, shoved it in his waistband and pushed her toward Liddell. Jack knelt and felt Jerrell's neck for a pulse. It was weak, but it was there. He was alive. "Handcuff her and call an ambulance," Jack said while examining Jerrell for other injuries and putting pressure on the chest wound. Foamy blood was coming from Jerrell's mouth. That's never a good sign.

Liddell pressed Shaunda against a wall, patted her down for other weapons, found a knife, and took it, said, "knife" to let Jack know while he pulled Shaunda's arms behind her and slipped hardened steel cuffs around her wrists. He helped her down to the floor, got on his cell phone and called 911. It seemed to take forever for the operator to stop asking questions and take any action and he was yelling at the dispatcher to 'hurry the hell up' by the time he ended the call. "Ambulance is on the way," Liddell said. "How bad?"

"He's been shot at least twice. Right side chest. Upper right arm. The arm might be broken. I can't see an exit wound on the chest. He's breathing and he's got a pulse but the ambulance better be close or he won't make it."

"It was Rosie," Shaunda said. "I told you I didn't shoot him. We're wasting time. Rosie has Pen."

"What happened?" Jack asked.

"I was downstairs with Pen. Troy showed up. He knew about Rosie. He confronted her and she shot him. I thought she was going to kill me, too. She's crazy, Jack. You've got to help me get Pen back. I'll tell you everything. I've got to find my daughter. Help me."

"Watch her," Jack said, and he went down the hall quickly checking the other rooms. He came back, pulled the big revolver from his waistband and smelled the barrel. It had been fired.

"I shot it earlier, remember. I just got it back from Troy. He gave it to me before he confronted Rosie. He said he'd figured something out and handed me my gun. He asked where Rosie was and I told him. He took off running up the stairs. I stayed here until I heard shots. I went upstairs and found him like this. Rosie and Pen were gone." More tears filled her eyes and her lips trembled.

Jack had gotten back on his knees holding pressure to Jerrell's chest wound. "You were standing over him with a gun," Jack said. "Why didn't you call it in? What the hell did you think you were doing?"

"I froze. Okay! I froze. Is he going to die?"

"How long ago did she leave?" Jack asked and when Shaunda didn't answer he yelled, "Answer me. How long?"

Shaunda raised her face. "Right before you came in. Maybe a couple of minutes. We have to go after her now. I don't know why she would take Pen. She loves Pen. Why would she do that?"

Human shield.

"Your call," Liddell said.

Jack hesitated and Shaunda said, "Troy said Rosie's name. He didn't say Shaunda. What the hell do you think he meant. Rosie shot him. Damn it, let me go or arrest me. If my daughter is hurt I'll..." Her face twisted into a mask of anger and she she didn't finish.

"I'll wait for the ambulance," Liddell said. "Go on. Get her daughter back."

Jack got Shaunda to her feet when he heard heavy boots on the stairway and Sergeant Ditterline came around the corner, gun in hand.

"What the hell?" Ditty said, taking in the scene. "Did she shoot the chief?"

Jack put Shaunda's revolver in his waistband and said, "I'm taking Chief Lynch with me. Liddell will explain everything. Check on that ambulance, will you?"

"Just did on my way up here, Agent Murphy. They'll be here any minute now," Ditty said.

Jack unlocked Shaunda's handcuffs and gave them to Liddell. "How's your side?" he asked Shaunda.

"I'll live. Let's get going. I think I know where she'll be taking Pen."

Sergeant Ditterline stood at the top of the stairs and yelled down to them, "Stay with Liddell and put out a BOLO on Rosie. She may be in that little Ford Ranger truck. She's got Pen with her."

"Let's take the Tahoe," Shaunda said. "We're going to be off-roading."

Chapter 43

"Where are we going?" Jack asked.

Shaunda had insisted on driving. She'd left a rooster tail of cinder and gravel and had a death grip on the steering wheel, leaning forward, mouth clamped shut. She said with a nervous tremble in her voice, "I know where she went. Or at least I think I know."

"That's what you said back at the bar. Where do you think she's gone?"

"The mine," Shaunda said.

"Which mine?"

"Dugger Mine. Or the old Sunflower. We'll go to the Dugger Mine first. We should see her truck." She continued to drive like a bat out of hell toward the lake where they'd fished out Brandon Dillingham's body only a day before.

"You said you'd tell me everything," Jack said.

"About Rosie and me? Well first off you know I lied about my aunt Eunice." Shaunda leaned back in the seat but maintained the tight grip on the wheel. "My aunt told you everything, so you know all about my shitty life growing up with religious sickos for parents. I had just found out I was pregnant when I came to live with her." She turned her head toward Jack and he nodded.

"I didn't tell you about Aunt Eunice because my past is long buried and I don't like digging into old dirt. I finished my sophomore year when I found out I was pregnant. My parents somehow found out and were forcing me to have an abortion." Her eyes teared up again at the thought. "Pen is my life. I snuck out and went to Aunt Eunice. She let me stay for a while but I had to leave."

She didn't mention the cousin that was molesting her so Jack didn't either.

"I quit school. I could never come back to my home. We would have been treated like lepers here. I couldn't do that to Pen. Do you understand?" When she asked she turned her head toward Jack and almost went off the road.

Jack said, "I get it. Now keep your eyes on the road. We can't do Penelope any good if we wreck."

Shaunda stared through the windshield and was in her own world. "When I was a sophomore, Lamont Washington and Daniel Winters were seniors. On the baseball team. Popular. Good looking and knew it. There was a pre-graduation party each year. Kind of a tradition for the seniors, but they invited some junior girls. The party was always held out at Dugger Mine. In the mine and down at the lake. I was a sophomore but Rosie was a junior and she was invited to go to the party. She had a crush on Leonard DiLegge. The high schools played against each other but DiLegge and Troy Junior had a bromance going with Washington and Winters. Where you saw one you saw them all."

She stopped talking long enough to cross into oncoming traffic going around a semi-truck and trailer. She whipped back in front of the truck as easy as if she were chewing gum. "Rosie got me invited too. DiLegge was supplying her with grass. Marijuana. She's never given the stuff up.

"No way I could get permission to leave the house at night much less go to a party of drunk teenagers. Rosie came by with some other girls and picked me up. We went to the party that night. There were fifty, maybe a hundred teenagers. They'd built small fires to keep their hands warm but they weren't warming their hands with the fire if you get my meaning. I'd see a little kiss here and there at high school, and maybe some necking in the parking lot, but I'd never seen anything like what was going on.

"I was a little scared, but excited too. I'd never done grown up stuff. Here, I was part of this. Rosie went somewhere with Leonard and Troy Junior came over. He was supposed to be a big man at school, but he acted like he was nervous or embarrassed to be talking to me. I found out later what he was nervous about."

She turned into the Dugger Mine property through a missing section of chain link fencing and continued across the rubble and brush. The Tahoe bounced and rocked but Shaunda didn't seem to notice. Jack had to hang on.

They topped a small rise and he could see the top of a vehicle the same color as Rosie's truck come into view. Shaunda slowed and came to a stop. "We need to go in on foot from here."

Jack agreed. "Do you think she'd shoot you?"

"I don't want to find out if you don't mind."

Jack said, "Finish your story so I know what I'm getting into here."

Shaunda took a deep breath, let it out and said, "Troy offered me a sip of what he was drinking. It was in a Coke can. He laughed when I told him I couldn't."

She saw Jack's eyebrows raise and said, "I know Aunt Eunice told you they drugged me. She was the one that suggested that that's what happened. I went along with her story because she couldn't believe I'd ever do anything like that, what with my upbringing."

Jack nodded.

"Rosie came back with Leonard, Winters and Washington. They were all smoking a joint. Rosie was giggling and she had been drinking. She told me to lighten up and enjoy the party. She promised nothing would happen and that she'd get me home before my parents woke up.

"I trusted her. She was my best friend. Like a sister. I'd never smoked or drank before and I was getting high. The boys wanted to go into the mine. It didn't seem like a big deal. Just us and the three boys. Troy said they were going to tell ghost stories and had built a small campfire down there. I should have known no one would build a fire inside a mine but I was with Rosie.

"The rest of what I told my aunt was true. I was high, drinking spiked drinks, smoking whatever they were and I remember feeling happy. I was free for once in my life. Then Troy started groping me. Rosie and Leonard were making out and the other two were just egging Troy on with these moronic grins on their faces. I tried to get Troy to stop. He slapped me hard and knocked me down. He straddled me and started ripping my blouse open. I heard Rosie yelling at him to stop and Leonard punched her. She fell down and we were looking at each other when they took turns with us. I'll never forget the look in her eyes. Betrayal, hurt, fear, anger. She looked dead. Like there was nothing behind those eyes."

Jack felt a chill run up his spine and down his arms. He wanted to kill the assholes himself. She went on in a fading voice.

"They were laughing and giving each other high fives when they left. They had taken our clothes. All except our underwear. It was cold. The ground was especially cold. It was in March, just like you guessed. We lay there a long time. Too ashamed I guess. I didn't want anyone to see me. I was afraid they were waiting."

"How did you get home?" Jack asked.

"Rosie had left her car at the party and came to pick me up with some other girls. Her car was still there. The party was breaking up and we were able to get to her car without seeing anyone. She had extra clothes in the trunk. She gave me a sweatshirt and pants but we had to go barefoot. We made a pact that we would never tell anyone what happened. Who would believe us anyway. They'd say it was our fault for leading those boys on. The baseball players were heroes to the school. They could do no wrong. We'd be labeled as sluts. Plus, I could never let my parents find out.

"I was able to sneak in and we saw each other at school. The next couple of months were a nightmare and then I figured out I was pregnant. I told Rosie and she said we should just take off somewhere out west. We could get jobs and no one would know. Her parents weren't much better than mine. They just had more money.

"School was over. Before we could come up with a plan my mom accused me of being pregnant. She found the pregnancy test I'd done in the trash. Her and my dad prayed and screamed and cried and prayed some more. I was going to hell. The baby was born in sin. That kind of stuff. They told me it would have to be aborted. Dad found a guy in Sullivan that would do it. I said I wouldn't go with him. He beat me. Said he would beat the demons out of me. Thought I was possessed. I packed that night and left. I slept in the woods for a night or two and finally had to go to Aunt Eunice."

"You left Eunice's and had the baby where?" Jack asked.

"St. Louis, Missouri. I was on the street for a long time until a cop caught me shoplifting food. He took me to a women's shelter and they had a doctor that delivered Pen. She was born with a spinal defect. Spina bifida. It got worse as she grew and her speech started to change and she was losing the use of her legs. They could do surgery but I couldn't afford it on a part-time waitressing job. I saved enough to get her in to a surgeon and he said he could do something but she may get worse even with the surgery and it was risky because of her particular condition. I think you know the rest."

"When did the killings start?" Jack asked. He hadn't heard any sirens like Sergeant Ditterline promised. He needed to call Liddell, but Liddell would have figured out what was happening after a few minutes of the ambulance not arriving.

"Baker was first," Shaunda said. She'd relaxed now. Telling a story that she'd kept inside all these years. "Rosie ran into him in a restaurant in Sullivan. He was with his wife. He recognized her and just sat there looking her up and down and smiling."

"Why kill Baker?"

"Baker was a substitute teacher at Union. He was at the party too. He came into the mine and saw what was happening to us but he just stood there and watched. He never tried to stop them. Never told anyone. In a way he was the worst of all."

"Who killed them, Shaunda? You? Rosie? Both of you?"

"Rosie did. I swear on my daughter's life. Rosie killed Baker and told me about it. I was going to come home but my parents were still alive and I just couldn't. When they died and Rosie hadn't done anything else crazy I decided to come home. I got the job I have and I let it go. She was my best friend. I couldn't arrest her. I thought she'd gotten her revenge and she was through. Look, Baker was a psycho. He molested children. He deserved what he got."

"What about the rest?" Jack asked.

Shaunda sat silent. She took the keys from the ignition and opened her door. "Let's go. If we come out of here alive I'll tell you the rest."

Jack said, "What if we both don't make it?"

"I plan on staying alive. How about you?"

"Good plan," Jack said and they exited the Tahoe.

They moved as quietly as they could across the rock strewn ground, circling around to the back of Rosie's truck. Jack looked in the bed and saw several blue tarps still in the package, a coil of boating rope, a shovel and several cinder blocks. It might have been there for legitimate purposes but he didn't believe that was the case.

They stopped at the wide entrance to the coal mine, their backs against the wall. Shaunda asked, "Can I have my gun back?"

"Only if you promise not to shoot me," Jack said and she gave a weak smile.

He took the gun from his waistband, opened the cylinder, snapped it shut and put it in the holster on her gun belt. She put the strap over it, snapped it down and nodded.

"Glad to have you back Chief," Jack said.

"Glad to be back. Not glad to be going up against my best friend. Promise me you won't kill her."

Jack said, "No one will get shot if we do this right. Let's get your daughter and get the hell out of there. We have her pinned in. There's no need to get in a gunfight, right?"

Shaunda put a cautioning hand on Jack's arm before they entered. "I'm familiar with these places. Don't touch the walls. Don't touch the supports. Don't make loud noises. Don't fire your gun unless absolutely necessary. I'll be right behind you."

"Yeah. Thanks partner."

"I'm injured remember. You're the man. You get to go first."

Jack gave her a sarcastic look.

She said, "That's what happens in all the movies."

"Bite me, Shaunda."

"Maybe if we live through this," she said, and gently pushed him into the entrance and followed close behind.

Chapter 44

After Jack and Shaunda left Liddell had begun to feel uneasy. Jerrell was in bad shape and he didn't hear the ambulance. He knew every minute was precious if Jerrell had a punctured lung and was bleeding internally.

"Where's that ambulance coming from?" Liddell said out loud. He should have heard something before now. "Hang in there, Chief. I've got you. You're going to be okay. I've got you."

Ditty had gone into one of the bedrooms and came back with a blanket. Liddell thought he was going to make a pillow from it, or use it to keep Jerrell warm, but Ditty just stood there looking down at them.

"I don't think he's going to make it," Ditty said.

"Of course, he is. We should get him comfortable and warm. Give me the blanket and see if you can find a pillow."

"I don't think he's going to need it," Ditty said.

Liddell thought it was a callous remark. He looked up into Ditty's face. He saw the flat eyed stare Ditty was giving him and a chill shot up his spine.

"See if you can hurry that ambulance up, Sergeant," Liddell said, thinking Ditty was in shock at losing his Chief.

"I can't do that, Agent," Ditty said, and pitched the blanket on top of Jerrell's face. "Use that to cover him up. Stay put where I can keep an eye on you." Ditty's duty weapon was in his hand and pointed at Liddell from five feet away.

* * * *

It was full dark now. Shaunda and Jack were fifty feet into the mine; no lights, feeling their way along the steel rails. Jack could feel the dampness that clung to his skin. There was a bad smell, like old sweat and dirty clothes and dust motes that hadn't settled out of the air for a hundred years. His throat had a sudden tickle. He put his arm across his nose and mouth but it didn't do much to muffle the cough.

Shaunda whispered from off to his right, "It's only going to get worse. That's coal dust and you won't ever get it out of your lungs. Don't worry. You'll get used to it in ten or twenty years."

"Just what I needed," Jack said. "Do you know where we're going?"

Instead of an answer a powerful flashlight beam came on and found him. "You got a light?" Shaunda asked.

Jack had one but he'd hoped to not use it if Shaunda knew where they were going. Not yet anyway. He pulled a small but powerful flashlight from his jacket pocket but didn't turn it on. "Get that light off of me," he ordered Shaunda. The light went off and the darkness seemed to deepen. He stepped over the rail, moving closer to Shaunda's last position with his gun in his hand and the other feeling for Shaunda, feeling for anything in this nothingness.

His fingers touched cloth with something soft and giving beneath.

"Whoa there sailor," Shaunda said.

Jack pulled his hand back and leaned in. In a low voice he said, "Use the light sparingly, on and off. Or at least hold it out to your side." He couldn't believe she'd gone through the police academy and hadn't learned the basics of not making yourself a target. Or making him a target.

Shaunda flipped the light on and off several times. "Like that?"

Jesus. "Better yet hold your hand over the end to limit the beam. Like a nightlight. She did so but still very close to her body. Jack took her hand and pulled the arm out to the side between waist and shoulder level. It was the best he could do for her.

He could see well enough with the dim light but felt in front with the toe of his shoe before planting a foot. He was glad he did because a moment later his shoe struck something hard and unmoving. He risked the low beam light and saw it was a light gauge rail for a coal car that was crossing the track they had followed. They were at a four way intersection. The ground and tracks were heavy with moisture. Where the tracks intersected one rail was bent outward and the ground beneath was half a foot lower than the rail.

"That's called a fall," Shaunda said. "These mines sometimes flooded or the ground was softer and the weight of the coal cars would put pressure on the intersections. Not a problem usually. It was flooding, or gas, cave-ins or fire that closed most of the mines."

"I feel much better now," Jack said.

"You're welcome. We go left here."

"How do you know?" Jack asked. He knew how to get back but he needed Shaunda to feel she was in charge.

"Because when I look that direction I get a sick feeling in the pit of my stomach."

This is where it happened.

They turned left. Jack had changed places with Shaunda putting her closer to the wall on his left. He kept his right foot close to the track. They were separated by just feet and she was falling behind. He could hear her regulation boots scuffing from time to time. She wasn't making a great attempt at being quiet and unnoticed except for whispering.

"Where are we going Shaunda," Jack said in a normal voice, not slowing.

She uncapped her hand from the front of her flashlight and shined the beam directly on him. He stopped and turned to face her. He heard her unsnap the holster. He could only make out her shape behind the blinding beam. The light glinted on the stainless steel gun barrel as she motioned he should keep going.

"I told you," she said. "We're going to find Rosie."

"Penelope?"

"Get moving," Shaunda said. "Or in the words of a stupid FBI agent, 'I'll kill you.'"

Jack bent his arms putting his hands up where she could see them and moved slowly forward. "Your daughter is in here."

"No. Penelope's safe and sound at home. Patty's with her watching television but they'll both be asleep before long. I put something in their tea."

"You get mom of the year," Jack said.

"Don't worry, it's doctor prescribed."

"Is Rosie alive?" Jack asked. "Or was this all you?"

Rosie answered from far down the dark shaft. "I'm alive, alone, and ready to rock and roll," she said happily. "I told you this would work, Shauny."

Jack saw Rosie's shape ahead in the dim light. He raised his voice. "She hates being called Shauny."

Rosie laughed out loud and said, "Get his gun."

Shaunda struggled a little to get Jack's gun out of his safety holster. There was a trick to drawing it, built in to keep the gun from being drawn by a bad guy. Jack told her how to get it out. She did and stuck it in her front waistband.

Jack felt the barrel of Shaunda's Colt Python against the back of his head.

"If my partner was here he'd have a joke for this. I think I've got one," Jack said.

"Tell me your joke, Agent Murphy," Rosie said. "I could use another laugh."

"Okay," Jack said. "A male and a female cop walk into a coal mine."

Rosie was already chuckling.

"The male cop says, "This isn't exactly what I had in mind when I said I wanted to get you in the dark.""

"You just made that up," Shaunda said and prodded the gun into his back again.

"You got me. Bigfoot is the jokester."

"Here's a better joke," Rosie said. "An FBI agent walks into a mine looking for a killer and disappears forever."

"What's the punchline?" Jack asked.

"You die."

"I like my joke better," Jack said.

"Shut up and move," Shaunda said and pushed the gun against his skull.

They moved forward and Jack could see Rosie was standing in front of a heavy door. Metal signs were attached to the door saying, "DANGER" and "NO ENTRY." Rosie was holding a small semi-automatic pistol in her hand pointed in their direction.

"Rosie, if you keep that pistol pointed at us you might accidentally shoot Shauny."

Shaunda cracked him on the back of the neck with the butt of the revolver. "Shut up."

Rosie lowered the barrel toward the ground.

Jack said, "If that gun goes off now the bullet will ricochet and we won't know what it'll hit."

"How should I point it smartass?" Rosie asked.

"Stick it up your ass," Jack suggested and ducked, expecting another blow but it didn't come.

* * * *

Liddell sat on the floor as ordered by Sergeant Ditterline. He was allowed to tear off a piece of the thin blanket and tie it off around Jerrell's bicep wound. He was allowed to keep checking Chief Jerrell's vitals and keep pressure on the chest wound.

"A waste of time," Ditty said.

"I've got nothing but time," Liddell responded.

It had been at least twenty minutes since Jack and Shaunda left and Jerrell was still hanging in there. By a thread.

"Says you," Ditterline said and grinned. "Just so you know, I never called for an ambulance."

"I thought he was your friend?" Liddell said.

"If I'd do that to a friend, imagine what I'd do to you if you pissed me off. I don't have a problem with you right now so let's keep it that way."

"Is that why you have that gun pointed at me? If we don't have a problem then let's get the chief to the hospital and I'll buy dinner. You like pizza?"

Ditty backed up a couple of steps. "I don't like what you're thinking. Someone gets a little too cocky I think they're up to something dumb. Don't do something dumb."

"I'll tell you what's dumb. You could have skated on all this. We only suspected Shaunda. We knew she shot the homeless guy in cold blood, but we couldn't really prove she did any of the other murders. You've gotten in way over your head, Ditty. It's not too late to stop this."

"Just how would I do that, Mr. FBI?"

"For starters, Sergeant, you can reholster that weapon, call an ambulance and help me save him. One of us needs to go and stop Shaunda from killing my partner."

"I just give up and you'll forget all about this I suppose," Ditty said and snorted. "I'll tell you what I'll do. After your partner is dead, I'll take his gun to shoot you and take your weapon and shoot him. Voila, you got lost in the dark and shot each other."

"Won't work," Liddell said. "You'd have to somehow get me and Jack together to make it plausible. I'm a big guy to have to haul somewhere. Besides, Jerrell's been shot with Shaunda's gun. Ballistics from the homeless guy will prove it."

Sergeant Ditterline said nothing.

"Also, you forgot one big thing."

"What's that?" Ditty asked.

"Jack."

Chapter 45

Shaunda pushed Jack forward. The ground was covered in grit and what felt like pieces of gravel under his shoes. Shaunda backed off as they neared Rosie but was still behind him.

Jack saw the door had heavy hinges that had started to rust. There was a small pass-through window near the top of the door. It was bolted shut and sealed with duct tape. The door itself was standing halfway open now. On the other side of the door all he could see was blackness and motes, maybe coal dust, suspended in the air.

"Get in," Rosie said, wagging her automatic toward the opening.

"You first," Jack said. "Equal in all things. That's my motto."

Rosie raised the gun pointing directly at Jack's face from ten feet away. Shaunda had put the barrel of the revolver in his back again and was pushing. It was the moment he'd been waiting for.

Jack pivoted on one foot, spun around, wrapped an arm around Shaunda's waist and pulled her against him. She was between himself and Rosie's gun. Rosie didn't shoot. Shaunda put the muzzle of her revolver against Jack's chest and squeezed the trigger several times.

* * * *

Liddell had rolled part of the blanket up and put it under Jerrell's head. "I'm your hostage in case this all goes to hell," Liddell said.

"I can see why you're FBI," Ditty said.

"You're going to kill me in any case," Liddell said indifferently.

"Who knows. Maybe your superman partner will fly here and save the day."

"Contrary to popular opinion, FBI agents can't fly," Liddell said.

"I could get to like you if I didn't have to kill you."

"I have an obvious question, Sergeant Ditterline."

"Wow. Just like on TV. This is the part where the hero gets the bad guy to confess to everything and then gets the drop on the bad guy. Everyone's happy. Except the bad guy that is."

Liddell shrugged.

Ditty said, "Go ahead. Ask your question. I might answer it."

"I have a couple of questions."

"We may run out of time."

"Okay. Biggest one first. Why are you doing this? Did Jerrell do something to you? Is it about money?" Liddell asked.

"Next question," Ditty said.

"You called Jack and told him Jerrell was on his way here. That means you're also the reason Jerrell came out here. It was a set up."

"Not bad. Not bad. But I had nothing to do with Jerrell coming here. He's in love with Shaunda in case you hadn't figured that out. I knew he'd come out here eventually. I took her gun out of evidence and waited for him to leave the station. I called Agent Murphy after Jerrell got here. He was inside talking to Rosie upstairs when I showed up. He was asking where Shaunda was. I told him upstairs but she was in the kitchen. I handed Shaunda her gun. She went upstairs and…well, here we are."

"I knew it was something like that," Liddell said.

"Yeah, right. You're so smart tell me why I'm doing this?" Ditty asked.

Liddell checked Jerrell's pulse again. It was weak. He said, "Number one reason. You're an asshole."

Ditty laughed.

"I'm guessing that Eunice's son didn't die in prison like Eunice believed. I think you're Shaunda's kissing cousin."

The laugh was erased and a shocked look took its place. The hand pointing the gun at Liddell was deadly still. "How did you know? It was that Angel gal that does all that computer stuff wasn't it?"

Liddell said simply, "I didn't know. Until right now."

Ditty stepped forward close enough to place the muzzle against Liddell's forehead. "You think you're smart…"

He didn't get to finish. Liddell grabbed the gun, pushed it up and grabbed Ditty's crotch with the other hand. He squeezed Ditty's wrist and crotch with all his considerable strength. The gun fell from Ditty's hand and Liddell got to his feet still hanging on to Ditty's damaged goods.

Liddell let go of the wrist, grabbed Ditty's neck and shoved him against the wall. He used all of his weight and strength to drive his fingers into the flesh, digging deep, feeling the larynx in his grip. Ditty forgot his wounded pride and joy and his hands went to his throat and clawed at Liddell's hands. Liddell head butted him in the nose again and again until Ditty's hands dropped to his sides.

Liddell let him drop to the floor, kicked the gun down the hallway and called for an ambulance. He then called Jack to warn him.

* * * *

Shaunda's head came up in surprise and she pulled the trigger twice more. Nothing. Jack spun her around with one arm around her throat while the other pulled his .45 Glock from her front waistband and shoved it in her side.

"Drop the gun Rosie," he said.

Rosie had fired one shot but it went wild and Jack heard it ricocheting down the shaft. She kept the little automatic pointed in his direction but she was caught between him and the way out. Shaunda struggled until Jack bore down on her neck and said in her ear, "I'll rip your head off and shit down your neck. Be still." She was.

"Take your handcuffs off your belt and toss them to her," he ordered Shaunda.

Shaunda hesitated and Jack tightened down until she made gagging sounds. Her hand went to her cuff case. She unsnapped it, removed the handcuffs and tossed them in Rosie's direction.

"Pitch the gun behind you and put the handcuffs on. Behind your back," Jack said.

Rosie didn't move. Jack could see the muscles in her neck tighten. He ducked his head behind Shaunda's just as he heard the crack of a gunshot. He felt Shaunda shudder and slump against him. He fired and the bullet struck Rosie somewhere in the face, twisting her head back. He fired again and a hole appeared in her shirt, just to the left of center on her upper chest. He fired again and this one hit her in the throat. Her gun clattered to the ground. Rosie collapsed straight down into a heap.

Chapter 46

Jack and Liddell had given statements all night to the State Police, Sullivan County Police, Greene County Police, and a special investigator with the FBI. Their guns had been taken and would be given back after a shooting board decided their fate. Chief of Police Pope had given them several days off with pay to recover and get the shooting board behind them. Deputy Chief Dick, aka Double Dick, had called Jack and advised him that there was paperwork to sign at headquarters but he had said it in a nice way and even asked Jack how they were getting on. Jack wasn't comfortable with this side of Double Dick after so many years of sparring with the man. He'd saved Double Dick's bacon not long ago and was owed big time. He wondered when the grace period would end and the Dickster would once again be an arrogant rampaging over-supervisor.

In the meantime, Director Toomey had heaped praise on them. Not. Toomey had been thoughtful enough to provide them with other weapons until they got theirs back. Being with the FBI, Toomey didn't know that police officers always had spares and then some.

The Coal Miner Bar was still a crime scene but Sergeant Crocker had been allowed to pack up their belongings and drop them off at Angelina's cottage. Penelope Lynch had been collected by Sergeant Crocker and his wife and the girl was currently staying with them until permanent arrangements could be made.

They'd stayed overnight, or over morning, at Angelina's in her spare bedrooms and slept until after noon. John Cline had come over and brought homemade cherry wine and pot stickers.

"I didn't forget you Agent Murphy," Cline said, and produced a gold colored box that bore the Glenmorangie twelve-year-old Scotch label. He handed it to Jack who didn't waste any time opening it and pouring four fingers into one of the old jelly jars they were using as tumblers.

"Would you care for some Mr. Cline?" Jack asked.

Cline filled a tumbler with homemade wine. "I prefer this but thank you. Angelina said it was your brand."

Jack rewarded him with a smile and held his tumbler out to the gathered group in a toast. "Sláinte."

Cline held his up and said, "Prost. That's German for 'cheers.'"

Liddell said, "This is really good," and ate another pot sticker.

Angelina merely nodded.

They finished the bottle of wine and a platter of the pot stickers and Jack made coffee. He said to Liddell, "I guess after we go see Jerrell in the hospital we'll have to make an appearance at Linton PD. I don't think they'll be mad at us, seeing as how you saved their chief's life."

"Yeah. Did you know the Town Council made Sergeant Crocker the interim chief until Jerrell's fit for duty?" Liddell asked.

"I did. He'll do a good job. Jerrell will have him on Facetime all day, digitally stalking the man."

Liddell smiled. "You know that's right. Give me some of that coffee."

Jack brought the pot to the table and Cline got up. "I'll leave you to it. I have to say this is the most excitement Pleasant Farms has ever seen." A smile crossed Cline's face. "There was that one wedding party…"

"I don't want to hear about it," Jack interrupted. "I'm getting married soon and I don't need bad thoughts."

Cline laughed and excused himself.

"I'd love to stay and drink Angelina," Jack said, "but we have business to attend to."

"If it's okay with you Angelina, maybe we could stay here tonight?" Liddell said.

"I'd be happy to house you, but tomorrow you have to go. I'm still on paid vacation and you two attract trouble. Toomey's already trying to give me orders."

"Speaking of which, we can order a couple of pizzas before we come back this evening," Liddell said.

"Marcie has you on a diet again, doesn't she?" Angelina asked.

"I've been eating vegetables until I feel like one."

"Pizza sound good to you, Angelina?" Jack asked.

"I'll go get the beer," she said.

Jack and Liddell headed to the hospital. They'd already been there once when Jerrell was taken to surgery. The sky had clouded up and there was a threatening blackness coming from the south by the time they found a place to park.

"He's a tough guy," Liddell said. "I thought for sure he was gone."

Jack put his hand on Liddell's shoulder. "If it wasn't for you he would be, Bigfoot. Tell me again how you took Ditty down."

"Quit it," Liddell said, but then rehashed his disabling of Sergeant Ditterline. Ditterline was barely alive when the medics arrived at Rosie's but he was DOA—dead on arrival—by the time he was packed into the ambulance with Chief Jerrell. Ditty's larynx was crushed and he'd choked to death on his own blood.

They entered the ER doors and Jack said, "Go ahead and say it. I know you're dying to."

Liddell grinned and said, "It was a 'nutty' take down. Get it. Nutty."

"I got it the first dozen times," Jack said.

"I got one for you, pod'na."

"I don't need one."

"This is what you should have said to Shaunda."

"Can I stop you?"

Liddell said, "When she tried to kill you, you could have said, 'Guns don't kill people. Unloaded guns don't kill people either.'"

"Did you just make that up?" Jack asked.

"You told me your mom used to say that."

Jack thought he might have told Liddell that at some time. "My mom would never say something like that. Shame on you."

"You also said she's the one that came up with, 'You get more flies with honey. But you get more attention with a gun.'"

"I did not."

"Did too."

"You're already back," the security guard said as they came in.

"Is he awake?" Jack asked.

"I hope so. His whole department is up there. The nurses want me to make them leave. I'll go with you. Maybe they'll listen to you."

They followed the guard to Jerrell's room and it was full of police and civilians. Even more were waiting in the hall and sitting in the lounge. The lounge was full of flowers and cards and several civilians were holding even more flowers.

The security guard said, "Troy told them to get those sissy assed flowers out of his room. Said they were stinking up the place."

Jack didn't think the guard was kidding. Liddell pushed his way through the door and yelled, "FBI. Make room boys."

The happy expressions suddenly turned sullen but they stepped back and opened a path to Jerrell's hospital bed. Last night Jerrell had lain unconscious with tubes and wires and whatever stuck in or to him everywhere. He had looked like death warmed over. Now, he was sitting propped up slightly and most of the devices had been removed. He had an IV drip going, and something on his fingertip to check his oxygen level.

Liddell said to the gathered officers, "Give him a remote and turn the game on and he's good to go."

Everyone laughed except Jerrell. He said to everyone, "Guys, I need the room. Thanks for coming but you don't have to hang around."

When they didn't move he said, "I'm still the ranking officer of this fine department and I want you to get your asses back to work. We have a city to protect. Remember?"

That got them moving and told Jack that Jerrell was truly on the mend. The room emptied and Liddell shut the door. When they were gone Jerrell closed his eyes and Jack noticed a fine patina of perspiration on his forehead and upper lip. He'd had his ass kicked and was putting on a brave face for his troops. Army strong.

"Shaunda?" Jerrell asked.

"I'm sorry," Jack answered. Actually, he was sorry she'd lived. But they needed someone alive to testify.

Jerrell's eyes closed again and Jack saw a fat teardrop run down his cheek.

"I'm sorry she got hurt, Chief," Jack said hurriedly. "She was shot, but she's alive and in the secured room down the hall."

"What are you sorry about? You the one that shot her?"

Jack told Jerrell what had happened at the mine and why he'd gone there with Shaunda. He told Jerrell about Sergeant Ditterline and that he was dead. Jerrell said nothing until the story was finished. He took a shallow breath and grimaced. Liddell pushed the "Call" button by Jerrell's bed and when the nurse came in he asked if she could bring something for Jerrell's pain.

"How's Pen?" Jerrell asked, when the nurse came in.

"Crocker and his wife took her home with them," Liddell advised him.

Jerrell's eyes welled up again. "I should have been there for her. I did something stupid and now that little girl's got to suffer for it."

"Let's get this straight," Jack said. "You didn't do anything but your job. This is all on those three idiots. I'm just sorry that Shaunda's the only one who'll be answering charges. They killed seven men. Almost killed all three of us."

Jerrell reached out his good hand to Liddell. "I think I owe you my life."

"You do," said Liddell. "I expect you to pay that back by staying in this job and being proud of yourself and your people. I think half the city is out there waiting to see their hero. You're a lucky man, Chief."

Jerrell seemed to want to say something but the words must have gotten stuck in his throat. He just nodded and squeezed Liddell's hand.

"Now for the bad news," Jack said.

Jerrell's mouth tightened into a straight line.

"The bad news is we are going back home in the morning. Angelina is putting us up overnight. She seems to have fallen in love with Greene County."

"That's the bad news?" Jerrell said sarcastically.

"Oh, and Crocker is the Acting Chief until you get back," Jack added.

Jerrell silently mouthed, "God save us."

Chapter 47

Jack and Liddell had gone to check on Shaunda after they'd talked to Jerrell. She was in a 'secure' room just down the hall from the man she'd shot and left to die. They didn't go into her room when the officer assured them she was still alive and out cold. They spent the evening with Angelina, eating pizza and watching old westerns on the big screen television. It seemed that Cline had a dozen or more DVDs of westerns. Gunsmoke, Palladin, The Rifleman, Bonanza, etc.

The evening was uneventful except for the fact that Liddell had too much garlic on his pizza and during the night created enough gas to run a turbine engine. Jack had to sleep with the window open and his T-shirt pulled over his face.

The next morning, they said their goodbyes to Angelina and found their way to highway 41 going south.

"It really is beautiful around here. I prefer small cities. Less noise. Less crime. Less people and cars and there's always a Pizza Hut or an Arby's nearby," Liddell said.

"Don't start on the pizza," Jack warned him.

"My momma always said, "Better out than in.""

"Your momma didn't have to sleep in the same house with you last night."

"Wasn't that bad," Liddell griped.

"I thought we had another crime scene. I was getting ready to call Rudy and Barr and maybe that K-9. Get out the caution tape…"

"Now that's just mean," Liddell said.

"Don't ask me to stop anywhere on the way home. That is unless you feel another gastric nuke coming on. I swear I'll pull over and leave you behind."

"You still love me, don't you?"

Jack said nothing.
"You wouldn't be mad unless you loved me."
Again, Jack said nothing.
Liddell said, "Pull my finger."

Epilogue

One month later...

There are adages that sometimes seem very appropriate. Such as "Time waits for no man." Jack and Liddell had come back to work to find their entire caseload had been left unworked, and new ones added. At least no one was trying to kill them here.

Jerrell hadn't stayed in touch, but Jack hadn't really expected him to. Jerrell wasn't the 'keep in touch' sort of guy. He didn't envy Jerrell cleaning up all the bodies and doing reams of paperwork. The Feds had turned all the cases over to the local agencies. The only one the Feds could charge was Shaunda Lynch, and it didn't make the national news. Jerrell had his work cut out for him. The rest of this was like shooting fish in a barrel but the paperwork was enough to make you want to shoot yourself.

Jack was eventually forgiven by Katie for not assisting with the wedding plans. He had, in turn, forgiven himself and didn't tell her that he'd made his own plans for their wedding. The downside of not telling her was that he'd put a rather large non-refundable deposit down for their wedding-moon in Maui. He'd have to tell her soon.

Liddell had assumed the role of daddy, which meant Jack had to listen to his incessant stories about Little Janie's teething, or the color and consistency of her stools, or how formula was good, but breastfeeding was better, and so on and so forth. Jack was Janie's godfather, and he loved the little girl, but his ears were bleeding by the end of each day. He didn't think he'd be that way when little Jake was born.

This morning Jack and Liddell arrested a burglar that had broken into a seventy-year-old widow's home, took her jewelry and cash, and then stabbed her because she wouldn't stop crying. He had left her for dead, but she'd been acting. She called police and within a half hour Jack and Liddell ran him to ground. He was still carrying the stolen goods.

"Can we put this guy on America's Dumbest Criminals?" Liddell asked after they'd booked him.

"This wasn't our case, Bigfoot. We officially poached on the turf of Violent Crimes or Property Crimes or whatever they call themselves this week."

Deputy Chief Richard Dick was the commander of Personnel and Training but somehow, he'd been allowed to rename the investigative units in the Detective's Division. He was having a grand old time coming up with names he considered more appropriate for the specialized units. He'd renamed the Burglary Unit as Property and Breaking and Entering. He'd changed Vice to Gambling and Prostitution. The only unit he'd left alone was Sex Crimes. He didn't have enough imagination to come up with something different that could still be politically correct. Some detective had suggested the "Me Too Unit" but that was shot down pretty quickly. Chief Pope was in the process of changing things back and taking Dick's new power away.

A uniformed officer caught the detectives in the hallway. "The chief wants you. I heard him asking for you. If you've done something wrong you'd better hotfoot it out of here."

They thanked the officer and decided they'd done nothing that could be proven. They went to the chief's office. The chief's secretary, Judy Mangold buzzed them in and told them they were expected. Jack heard voices coming from the chief's office and they knocked on his door.

The door was opened by Captain Franklin. Franklin was smiling. Jack thought maybe it wouldn't be too bad. Jack was wrong.

In the room were Chief Pope, Deputy Director Toomey, and two suits. The two suits were a man and a woman, both dressed in FBI attire, blue suits, starched white shirts, red ties, and highly polished wing tip shoes. Jack didn't know them and that worried him.

Toomey made introductions and the suits stood and held out a well-manicured hand each.

"Jack Murphy and Liddell Blanchard. This is Special Agent Saundra Lane and Special Agent Steve Offerman."

Jack barely resisted saying, "Well, isn't that special," but Liddell beat him to it. Chief Pope looked at the floor, Toomey looked uncomfortable, Jack was just glad Liddell hadn't told them to pull his finger.

The two Special Agents stood like statues. Jack shook their hands. Agent Lane's grip was strong, but Agent Offerman wanted a contest to see who could crush the other one's hand. Jack pegged Offerman as passive aggressive and let him win.

"If you're here to arrest us, I want my attorney," Jack said.

The agents didn't crack a smile.

Toomey cut the tension. "They're not here to arrest you, Jack." To the agents he said, "I told you these two were wiseacres."

Chief Pope asked everyone to take a seat. Franklin shut the door. Their only way out.

Chief Pope said, "Before we tell you why the Special Agents are here, I want to once again tell you how impressed we all were with the way you handled those cases up north."

Toomey said, "Excellent results."

Franklin stayed by the door. Jack thought maybe he should make a break for it. He was being fattened up for the slaughter. The Special Agents looked like paid assassins for the IRS. Paid for with Jack's tax dollars.

"Thank you all," Jack said. "If we're through here we've still got a lot of paperwork." He and Liddell started to get up but sat again seeing the look on Pope's face.

Toomey said, "I thought you should know that Angelina's new software was a big success. We're still—I mean *she's* still tweaking it, but I have no doubt it will be helpful for years to come. We found another victim thanks to Angelina's due diligence. This one was murdered by Rosie right after Shaunda left town. We've confirmed that Shaunda was in St. Louis having the baby when this one was killed. Who knows how many more they would have killed if you two hadn't stopped them."

Jack noticed the two Special Agents were giving Toomey an impatient look.

Jack asked Toomey, "Did you find out who Sergeant Ditterline really was?"

Toomey gave a weak smile. "We ran him down. He was Eunice Lynch's son, Danny Lynch."

He went to prison right after Shaunda left her aunt's house. He was convicted of premeditated murder and got a life sentence. He made friends with another inmate in prison and made some kind of deal to trade identities. They looked alike. He got away with it until the other guy was stabbed to death and the prison discovered the dead guy's prints didn't match Danny's. By then Danny had created another identity for himself, all fake, but it held up to a police background check. He's worked for Linton PD for seven years.

The same amount of years since Baker, the first victim, was killed.

"We were never informed about the lab results on the phones or the other evidence," Jack said.

Toomey pulled out a notebook. "You got nothing on the phones as far as DNA. The sim cards were missing from all but the Dillingham kid and it had nothing useful. The dispatch tapes were inconclusive as to a match, but we don't have Rosie Denton's voice to compare with, and Shaunda's wasn't very clear either. I'm only the messenger. Oh, but the drill bit was matched to all the head wounds of every victim except the last. Of course, that's not conclusive either because all we had to work with were photos and X-rays. The bullet that struck Chief Jerrell was from the gun you took from Shaunda. As was the bullet that killed the last victim, Anderson."

Jack saw Offerman was even more impatient so he decided to push it. "One more thing, Director. Is Shaunda cooperating, or is she just trying to avoid the death penalty?"

"She's cooperating. It's the only way we'll let her daughter have visits."

Jack asked, "Is Penelope still with Sergeant Crocker and his wife?"

Offerman interrupted. "We have other matters to deal with today Director if you don't mind."

Toomey said, "Cut right to the chase. That's how these boys operate. I think you all were made for each other."

Special Agent Offerman smiled at Jack. "I can see that. I'll be glad to take him off your hands for a while Chief Pope."

"Oh boy!" Liddell said.

"I have another job for you," Toomey said.

Acknowledgments

I would like to acknowledge some special people for their help with research and for allowing me the use of their names as characters and/or locations in this story. Shaunda Lynch, Troy Jerrell, William Ditterline, Rosie Benton, Nonnie Murray, The Dugger Coal Museum and Dugger Town Library showed great patience with me. They are all wonderful people and new friends who have allowed me to take liberties with their personalities. I would also like to give a special thanks to John Cline and Kenneth Dowling at Pleasant Grove Farm in Lyons and Jeff Thom at Francisco de Borja Café in Linton where the beginning of this book was written.

I would also like to acknowledge the men and women of the Linton Police Department and Dugger Police Department. This book does not come close to giving these officers credit for the hard and professional work they do. I can't imagine a world without law enforcement. Be safe. Thank you for everything you do.

The existence of this ninth book in the Jack Murphy thriller series is due in no small part to Michaela Hamilton, my editor, who I consider my friend and mentor. And kudos to my excellent team at Kensington who are experts at publicity, marketing, proofing, editing, legalese, cover design, distribution, publicity and so many other things. Without all of you this book would still be a file on my computer.

If I have not mentioned you, I hope I have thanked you in some way and that you will forgive my omission.

USOC, or Unsolved Serial and Organized Crime, is not a real FBI Task Force and is solely my creation.

Sneak Peek

In case you missed the first Jack Murphy thriller, keep reading to enjoy an excerpt from the book that started it all . . .

THE CRUELEST CUT

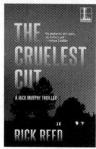

WHEN A KILLER PLAYS MIND GAMES WITH A COP, THERE ARE NO RULES.

The first victim is attacked in her home. Tied to her bed. Forced to watch every unspeakable act of cruelty—but unable to scream. The second murder is even more twisted. Signed, sealed, and delivered with a message for the police, stuffed in the victim's throat. A fractured nursery rhyme that ends with a warning: "There will be more." For detective Jack Murphy, it's more than a threat. It's a personal invitation to play. And no one plays rougher than Jack. Especially when the killer's pawns are the people he loves . . .

Prologue

The late-May rain came down hard as the Evansville PD detectives, uniformed officers, and SWAT team staked out the downtown alley behind Turley's Jewelers. Thanks to a tip from a reliable informant, today they would take down the Solazzo gang, armed robbers who had done a Godzilla on the downtown small businesses recently.

Bobby Solazzo had recruited the team carefully, finding only the most vicious and psychotic bastards and leaving the ones with an ounce of compassion in them to join Kiwanis or Civitan. Solazzo's crew were the kind of guys that said, "Give me the money and I'll kill you."

Solazzo and company had already eluded authorities in a high-speed chase and a shoot-out at a liquor store that left two employees dead in a pool of blood, and had been lying low for the past ten days, but now they were ready for their next heist.

Detective Jack Murphy was in charge of the stakeout. He was crouched uncomfortably behind a Dumpster, wiping rain from his eyes, while the deputy chief of detectives was on the store's rooftop, along with a reporter from the local rag who was pressing for the perfect shot for their headline: SOLAZZO GANG GOES DOWN. Other sharpshooters were strategically located in vantage points overlooking the alley, already designated the "kill zone." They didn't have to wait long.

An older black Suburban with darkened windows slid into the mouth of the narrow alley and eased along, coming to a stop directly behind Turley's Jewelers. The next two minutes seemed to run in slow motion, beginning with the doors of the Suburban flying open and four large and well- armed men emerging.

One man approached the back door of Turley's and pointed a sawed-off shotgun at the door's lock. The shotgun blast that shattered the lock on the door spooked one of the cops, who had his pistol pointed into the alleyway, and some reflex caused him to yank the trigger. Jack half-stood and looked around, thinking, Must be the deputy chief. Leave it to him to screw things up.

The shot went wild, but the reaction of the four men below was that of a well-trained military squad, as two men rushed into the back entrance of Turley's, and the remaining two returned fire at the rooftop snipers' position and back down the alleyway. Although the original orders to all of the ground team were that no one fired except the SWAT snipers, the air was suddenly filled with deadly projectiles. A bullet zinged into a nearby quad of electrical transformers high up on a telephone pole just above the west half of the stakeout team, sending a shower of fiery debris down on them. The uniformed cops positioned above the kill zone continued their barrage of gunfire, effectively immobilizing their team members on the ground.

Murphy had been waiting for the Suburban to come to a stop before giving the order to the SWAT commander to move in when he'd heard the single gunshot and then all hell breaking loose. Now he was in the middle of a goddamned war, and he was fucked no matter which way he ran. He could flee into the raging fire at the west end of the alley where there were some backup officers at least. Or he could chase the asshole he saw take off east down the alley when the shooting started. Staying put was not an option.

He bolted from his hole and chased the lone runner. The good news was that he'd gotten a pretty good look at this character and was pretty sure it was the leader of the pack, Bobby Solazzo. The bad news was that it was Bobby Solazzo, and Bobby had a sawed-off shotgun and liked to use it.

What kind of moron chases a guy who's got a shotgun? Murphy thought. But he plowed ahead through cascading rain, the smooth soles of his dress loafers slipping on the wet brick-worked street surface, the smell of sewage from the overflowing storm sewers barely registering.

He gripped the polymer handle of his Glock .45 standard police issue semiautomatic and slowed his pace—listening, watching for any movement or lack of movement. The alley was so narrow that a shotgun blast down the middle would take out anyone standing there. Not Jack's idea of a fun time. With the damn rain coming down in waves he could only see a few feet in any direction. For all Jack knew, Bobby was ten feet away, just waiting for him to come into view.

Murphy's Law says, "Never take a pistol to a shotgun fight." But, then, he wasn't supposed to be taking on Bobby's gang alone, was he? He was a detective. He was supposed to be directing the stakeout at a safe distance, watching the action as the uniformed officers and SWAT team took these assholes down. And that reminded him that Murphy's Law also says, "Anything that can go wrong, will always fuck you sideways."

He took a deep breath, let it out, and then moved forward again. Bobby's got to be close now, he thought, as he neared the end of the alley where it turned to the right. He stopped and, blading his body against the concrete-block wall, he glanced around the corner and spotted a shotgun lying on a pile of trash.

He's unarmed! Jack thought, as lightning flashed overhead. The resultant thunderclap was immediate and deafening in the tight alleyway, and it couldn't have come at a worse time. He had just moved out from cover when another flash caught his eye. This one close. Too close. Moving at him with the speed of lightning. But not lightning. A blade, he thought, then, too late, and tried to turn away, but he felt the point of the blade cut into his face and scrape downward, gouging a path through flesh and bone.

He lifted his .45 toward the direction of the attack . . .

Chapter One

Dr. Anne Lewis stood in the doorway of her garage and looked toward the back door of her house. The television weatherman had it wrong again. "Partly cloudy with a ten percent chance of rain" had turned into a raging thunderstorm. If I wait it will stop soon. It can't rain this hard for long, can it? she wondered.

Then she heard the phone ringing inside the house.

She muttered an expletive and ran. She was thoroughly soaked when she got inside and, of course, the phone had stopped ringing.

"Probably just a telemarketer," she said out loud, a little put out that her husband, Don, had not answered the phone. Since his retirement last year, all he had done was lie around the house, read the newspapers, watch sports, and make a mess.

She sighed and straightened a picture frame near the back door on her way into the bathroom for a towel. At the sink she dried herself and looked in the mirror. Her hair had turned prematurely gray in college—many years ago—but still had a shine to it that made it remarkable. Not that Don noticed anymore.

But she wasn't really being fair to him. After all, they had been married forty-three years. Both of them had been driven by careers, so they had never found time for children. Also not his fault, but still she wondered sometimes what her life would have been like if they'd had kids.

With Don's retirement last year, and her planned retirement at the end of this year, maybe she was just going through growing pains. Thirty-plus years of working in the psychiatric field had made her too introspective. She leaned close to the mirror and looked into her sky blue eyes.

What do psychiatrists do when they retire? she wondered. Teach? Travel? Slowly go insane?

She pushed the thought away and glanced once more at herself, smoothed her damp hair, and then dabbed a tissue at the eyeliner that streaked her face.

"Not bad for an old dame," she said and smiled. But as she started to leave the bathroom she noticed an odor. "My God, something smells like a wet dog!" she said and sniffed the hand towel. That wasn't it. "Please don't let it be the septic." The last time it had cost them a small fortune to repair the septic system, and then there was the smell and the mess with the whole backyard dug up.

How could he put up with this smell all day? Where is he?

She left the downstairs bathroom and walked through the house.

Surely he isn't still in bed!

She started up the stairs but stopped at the top step; a cold chill ran the length of her spine.

"Hi, Doc. Remember us?" A fist slammed into her sternum, crushing the breath from her and causing an explosion behind her eyes.

* * * * *

She woke to the most extreme pain she had ever experienced. Wherever she was, it was pitch black and her eyes hurt.

How long have I been unconscious? What happened?

She couldn't see, but she could tell she was propped into a sitting position against something hard. She tried to move but could only turn her head from side to side. She managed to wiggle her fingers and toes but could barely feel them. Something was crammed into her mouth, causing her jaws to ache.

Then she remembered the man. Although she couldn't place him, he had looked familiar. The professional, analytical part of her mind kicked in. Had she seen him in the newspaper or on television recently? No, that wasn't it. Was he a patient?

Whoever he was, it was clear that he was angry and quite capable of hurting her. And where was her husband? She wondered if Don, too, had been tied up somewhere.

Sudden pain. A blindingly bright light shone in her eyes. She tried to close them but couldn't.

"Wakey, wakey," a voice said.

She tried again to shut her eyes.

"Your eyelids are taped open. We don't want you to miss anything, Dr. Lewis."

He knows my name!

She tried to talk, to ask him what he wanted, why he was doing this to her, but was unable to speak because of the gag.

"Yeah—taped your mouth shut, too."

Oh my God, where is Don? What has happened to my husband, you bastard?

As if he had read her mind, the intruder trained the flashlight beam next to her and, with a gloved hand, turned her head in that direction.

Anne Lewis looked into the bloody and empty eye sockets of her husband's face. His body was bound and propped on the bed beside her. Where his mouth should have been was a bloody, cavernous hole. His lips had been crudely cut off, most of his teeth smashed out or broken, tongue cut out. She tried to look away but couldn't. Hot bile rose from her stomach and, finding no other avenue, it erupted from her nose.

"Now look what you've done, Anne," the voice chastised softly, as if correcting an errant child. "And you're supposed to be a professional woman."

The blow to her face came unexpectedly, and she almost choked on the gag. Her vision blurred, and she felt herself blacking out.

"Don't you pass out on us, bitch!"

The intruder yanked her head up by her hair, slamming the back of her skull into the headboard hard enough to make stars swim behind her eyes. Another blow to her chest took her breath, and she felt an explosion inside her skull as the world danced around her.

She heard something ripping and then felt her head being secured to the upright rails of the headboard with something sticky. Tape.

His voice took on a childlike tone. "Punch and Judy fought for a pie. Punch gave Judy a knock in the eye. Says Punch to Judy, will you have any more? Says Judy to Punch, my eyes are too sore." He laughed heartily.

Fear racked her body as she, too late, recognized her assailant. She was quite certain she was going to die.

"Well, Anne, Bobby's waiting, and I promised that I'd make this quick." He grabbed her by the throat, and said, "But I lied. I'm gonna make it as painful as I can. Practice makes perfect, you know."

About the Author

photo by George Routt

Sergeant Rick Reed (Ret.), author of the Jack Murphy thriller series, is a twenty-plus-year veteran police detective. During his career he successfully investigated numerous high-profile criminal cases, including a serial killer who claimed thirteen lives before strangling and dismembering his fourteenth and last victim. He recounted that story in his acclaimed true-crime book, *Blood Trail.* Rick spent his last three years on the force as the Commander of the police department's Internal Affairs Section. He has two master's degrees and upon retiring from the police force, took a fulltime teaching position with a community college. He currently teaches criminal justice at Volunteer State Community College in Tennessee and writes thrillers. He lives near Nashville with his wife and two furry friends, Lexie and Luther.

Please visit him on Facebook, Goodreads,
or at his website, www.rickreedbooks.com.

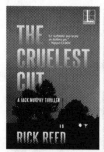

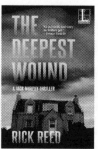
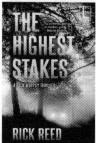

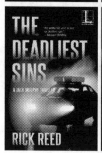

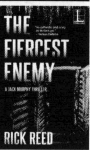

Printed in the United States
by Baker & Taylor Publisher Services